# HIDDEN RELICS

## RELICS OF THE ANCIENTS BOOK 2

### M.G. HERRON

# NEXT IN THE SERIES

*Starfighter Down*
*Hidden Relics*
*Rogue Swarm*

# ONE

"My family and I are at your mercy, Mr. Chairman," said the frail man who bowed his head before the might of the Colonization Board.

The man couldn't have been older than forty-five, but appeared to be in his mid-sixties with a tangled mop of gray hair, leathery skin and a puckered hole where his left eye had once been. The man reached out and put an arm around his wife's shoulders and even from where she stood at the back of the assembly hall, Admiral Kira Miyaru recognized the long, curved scars of someone who'd fended off a groundling attack with his bare hands. Pinkish lines criss-crossed weathered skin to the man's elbow, ending in a large circular welt of tissue on the joint.

His wife leaned against him, propping herself up with his strength. On his other side, a starved-looking young boy shuffled his feet, head bowed and eyes cast down like some kind of abused creature. All three of them were too thin, dressed in threadbare clothes made of some colorless synthetic, their shoes patched and repatched until not even the original manufacturer would have recognized their make. The tablets on their wrists were generations out of date, with cracked and battered screens—a far cry from the high-tech, invisible neural interfaces the Empire paid to put in *her* head.

Chairman Alvin Card leaned back in his seat of state and regarded the impoverished family down the slope of his bulbous nose. They were one of a hundred such families the Colonization Board would be seeing today. A line of suppliants ran along one wall of the cavernous room, out the front door of the state building, and down the marble steps.

It had only been a few months since Kira had last seen Card, but in that time the fringe of brown hair ringing his shining pate like a poor man's crown seemed to have receded further. He'd also put on an extra ten pounds, and that was being generous.

"The next colony ship embarks in a month," Card said, "but it is nearly full. There are two cabins left in first class, however..."

The man's wife slumped visibly.

"Please, sir," he said, "we can't afford first class tickets. Won't you make an exception?"

"Do you have any money?"

As if the fat bastard didn't already know the answer.

"Enough to eat, but little besides," said the man. "We live in Camp Six, near the water treatment facility." Translation: in a stinking smog. "I've been looking for work since we arrived three years ago, but with the unemployment rate so high and employers giving precedence to natural born Ariadneans, I can't get work, not even with my training as a robotics engineer."

Card frowned and pretended to consider it, but Kira could tell that mention of the man's work experience had piqued his interest. The chairman asked several more questions in a disinterested tone. Where had the man been schooled? What jobs had he held previously? Card finally traded a look with another of the board members, a tall, severe woman with full fake lips who sat in front of a holo-screen. She tapped on the translucent crystal touchpad for a minute. Passenger lists and diagrams scrolled down through the air before her faster than Kira could follow. She finally leaned over and whispered something in the chairman's ear.

"There is one other possibility." The edge of a predatory smile appeared briefly on Chairman Card's face before he swallowed it with a practiced smoothing of his facial muscles.

The young boy looked up. The whole family held their breath as one organism. They had to be tight knit to survive the destitute poverty of Ariadne's filthy, overflowing refugee camps. Those who went it alone rarely made it out alive.

"If you agree to this, all three of you must sign a contract to serve the Colonization Board for a term of no less than ten solar cycles, galactic standard time."

The woman began to protest, but her husband gently hushed her.

"In exchange for your service, you will be provided passage to New Kali in the Elturis System, plus room and board in shared lodging upon your arrival."

The whole audience, including Kira's normally aloof security guards, held their breath, still and silent. It was a rare thing for a family to be offered free passage to a new colony. Everyone waited with rapt anticipation.

Everyone except for her. Was New Kali a chance to start a new life? Sure. Would Card and the Colonization Board profit greatly if he made this deal? Without a shred of doubt. And if this family accepted his offer, they would move from a refugee camp to a potentially worse situation. Founding a new colony was no walk in the park. She clicked her tongue disdainfully.

Card glanced in her direction, but seemed unable to pick her out among the crowd of journalists, attorneys, family, friends, and other observers who stood near.

"Mr. Chairman," said the old-looking robotics engineer. "I beg your pardon, sir, but my wife has been dealing with some health issues. What kind of work will she be required to do?"

The secretary tapped on the crystal. The holograms facing the chairman changed their layout and configuration.

"We don't have anything in our records. What is her condition?"

"Lung damage due to smoke inhalation during a Kryl invasion. Insurance won't cover it."

Card grunted. No more explanation was required.

They went through a series of different options until she finally agreed to take a cooking and cleaning job—essentially indentured servitude. While some Solaran bureaucrat, the son of a rich senator, helped set up a tax-collection system and monopolized industry on the new world, this poor woman would scrub his toilets or serve him home-cooked meals made from the best vegetables the hydroponics farms could grow. Meanwhile, her husband and son would break their backs doing manual labor and eating gruel.

The Colonization Board was *oh so* magnanimous.

Kira glared at Card and knotted the cloth bag she'd brought with her between her fingers. It was not often she felt ashamed to wear the crimson-trimmed navy uniform as a Rear Admiral in the Solaran Defense Forces, but today was one of those days.

They could do so much *more* for these people.

If only it wasn't so profitable for the Solaran Empire to do less.

For the hundredth time that day, Kira wondered how her request to halt colonization efforts would be received by the populace. Life on new colonies was hard… but was life in a refugee camp on the overpopulated city-planet of Ariadne any better?

Not in the eyes of these three. At least on the new colony they had a chance to start fresh.

Once they agreed to the woman's job, the father of the family said, "Very good, sir. Thank you, Mr. Chairman. We accept."

His wife covered her mouth with both hands and choked back tears—tears of relief. Tears of happiness.

Tears of hope.

Kira took a deep, steadying breath and steeled herself. Even if she got what she wanted, this wasn't going to be easy.

The family departed with a bounce in their step. The next group of petitioners in line watched them go with hungry, jealous eyes.

The secretary stood and leaned down to whisper in Chairman Card's ear.

"What?" he whispered fiercely. "This is our busiest day in months. The *Maiden of Kali* departs in less than a week. No, dammit, I don't care if the Emperor himself booked the appoint—" He strangled the word in his throat as another member snapped at him, something about decorum and points of order. "Of course. Yes. Okay, fine, fine. It won't take long in any case, I promise you that."

Kira's name flashed into the secretary's holoscreen, the letters reversed from her perspective. She hadn't had to wait in line with the other petitioners. She strode into the building on the power of her rank and uniform, having been granted an urgent appointment by the Solaran Defense Forces on grounds of galactic security. When they learned this, the guards at the building's entrance had saluted her and then parted like the ink-dark seas on Posibar.

Yet despite her station and the authority she bore on

orders from the Executive Council, after seeing that family eagerly gather up their scraps she felt like a fly before the swatting machine.

*Don't let this insolent bureaucrat intimidate you*, Kira told herself firmly. *Stand tall.*

The Chairman lifted his chin as she approached and clasped his hands together so hard his knuckles turned white. "I didn't recognize you at first, Admiral Miyaru. Good to see you again."

*Sure it is.* "Likewise, Mr. Chairman," Kira said, careful to keep any malice out of her tone. "I hope life has been treating you well."

"Of course, Admiral. Busy season, you know, as it always is before a colonial voyager departs. Now you are here to discuss..." He glanced over at the holoscreen in front of the severe secretary, whose lips were pursed into a firm rosebud of disapproval. The Executive Council must have thrown their weight around to get her this appointment on such short notice, and these people obviously did not take kindly to it. "A matter of galactic security. Is that right?"

"Yes, Mr. Chairman. My pilots discovered something while evacuating Robichar that poses a great danger to the Solaran Empire's colonization missions. I thought you should be made aware of it as soon as possible." It would have been sooner if they hadn't rejected her request for an audience so many times she'd been forced to go to the Executive Council.

The waiting queue of supplicants began to stir and murmur amongst themselves. She felt a sense of hostility float toward her. It was thick and cloying, like steam on a hot summer's day.

"Which is?" Card asked.

Kira forced herself not to glance to the side. "It is a sensitive matter. Can we please speak in private?"

"I don't have time for this. Whatever you have to say can be said right here."

"May I approach, Mr. Chairman?"

He sighed and rolled his eyes. "Very well, come forward."

The Chairman of the Colonization Board was as much a judge as an administrator. In matters of colonial expansion, Card was invested with the power of the Emperor himself. In the rare instances where appeals were sought, the decision went to a vote of the whole board and, if no majority decision could be reached there, on up to the crown. Before coming today, Kira had checked the records. Card had been appointed Chairman at the end of the Kryl War twelve years ago. Since then, not a single appeal had gone to the Emperor.

She must choose her words wisely if she didn't want to get sucked into a bureaucratic quagmire. She composed herself as she strode up to the high bench. She was just tall enough to see over the desk—and Kira was usually the tallest person in the room.

"What is so important that you cannot speak in front of the board like everyone else?" Card demanded in a whisper.

"This is a matter of galactic security, Mr. Chairman, and not everyone here has clearance."

"Why did you not seek a private appointment with my office?"

*You weasel*, Kira thought furiously. She almost lost her cool then, but managed to reign her temper back in with a supreme effort of will. She took a deep breath before saying, "I tried, Alvin. Your office denied five requests in the weeks since the *Paladin of Abniss* returned to port."

"It is our busy season, as I've said. They have instructions to delay any non-urgent matters."

"This *is* urgent, Mr. Chairman. A Kryl hive led by a rogue Overmind has already forced us to evacuate one colony and—"

"I am *well aware,*"—he twisted each word into a knot as it passed over his tongue—"of your previous mission. Which is why it is imperative that we not fall further behind schedule. We've had to divert fifty thousand refugees previously bound for Robichar to other colonies, and you brought back another million we are still scrambling to find housing for!" His voice had risen in volume to match his anger. She felt the audience leaning forward, listening in. Though they were dozens of feet away, it felt as if the refugees were all crowding in at her back, breathing down her neck. She stretched her neck and cleared her throat softly.

"Would you rather we left them on Robichar to be slaughtered by the Kryl?" Her words echoed sharply through the large chamber. She hadn't meant for her voice to rise quite so high or fast, but the words were out before she was able to contain them.

Card practically choked. A bead of sweat dripped from a neatly plucked eyebrow and splattered onto the tabletop. "I would *rather* you stay in line, Admiral. Matters of colonial expansion are the Board's responsibility, not the Fleet's."

"Except when it puts the people of the Solaran Empire in danger."

"You got what you wanted—we evacuated Robichar. Now do your job and eliminate this rogue Overmind so that no more of our citizens have to suffer."

"We eliminated as many of the Kryl as we could without endangering the civilians we were there to rescue, Mr. Chairman, and we continue to monitor their movements. Had we been given the support I had *asked* for, things may have gone differently, but the Fleet was too busy running patrols on trade routes to your colonies to deploy a sizable force to Robichar."

"That is a military matter, and none of my concern."

*Yes, it is, you slimy, pedantic son of a xeno.*

8

The Solaran Defense Forces had the Fleet stretched so thin that she had been forced to evacuate Robichar with a single destroyer and half a dozen wings of starfighters and their support craft. It was only due to their ability to track the hive's movements, her tactical prowess, and a good bit of luck that they got the colonists out in time. And not all of them had made it.

Not that Card gave a damn.

Kira was a tall, broad-shouldered woman, but even despite her six-plus feet in height, she still had to gaze upward to meet Chairman Card's eyes where he sat at the center of the long, curved desk. She reached up and dropped the cloth bag in front of him. It landed on the table with a thunk.

So he wanted this to be public? Fine. Without so much as an explanation, she whipped the cloth bag off the sealed, aluminite container it concealed.

Card hissed a breath in through his teeth and leaned back in his chair. "By Animus! What in the name of Earth is that?"

"What we discovered on Robichar."

Inside the transparent, sealed jar was a Kryl parasite about the length of her pinky finger. Its thin, segmented body sprouted eight legs, each ending in hair-thin multi-pronged talons. Its body was translucent, and through its skin a network of veins pulsed with silvery-blue blood.

Exposed to the light, the creature had swelled up to five times its original size, opening its petal-shaped mouth in a silent scream, and was now flinging itself violently against the wall of the jar closest to the chairman. The container rocked on the desktop, causing the chairman to flinch and shove his chair backward.

"This parasite was pulled from the body of one of my starfighter pilots by a surgical bot."

Card narrowed his eyes and stared down his round nose

at her. "And what, pray tell, does this have to do with the Solaran Empire's moral imperative to find a home for *every* citizen?"

She heard the shouts of "Yeah!" and "That's right!" from the crowd of petitioners behind her.

Card recovered from his shock faster than she expected. He may have been an obese, balding bureaucrat, but she had better be careful not to assume he was a dimwit. His unkempt physical appearance had caused her to lower her expectations. Appearances always presented a real danger in politics, something she did not consider herself very good at.

Instead of falling into the trap of playing his games, Kira did what she knew how to do best in difficult situations—she boldly stated the unvarnished truth.

"The pilot we found this parasite in was hallucinating so badly he thought his comrades-in-arms were xenos trying to kill him. He attacked them and had to be detained by force. This same parasite took another pilot, who caused an explosion in my hangar that killed seven good soldiers and injured dozens more. On Robichar, another one of my pilots uncovered a Kryl plot to kidnap children and convert them into mutant Kryl-human hybrids using the same parasite you're looking at. Does that count as a clear and present danger to the Solaran Empire, Mr. Chairman?"

She left the bit about the Telos relics out of her story. The idea of a relic that could be weaponized against the Kryl would have been laughable if she hadn't seen it with her own eyes. She couldn't very well include that part without revealing the relic, and while she had been willing to make a scene if the chairman gave her no other choice, she still hadn't been willing to expose such a dangerous weapon to the public. The relic was stored securely on her destroyer and would remain so until she had assurances. And it wasn't the chairman she'd hand it over to when she did.

He just stared at her, fury rising in his clenched face.

"So, what does this have to do with the Empire's moral imperative to expand?" Kira went on, turning from the chairman and raising her voice to address everyone in the room. "Everything."

If these people were going to be sent to colonize a new world, they deserved to know the danger they would potentially be facing. "Before I left on the mission to evacuate Robichar, I told you the Kryl were up to something, but I didn't know what. Well, now I do, and here's the proof. The Kryl are roaming again. They're developing dangerous new abilities, ones that involve kidnapping and turning our people—our *children*—into xeno mutants. This new, rogue Overmind is the greatest danger the Empire and her colonies have faced since the end of the Kryl War." She turned back to Card and met his eyes. "So I'm asking, Mr. Chairman, for you to pause colonial expansion until the threat has been eradicated. Until we can ensure the safety of all of our citizens."

A worried murmuring broke out among the crowd. Husbands turned to their wives. Mothers clutched their children to their skirts. Friends whispered worriedly in each other's ears.

Meanwhile, Chairman Card's face had darkened to a livid shade of red. "Request denied."

"Sir, please. Galactic security—"

"I have made my decision!" he shouted, shooting to his feet and knocking his chair over, the wood—the rare, expensive, and elegantly carved wood—of its frame clattering carelessly on the marble floor behind him. He strode away and departed through a door set flush with the wall. His secretary gathered her things and followed her boss. After a moment's hesitation, the other members of the board went, too.

When Kira turned back to the people, she found no

sympathy. A sea of agate-hard eyes stared back at her, faces set in sneers, jaws clenched in anger.

In that moment, Kira realized she'd made a fatal mistake. Knowing the chairman would deny her request, she had let her temper get the best of her. She'd used the moment and her position to publicly humiliate him. And in her desire to crush his ego, she had inadvertently turned the people she was trying to protect against her.

Kira turned her eyes down in shame. She was a soldier, not a politician.

Taking a deep breath, she wiped her expression smooth and pulled her shoulders back. One day, they would understand. And until then, she could deal with their judgment. She'd lived long enough as a false war hero in the public eye. This wasn't much different. On some level, she even welcomed the change.

But by the Spirit of Old Earth, she hated playing politics.

# TWO

Captain Elya Nevers' breath came hard and fast.

Sweat streamed down his face, burning his eyes and matting his hair to his temples.

He cast around, searching for Hedgebot's comforting blue nimbus as his chest heaved. It was full dark in the building. No light, not even the soft glow the bot usually gave off.

He was trapped.

Groundlings prowled around him, toying with him while his heart thundered. He heard the click of their talons against the stone floor, the burbling, growling sounds they made when they were hungry. The metallic scent of blood filled his nostrils.

He followed the dim outlines of their hunched backs as they circled. Between three and six Kryl were in the room. He couldn't be sure. Seeing what he took to be a narrow gap, Elya lunged forward, hoping to squeeze between them while he had an opportunity.

He was too slow. Their talons sank into his soft flesh like hooks into fish. He screamed so loud it felt like he had torn open his throat. They dragged him across the floor by the shoulders and thighs, leaving a wet streak of blood in his wake. His palms slicked up as he scrabbled for purchase.

His fingernails tore as they caught on cracks in the floor. His flesh rent with a moist ripping sound and a shock of pain as the groundlings hauled him over a semi-soft object. He managed to get his bloody fingers wrapped up in some kind of cloth covering a lump, and used its weight like an anchor to delay the inevitable.

The groundlings yanked on him like a pack of rabid dogs fighting over a rope chew, before retracting their talons and withdrawing suddenly, leaving him aching and panting and cold, leaning on the cloth-covered mound.

Hope flared in his chest. A bulb sparked to life overhead and he saw the object he'd been grasping onto.

It was a body.

And not just any body. It was his mother's body. Glassy-eyed and open-mouthed, with old talon wounds exposing her neck and chest.

He gasped and scrambled backward, horrified. A hollow pit formed in his stomach. Like a bottomless hole, no matter how much fear poured in, nothing seemed to fill it.

When he managed to haul his gaze away from his mother, he saw two more bodies. His older brothers, Arn and Rojer—missing limbs, their guts trailing along the floor like a pile of white snakes. Captain Osprey lay to his left, still and pale, blood matting her short blonde hair. Beside her, Lieutenant Yorra and Lieutenant Park, his squadmates in the Furies, had died in each other's arms.

Everyone he loved, murdered by xenos.

The groundlings surrounded him but didn't attack. They watched him with bulging eyes. Strands of yellowish saliva dripped from their toothy jaws.

He was trapped. No escape.

"It doesn't have to end this way," Subject Zero said

14

through the clicking mandible that had replaced his human jaw. The spider-like legs that had grown out of his back were fully extended, each ending in a bloodied, talon-bearing foot.

The Kryl-mutant hybrid he'd fought on Robichar stood over the bodies of his loved ones. Once known as Captain Omar Ruidiaz, a decorated starfighter pilot and hero of the Kryl War, he'd been turned into Subject Zero by the xenos and their parasites. Behind Subject Zero, an enormous, slavering xeno lurked in the shadows. Though he'd never seen one before, Elya took this to be Overmind X, the rogue queen who controlled Subject Zero and the rest of the hive— the same xeno queen who invaded Robichar in search of the Telos relic he'd recovered.

*Join us, Captain.* She spoke directly into his mind. No way to block out the sound since there was no sound. *Join us and inherit the galaxy...*

"No," Elya rasped. "It doesn't belong to you!"

*Join us or die. Your future holds nothing but pain and sorrow.* Her voice scraped around the inside of his skull. Though he tried to fight her off, she crashed through his resistance and pawed through the contents of his memories. *Join us or be eradicated like the rest of your kin.*

Subject Zero raised his one remaining human hand. In his palm sat a tiny parasite, its thin body upraised and trembling in anticipation.

*Resistance is futile...*

Elya's pain suddenly intensified and then, just as quickly, vanished. He lumbered to his feet like a marionette being lifted by its puppetmaster, and stumbled jerkily toward Subject Zero. His whole body shook with terrified tremors as he fought to resist. But the queen was just too powerful.

As he approached, Subject Zero reached out his other hand, the one attached to his monstrous Kryl arm, and wrapped it around Elya's neck. The hand was so large his

15

clawed fingers met behind his skull, fully enclosing his throat.

He dropped the parasite onto Elya's nose. The little worm sniffed his open nostril, clambered over his cheekbone, and vanished into a tear duct.

Elya felt a minor discomfort, an itching like a few grains of sand had blown into his eyeball.

Then blinding pain that blotted out the world.

He shot up in bed, gasping and half naked, clawing instinctively at his face. He'd scratched a furrow across the bridge of his nose and eyelid before he realized the parasite wasn't actually there, but only existed in his mind.

The thought of trying to go back to sleep after that nightmare was inconceivable, so he stumbled out of bed and splashed cold water on his face. He barely recognized the man in the mirror. Medium length black hair fell into his eyes, which had shadowed bags beneath them. The wound he'd inflicted with his scratching fell squarely across the bump on the bridge of his nose. Bushy eyebrows and light brown skin matched his eyes. Elya wasn't tall, but he wasn't short either. A prominent Adam's apple protruded from his long neck.

Every night since he'd been rescued from Robichar and the clutches of Subject Zero, he'd had the same awful dream. Attacked and harried by groundlings, finding his family and friends murdered, and Subject Zero or the Overmind—or both—dropping a parasite into his brain to control and then turn him into some kind of xeno mutant.

He hadn't had nightmares this awful since he was a child, after his family narrowly escaped a Kryl invasion on Yuzosix —now a Kryl hive. That's why he had joined the Solaran Defense Forces and worked so hard to become a starfighter pilot. The bad dreams had faded away when he figured out what he could do to fight back.

But now the xenos had faces and names. They had smells and sounds and a horrible specificity. His doubting brain just loved that. All the fodder his subconscious needed to reproduce childhood terrors as vivid as big budget holofilms.

What a treat.

Elya checked the clock in the upper lefthand corner of the mirror—two hours 'til sunrise. Might as well stay awake at this point.

Next to the clock, a small window played newsreel reruns from yesterday, coverage of the *Maiden of Kali* being outfitted for its upcoming colonial voyage. They were currently showing interviews with the captain and crew on a tour of the ship. No wonder the lists to get approved for colonization were so long. Exhaustive coverage like this was shoved in everyone's face all day, every day, on an endless loop.

He swiped it away with a finger and a sigh.

Back in bed, Elya had just entered his passcode and logged into his tablet when a pillow struck him squarely in the face.

"Go to sleep, Fancypants." Lieutenant Innovesh Park groaned as he buried his own face beneath the covers. It used to be that a pilot got his own room when they docked at port on Ariadne. However, with Ariadne's housing shortage and their overflowing refugee population, those days were nothing but a blurry memory in the minds of aging veterans.

"Can't."

"Try harder."

Elya ignored his wingman and navigated to the research folder on the glowing holoscreen of his tab.

"You're the most stubborn person I know," Park said, his voice muffled through the bedsheets.

Elya snorted and dimmed the light of his holoscreen. In five seconds, Park was snoring softly once more.

Elya envied the man. He may have been the most stubborn person in their flight, but Park could sleep anywhere provided his normal outlets of gambling, tobacco and pretty girls were available in plenty. On Ariadne, humanity's favorite vices were easy to obtain, especially for SDF soldiers with reliable paychecks.

Elya pulled up his notes and opened half a dozen applications in different windows, tiling them in a curved surface around his head like a cockpit so he could take them all in together. He picked up reading where he'd left off.

Remarkably little was known about the Telos. Despite several long days and sleepless nights spent reading, and thousands of destinations scoured, from niche history sites to a visit to the capital library of Ariadne for the holovidi records, all of Elya's notes fit in a single window.

Thought to be extinct, no Solaran alive or dead had ever encountered one of the ancient aliens, nor their buried remains, so only conjecture could be made about their appearance. If you asked a thousand xenobiologists, you'd get a thousand different physical descriptions.

Ruins of Telos temples and cities were scattered across hundreds of worlds—that they knew—some of which were habitable, many of which were not. Scientists believed the Telos had been carbon-based life forms, like Solarans and Kryl, but no one had been able to prove the theory due to the wide variety of planetary atmospheres on which their ruins had been found.

Even less was known about their relics. Oh, plenty of artifacts had been recovered: petroglyphs, small statues, hand tools, bladed weapons, and containers of various sorts. But other relics with power, like the geode he'd found on Robichar? Nothing.

He held this absence of information up next to what he knew from his own personal experience.

The artifact he'd possessed for a short time looked like a lantern, about the size of a man's fist with an almost delicate-looking U-shaped handle. It was made of some kind of stone, but hollow inside. When activated, it emitted an ambient green glow that made any Kryl creature within fifty meters scream in pain and flee, repelling them more effectively than the sound cannons used for riot dispersement. The only xeno who'd been able to resist the effects of the relic (and then only partially) was Subject Zero. Being partially human, the relic didn't debilitate it the way it did other full-bred Kryl.

Elya had been able to corroborate absolutely *none* of his theories about the geode with information on the net or in the library. On nights when he couldn't sleep, it had gotten to the point where he'd begun to doubt if what he'd seen on Robichar had been real.

Had he really found a Telos relic, like Subject Zero and his Overmind controller had confirmed? Or was there another explanation?

He didn't know.

Some days, he wished he hadn't handed the relic over to the admiral so quickly. He would have liked the chance to study it more carefully.

He hadn't been given a choice after his chaotic rescue.

The only thing he was certain of at this point was he had to keep digging until he found some verifiable *facts*.

He booted up a virtual private network to obscure his tracks, skipped over to the xenoarchaeology chat room he'd been using as a jumping off point, and logged in under his pseudonym. The usual characters were there, animatedly arguing over theories and sharing photos of ruins he'd seen a hundred times. He'd begun to recognize when a photograph or video had been doctored. At first it had been almost impossible to tell a deepfake from the real deal, but after a little practice and access to the right software, it became more obvious (if somewhat time consuming).

A link he'd followed several times before came through the chat. Elya clicked it without thinking, only to hit an error page that made him gape in shock. The popular xeno forum had been taken down.

Chills crawled up his spine.

He snapped his jaw shut and scrolled up through the chat. The conspiracy theory they'd been discussing was, in fact, no conspiracy at all. A dozen such sites on the net had been shut down recently, some through distributed denial of service attacks, others inexplicably censored by their hosting providers, who provided zero explanation for their removal. Checking his notes against the circulated list of ghosted sites, Elya realized he'd visited every single one of them since he'd returned to Ariadne. They were all hubs for discussing xenos and their many related fields of study.

The conversation in the chat circled around possible perpetrators. Some thought it was a hacker, others a network of hackers known as Veritas. One person blamed the military, others the various Imperial intelligence organizations.

One thing they all agreed on, however, was that the Ministry of Xeno Affairs was historically known to be critical of any group putting forward theories of ancient alien intelligence or the Telos. Several years ago, MOXA had waged a campaign to debunk the mystery of the hyperspace drive's origin. The campaign had been poorly received by the public, partly because it was an obvious propaganda attempt to credit the Empire with the ancient innovation, and partly because if they were right, it ruined the fun of the mystery.

Historians largely agreed that the discovery of the hyperspace drive post-dated humanity's ancestral departure from the desiccated husk of Old Earth, and pre-dated the founding of Ariadne. However, the specifics, like most details from the Great Migration, had been lost to time. No one could really pinpoint when or how the hyperspace drive was invented, only that it had been used to find the world that became known as Ariadne.

A new chat window appeared in the air before him. It was from a pseudonym he didn't recognize. Screen name: Xenophile7643. With a wry smile, Elya tapped to accept.

The message said, *I can help you find what you're looking for.*

His breath came hard and fast.

Elya deleted the message without responding, then logged off the network, erasing his history as he went.

He hadn't told anyone what he was looking for, had he? He logged back in under a new virtual private network to obscure his true source address. A quick search revealed all of his publicly available chats.

He couldn't find anything that would indicate he'd given away his motivation. He certainly hadn't given away any information about the relic now in SDF's possession.

The message must have been a scam—someone looking to bait him in order to gain information, or money, or access to his accounts.

Maybe someone had figured out he was an SDF pilot and wanted to use him for his security clearance.

If that was true, the joke was on them. He didn't have any kind of special clearance. At least not the kind that would help answer questions about the relic.

Still, the timing of it ate at him. First, the sites with the best information disappeared shortly after he'd visited each of them. Then someone messages him out of the blue with the kind of offer he'd been searching for?

It smelled fishy.

His skin crawled like it was being trodden by a thousand tiny parasites. He shivered and pulled the covers up to his neck.

By now, sunlight had begun to drip in through the high slot windows in the barracks dorm. Park was sound asleep and would be for another hour. Hedgebot was curled up on his charging pad with a full battery. If he got up now, Elya could get a workout in and maybe a flight sim before breakfast. And he'd still have time to stop by the library before Lt. Colonel Walcott's funeral. He powered off his tab, dressed quietly, and snuck out the door with Hedgebot trotting at his heels.

Though he didn't see anyone following him when he looked over his shoulder, Elya couldn't shake the feeling that he was being watched.

# THREE

Family, friends and loved ones of Lieutenant Colonel Pershus Walcott flooded into the church for his memorial service.

Standing at a pew near the rear of the great sanctuary, Captain Casey Osprey greeted people she recognized and clasped her hands in front of her, forcing herself to stand in a calm, confident manner the way her former commander would have appreciated—shoulders pulled back, chin raised, professionally neutral expression worn carefully on her face —and tried to stop shifting her weight nervously from one foot to the other. Walcott had not been a critical person. He mostly kept his thoughts to himself, which had always caused Casey to work harder to impress him. She could clearly visualize the slight frown marring his smooth, dark face whenever he saw something he didn't like.

"People look to their leaders during troubled times," he would have said. "To be good at this job, you have to be prepared to bear up under that kind of pressure."

He'd never said those words to her. Not exactly. But the sentiment remained true. Since Robichar, she'd had more than her fair share of time to imagine the ways in which she was letting Walcott down.

The Furies needed strong, steady leadership. Now more than ever.

That's why Casey watched the crowd and kept an eye peeled for Admiral Miyaru. The broad-shouldered, bronze-skinned figure, crowned by a hallmark shock of silver-white hair, would be unmistakable. The admiral towered over most people at a height that Casey found extremely intimidating until she had learned how deeply the admiral cared about the people under her command, and the civilians she'd been sworn to defend. It had always been hard for Casey to trust her commanders (she had her father's constant criticism and ability to unbalance her to thank for that), but Admiral Miyaru's refusal to leave Captain Nevers behind after he crashed on Robichar, even in the face of a Kryl invasion, had earned Casey's respect in a deep and permanent way.

That's probably why she held onto the thin hope that this bond, new though it may have been, would make the admiral receptive to her recommendations.

She dug a thumb nail into her skin, leaving crescent-shaped marks alongside the tattoos of Old Earth hawks—Ospreys, her namesake—up and down her forearms.

"Heya, Raptor, what's the haps?"

Casey smiled and threw an arm around Park's shoulders. "Naab," she said, using his call sign. "You look nice."

"I know how to clean up when I need to." The pilot from Taj Su winked at her and dug around in the inside breast pocket of his crisply ironed formal blues. He withdrew a hand-rolled cigarette that looked as neat as his freshly shaved face. "You look like you could use a smoke."

She grunted. "That obvious, huh? Hey, Fancypants."

Nevers nodded to her, the bags under his eyes more pronounced than the last time she'd seen him. They'd all been given a brief shore leave after the Robichar mission, to rest and recover and attend this service. As usual, Nevers had been spending his free time with his head buried in some obsession. Hedgebot scampered up onto his shoulder and let out a triumphant little chirrup that made her smile. "You're still having trouble sleeping."

"I've been busy. Don't worry, I'm not letting it affect my training. Hit the gym this morning while this lazy bum slept in." He thumbed at Park, who separated from her and jostled Nevers playfully with an elbow.

"Aw, come on, man! I was out late."

"At the brothel, no doubt."

"Me? Nahhh."

Nevers snorted a laugh and studied the room. "Big crowd," he muttered. "Where's Yorra?"

"Helping them finish setting up. She should be back in just a minute… speak of the devil."

"Gears," Nevers said, nodding at the petite, dark-haired woman. "How's it going?"

She blew a raspberry and gave them a thin smile that didn't touch her canted brown eyes. "Busy. Glad I could be here for the family, though. I think Mrs. Walcott is still in shock. And they haven't gotten Pershus Junior to speak a word since he heard the news."

"Oof," Nevers said, clutching his stomach. "Kids always like Hedgebot, maybe I should try to talk to him?"

Yorra nodded. "Worth a shot."

"Where they at?" Park asked. "I want to pay my respects before it gets too crazy."

"Outside," Yorra said. "Did you know that Walcott's the highest ranking officer we've lost in combat since the end of the Kryl War? We planned for high attendance, but I don't think anyone expected it would be standing room only. For the family's sake, I'm glad the Empire's footing the bill."

Walcott had been the victim of one of the xeno parasites, which had attached itself to a petty officer and then driven him into a fit of paranoid rage. In his delusional state he had taken a torch to a tank of compressed gas. The massive explosion had killed Walcott and severely damaged the hangar of the *Paladin of Abniss*.

"Thank Animus for that. Come on." Casey slid into a pew and led the others through the far aisle and out a side door. Hundreds of people mingled in the courtyard outside the enormous stone church of Animus, a rare structure because it stood on five acres of manicured lawns and paved paths—unheard of in the vast majority of the city-planet. Shielded by laws of the Empire that held the church of Animus as a protected institution, this sanctuary had stood stalwart for hundreds of years as the city encroached upon it. Hundred-story condo and office buildings surrounded the property on all sides like a ring of giant spikes, casting the grounds in shadow except at mid-day, when the sun was straight over-head, like it was now.

They wove through the crowd until they spotted the widow in a conservative black dress, fringed with black lace. Her six-year-old son wore a suit of the same color. Nevers whispered something to Hedgebot and sent the little scamperbeast ahead, drawing a delighted gasp from Pershus Junior, who chased the hedgehog bot around in circles. Nevers hugged Mrs. Walcott and exchanged a few quiet words, and then played tag with the boy and the bot while the rest of them gave their condolences.

Words had never seemed so inadequate, but Casey said them anyway. Park told his favorite story about the time they pranked Lieutenant Colonel Walcott with a hologram and water balloons. The commander made them run laps in the rain the next day, grinning the whole time while he sat dry beneath an umbrella and sipped lemonade. He was a tough squadron commander, but always fair. He had a knack for driving them to better themselves even when they didn't want to do the work needed to get there.

That was the kind of flight lead Casey wanted to be. Maybe one day she'd get promoted to Lt. Colonel and make squadron commander. But until then...

She spotted the platinum mohawk she'd been searching for and parted ways with the widow Walcott. Her squad saw where she was headed and trailed after her. Casey waved at them to stay back, and they broke off, casually pretending not to pay attention.

She wiped sweaty palms against her trousers and forced herself to take several deep breaths. "Admiral Miyaru." She clicked her heels together and gave a sharp salute. "Good to see you, sir."

The troopers that served as the admiral's security escort had swapped out their crimson armor and carbines for loose-fitting suits, but the tiny comms bugs in their ears, and the bulges beneath their jackets, gave them away as they moved in around the admiral cautiously. Perhaps with the knowledge of what had happened to Walcott, they were a little more tense than usual.

The admiral inclined her head. "At ease, Captain. This isn't an inspection."

Casey relaxed her posture and spread her feet, once more clasping her hands behind her back and digging that too-long thumbnail into her wrist. The stinging pain helped calm her. "Somber day, sir."

"It's been a long time since I've been to a memorial service for an officer under my command."

"Never long enough, sir."

"Couldn't have said it better myself." She cocked her head. "Even though you're supposed to be on shore leave, you look like you're on a mission."

"Not a mission, exactly, sir, but I do have something I'd like to speak to you about."

"This isn't the appropriate venue to discuss business, Captain."

Casey hesitated. She supposed that was true, but the longer she held onto her recommendations, the more likely it became that the position would get filled. "I tried to reach you a few times, but your secretary said you were not to be disturbed as the project you were working on was time sensitive. I'll be quick about it," she rushed to add, as some movement among the security guards drew the admiral's attention away.

"Just a second, Captain."

"But sir, I—"

Admiral Miyaru raised her eyebrows and met Casey's eyes. "I'll hear you out, Captain. Be patient."

"Sorry, sir. Of course." *You should know better,* she berated herself. *Never interrupt your commanding officer.* How many times had her father told her that? And she still had to learn it the hard way.

She had to learn everything the hard way. It was incredible Lieutenant Colonel Walcott had even made her flight lead in the first place, for all the times she'd screwed up.

"You control your thoughts. Don't let them control you," Walcott would have said. His voice had a calming effect, even from beyond the grave.

Casey studied the man who had absorbed Admiral Miyaru's attention. He wore the crimson robes of an Imperial official, made of expensive silk and stitched with gold in a double helix pattern, with sleeves big enough to fold his hands into and a fitted cloth cap. The man's lips were bordered by severe lines on both sides, and he had a thin black mustache with flecks of gray in it. She didn't recognize him, but he was obviously pretty high up in the Empire's bureaucracy.

"Minister Aganaki," said the admiral in a cool tone that, had Casey not worked with her so closely during the evacuation of Robichar, she wouldn't have recognized as on guard, if not outright hostile. "So good of you to attend the service."

The minister didn't seem to notice anything amiss. He gave the admiral a smile that didn't touch his eyes, laid his palms together in opposite directions, reminding Casey just how much influence the Church of Animus had over Imperial politics, and bowed his head. "I wouldn't have missed it for the worlds. It's the least I can do for those who give their lives to protect the Solaran Empire."

They exchanged a few more pleasantries. The conversation concluded with an invitation to lunch. It seemed a rather innocuous request, but something about the subtext must have been lost on Casey because, judging by Admiral Miyaru's body language, the offer was tantamount to being asked to share a meal with a sea serpent.

The minister bowed again. As he walked away, Casey noticed Fancypants squinting at the man. Hedgebot scampered down from his perch on Nevers' shoulder and followed the minister with Nevers trailing behind.

She exchanged a questioning glance with Park, who shrugged. Casey jerked her head. He nodded, gestured to Gears, and they followed Fancypants.

She didn't think he'd do anything stupid, but she didn't want to take any chances.

"Sorry about that, Captain. What is it you wanted to ask me about?"

Casey forced herself to stop rubbing her sweaty hands on her trousers and met the admiral's eyes. "I wanted to make a recommendation for our next squadron commander, sir."

Admiral Miyaru's eyebrows shot skyward.

"I know it's unusual, sir, for a flight lead to make a recommendation for her next commander, but I know of several excellent candidates the Furies would be honored to fly for. I've brought a short list with me, which I had independently vetted."

"By your father?" It was no secret that her father was Eben Osprey, a war hero who served as an admiral and for a decade as an Inquisitor—the Empire's traveling investigators and judges—before he retired.

"No, sir. I wanted the list to be objective. I reached out to some of my training officers and asked them to look it over. Would you mind if I sent it to your tab?"

"Prudent." Her tone was one of surprise and admiration. A good sign. "Can I take a look, Captain?"

Before the admiral could change her mind, Casey pulled the thin crystal tab out of her pocket and transferred the list over the air. A motion of her eyes and a slight nod told Casey that the admiral had accepted it with hands-free holocontrols enabled by the hardware embedded in every SDF admiral's skull.

"Not a bad list. They all have plenty of combat experience, a good track record as a commanding officer, and some have even been awarded commendations." She sighed and looked down at Casey with a strained smile that didn't show any teeth. "But I'm afraid we've already chosen your new squadron commander. Allow me to introduce you."

Casey's heart dropped into her shoes. Damn it all. She *knew* she should have gotten the list in front of Admiral Miyaru sooner. She wasn't the type to sit on a decision like this.

"Things didn't go your way? Good," Walcott would have said. "You've been given the opportunity to rise to the challenge."

As she was imagining Walcott's words, her father's voice

intruded. "Don't be such a pushover, kid. You give up too easy! Soldiers fight because their lives depend on it!" She didn't have to make up those words—she'd been just five when she heard them the first time. They'd been repeated so often throughout her childhood that they'd been burned in.

She didn't have a chance to decide which voice to listen to. Before she could make a decision, a middle-aged colonel with a bald head and a uniform that slouched on his frame ambled up. "Admiral," he said as his eyes skipped briefly over Casey.

Colonel Volk had been Admiral Miyaru's executive officer since long before Casey joined the Furies. He had a taste for whiskey, which was probably the reason he looked frumpy next to the admiral's towering fitness, but he'd served honorably and stood strong in a fight next to Casey, so he'd earned her respect. All the same, she didn't like him too much. But it didn't have to be personal. She saluted him, which caused Volk to draw down his eyebrows and glance between her and the admiral.

"Did we interrupt something?" Volk asked.

From behind him stepped a woman with hair the color of oak trees in the sun. She had a lean face with full, annoyingly perfect lips, cheekbones that could cut glass, and a pointed chin. Something about her immediately seemed familiar. For a moment, Casey struggled to place her. Shiny Lieutenant Colonel's shields had been freshly sewn onto the woman's shoulders. She was about Casey's height, six or eight years her senior, but still far too young to be a Lieutenant Colonel.

Young enough to make Casey suspicious.

Her suspicion fell to oceanic depths when a spark of recognition allowed Casey to place the officer. A tinny, echoey sound filled her ears. She stared, eyes fixed upon the beautiful woman.

She didn't realize she was clenching her teeth until Colonel Volk said, "Captain, are you all right?"

Casey blinked and forced a smile onto her face. "Fine, thank you, sir."

"Captain, I'd like you to meet your new squadron commander." Admiral Miyaru held out a hand. "This is Major—excuse me—*Lieutenant Colonel* Renata Spector."

Even though she knew it was coming, the admiral's words caused the bottom of her stomach to drop out. She felt suddenly queasy and tried her best not to show it.

"We've met," she managed to whisper. "Renata."

"Why, don't be disrespectful, little bird. It's Colonel Spector, *sir*, to you now."

The *nerve*. Casey hated the nickname Renata had used for her in military prep school, back when Casey had still been a scrawny thing whose growth spurt had come late. She would rather eject herself into deep space and freeze her ass off than face that shame again.

One of the voices vying for influence in her head finally won out—it wasn't Walcott's *or* her father's.

"Is that so?" Casey said. "I didn't realize the qualification standards for Lieutenant Colonel posts had been lowered so substantially."

"Captain!" Colonel Volk barked. "Apologize right now."

"Sorry, sir. I don't know what I was thinking."

"I do, little bird." Renata's wicked smile spread. "You always did know how to hold a grudge."

"And you always did know how to kiss major league ass."

"You'll regret saying that."

"And I will bear my punishment with grace, which is more than you ever did." She turned to Admiral Miyaru, whose face flushed with rage. "My sincere apologies, Admiral Miyaru. Thank you for agreeing to speak with me, even if the outcome was not what I'd been hoping for."

"Captain." The tone of her voice was a warning: walk away now before you regret it.

She spun and fled, being careful not to run, before she said anything else she'd regret. Casey cursed herself for reacting out of her basest instincts. Of all the thousands of people in the Fleet, what were the odds of her childhood tormentor becoming her new commander? And what kind of twisted universe did she live in where she lost the best boss she'd ever had, only to have him replaced by the likes of Renata freaking Spector?

She knew what Walcott would have said. He'd have said, "Good. She'll be hard on you, and it will make you stronger."

*Well, screw that.*

# FOUR

**W**hat luck, running into the Minister of Xeno Affairs at Walcott's memorial service!

Elya recognized Aganaki from a photo he'd found on the net. He dogged the man through the crowd. The minister was older, more wrinkled and gray than he had been when the photo was taken, yet still hale and lean and healthy-looking. Before he could make contact, Park and Yorra caught up to him and corralled him in another direction.

"Don't make a scene," Yorra whispered in his ear.

"What? I just want to ask him a question."

"About what?" asked Park.

Elya clammed up. Not yet. He'd always planned on telling them more, but not until he had something concrete.

They should have been more worried about Raptor. She was the one who was causing a scene. A sharp rebuke from Colonel Volk drew the crowd's eyes, followed by a ripple of stunned silence. The look on Admiral Miyaru's face as Osprey retreated could have melted aluminite.

Captain Osprey did have a way of speaking her mind, but that kind of outburst was unusual—something must have triggered her. There would be fallout, he had no doubt, and they'd all suffer for it.

By the time Elya turned his attention back to the minister, a crowd had surrounded the man. High level Imperial officials were rarely seen in public and everyone wanted to shake the hand of the influential bureaucrat. You never knew when you might need a favor to cut through the thick barricades of Imperial red tape.

Elya could use a favor about now. If anyone knew more about the Telos and their relics, it was the Minister of Xeno Affairs.

He lost his opportunity when someone announced that a flight of Sabres were doing an honorary pass to commence the service. Engines roared as the starfighters bore down on them from the north. The purr of engine fire increased as they passed rapidly overhead, leaving vapor trails in their wake like eight cloudy fingers.

After that, soft bells chimed to announce the service was starting. Elya reluctantly followed Park and Yorra back inside, meeting Osprey along the way. The four of them found a seat in a crowded pew. Elya scooted into the middle, between Park and some friends of the family.

His neck immediately began to itch. Were those security guards in the back of the sanctuary watching him?

*Or am I just being paranoid?* he thought.

Though he craned his neck around, he saw no one keeping an eye on him in particular. At least, not any more than normal in a crowded church service. Parishioners did love to gawk. He pressed his palms into his gritty eyes and forced himself to relax. The paranoia he'd left with that morning hung around him like a bad smell in the barracks.

A High Priest of Animus mounted the pulpit to perform introductory rites. Elya barely heard the rote phrases and familiar hymns. He did his best yo-yo impersonation, rising, sitting, rising, and sitting again in time with the rest of the congregation. The set of hymns chosen for today tugged at his heart. One young priest, a short plump man with a hawkish nose, had a voice that soared in a wailing minor key. Candles were lit and given to children who bobbed up and down the aisles, symbolically spreading the light of Sol, humanity's ancestral sun.

The ceremony ended with the widow and her son coming to the front and receiving an offering from the priests—a traditional haiwood sapling, representing new life, its roots bound up in the soil of Earth (symbolic Earth, anyway) and infused with the spirit of Animus. Funny gift to give someone on a city-planet whose only remaining green space had been overrun by refugee camps. Did they expect her to plant it on her thumbnail of a lot? What if she lived in an apartment like ninety percent of military families? But ancient religious institutions weren't exactly quick to change with the times.

The back of Elya's neck continued to tingle, as did his fingers, which wanted to look up Telos relics on his tab. A half-dozen search phrases he hadn't tried yet floated through his brain. Too bad he didn't rank high enough to get one of those implants all commanding officers received. It would allow him to search the net without looking at a device. One of those shipboard AIs would surely come in handy, too.

Assuming they could keep a secret...

Could they? Or was data shared when a shipboard AI was wired into the Ansible network?

With an effort, Elya dismissed the questions as curiosities for another time. *Man,* he thought, *My mind is easily distracted when I'm this exhausted. I really need to try to get more shut-eye.*

The coterie of priests in their green and brown robes faded into the background like the trees this world hadn't seen in centuries. Speeches started up next. Walcott's younger brother, the spitting image of the man, delivered a real tear jerker. Cousins, friends, and colleagues filed up to have their say. Mrs. Walcott dabbed at her eyes with a black handkerchief and rubbed her son's back while they pontificated. The boy sat straight and stone-faced.

Brave kid. Elya had lost his father to the Kryl when he was young, too, so he knew what the boy was going through. It would hurt—bad, and for a long while. But the boy was young enough that he would rebound within six months to a year, if he had good people around him. And it seemed like he did.

He ought to buy a tinkerbox and send it to Mrs. Walcott to give to her son. Anonymously, of course. Just a little something to keep the kid's mind occupied and his hands busy. That's how Elya first started working with bots, a skill that later helped him get into the SDF.

Once he made up his mind to send the boy the gift—after a polite delay, of course, to give him time to grieve—it set his mind at ease. He stopped fidgeting, and the rest of the service passed fairly quickly. The speeches drew to a close. Priests came back up to give their final remarks. He couldn't wait any longer. Before the congregation was dismissed, Elya dug out his tablet. He marked where the Minister of Xeno Affairs was sitting near the front of the chapel, then his fingers went to work.

Osprey hissed at him. When he didn't respond, she whispered, "What do you think you're doing?"

"Looking something up."

"The service isn't over."

She was worse than his nagging mother, sometimes. "Hedgebot, crawl up into Raptor's lap and give her the chill pill she forgot to take." The bot dutifully obeyed, hopping up onto Osprey's legs and cocking his head at her with a soft, *Meep?*

37

Osprey ground her teeth so loud people three rows up could have heard a molar chip.

The service ended as a priest thanked everyone for coming. Murmuring voices and the shuffle of feet filled the vast, echoey chapel as people rose and began to chatter with their neighbors.

He glanced up. The minister was already surrounded by eager citizens again. That bought him a little time.

Raptor's next words came in a normal voice and bearing a hard edge. "You've been buried in that screen since we got back."

He'd take that edge to the neck if he wasn't careful. "I'm doing research."

"On what?"

He looked up at her from under hooded brows.

"Oh, that."

She knew as much about the Telos relics as he did, since she was with him when he demonstrated the geode's power on the Kryl parasite and then handed it over to Fleet security. But she was better at following orders, content to let sleeping dogs lie until they received word to do otherwise, whereas Elya's nightmares didn't give him the luxury to leave it alone. And on the off chance his sleepless paranoia had the slightest basis in reality, time was of the essence.

"Ahh, here it is." His memory of the mystery had been true, but he'd forgotten the details.

A few years back, there had been a bunch of media consternation about a series of discretionary items a journalist discovered in the MOXA budget marked, "General Contracting & Repairs." The event had sparked a flood of wild speculation for two reasons:

One, financial regulations demanded such descriptions be specific.

Two, the amounts rose to the exorbitant sum of a hundred million credits.

Some theorized that the ministry was experimenting on Kryl in a secret laboratory located in a sub-basement beneath their building on Nebula Drive. More imaginative rumors held they were spending the money developing a "final solution" for the bugs, something war hawks in Parliament had suggested on more than one occasion. This idea sparked outrage from the scientific community, as well the Church of Animus, and was usually not taken seriously. Even though they hated the Kryl, the general public did not, as a rule, respond positively to the idea of government-sanctioned genocide.

As is the case with most conspiracy theories, a small intersection of speculators believed both rumors to be true.

It eventually came to light that the vague classification was a clerical error. MOXA officials claimed the budget was spent on repairs to the crumbling foundation of their headquarters building—and the foundation contractors who'd done the repairs had originated the fantasies about underground labs. No, they weren't holding Kryl prisoner in secret labs, and no they weren't researching a "final solution."

Or so they claimed.

Anti-Kryl activists had been disappointed to hear that one. You could almost hear the outrage and denial ringing out across the net.

No one had been truly satisfied by the ministry's explanation, but that was the official line and they stuck to it. Eventually, the story faded into the background of life as parliamentary elections and ministry appointments took precedence.

Except that, here on his screen, Elya had located one lone theory, backed up by no evidence and scoffed at by all the

Kryl-obsessed conspiracy theorists, saying the ministry had been funding research looking into "tools of the Telos."

Just a single line buried within a much longer discussion. But it fleshed out the idea his subconscious had sniffed out.

Exploration of Telos ruins also fell under the purview of the Ministry of Xeno Affairs. They had a whole division of xenoarchaeologists who mounted expeditions every year or two with a mandate to explore newly discovered sites—shrines, temples, small habitats excavated from the sand. MOXA would be interested in hearing more about the Telos shrine on Robichar. The boy Elya had saved from the Kryl once described it as a glowing golden room hidden at the back of a cave. Two relics had been found there—the geode Elya ultimately recovered and another one that, at least according to the boy, projected a holographic map of the stars.

Admiral Miyaru had told him not to speak to anyone about the relics. Technically, she hadn't ordered him not to speak about the room where those relics had been found.

Perhaps it was time he stopped passively researching and took matters into his own hands... before whoever was stalking his movements on the darknet caught up to him.

Besides, what harm could a little suggestion do? Worst case scenario, the minister ignored him and nothing came of it. They'd never be able to connect it to *him*. He'd been careful to cover his tracks.

Just in case, Elya quickly wiped his search history.

"Earth to Nevers. Come in, Fancypants."

He ignored Osprey and located the minister's crimson robes. The man had slipped through the crowd with the help of his body-blocking security retinue. Elya shuffled out of the pew, but got stuck in the outermost aisle by a group of people gabbing to each other and exchanging teary hugs.

"By the black hole of Damitron, move people," he muttered.

"Nevers!" barked Osprey behind him. "Show some respect."

The minister slipped out the fire exit door near the pulpit.

"*Not now*, Raptor," he muttered.

"You can be an insubordinate bastard sometimes."

Who was she to talk about respect when she'd just insulted their new squadron commander? "After that scene you made? Takes one to know one I guess."

Her face turned a red the same shade as the minister's robes.

"I promise to tell you all about it later," he added to soften the blow, "but I can't lose the minister. I need to get a message to him while I have the chance."

She blinked a few times before making the connection. Her mouth opened in a slight O-shape. She nodded. "You better not be disobeying orders. I'm already on thin ice."

"Not technically," Elya said, "Hedgebot, find the minister and try to delay him."

"This way," Osprey said. "You better not make me regret this."

He heard the fear in her voice. *I've already screwed up once today*, it said. *I can't afford another mistake.*

He understood how she felt. But he'd learned on Robichar that you can't let fear keep you from taking action. This was no life or death scenario, but the fate of the Solaran people was at stake. If they didn't find out more about those relics, the Kryl would get to them first and use them to attack the Solaran Empire—or Animus knew what else.

Hedgebot darted under the feet of the people blocking the aisle, and scurried out the fire exit at the next opportunity. Elya turned and followed Osprey to the front entrance. They ran around the outside of the building.

He was breathing hard when he reached the far corner, casting about as he searched for Hedgebot.

Because of the daylight, he didn't notice the red warning light his bot was giving off until the cold barrel of a blaster pistol pressed against his temple.

"This bot belong to you?"

Elya glanced down without moving his head. Hedgebot was stuck firmly under the black combat boot of a security officer. Two more stood behind him with their hands on their weapons. The minister was nowhere to be seen.

*Earth damn it all.* "It does."

"Why'd you send him after the minister, Captain...?" The man leaned in close enough that Elya could smell the menthol of chewing tabac on his breath. "Captain Nevers?"

"I just wanted to speak to him."

"If you weren't an SDF officer, I'd have you arrested right here for pulling that crap."

"At a funeral?"

The security guard glared.

"Uniform comes in handy, I guess," Elya added, his voice wobbling with a nervous chuckle.

"Do you know what the punishment is for attacking a minister of the Solaran Empire?"

"I didn't attack anybo—"

"Twenty years in the Cage." Short for the Molten Cage, the maximum security prison was an isolated habitat which orbited Ariadne like a small moon. It was big enough that you could see it from the surface if it weren't for all the light pollution (not to mention *actual* pollution).

"No one's attacked anyone," he said. "Hedgebot isn't designed to cause any harm. He's a colonial danger detector I converted to an astrobot. You want to see my license? I only sent him to distract and delay you so I had time to catch up before the minister left."

"Well, you missed your chance."

Raptor finally had enough of the exchange and stepped in front of him. "Would you mind not pointing your *weapon* at the head of my *pilot*? If anything happens to him, Admiral Miyaru will be furious."

The guard thrust his chin out and twisted his lips before slowly lowering the pistol. Elya took two steps back, exhaled shakily, and took the man in. He was a head taller than Elya, with a thick jutting brow and a nose that had been broken several times. His straight chestnut hair had been shaved close to the scalp on the sides, leaving greasy bangs to frame empty gray eyes. "She's already pissed at you. I saw that exchange earlier. I doubt she'd mind if I taught you a lesson, either, girl."

This time Osprey didn't blush. She lifted her chin in challenge and met the security guard's gray eyes with her unflinching sapphire gems. He'd never seen her back down from a challenge. Why start now? "Call me 'girl' again and you'll regret it."

"Easy," Elya said, holding up his open hands and stepping forward again, "Listen, I just wanted to give the minister some information. It's important. I didn't mean any harm. We'll act like this never happened if you relay a message to him for me."

Bangs adjusted his grip on the pistol held at his side. It had a squat silencer mounted to the barrel. His booted foot remained on top of Hedgebot, pinning his bot to the ground. "What message?"

Elya clenched his fists even as he tried to keep his voice calm. "Tell him I know the location of some Telos ruins on Robichar." Elya wished he could see the minister's face when he delivered the next part of the message. His reaction would tell him how close he'd come to the truth. But beggars couldn't be choosers. "They might have the relics he's been looking for."

The man snorted and lifted his foot. A bolt of plasma erupted from his pistol and ripped through Hedgebot's shell with a soft pop, killing its motors and putting out the bot's lights.

"Hey!" Elya's cheeks shook with anger. "What was that for!?"

He knelt beside the damaged bot, his heart thudding and aching at the same time as he lifted his carbon-stained companion in his hands and inspected the damage. Thank Animus, its protective armor plating had taken the brunt of the blast. Hedgebot's main electrical conduit had been severed by the blaster, but his central processing unit and power core seemed to be intact.

"My message to you," the guard said. "Keep your distance. Next time, that'll be you."

"Will you give him my message or not?" Elya forced the words out between clenched teeth.

The man glared down at him for a long minute before nodding, ever so slightly.

"Hope you enjoyed the service," Osprey called as the three guards turned and strode away. Her voice dropped to a whisper. "Asshole."

# FIVE

K ira spit a burnt yet chewy wad of bacon-wrapped shallot into a napkin and deposited it on a tray held out by a passing servant bot. Vat grown bacon was especially disgusting. She knew she should eat something and had tried several of the foods being served at the reception, but everything she put in her mouth tasted like ash.

She forced a smile onto her face as Colonel Volk made a joke to a group of younger officers. Not only did her gut feel like a pit, but she'd also lost her sense of humor since Captain Osprey's public outburst. It wasn't insubordination, not exactly, but it had pissed her right off.

She spent an embarrassing amount of Walcott's service imagining creative punishments for the young flight lead. Hang her upside down from a suspended starfighter? Order her to clean carbon marks off a battle-scarred bot with a toothbrush? Put her in the brig for a month with her own words played back on a loop?

Nothing was satisfying. Not only could she not afford to lose a good pilot and a capable leader during a command transition, but it wasn't her place to punish Captain Osprey.

That was Lt. Colonel Renata Spector's job now.

She grabbed the woman's arm as she walked by. "I need the Furies in fighting shape," Kira whispered.

Renata's finely plucked eyebrows lifted slightly. "Of course, Admiral. Is there something particular I should be preparing them for?"

"I don't expect we'll be in port for long." Word of that morning's events would spread, no doubt. She'd figure it out.

"I see. And what do you recommend I do with Captain Osprey, sir?"

Kira kept her imaginative punishments to herself. "You're the squadron commander. I expect you'll handle that how you see fit."

Spector took a breath in as if to speak, then held it, pursing her lips. After a moment, she said, "I wonder if she has the temperament to be flight lead, sir."

"Give her a pass on this one." In spite of her emotional outburst today, Kira had seen Captain Osprey perform well under pressure, in a job that she had no business doing. She'd seen her stand her ground in the face of danger, and put her life and career on the line to save a fellow pilot. That was, perhaps, why Kira had been dreaming up such imaginative punishments for the young woman. She *liked* Captain Osprey, and Kira had always demanded the most out of the people she cared about.

"Captain Osprey has much to learn, but keep in mind she buried her squadron commander today. There's obviously some history between you two. That's on me for not real- izing it. Since you don't officially take this post until tomor- row, start with a clean slate. If she made this personal, as her squadron commander, I expect you *not* to." It was so much easier to give other people advice that you didn't want to take yourself. Did she want to punish Osprey for the embar- rassing outburst? Affirmative. Was she asking Renata not to?

Also yes. She didn't want any animosity among the squad. "Are we clear?"

Two vertical lines made a brief appearance between Renata's perfectly plucked brows. If she hadn't been watching closely, she wouldn't have seen the hesitation. "Yes, Admiral. Crystal."

"Good. From here on, she's yours to command, but do so fairly and with discretion."

Spector saluted. Kira returned the gesture then departed, leaving the reception without a word or a backward glance. Colonel Volk would forgive her for not saying goodbye and she didn't care what anyone else thought.

An untrusted leader is a danger in battle, and this was Spector's first command position as Lt. Colonel. She'd made the rank young and while she came highly recommended, with experience patrolling Kryl space, the SDF had grown soft in the last decade of peace; Kira wondered if anyone except a veteran of the Kryl War would be truly ready for what she feared was coming.

Especially if Chairman Card didn't heed her warnings.

The day was unseasonably warm. Kira shrugged out of the jacket of her formal dress and folded it over one arm, hoping that the white undershirt would help her blend in with the crowd better. She needn't have worried. The four story market square was thronged with people, crowded and noisy and filled with smoke. No one paid her the slightest attention.

She inhaled the aroma of fresh-brewed coffee, flowers, and roasting meat—*real* meat, not that vat-grown rubber—as her mind returned to mulling over the problem of the Colonization Board.

Embarrassing Chairman Card in a public hearing had been a grave error. She saw that now with clear eyes. In a battle, outmaneuvering her opponent usually got her what she wanted. Politics was a much more delicate operation.

She needed Card to be willing to listen to her. She'd already shown him the parasite. It had moved him, but not in the right way. To get him to hear her out, she needed him to have an open mind. And to get him to be open minded, she'd need to offer him something that he wanted.

So what did he want? To act on what he called the Solaran Empire's "imperative to expand." To redistribute the refugees crowding Ariadne out into the galaxy so they stopped crowding his front yard. She'd already publicly opposed Card in the hearing. Imagining what she'd have to do to walk that back left a sour taste in her mouth.

The other option was to get someone Card trusted to calm him down—a neutral third party—so he'd be willing to entertain her way of thinking. Maybe then they could meet behind closed doors. He'd never agree to another public hearing. What Kira needed was an ally.

Short of going to the Emperor himself, Kira didn't have the connections to make this happen. She only had one card left to play—the Telos relic Captain Nevers had found. And she wasn't ready to reveal that yet.

"You have such a talent for getting yourself into impossible situations."

Kira smiled at the return of Harmony's sardonic words, ones which mirrored her own thoughts with uncanny ease. The shipboard AI had access to her thoughts through the silicate chip embedded at the base of her skull, right next to the spinal port that all pilots were given for chemical administration while piloting high-velocity spacecraft. She didn't make use of her spinal taps much these days, not unless she took a joy ride in a Sabre, but she had come to consider the companionship and support the AI provided indispensable.

"Welcome back, Harmony. Didn't realize I'd come within range of the *Paladin*. How long have you been with me?"

"Long enough to know you had an interesting morning."

It had taken her years to get used to Harmony's presence. Now, she couldn't imagine her job without her. She was a confidante, a comrade, and the pilot of *Paladin of Abniss*, her great Imperial destroyer. Outside of the ship, away from the hologram arrays, Harmony wasn't able to manifest the nodes of light that made up her physical presence like she did when Kira was aboard the ship. However, even without a physical presence, within a certain radius of the ship she was fully present in Kira's mind.

"The new software upgrade we received this week extended my range on Ariadne by another three kilometers," Harmony said proudly. "I've been with you since you reached the market."

"Neat. Now everyone here will think I'm a crazy person talking to myself."

Harmony chuckled. "But much better dressed. Can't remember the last time I saw you in this uniform."

A ragged beggar limped through the market muttering to himself with outstretched hands. His hair was matted into a single tangled dreadlock and his patchy beard stuck up in all directions. Shoppers gave him a wide berth. Kira frowned at the faded Imperial patch on the old jacket he wore. She veered past him, swiping her tab against the wrist-mounted device he held.

"Thank you, miss," he croaked.

She smiled. "Take care."

On her walk she saw a dozen more like him. She donated to a few, but couldn't afford to help them all, and eventually had to cut herself off.

"It's too bad you couldn't make it to the hearing this morning, Harmony."

"I watched the highlight reel."

Kira sighed. "Promise me you'll put me out of my misery if I ever contemplate a move into politics."

"You have my word."

She spotted a pub up ahead, a comfortable, dingy place full of old wood and older music frequented by officers of the SDF and playfully named *Nuke It From Orbit*. She realized her feet had been taking her here the whole time.

Her stomach rumbled. Maybe she was finally ready to eat. A drink would be nice, too.

"You are a creature of habit, Admiral."

"Oh, hush. It isn't often I drink."

"I meant the bar. You always come here when you're feeling contemplative."

Kira hung her formal jacket on a hook beneath the bar and slid onto a stool at the far end, as far away from other people as she could get. She ordered a double shot bloody mary and snacked on a cup of mixed nuts—also lab grown, but salty enough that she didn't care—while she waited for her drink. When it arrived and she went to pay for it, the bartender shook her hand and pointed down the bar at an older woman with tight curls of steel gray. A face with a broad nose and square chin looked back at her. Kira gestured to the open stool beside her. The woman picked up her pint glass and walked around the bar.

"Admiral Gitano," Kira said. "What a lovely surprise. Thanks for the drink."

"Looked like you could use it."

Kira grimaced. "That obvious?"

"Cheers."

She met Gitano's large, watery eyes as they clinked their glasses. The admiral sat on the Executive Council, a group of senior-ranking military personnel who governed the Solaran Defense Forces—the same council who got her the appointment with Chairman Card. Gitano's area of focus was the space navy, more commonly known as "the Fleet," but ExCo governed all military branches; they approved new policies, managed funding, assigned key strategic missions, and generally governed the vast bureaucracy the SDF had become since the beginning of the Kryl War.

Gitano also governed the Fleet's spy apparatus. It was no coincidence that they'd run into each other here.

They chit-chatted about mutual colleagues and work while Kira ginned up courage to ask the question she was dying to ask. She wasn't quite there yet, so she stuck with small talk.

"How long have you been part of the Council now, Vice Admiral?"

The corners of Gitano's mouth pulled down, creasing her otherwise smooth, unblemished dark skin. "Almost a decade."

"You don't like it?"

"Fah. Not most days. They seemed to think my appointment was some kind of award for my service. I would rather be leading an armada into battle, but battle commanders were not what the SDF needed after the Kryl War."

Kira had been a colonel at the end of the Kryl War, and was only promoted to admiral for her heroics in helping that end come about. Her first years in the peace that followed were spent running around the galaxy mopping up straggling Kryl forces and chasing aggressive hives back to Kryl space—not that she'd minded. With her heart so recently broken, she had needed the distraction and liked being far away from home, where everything reminded her of what she'd lost. Nevertheless, Kira had been deployed while the transition Gitano was talking about took place. "What *was* needed?"

"Politicians."

Kira nodded. She had been deployed when the war leaders were forced into retirement and people like Gitano were appointed to the Executive Council, but she paid enough attention to know it was happening, and why. "You must be good at it to have lasted this long."

Gitano shrugged, drained her glass and signaled the bartender for a refill. "My curse."

"Maybe your curse is my blessing." She finally decided to just go for it. "Did you see the feeds this morning?"

Gitano grimaced, but her eyes glittered. "Quite the performance you put on. Card's a stubborn one, though. Didn't really expect anything less."

Kira answered with a groan. "I know, I know. I misjudged."

"Like anything, it takes practice."

"So can you help me?"

The barkeep dropped Gitano's new pint on the counter in a chilled glass. She picked at the frost on the outside with a thumbnail. "Not officially. You probably already know this, but the SDF has been downsizing for years. We're more of a colonial security force these days than a space navy."

"I'd noticed," Kira said, her voice flat and hard.

"As our star falls, the Colonization Board's rises. Next year their budget will be three quarters the size of ours, and in the next five years it will be larger than the SDF's. It has taken almost all of my energy over the last three years to prevent substantial forces from being transferred into their control."

Kira inhaled sharply. "I didn't know that."

"Because I didn't let it happen. The only way to prevent it in the long term, though, is to cooperate with them. As you know, the Fleet escorts the *Maidens* on their voyages." She was referring to the ships carrying colonists to new worlds.

"And we give them free security for the first five years of construction."

"That, and he was opposed to the mission to Robichar because it delayed the voyage to New Kali that's scheduled to depart at the end of this week."

*Aha.* She hadn't realized that sending a single destroyer and a couple wings of starfighters to Robichar meant that he didn't have the required security escort to launch the *Maiden of Kali* when he wanted to. "Talk about being spread too thin. No wonder Card was so hostile towards me." Kira cussed into her bloody mary for a minute as she angrily gobbled up the rest of the olives and pickles in her glass. It was her turn to signal for another. They watched the bartender in silence while he prepared it.

After her drink arrived, Kira took a sip and said, "Did you read my report about what we discovered on Robichar?" She'd kept any mention of Captain Omar Ruidiaz out of her official report. It disturbed her deeply to learn that her former lover had not, in fact, died, but had become a Kryl mutant known as Subject Zero. She wasn't ready to share that information with anyone. It didn't change what she learned about the parasite or the Telos weapon, or what needed to be done about them, so there was no reason to tear open old wounds by mentioning him. Whatever he was now, he wasn't the Omar she'd once known. That man died a long time ago.

"I read it," Gitano said.

"So you know what's at stake. The Kryl are evolving new capabilities. They're roaming again, and this time they seem to be after these Telos relics—the stuff of legends. I wouldn't believe it if I hadn't seen the weapon with my own eyes. It's dangerous to them, so no wonder they don't want us to have it. If we don't act fast, the Overmind will soon perfect the parasite as a means to capture human intelligence, and potentially acquire more relics with Earth knows what kind of power. If that happens, we've got another galactic war on our hands."

Gitano swirled the beer in her glass. "Did you turn the Kryl parasite over to the Ministry of Xeno Affairs for study yet?"

She'd been ordered to do so by the Executive Council. And after the confrontation with Chairman Card, the press was clamoring for her to turn it over to the proper authorities—no doubt so they could write lurid articles about it. Kira hesitated. Could she be honest?

"You did say you needed an ally..." Harmony added silently.

"Not yet," Kira said aloud.

Gitano nodded. "Then there's still a chance."

Maybe she wasn't as bad at politics as she thought.

"What do I do?"

"Meet with Minister Aganaki."

She exhaled forcefully. "That snake?"

"Yes. He is a snake, but he's a consistent snake. He knows about the parasite now, and he wants it. Use it as a bargaining chip to get him to help you convince Card that the threat is real."

"You... you want me to bribe him?"

"I didn't say that, Admiral."

"I just need to get Chairman Card to meet with me in private. If you can get him to listen to reason, I—"

"I can't. I told you about our funding problems. If I intervene, I'll jeopardize a number of efforts already in motion. I can't risk it. If we do have to go to war again, it's imperative that we keep the Fleet intact."

Kira stared at her hands. "If this were a war, I'd know exactly what to do."

"Aganaki is your best bet. Remember, he's a snake, but

he's a *consistent* snake." Gitano reached over the bar and grabbed a napkin and a pen. "Here are a couple more people who might be able to render aid. Tread carefully."

"Oh, fascinating," said Harmony's voice in Kira's head. "I haven't seen *him* in years."

Kira ignored the AI and shoved the napkin into her pocket. She drained the rest of her drink and stood. Her stomach roiled, and not from the vodka.

"One more thing, Admiral," said Gitano. "I was asked to pass along a report we received this morning. The Kryl intelligence you are calling Overmind X has left Robichar. They're on the move again."

"Earth's last light... so soon." Kira said. "They must have found what they were looking for."

"It's unclear where they're headed, but my people are tracking them."

Clearly, running into Gitano at her favorite bar hadn't been a happy accident. The meeting had been engineered. Kira took a deep breath, trying to maintain her composure in front of a member of the Executive Council—a leader she trusted.

And who, despite her many mistakes, trusted her.

She didn't want to ask the minister for help. But what choice did she have?

"Remember, Kira, this is politics, not war. At least not yet," Gitano said. "Good luck."

# SIX

Elya braced against the fence and dry heaved between panting breaths.

"We've run drills for your smartass mouth before," he said after the convulsions passed. "But this is by far the worst."

"Quit your whining," Osprey panted, shooting him a wry grin. "What doesn't kill you—"

"Makes you sore and tired," Park finished for her. "This makes boot camp seem like recess for Kindergarteners, Raptor. We've been going nonstop for *days*."

"Shut up, the lot of you," Yorra whispered. "She'll eat us alive."

"Flight 18!" Spector barked across the empty runway, her voice tinny and sharp as it was projected through the speakers of a blocky surveillance drone hovering fifty meters away. Its tiny engines hummed as it drifted over, illuminating them with a spotlight in the pre-dawn darkness. "Did anyone tell you it was okay to stop and chit chat? Do you think this is some kind of happy hour?"

"Sir, no, sir!" Raptor shouted back.

"I don't appreciate your snark, little bird."

56

"Snark? What, I just—"

"I'm docking a hundred points on your flight's ratings for mouthing off. Now drop and give me fifty!"

They hit the ground as a unit. Between pushups, Osprey glared across the tarmac to where Spector stood watching them. Yorra was the first to finish. She bounced up and laced her hands over her head, catching her breath.

"No fair," Elya said, "You have less distance to travel with those short arms."

"NEVERS, DID I SAY YOU COULD SPEAK?" the commander shouted. "YOUR WHOLE FLIGHT GETS ANOTHER FIFTY!"

Colonel Volk, who had joined them at O' Dark Thirty for conditioning, clutched his beer belly and chuckled as he and Spector sipped their hot coffees.

The others groaned as they dropped to the ground. Park gave him the finger as he did a one-handed pushup. Yorra muttered some very colorful cuss words as she lowered back down and started on another set. Osprey counted out loud.

*Overachiever*, Elya thought darkly.

When they were done, they hauled themselves to their feet and sprinted across the tarmac to the next station, where they jumped rope for five minutes.

And on and on it went.

This was the fifth day of punishment—er, training—the new squadron commander had put them through. With the way he was tossing and turning at night, waking up every couple hours with terrible nightmares in a flood of adrenaline, Elya struggled to drag himself out of bed before dawn, let alone find time to continue his research into the relics.

He hadn't heard back from the Minister of Xeno Affairs and, at this point, he didn't expect to. The chatrooms were aflame with news of the parasite the admiral had shown the Colonization Board. It was a ballsy move, and one that he

57

hadn't expected from the cool-headed admiral. But it sure had made a point and it was fascinating to see how people were responding—from excitement to panicked terror and everything in between.

He had also received several more messages with offers of help and random tidbits of information. One out of ten seemed legit, and of those, the majority talked nonsense, like bots with crossed wires or faulty power cells. There was one source that made some sense, but they were making him jump through hoops consisting of private addresses, secret keys and code phrases just to chat, which made him even more suspicious of their intentions. To make his paranoia worse, every time he left the base by himself, the back of his neck itched like someone was pulling a bead on him. Given all of this, it was, frankly, a relief to be training. At least on base, only people with valid identification got through the security gates.

Spector drove them hard. Physical training in the morning, practice maneuvers in their Sabres during the day, and at night they alternated shooting range drills with ground school.

But Osprey was even more ruthless. If the commander didn't make them run enough to suit her, she dragged them to the gym to lift weights. She made them show up early for pre-flight, and stay late after ground school for extra "bonding time." Their flight was always the last to leave the shooting range. They burned through more charge mags than any other flight in the squad.

Elya liked working hard; it's how he had got into officer school and how he made the cut for the starfighter pilot program once he was there. Training more than everyone else had always been his *thing*. It used to drive Osprey crazy when he would pass up time playing cards to squeeze in an extra sim.

Now, it was Osprey who pushed them forward with relentless determination. He'd never seen the masochistic side of her, and he wasn't sure he liked it. She obviously held some kind of grudge against the new squadron commander, too, because everything was "yes, sir" this and "no, sir" that—far too stiff to be a sign of respect.

But he wasn't going to be the one to point that out to her.

Fortunately, he didn't have to.

"What's your deal with Renny Stickbum anyway?" Yorra asked in the locker room after physical training ended. She used Park's name for their new commander, a nickname he'd invented days ago when she made them stand in parade formation to criticize the creases on their uniforms and inform them that their every waking minute now belonged to her. He wondered if all new squads went through this kind of hazing with a new commander or if it was just her style as a hardass.

"What do you mean?" Osprey asked, pulling off her sneakers and tossing them into her locker from a seated position on the bench. She was the last to change out of her training clothes, as usual, as if she felt like changing was tantamount to giving up. The rest of them were standing, already dressed in casual clothes for breakfast.

"Come on, Rap, don't play dumb. You push us harder than she does. And I see the way you look at her, like your eyes were blaster bolts and you have the power to burn her tits off."

Reserved and quiet in public, Yorra had a way of making a person listen when she spoke.

Osprey glanced at Elya for support. He shrugged and rubbed the back of his neck. When Park refused to meet her eyes, either, her mouth fell open in astonishment. "You're ganging up on me."

Elya exchanged looks with Park and Yorra. "Well, we

didn't plan anything ahead of time, if that's what you're asking. But I agree with her."

"Fine. You can sleep in tomorrow."

"And you'll let us go early after ground school tonight?" Park asked hopefully.

"I was kind of hoping we'd review the playbook together..." Osprey was referring to the file of a hundred flight maneuvers the new commander had given them to memorize as homework. It was complex stuff that made even Elya's eyes roll into the back of his head. "It's good bonding time. We could do it over beers!"

Park groaned. "What happened to you, Raptor? Used to be bonding meant playing games in the rec or going out to bars when we were back on base. Now all you wanna do is train! It's like you and Nevers switched places."

Elya felt himself blush. "That's not all I want to do."

"Oh yeah, you like reading conspiracy theory crap on those darknet forums too."

Raptor blinked. "Conspiracy theories? I thought you told me you were just fact checking what you learned about the Kryl on Robichar."

Elya felt his blush deepening. He'd brought her into the tent after their encounter with the MOXA security guard. He kept his suspicions that he was being followed to himself, and only shared a few of the more, uh, reputable theories. He didn't tell her anything about the anonymous messages he'd been receiving. He coughed into a hand. "This isn't about me."

"We'll come back to you, Nevers." Yorra's narrowed eyes were hard, and she planted a fist on one hip. "So, 'little bird,' what's your deal with the commander?"

Osprey hung her head between her legs for a second, rubbing at her temples. "I'm your flight lead, show a little more respect." Though she said the words, there was no conviction behind them. After a moment, she pushed herself to her feet and sighed.

She paced around the locker room barefoot for a minute while she gathered her thoughts. The three of them sat down on the bench and waited.

"My dad shipped me off to the Capital Military Academy on Ariadne when I was ten. Renata went to the same school. She was older, I think she was junior grade when I got there. She was popular. Had a ton of friends. Head of her class academically and she dated the most popular boy in school, Avis Perjeron."

"Wait," Park said. "*Major* Avis Pejeron?"

"The very same."

"Damn."

"But that only makes her, what, six or seven years older than you?" Elya said. "And you're a year older than me, so... she's, what, thirty-three?"

Osprey nodded. "Thirty four, I think. Her parents held her back a year so she would be bigger and smarter than the other kids."

"Who the hell makes Lt. Colonel at thirty-four?"

"Renata does." Her mouth twisted with distaste.

"I still don't understand," Yorra said. "Why do you hate her so much?"

"Because she tormented me most of the year we went to school together."

"'Little bird.'" Elya used his fingers to wrap air quotes around the phrase.

Osprey scrunched up her nose and made a growling noise in her throat. "Yeah. That."

"What did you do to piss her off?" Park asked.

"I didn't *do* anything."

"Uh huh," Yorra said.

"At first, I looked up to her. Wanted to *be* her. What

impressionable teenager wouldn't want to be the popular girl? All the teachers loved her. All the boys wanted to date her. But then one day I walked into a classroom looking for one of my teachers—I don't even remember what I wanted to ask them—and found her there with two of her friends. They were doing something on a school terminal, and when I tried to turn and leave they grabbed me by the arms and legs, pinned me down and told me to keep quiet about what I saw or they'd have a bot cut all my hair off."

Elya shuddered involuntarily. He'd had bots sicced on him by bullies before. It wasn't an experience he'd wish on anyone.

"Well, don't keep us in suspense, Raptor," Park said, leaning forward. He was into it now. "What was on the tab?"

"At first I didn't understand it. But they gave it away when they threatened me. They were cheating."

"Like cheating on a test?"

"Worse. They were fixing the vote for class captain so that Renata would win."

Yorra's eyebrows shot up. "Did you tell anyone?"

"I did, but it was my word against all of theirs. I got in trouble. Suspended for three days. They got a slap on the wrist, and none of the teachers found any evidence of trying to fix the election."

"Let me guess," Yorra said. "She was elected class captain."

Osprey twisted her mouth so her jaw stuck out to one side. She nodded.

"What!" Park said, outraged. "That's not fair!"

Raptor shrugged. "I know. But none of the teachers believed me. They thought I was jealous of her or something. You asked who makes Lt. Colonel at thirty-four? She's probably the youngest Lieutenant Colonel the Solaran Defense Forces have ever had, and I'd bet my life she didn't come by it honestly."

"Are you saying she fixed her promotion like she fixed the school election? The SDF isn't some high school popularity contest."

"I'm saying that she'll do anything it takes to climb the ladder and make herself look good in the process. I don't know if she bribed, blackmailed, kissed ass or called in favors to make it happen, but I guarantee there's a story there. Anyway, after my suspension ended, the tormenting began. They teased me endlessly. That's when 'little bird' started. They pulled pranks on me. They put vinegar in my toothpaste and baking soda in my pillow. One time, they stole my clothes and towel when I was in the shower after gym class, forcing me to walk naked back to my dorm. The whole school talked about that for weeks. They beat me up between classes, locked me into lockers, hid my tab from me when I had a paper due. Looking back, I guess it made me tough. I got my tattoos to spite Renata, you know." She bared her forearms, where there were tattoos of the hawk that was her namesake in flight. It didn't look like a little bird—it was ferocious, its eyes narrowed hard. One of them had a fish gripped firmly in its talons.

"Sorry, Rap, we didn't know. I feel you about the nickname, though, believe me." Elya had come to accept and even enjoy his own moniker, but that was a recent development borne of the respect he'd earned from his friends for surviving the crash landing on Robichar, rescuing two civvies from the clutches of the Kryl and bringing a Telos relic back with him.

"Hey, Fancypants, we offered to change your name to Skid. You declined."

Elya shrugged. "What can I say? It's grown on me."

"It's fine, guys, really," Osprey said. "I shouldn't let it get to me so much."

"Little bird is way better than Renny Stickbum, in any case."

"I'll admit, it did make me feel a little better when you started calling her that." A smile slowly spread across Osprey's face to match Park's wry smirk.

"And now we know why you laughed so hard about it."

"You don't have to prove anything to her," Yorra said. "We're with you."

"That's right," Park said.

"Always," Nevers added. "We've got each other's backs."

Osprey blinked a few times before inhaling deeply through her nose and shaking her head slowly. "I just… I don't want there to be any doubts. Even if we were the best flight in the Furies, that wouldn't be enough for her. We also have to work the hardest."

"You know I like training hard," Elya said. "Gears is tough, she can take it. Naab's lazy, but he keeps up most of the time."

"Ow, Fancy, that hurts. Right here." He tapped his chest with two fingers.

"You have a heart?" Elya asked. "This is news to me. Tell me you didn't share that with the one-night stand you brought home last week. She might get attached."

Park picked up a sweaty t-shirt and threw it at him. "Wiseass."

Yorra frowned at Park and turned to dig in her gym bag.

A ping sounded from his locker. While the other two comforted Raptor, Elya retrieved his tablet and checked his messages.

"Speaking of Renny Stickbum, we just got a note from her. Went out on squad comms." He scanned through the message and glanced up. "She ranked all twenty-five flights."

Osprey's breath caught in her throat. "And where is Flight 18?"

"You don't want to know."

Her face darkened. "Yes, I do."

"Well... we're not in last place."

"What's our rank, Nevers?"

He squinted as he said it. "Twentieth."

A metal sound deafened them as Osprey stood and kicked the door of an open locker, rattling it loudly.

"Come on, that can't be right," Park said. "Did she say why?"

"I don't see anyth—oh. She sent another message to each flight individually. Let's see."

Elya read it, paused, looked from Yorra to Park.

"Well?" Osprey said. "Read it to us."

"It's bullshit, Captain."

"Read it anyway."

"It says, 'Physical fitness good. Flying skills adequate. Leadership leaves something to be desired. Work ethic doesn't seem genuine. Leaders should inspire, not coerce.'"

This time Osprey didn't kick the locker. She held in her anger, and her face grew hard and cold. "That dishonest, rotten, two-faced, backstabbing bitch. She's doing this to punish me, I know she is."

"We'll stay late tonight," Park said. "Go over that playbook."

"And get up early tomorrow," Yorra added.

"Flying skills *adequate*," Elya said, chewing over the words as he reread them. "Now I know she's full of shit. I'm the best pilot in the squadron!"

"And humble too."

Elya threw a half-hearted swing in Park's direction, which the shorter pilot ducked easily as he brought his hands up to a high guard, bouncing back and forth.

But Osprey was in no mood for games. She dressed quickly and silently, tying her shoelaces like she was trussing

65

a wild boar. "Do breakfast without me," she said as she strode past them. "And take tonight off, too."

"Where are you going?"

"We worked too hard to get here," she called over her shoulder. "I'm not going to let Lieutenant Colonel Renny Stickbum take that away from us."

# SEVEN

Spector ran them through a brutal physical workout the
next day followed by six hours of high altitude pattern
work. The mental stimulation of that many takeoffs and
landings could be taxing on a normal day, but after a week of
strenuous workouts and drills, it was a miracle Casey's team
didn't have any accidents.

Debrief ran an hour longer than usual, with half the
squad on the verge of collapse. Squadron Commander
Spector seemed to delight in startling people who fell asleep
while she was talking.

Then she abruptly gave them the weekend off.

Which was a relief. But also a subversive way to endear
the pilots to their new commander, softening the punishment by following it with a wonderful reward. Casey recognized the pattern. Her father had used the same tactics on
her when she was a child, pushing her and pushing her until
even a routine kindness like letting her sleep in on a
Saturday morning seemed like a magnanimous gesture.

And it was working. The other pilots in the squadron
were warming to Spector. She overheard one of the older

guys, a major from flight two, say, "Work hard, play hard—I can get behind that," as he rushed off to blow his paycheck at the nearest strip club.

Park, Yorra and Nevers remained supportive, insisting they believed her story about Renata's prep school misbehavior. But she could see a glimmer of doubt in their eyes, too. They thought it was possible Spector had changed, that she wasn't as bad as Casey said she was.

She went to bed furious that night, and slept fitfully.

The next morning, Yorra suggested they all go down to watch the last shuttle ferry people up to the *Maiden of Kali* before it embarked on its maiden voyage. Casey jumped on the idea, calling a hovercab to take the four of them to the Colonization Board's dedicated spaceport.

While Park and Yorra spent the ride cracking jokes, Nevers tapped on his tab, chewing his nails and ignoring them all. It always got under her skin when he held himself aloof from the rest of the team, and she found herself seething over his behavior, clenching and unclenching her jaw and staring at him across the back seat.

A part of her recognized she was most likely directing her frustration with Renata toward the other captain when he hadn't done anything to deserve it.

Another part of her didn't care.

She fumed.

The hovercab slowed as the crowd thickened, edging to a standstill at the observation deck adjacent to the spaceport, which was mobbed with people.

"Here's good," Casey said, swiping her tab to stop the autonomous cab and pay at the same time. She jumped out while the vehicle was still moving.

Yorra unfolded from the front passenger seat with an audible gasp. "Wow," she breathed. "It makes the *Paladin* look like a little dinghy."

The *Maiden of Kali* stretched overhead, its shining alumi-nite hull rising up and out of sight. It spanned the length of the deck, two kilometers at least, and curved out of sight for another klick in either direction. A grouping of six powerful engines mounted together at the back of the starship were each larger than Ariadne's tallest skyscrapers and powerful enough to burn one of the buildings they resembled to ash with a single burst.

At least, it would have been if it were here on Ariadne. Due to its massive size and weight, colonial voyagers had to be constructed in orbit. It would take too much fuel to launch a starship of this size from the surface of Ariadne. But the Colonization Board wanted everyone to be able to marvel at it, and celebrate its departure, so they spent the money to pipe in a scale model, live holovid and host this launch party where everyone could watch the final passenger shuttle fly up to board the craft.

"You've never seen a voyager before?" Park asked.

"Not like this," Yorra said. "Oltanis was settled long before I was born, and since I enlisted I've always been in training or on missions when a colony ship launched."

"When they get to New Kali, the ship is designed to set down and serve as their habitat for three years," Park said. "After that, they take it to pieces and reuse its parts to construct the colony's first permanent settlements."

Yorra rolled her eyes. "I said I'd never seen one in person, not that I learned about colonies yesterday."

"Oh." He frowned, pulling out his loose tabac and rolling a cigarette.

"The original command deck of the *Maiden of Oltanis* still operates as a museum near my hometown, you know, and the greenhouse grew vegetables until I was ten. Bet they don't have anything like *that* on Taj Su."

"You know the first wave of colonies didn't get all the

bells and whistles, not like yours did. And the new ones get support from the Fleet, now, too."

"Lucky them. My parents' generation built Oltanis with their bare hands. We grew up really poor, you know."

"Us, too. It still won't be a walk in the park, but most people would pay a lot for a chance at a new life."

Casey let the pair drift ahead as they chatted, their shoulders brushing. She slowed her pace until Nevers came alongside her. He was walking without watching where he was going, totally engrossed in his tab. She wasn't sure he'd even lifted his head up to look at the voyager yet. Hedgebot, which he'd finally finished repairing last night after they were dismissed from ground school, was perched on his shoulder, watching the crowd with a keen interest.

The bot noticed her before the pilot did. Nevers cycled between an image of a blueprint of a large building, a busy chatroom and a dense page of text on his tablet.

"Planning a heist, Fancypants?"

He jumped and fumbled the tablet, catching it halfway to the pavement. "Earth's last light, you startled me."

"Think it's high time you told me what the hell you're doing that's got you so wrapped up you aren't even watching where you're walking."

"I told you, it's that Earth-blasted relic." Nevers folded and pocketed his tablet. "I'm not sleeping well, either. I keep having the same nightmare over and over." He rubbed at his eyes with his knuckles.

"Why?"

"What happened on Robichar I guess, with Subject Zero and the geode, and that nasty little parasite."

She grunted. Casey could understand that. On Robichar, he'd been forced to face his mortality in a way she never had. Her own experience with the parasite had been harrowing, but at least she had the support of Admiral Miyaru. Nevers had been down on that planet alone, with no guarantee of a rescue.

Her heart hardened. He was avoiding the question and she was falling for it again. "So what *are* you researching, then?"

Nevers licked his lips and looked over his shoulder, studying the people around them. Hawkers shouted from market stalls along one entire edge of the observation deck. Buskers and performance artists played music, made living statues, or danced in various spots, causing the flow of people to stream around and between them. The crowd was made up of Solarans from all walks of life, from the aristocrat in an angular high fashion suit trailed by a bot hung with a dozen shopping bags, to a young family pushing twins in a double stroller, to shabby-looking refugees begging for spare credits. Dozens of SDF personnel were here, in casual clothes but recognizable by the port on the back of their heads and their shaved, regulation haircuts. Some were with their spouses and children, others with their squadmates, like the four of them.

Among all of this noise and movement, Colonization Board security guards in gray body armor and helmets, with semi-automatic rifles slung over their shoulders, meandered, keeping watch. To any average person, their movements seemed random, their stoic expressions bored. Casey had been around military forces long enough to know that wasn't the case at all. The patrol patterns they walked were purposeful and well designed. Their eyes took in everything.

"Tell me this," Nevers said as he lifted Hedgebot off his shoulder and set him on the ground. With a spiraling motion of one pointer finger, he deployed the danger detector in a patrol pattern of his own. Nevers took his tablet back out and kept one eye on a blinking beacon. Casey realized after a beat that it was tracking Hedgebot. He must have made some improvements to the bot during his repairs. "Why weren't we briefed on the possibility of Telos relics before I stumbled on one on Robichar?"

She shrugged. "Because you found a new and remarkable alien technology?"

He bobbed his head from side to side in a non-committal gesture. "Too easy. I don't think so. There are tons of theories floating around the darknet about the Telos, including about the artifacts they left behind. Rumors and guesses, mostly."

"Did they say anything about relics?"

"Nothing solid I can confirm. There's no peer-reviewed scientific literature on the subject, which strikes me as extremely strange. Oh sure, there are papers and books about the Telos published by MOXA, and tons of xenobiology and military strategy stuff about fighting the Kryl, but nothing specifically about relics. Don't you think that's weird?"

"Not really. What's it matter?"

"If the SDF knew Telos relics existed and were dangerous —hell, if they knew the relics even had the *potential* to be used as a weapon against the Kryl, why weren't we briefed?"

"Because it's a military matter that requires the right clearance."

"Or," Nevers said, "is it because they don't want us to know that they exist in the first place?"

She snorted. "How did you make that connection?"

"Think about it. It's the absence of reliable information that's so damning. Not a single reliable source has anything to say for certain about the relics—not historians, not xenoarchaeologists, not xenobiologists. The Ministry of Xeno Affairs have been silent on the matter, never once making a public statement about relics of any sort. Same with the SDF. And if it's MOXA's job to explore Telos ruins, don't you think they'd have found *something* by now? Don't you think they'd at least have theories of their own?"

"And you got all of this from the darknet. Which is the most *reliable* place to get your information." Casey'd lost count of how many crackpot theories and fake findings had been debunked by actual journalists once they came to the forefront of public awareness.

"And other sources. I checked the Ariadne public library, too, plus the one on base. But are you really trying to tell me that in the hundreds of years we've known about the Telos, not a single person has found a clue pointing to the existence of these artifacts?"

Casey shrugged. "Maybe because there's no *there* there, Fancypants. Hey, you think you could do something useful with your research skills and dig up some dirt on Renata for me instead?"

He pinched the bridge of his nose and sighed. "The squadron commander again? You really gotta let this old grudge go, Rap. Besides, I thought that's what you were doing the other night."

She crossed her arms. "I called around to some of our mutual acquaintances. Didn't find anything yet. But I will. I'm telling you, she's bad news. No one makes lieutenant colonel at thirty-four without breaking the rules somewhere along the way."

He grunted. "Back to my point. Tell me this. Why haven't we heard anything about the geode since I handed it over to Admiral Miyaru?"

"Well everyone knows about that parasite now. But the relics are in a class by themselves. I'm sure it's working its way through the right channels."

Nevers snorted with contempt. He checked Hedgebot's beacon on his tablet and frowned.

"What is it?"

M.G. HERRON

"Hedgebot broke his search pattern."

"Probably skirting around one of those security guards."

Nevers glanced in the direction of Hedgebot's beacon on his tab. His eyes widened. "I think we're being followed."

Casey looked back and caught sight of the bored security guard she'd noticed earlier. He pressed a finger to the earpiece, then exchanged words with a stocky man with a thick brow, a broken nose, and bangs framing dead gray eyes. The gray-armored security guard suddenly backed off, as if yielding his position to the newcomer.

That wasn't normal.

"By the breath of Animus," Nevers muttered as he rapidly tapped his fingers on his tab. The blinking dot representing Hedgebot cut its patrol and made a B-line for them, scurrying between the reaching hands of two children a moment later as it sprinted past them.

He grabbed Casey's elbow and pushed her forward. "Follow the bot."

"What is your deal?"

"Not now."

"Stars, you're being so paranoid."

"Don't you recognize him? It's the MOXA security goon from the other day, only this time he's wearing plain clothes."

"Of course I recognize him, but if we run like criminals, we'll *look* like criminals. We haven't done anything wrong!"

She searched until she found his eyes. Nevers swallowed and glanced away, searching for the MOXA guy.

The bottom dropped out of her stomach. "What have you done?"

"Nothing."

"Obviously not."

"Someone's been tracking my movements on the darknet."

74

"Is that why you wanted to give a message to the minister?"

"Well, no, I just wanted to talk to him. Ask him about the relics. But maybe I should have been more careful…"

Nevers stood on his tiptoes and peered through the mob. "He's moving in this direction. How the hell is he tracking me?"

"How does he even know it's you? I thought you said you were on the darknet."

"I am. And he shouldn't be able to." Nevers blinked. "He doesn't know it's me. But that means…"

He stared down at his tab. Then he dropped it on the pavement, stomped a heel on a corner of it, and began to haul on the opposite edge.

"What are you doing?!"

"Testing a theory." He groaned as he heaved. She shoved him off of it before he had a chance to do any damage.

"You idiot. You don't need to break it in half, just pull the battery out."

"Oh. Right."

Hedgebot spat out a multitool he kept somewhere within his compact body. Nevers caught it and flipped open a thin metal screwdriver. While Casey turned off the tab and held it firm, Nevers wedged the screwdriver into a seam in the tab's casing, popped off the shield over the battery, and removed it. He dropped the tool, which Hedgebot stowed, followed by the battery, which Hedgebot also swallowed. Then Nevers folded the tablet back up and put it in his pocket.

He must really have been panicked. It wasn't like Nevers to react so rashly. She looked into his eyes, which darted around, searching. They were puffy, with dark circles beneath them, and shot through with red.

But paranoid and exhausted didn't mean he was wrong.

The plainclothes MOXA guard stopped and held up a fist.

He spoke into an earpiece, then pointed left and right. *Fan out*, the signals said. *Search.*

"By the Spirit of Old Earth," Casey cussed. "You were right."

"I hate being right," Nevers muttered.

"No you don't."

"In this case, I'll make an exception. What now?"

"Act normal."

"What's normal?"

"We're here to watch the last shuttle launch. So we watch."

She spotted Park and Yorra and directed Nevers toward them.

"You two look like you've seen a ghost," Park said when they reached them. "Are you okay?"

Nevers brushed his hand through his short black hair and chuckled nervously. "Us? Of course, what do you mean?"

"Liar," Yorra said. "Something happened."

"Later," Casey whispered. "When's the shuttle take off?"

Yorra jerked her chin upward. "Any minute now."

She realized that while she and Nevers had been fiddling with the tablet, the whole crowd had slowly paused and turned, as one, to gaze up at the shuttle at the far end of the spaceport runway. She pushed them deeper into the thick of the crowd as a mechanical racket poured out of the sky, followed by pneumatic exhalations as the shuttle's supports detached themselves and pulled away from the ship. People lifted handheld devices over their heads to snap photos. Some stayed up to stream video.

"The shuttle is clear for launch," said a voice over a loud-speaker. A cheer went up in the crowd.

"Yeah!" Park shouted.

Yorra whistled.

"Clap, Fancypants," Casey said. "That's an order."

Nevers quit looking over his shoulder and clapped along with everyone else.

Casey cupped her hands and let out a high-pitched "WOOOO!" right as the MOXA goons waded into the dense crowd behind them. One of the agents passed close enough that she felt the concealed-carry blaster pistol on his hip brush up against the small of her back. He winced at the sound of her scream and veered away from the press of people.

Out of the corner of her eye, about a hundred meters west of their position, she saw the men huddle up. Their leader, the one with the jutting brow and broken nose, cussed and then signaled for them to move away.

When they were out of sight, Nevers stopped clapping and braced himself on his knees. Casey set her hand on his back as he exhaled shakily. She, too, was shaking with the rush of adrenaline.

"Close call," he said. In all the racket, they had to shout just to hear one another.

"What the hell did you do?"

"I was careful! I covered my tracks. There's no way they could have backtraced it to my tab."

"Clearly not. Tell me what you did."

Nevers' skin had gone very pale. He looked like he might puke.

Behind them, the shuttle's enormous engines fired, sending a great rumble through her chest. The roar of the crowd rose to join it.

"I may have hacked into MOXA's servers."

"What! How?"

"It wasn't all that hard. Others have done it before. There were straightforward instructions on the darknet. When I got in, I found the blueprints and... Oh, Animus," he said as the realization hit him. "It was a trap. Those blueprints are fakes. They *want* people to hack their servers to get them. That's how they discredit the theories!"

"Ok, let's pretend for a second that I'm not furious with you. What theories? What are you talking about?"

"People think MOXA was conducting some kind of Kryl experiments in secret labs under their building. I thought I might find something about the relics or something else there if I went snooping around. Instead, I found these blue-prints of their building—blueprints that don't show any kind of underground labs or even a sub-basement of any kind. But of course they don't! The blueprints were planted by MOXA themselves. They *want* people to find them!"

"Because the files contain some kind of tracking script."

"They must. I don't know how. I scanned them first. It must have been a concealed trojan virus…"

"We have to destroy the files. And probably your tablet, just to be safe."

"Oh, *now* you want to destroy it."

Another wave of cheers erupted from the crowd as the shuttle's distant engines sparked to life, burning against the runway. As it rose, the whole deck was momentarily cast in shadow. That's when the thrusters really began to burn, taking the ship vertical as it left the atmosphere. The noise was enormous and Casey could feel it shaking through her whole body.

"You've left me no choice," she shouted into the noise. "As your flight leader, I forbid you from researching anything about the relics or the Telos. No more darknet!" She pried the tab out of his hands and slammed the screen over one knee.

"But, Raptor, hear me out—stop! Dammit, stop it!"

She kept slamming it down until the screen cracked and she ripped the thin, translucent crystal in twain along the folding seam. She shoved the pieces back into his hands.

*How dare he put the whole flight at risk like that!*

"I don't want to hear it. You did this to yourself. What if Renata found out? What if she caught you? You'd be court martialed! We'd all lose our jobs! You're lucky I don't report you to the admiral myself." Her whole body was shaking with anger. She was breathing hard. Park and Yorra were both staring at them with mouths hanging open.

Nevers stared at her for a while, at a loss for words, which was rare for him. Hedgebot cocked his head at an angle and beeped questioningly.

"Loud and clear, Captain," Nevers finally said after the shuttle had receded into the sky so they could hear each other more clearly again. He may have been stubborn, but at least he knew when to acknowledge defeat.

In the distance, the shuttle's engines burned white hot. The ship rose through a thin layer of wispy clouds, rising and rising until it was a tiny speck in the sky. And then it was gone.

When she turned back to look at Nevers, so was he.

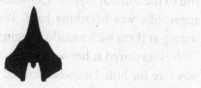

# EIGHT

K ira watched the shuttle until it was a tiny speck in the overcast sky before she turned and trudged back into the city, her footfalls heavier with each step.

To say she was reluctant would be the understatement of the century. The very *idea* of asking Minister Aganaki for his help repulsed her the way the Kryl did when she saw them in person.

Yet Admiral Gitano thought it was a good idea, and she trusted the older, more experienced woman. In this situation more than perhaps any other, Kira thought she should take the advice of one of the few Fleet officers who'd made the transition from military commander to military bureaucrat successfully.

But her respect for Gitano made the deed no less distasteful.

"If this is what political appointments are like, I don't want the job."

"You're not cut out for politics," Harmony responded. "Too self-righteous."

Kira barked out a laugh. "Too attached to those squibbly little ideas like honor and truth."

"Precisely. Inconvenient, to say the least. Chairman Card never has any such hangups. And look at him!"

"If you're saying I should be more like Alvin Card, you can blow a circuit."

"You're turning me on, Kira."

"Careful. I know how to turn you off, too."

While she walked the rest of the way through the crowded city streets to her appointment, the mention of honor and truth caused Kira's mind to drift back to the final days of the Kryl War.

Gitano had been a Rear Admiral then, the same rank Kira held now. Unlike Kira, however, she commanded four destroyers, a dozen cruisers and twice as many wings of starfighters under her command—a properly outfitted armada with which to defend the Empire against the Kryl scourge.

Kira had been a colonel then, a younger woman with her own command who'd fallen in love with a captain several years her junior. It was frowned upon to date a younger officer, especially one she outranked, but thankfully he reported to a different commander. In war, everyone needed an outlet for their stress, and she had been filled with boundless joy every time she remembered that Omar Ruidiaz had been hers.

He was the best starfighter pilot she'd ever met. He flew the Scimitar-model jet like it was an extension of his long, athletic body. He also shared her ideals—honor and truth and selfless service were the foundations that man had built his life upon. That, and flying. He loved flying and he loved fighting with a joy that rivaled her own.

Like her, he'd joined the SDF and become a pilot in order to protect his family and the people of the Solaran Empire

81

from the xenos, who were raiding outposts and razing colonies, taking millions of human lives over the course of the war. They'd both dedicated their lives to the cause—to defend the Empire at all costs.

Little did she know this cause would lead to his death. When their mission to nuke the Queen Mother failed, he delivered the payload to its destination personally, sacrificing himself in the process.

He ended the war and broke her heart in one fell swoop. In one glorious and tragic explosion.

She didn't know how he could possibly have survived. The Kryl must have protected him from the worst of the blast, and then turned him. Or something. She didn't know. It made no sense. It felt like his ghost had been hauled back from beyond the grave in a horrible sin against creation itself.

"Still hurts?" Harmony asked, her voice soft. The AI didn't know how to show sympathy, not exactly, but she did a good job of saying the right things at the right time.

"You have no idea."

"No," she answered wistfully. "I don't."

"Feelings aren't all they're cracked up to be," Kira muttered. "Look where they got Omar. Look where they got me."

"That's the spirit! Today will be a cinch compared to that experience. Perspective is everything."

"You're a brat, you know that?"

"You programmed the personality guiding our interactions."

"Touché."

"Humanity has always prided itself on being adaptable, but if you can't muffle your core values for a temporary discomfort, how adaptable are you *really*?"

Kira snorted and then paused. Her laughter trailed off.

She had arrived.

The squat gray block of a building before her had MINISTRY OF XENO AFFAIRS printed in tall gold letters over the wide stone doorway. Gold-framed glass windows were spaced evenly to either side, eight per level on every floor except the top story, where a solid wall of one-way glass framed the office of Minister Aganaki.

"I don't see as I have much choice."

"Just think about it like you're following orders. Good, obedient little soldier."

"You can't come in with me, right?"

"Negative. They're the most paranoid of the government ministries. They don't permit neural networks in their building. Not even your tab will work inside unless they grant you guest access to their local network—and then they'll monitor your every move."

"Wish me luck."

"Godspeed, Commander."

As she pushed into the building, Harmony's presence fell away from her mind with a tingle at her spinal port. Between one breath and the next, the AI's familiar presence was simply gone. Kira stood just inside the lobby for a moment longer, adjusting to the sudden absence and trying to gin up her courage.

Like most of the danger she faced as a soldier, there came a moment where your fear of a task would not dwindle any further. You just had to go for it. So she recognized her fear, thanked it for the important job it was doing, and stepped through it.

The receptionist at the front desk noticed Kira before she'd introduced herself. Within moments, she was swept toward an elevator and escorted to the top floor.

The elevator took longer than she expected to reach its apex. She forgot that the building only looked squat in comparison to the relatively newer buildings that had, by necessity, been built to soaring new heights around it. When Ariadne ran out of space, they had no choice but to build up, especially in the high-demand real estate districts in and around Parliament and the Ministries.

Soon she arrived. The double doors slid open to reveal a luxurious lounge, all white leather and shining metal. She stepped through, between two crimson-armored security guards, and was directed to wait in a comfortable recliner. Kira nodded to the two guards—she'd left her own security detail behind, knowing both that they couldn't enter the ministry building, and that she'd rather people under her command didn't witness her doing something that turned her own stomach, even if she had good reasons for it.

She was served ice-cold sparkling water by a secretary and told to wait in a spacious lounge for another fifteen minutes before finally being shown into an office at the back.

If the lounge where she waited was luxe, the minister's office itself was reminiscent of an ornate museum. It took up ninety percent of the top floor and not only was it trimmed in gold like the rest of the building, but it housed all manner of xeno trophies.

Just inside the door to her left, a stuffed Kryl groundling sat on its haunches, its fanged mouth hanging open, leering at her with glassy eyes. Mounted on the wall beside it was the long stabbing tail of another Kryl predator. Individual teeth, talons, preserved organs, jaw bones, and more ran along the side of the room, some in glass cases, others standing in the open like the first two. Elaborate replicas of flower blossom-shaped ships hung next to a hologram of an Overmind with its invisible psychic connections mapped out in every color of the rainbow. The Overmind and her hive were in orbit around a planet, which Kira realized must have been a model of the Kryl homeworld. Only a few forces had ever been close to Ambixuan, let alone to the solar system in which the rock orbited, but the Empire's greatest xenobiologists and astronomers had studied it from afar for decades.

On her right-hand side, opposite the wall of Kryl paraphernalia, was a similar exhibit featuring Telos keepsakes. Two enormous carved hands of stone, presumably taken from one of their ruined temples, were mounted in the center of the wall. They were huge and long-fingered, bony with an extra set of knuckles that made them look almost human—but not quite. Arranged on either side of the pair of hands was the rest of what looked like an entire Telos ruin airdropped in and spread out in both directions. Once again, there were theoretical models in hologram alongside other objects. In this case, intricately patterned tapestries, pottery, and a plate of gold—actual solid gold—carved with runes patterned in an unrecognizable language of intricate symbology. There was no taxidermy on this side, for apart from the pair of oversized stone hands—a feature commonly found in Telos ruins—no one had ever seen the Telos themselves. They never drew pictures of their own people so xenoarchaeologists could only guess at their appearance based on what little had been left behind. Their computer models showed a tall humanoid being with arms that hung down to a pair of reversed knees, enormous and vaguely reptilian feet, and an overlarge, oblong head—a complete fantasy! They looked almost human. How could anyone possibly know what a Telos looked like? To her knowledge, not a single burial site or body had ever been found.

At the far end of the room, framed between the two exhibits, Minister Aganaki sat behind a large glass desk, smiling at her with his thin lips pressed together.

*Look*, she thought, *the serpent smiles.*

"Admiral Miyaru, thank you for coming all the way up here." He came around the desk and shook her hand, then gestured to a large, wing-backed chair—also upholstered in white leather. She lowered herself reluctantly into it and sat straight, careful not to relax into the upholstery, though it looked comfortable. She needed to stay on her guard.

"To what do I owe the pleasure of your visit?"

She inclined her head politely. Start with small talk, the political advisor Gitano had referred her to had said. "After seeing you at the memorial service, I thought I should return the favor and pay my respects."

"Is that so?"

"It's not every day that a minister attends the funeral of an officer of the Solaran Defense Forces."

"It's not every day that a xeno kills one of the Fleet's finest. In fact, it's been over a decade."

"Eleven years and seven months," Kira said. The last person to give his life to the Kryl had been Captain Omar Ruidiaz himself—during the attack that ended the war. "But who's counting?"

"Considering my position as the Minster of Xeno Affairs, it could have been construed as an insult had someone from my office *not* attended the service."

She hadn't thought of it that way. He had a good point. "All the same, you could have sent someone in your place. Your director of research, for example."

He gave her that thin-lipped smile again—no teeth—and changed the subject. "I heard the speech you gave to the Colonization Board, not to mention five hundred petitioners present. You made quite the impression."

Kira forced a smile onto her face. "Did I?"

"I haven't seen Chairman Card lose his temper publicly like that for *years*."

"That was not my intention," she muttered darkly.

"Certain people do appreciate you putting Alvin in his place. Lord knows the man's ego has inflated recently. Still, one is left to wonder if what you shared was wise to reveal to the public."

"You're referring to the parasite."

"Quite so."

"I think it's important that the people know the dangers the Kryl pose."

His smile tightened against his teeth. "That is the purpose of my office, is it not? To decide when and how to tell people about the dangers the xenos pose to them?"

*So, he didn't like that she made the decision for him. Be smart,* she reminded herself. *You're playing politics, remember?*

"You're right, of course," Kira said. "I should have consulted you first. I'm sorry." The snake blinked. He hadn't expected an apology.

He inclined his head.

Kira saw her opening. She jumped for it before she had time to think about how it made her feel. "Speaking of Chairman Card, I'm told you might have some influence with him."

"That depends on the subject in question."

*Playing hard to get, I see.* "I would greatly appreciate it if he agreed to sit down with me and discuss this matter privately."

Aganaki steepled his fingertips together. "I may be willing to offer you my assistance… in exchange for some considerations of my own."

"And what would those be?" She tried to smile, but it felt like it came off as more of a grimace.

"For starters, tell me what you discovered on Robichar and how this parasite you frightened the chairman with came into your possession."

So Kira did. She told Minister Aganaki how the parasite snuck aboard her ship and got into the head of a starfighter mechanic, causing the death of Lt. Colonel Walcott and several others. She told him how another one climbed into the head of a pilot, causing more trouble in the sick bay, and how the parasite made them both hallucinate so vividly they mistook their comrades for xenos with murderous intent.

"Fascinating," Minister Aganaki said. "And what do you think the Kryl wish to accomplish with this parasite?"

"Well, I'm not sure. I was hoping your people would have some theories."

"Nothing in our files or research about the Kryl ever indicated that such a thing is even possible. This is, as you put it, a 'dangerous new ability'."

She stared at him.

"Now, don't look surprised," Aganaki said. "It is my job to stay abreast of any new developments about the Kryl."

Good thing she hadn't said anything about the geode at the hearing. But she needed something to hook him. It was time to start playing her hand.

"My pilot saw something else on Robichar: they put one of these parasites into the head of an innocent child. He believes they were trying to turn him into a Kryl."

"A child?" Even the scheming minister looked appalled as he shook his head. "So... what? Do you think they're trying to develop some kind of mutant army?"

"I can't be sure. I know the hive is on the move again. They left Robichar and no doubt they've got more of those parasites with them. I fear for the safety of our colonies. What Card doesn't realize is that colonization efforts have spread the Fleet thin. The SDF is no longer building new warships. We're too busy building voyagers for the new colonies. All of our funding is going in that direction."

"Surely you see his point though," Aganaki said. "There's no reason to build warships if the war is over."

"The war may be over, but the threat still exists. If we spread ourselves too thin, we won't be able to defend the colonies, let alone Ariadne, in the event of a coordinated attack. This unquestioned faith that the peace is permanent is... misguided. Doesn't it worry you that the new hive is on the move? That they've started to evolve?"

"Indeed it does," Aganaki said. "But you're the first one to publicly express such sentiments. And the first one to take an unpopular position is rarely rewarded for the effort."

"So will you help me or not?"

"Hmm," the minister bobbed his head back and forth. "Perhaps. What's in it for me?"

"I'll give you the parasite to study and any additional intelligence we gather about the Kryl's intentions."

"Admiral please don't insult me," he said. "Once you made the parasite public knowledge, you wouldn't have been able to keep it from us for long. One could hardly consider that a favor."

"That's all I have."

"I think not... I heard there was something else you recovered on Robichar."

Kira clenched her jaw. Had Gitano told him about the relic ahead of time? No, the admiral wouldn't do that. How then? How did he discover it?

"We did recover a geode with some interesting abilities," she said. "Telos in origin, or so we believe."

"What does it do?"

"It has the ability to repel the Kryl."

Aganaki's tongue darted out to wet his lips. "That would be sufficient. Give me the parasite and the geode and I'll see what I can do about Alvin."

Kira had overplayed her hand with Chairman Card. She wasn't about to do the same with the minister, no matter what guarantees he gave her.

"You deliver a cooperative Chairman Card, and in

exchange I'll give you access to the parasite. Then we can talk about the Telos artifact."

Aganaki narrowed his eyes. "Very well." That tongue darted out again, like the viper he was. "I cannot guarantee that Card will cooperate."

"But you can soften him up for me. Make him aware of the risk the rogue Overmind and her roaming hive pose. Once he understands that, I'll convince him that temporarily halting colonization efforts is the wisest course of action."

"Sounds like we have a deal." He held out his hand. She took it in her own and they shook. His palm was damp and greasy, as if it had recently been oiled.

He watched her go, his eyes never leaving her. It took all her effort not to wipe her hand on her pants as she exited his office. Once the elevator doors closed behind her, she did, but the action did nothing to dispel the dirty feeling.

The slime of politics had gotten on her, and no amount of washing could clean off the filth.

# NINE

The sun fell behind the skyscrapers of Ariadne's capital as Elya paced through the city.

He walked until his feet were sore. He walked until his leg muscles ached.

He walked, and he racked his brain.

*How could I have been so naive?*

He'd left the spaceport alone and vanished into the high streets of the metropolis to clear his head after the near brush with the MOXA security goons, eager to make himself scarce and needing time to think. Hedgebot roamed in front of him, blue light pulsing ever brighter in the fading dusk.

He'd been too eager to believe what he wanted to see: that the Ministry of Xeno Affairs was keeping secrets. But of course they were! What government ministry wasn't?

He'd fallen for their trap. They didn't seem to know his true identity yet, but they could track his tablet when he was connected to Ariadne's public network. Unless he ditched the tab, it was only a matter of time before they found him again.

Elya thought back through each decision he'd made over

the last week, searching for where he went wrong. One thing became clear: he should have listened to his sources. He'd received several messages since the first from Xenophile7643, under a dozen different pseudonyms. Almost all of them were obvious fishing expeditions, transparent attempts to get him to divulge personal information under the guise of common interests.

But one had been different. A hacker—man or woman, Elya couldn't be sure—who called themselves Backspace. Backspace told him that he wasn't going to find what he hoped to find if he went digging around the ministry's servers. Elya had ignored their warning, thinking that they were lying to mislead him, that if they warned him away from something, then that something was worth digging into.

He'd been wrong. Backspace's warning had been sent in good faith. He could see that now. He needed to make contact with them again so he could ask more questions. If Backspace knew that the blueprints were a trap, it stood to reason that they had more information that would help him in his hunt for the truth about the Telos relics.

But in order to make contact, he'd have to get his secret key—a random string of letters and numbers—off his tab.

The tab that Casey had broken over her knee.

He was conscious of the two pieces of the device pressing against his leg. It didn't look conspicuous, but he couldn't help feeling like he was carrying a ticking time bomb in his pocket. He needed to get the data off it and ditch the machine, stat.

So after hours of walking and thinking and planning for a worst case scenario, he headed to a robotics shop a couple klicks from the base, commonly frequented by pilots.

The sun had long since set on the city, and without the light of the star to warm the overcast atmosphere, the temperature had plummeted. A bell chimed as he pushed the door open and ducked in out of the cold.

"Elya," said Klayton, the old shopkeeper. He had muscular arms marbled with thick veins, and his fingertips were calloused and blackened with grease. His bald head shone in the fluorescent light. "Surprised to see you back so soon. Something wrong with Hedgebot?"

The little bot scampered through the door behind him and beeped a greeting. "Not at all. It was a good idea to replace the photometer. His new conduits are working great, too, and he's a lot better at keeping his distance from strangers now."

Elya glanced furtively around. The normally busy shop was empty. Perfect. He'd intentionally waited until right before closing time to show up.

"Glad to hear it. So what can I do ya for?"

The old man always had a friendly smile for Elya. After he first moved to Ariadne, Klayton had quickly become his favorite machinist in the city. In fact, it had been Klayton who sold Elya the parts needed to modify Hedgebot for approved use in a Sabre. He trusted the man.

"I need your help with something."

Klayton nodded. "Name it."

Elya wasn't surprised. The man was a natural helper, and he'd spent enough money here over the years to earn a little goodwill. He fished the two pieces of his tab out of his pocket. "I need this fixed long enough to pull some data off it."

The old man whistled. "What happened?"

"Long story."

"Oookay," he said, dragging the word out and raising an eyebrow in Elya's direction. That was the other reason he liked Klayton. Nothing skipped by him.

Klayton reached out to grab the pieces of mangled glass

and metal. Elya put his long-fingered hand over the other man's grease-stained paw.

"Can't be on network."

Klayton's caterpillar eyebrows knit down. He may have been bald, but his eyebrows were still thick and dark.

"You in some kind of trouble, kid?"

"Maybe a little," Elya admitted. "Need your help on this one."

Klayton nodded. "Off network. Got it. Transfer the data for you?"

"I'll do it. Need to buy some backup storage."

"New drives in the back."

"Thanks. I'll grab a couple while I wait."

Klayton studied the rectangular aluminite housing that held the battery core, and the data ports that would connect it to external hardware. He flipped open the battery cover.

"You got the battery?"

"Right." Elya fished it out of his coat pocket and passed it over. "Remember, off network."

"I heard ya, kid. Let me see what I can do." Klayton dug a pair of needle-nosed pliers out of his pocket. Long dark hairs sticking out of his nostrils wavered as he exhaled heavily. He turned and ducked into the back room where his workshop was located.

While he waited, Elya picked through spare parts: circuit boards, batteries, wheels and rotors and grabbing arms. It felt safe in here. Familiar. Unlike the world of the relics and xeno mysteries he'd been digging into, he knew the shape of each of these pieces, their model numbers and configurations.

Elya found a retired military SecBot standing in a corner at the back of the room. He recognized the model. It was about twenty years old. He'd encountered one, once, as a refugee. It had saved his life after a bully cornered Elya on a Mammoth-class longhauler. Amazing to think about. The bot had seemed so frightening back then. Now, it just looked small and old, its edges too square, inelegant compared to the newer models.

Elya finally picked out two drives in plastic packaging, each a tiny card the size of his pinky nail, and headed back to the front desk.

"Good news and bad news," Klayton said when he came out of the workshop a minute later. He only held one piece of the tab. The other lay on a workbench that Elya could see through the open door behind him.

"Bad news is, you're not getting that screen back together. Good news, I routed the interface to this side so you can take what you need off it."

"Thanks. I need to use the room."

"You know where it is." Klayton jerked his head toward the door he'd just come through.

Elya grabbed a connector cable off the workbench on his way back. A door in the corner opened to a tiny, padded room the size of a small closet. Its walls were barely broader than Elya's shoulders. He sat down on the bench inside and shut the door.

The room looked a little bit like a recording studio and served dual purposes. It blocked sound, so a person could use it to record a private message. Those who couldn't afford to rent frequency on the Empire's intergalactic ansible network sometimes came to bot shops like this to record messages for their loved ones, and have them shipped across the galaxy. The room provided a measure of privacy when they were making their recordings. Klayton charged a small fee to ship the recordings on cargo ships with extra space.

But the padding on the walls did more than block sound waves. It also blocked data scanners. He could safely turn on his tablet here without fear of the MOXA security goons geolocating his signal in the process.

He connected the cable to the tab, booted it up and slipped the first drive into the housing at the end of the cable. He began to selectively group files into folders on the screen's two dimensional interface, since the holograms couldn't project in this condition. Once he was satisfied he had everything he needed—transcript logs, notes, his secret keys and secure access tokens—he made the transfer, first to one backup drive and then to the other.

As a precaution, he took a few more minutes to commit his secret keys and secure access tokens to memory. They were random strings of letters and numbers, and it was difficult work, but eventually he got them.

Then he wiped the tablet clean.

While he waited for the wipe to complete, which took about ten minutes, he slipped one of the tiny drives into a small gap between the floor and the padding on the walls.

The other went into his sock.

He shut the door to the secure room behind him and slipped back around to the customer side of the front desk. Klayton was waiting there with his thick brows knit into a troubled frown, his chin held in one grease-stained hand.

"Sorry I can't tell you more," Elya said.

"I understand," Klayton responded, straightening. "Appreciate your discretion."

The old man nodded. "Sure, sure."

"And your planning. Can't tell you how many times that room's come in handy."

Klayton smiled. "That's why I built it."

"One more thing. I want to send a bot tinkerbox to a friend's kid." He gave Klayton the address of the Walcott's flat, which he'd obtained with discreet inquiries a couple days ago. He picked out the kit he wanted, one that would result in an articulating, ambulatory playmate about half Hedgebot's size, but without his expensive sensory tech.

"Mark it as an anonymous gift. Now, what do I owe you for all of that?"

"Ehh." The old man shook his head and waved his hands. "Your money's no good today. This one's on the house."

Elya blinked. "You sure?"

Klayton nodded. "Absolutely. Take care, Captain Nevers." He turned and went back into his workshop without another word.

*Well,* he thought, *I have spent thousands of credits here over the years.* The old man probably thought five minutes of work, a kid's tinkerbox, and a couple backup drives were nothing in the grand scheme of things.

Elya whistled for Hedgebot and slipped out into the cold, shivering as a gust of icy wind blew through his thin jacket. He took his bearings and began to trudge home.

His legs were so tired now he had to force them to keep moving. To distract himself from the numbness in his fingers, Elya's mind played back over the facts he'd learned about the relics.

Fact number one: Stories about the Telos were as old as the Empire itself. Legend had it that the survivors of Old Earth, after leaving the dying planet in their generation ships, first encountered the Telos on their journey—long before Ariadne was established. Some believe that the Telos helped humanity locate the first habitable exoplanet, which they named Ariadne, over 5,000 years ago.

Fact number two: The Church of Animus considered this legend heresy. They believed that Animus, the Spirit of Old Earth, led the colonists who eventually became the founders of the Solaran Empire to Ariadne, not hyper-intelligent aliens who were never heard from again. They maintained that humanity's ingenuity and, more importantly their faith, led them out of the long darkness and endless night.

Fact number three: Ignoring conspiracy theories about

what the Ministry of Xeno Affairs may or may not know, it was indisputable that they knew more than they were letting on. The ministry had been established when the Kryl first made contact with the Solaran Empire, decades before the big war broke out. Their mission was to gather knowledge about the Kryl and later, when the Kryl War burned at its hottest, their mission was to supply intelligence to the Solaran Defense Forces in order to help them beat back the encroaching alien horde.

Whether or not there was a secret lab beneath the MOXA headquarters building remained to be proven. That blueprint didn't have one, but since it had been a plant, he wasn't willing to rule out the existence of a secret lab. Were they experimenting on captured Kryl? Were they developing some kind of secret weapon to eradicate the xeno scourge once and for all? No one knew.

Fact number four: The Ministry of Xeno Affairs was responsible for exploring Telos ruins and cataloging their findings. Teams of archaeologists were tasked with exploring the ruins and bringing back any artifacts and knowledge they discovered there. All the information he'd seen said that they had discovered shrines, glyphs, and carvings. The descriptions of such ruins seemed to match—roughly—the description the boy Hedrick had given Elya about the site he'd stumbled upon on Robichar. Once again, no information about any relics with power discovered at these sites could be found. That was suspicious, to say the least.

Fact number five: Despite having discovered the geode on Robichar, the SDF had made no public acknowledgment of its existence or any other kinds of relics. They didn't brief him on the possibility of relics when they were sent out to fight the Kryl, and they didn't *de*brief him on what he'd discovered when he returned, despite what he discussed with Admiral Miyaru. The relic had disappeared into the vast machinery of military bureaucracy. For all he knew, that was the last he'd ever hear of it.

Despite weeks of research, those facts were all he'd been able to confirm. All the rest—legends of Telos assisting ancient humanity, giving them knowledge and technology, rumors of MOXA conducting top secret projects and collecting a curio shop of Telos relics and Kryl genetics—none of it could be verified with information available to the public.

And this last one—fact number six, if you could call it that—wasn't so much a fact as an absence of information: No one had published any credible books or studies on Telos relics.

Ever.

Not one book in the history of scientific literature.

So either Elya was the first to discover a Telos relic with powers that could be weaponized… or any such previous discoveries had been erased from the public record.

The sound of a stone pinging off a curb snapped Elya's head up. He pulled his hands from his pockets and looked around. It was full dark now. He was alone in the city streets, and feeling naked without his sidearm.

Hedgebot paused and stood on its hind legs ahead of him, pulsing a warm orange-yellow—a few shades shy of the red that signaled danger.

Elya made his way into the middle of the street so that he would see any potential attack coming. The road ran through a commercial district that would take him to the south gate of the base. There were no vehicles and no other pedestrians around at this time of night. He was still a couple kilometers from home.

When Hedgebot's light faded to a cold blue, Elya began to walk forward again. He'd gone another twenty yards when there was a soft whirling sound. When Hedgebot flashed red,

Elya broke into a sprint, but the moment his back foot lifted, it caught on something and he slammed to the ground, knocking his head against the pavement.

He tried to get up and found his ankles were stuck together. He looked down and saw a bola wrapped around them.

"Hedgebot, run!" he shouted.

The bot disappeared down a side alley and scurried up the side of a building seconds before a team of four men, all clad in dark clothing, sprinted into the street, lifted him up and carried him toward a dark office building.

"Get offa me," Elya hissed, thrashing out with elbows and fists. His legs were still tied together but they hadn't secured his arms. He landed an elbow against the back of someone's skull. A man grunted and stumbled forward, but didn't let go. Another person pulled Elya's arms behind him and wrapped them quickly with some kind of metal wire.

Now he was tied up good, helpless and being carried by four strong men down a dark alley. They knocked an unrecognizable pattern on a door with no handle, and the door opened from the inside. They stepped into the building and shut him into the darkness.

A flashlight shone directly into his eyes, blinding him and preventing him from seeing any of their faces.

"Don't know why I'm surprised, but I am." The voice was vaguely familiar, but he couldn't place it.

"I'm a Fleet officer!" Elya said. "If you harm me in any way, the military industrial complex is going to come down on your neck."

He couldn't see the man's face, but he heard the wicked smile in his voice. "We operate outside of their jurisdiction."

Elya felt a chill shiver through his body that had nothing to do with the cold weather. "Who are you? What do you want with me?"

"Better question is," the man said, "what do *you* want? And why do you keep sticking your nose where it doesn't belong?"

A cold shiver crawled over Elya's skin and buried itself in the pit of his stomach.

"Search him," the man said.

They dropped him on the ground, hard, and turned him over on his stomach.

"At least buy me dinner first," he mumbled.

Someone cuffed him on the side of the head and stuffed a sour-tasting cloth into his mouth, maybe a bandana or dirty rag.

They pulled out his wallet, removed his military ID, examined pictures of his mom and his brothers, and studied the challenge coin his flight instructor had given him when he graduated from flight school.

"Well?" the man in charge asked.

The others shook their heads.

"Take off his shoes."

Elya's stomach dropped. They removed his shoes and socks and finally found the backup drive he'd stowed there.

"We'll be taking that and any backups you've got in your bunk, too, Captain—" He glanced down at Elya's ID "—Nevers." That's when he finally placed the voice. This was the MOXA security guard, the one he'd run into after Walcott's memorial service. The same man who had been searching for him at the spaceport. His eyes had adjusted somewhat to the flashlight beam they still held in his eyes. Elya saw enough to recognize the crooked nose, the bangs brushing over dead gray eyes.

"Did you ever deliver my message to the minister?"

The man snorted. "I did. He told me to keep an eye on you."

A pack of tiny spiders crawled down his spine. His gut had been right. Someone *had* been watching him.

"Little did we know that the hacker poking around MOXA's servers would turn out to be some punk kid pilot. Two birds with one stone. Must be my lucky day."

For all they knew, it could have been two different people. They hadn't known it was him until they caught him.

*So how did they catch me?*

His mind raced trying to figure it out. Sure, they'd been watching him, but if they didn't know he was the hacker, why did they jump him on the street? He'd been careful. He used the secure room to make backups, hadn't powered it on or connected it to Ariadne's wireless network. He covered his tracks as he moved through the darknet. How then? How did they...

"Earth be damned," Elya muttered as it hit him. Klayton. The old man told him to "take care"—told him his money was no good there tonight. He hadn't just been acting nice. He'd been feeling guilty for reporting him.

When he looked at Elya's tab in maintenance mode, the embedded tracking script must have given Klayton some kind of Imperial order to turn him in.

"The bot machinist," he whispered.

MOXA's head of security smiled at him. "Very good. You're a clever kid. It's too bad you make such stupid decisions."

Suddenly the man was on him, a small boot knife held at his throat.

"Stupid'll get you killed," the man said. "Stop digging around or it won't just be your career as a starfighter pilot that ends."

Elya leaned away from the blade, but the threat pissed him off enough to make him buck in the face of danger. "People deserve to know the truth!"

"People need to know what we deem it necessary for them to know. This is not one of those things. So either you back off..."

The man pressed the knife against Elya's throat and pulled it to the side. Something snapped, loudly, making him flinch, at the same time as his hands were suddenly released from their bindings. He clutched his throat, desperate to hold his bodily fluids in before they gushed onto the floor.

But all he found was sweaty, clammy cold skin.

"Or next time," the MOXA head of security said, holding the dangling ends of a thick rubber band in his hand, "I'm going to hurt you so bad you'll wish you were dead."

The dark-clad men slipped out the door and shut it behind them before Elya even had time to realize what had happened. He caught his breath. With shaky hands, he untangled the bola from his ankles.

He opened the door and found Hedgebot there waiting for him. *Me-meep?* The bot asked in a worried tone.

"I'm all right, buddy."

He hurried back to his barracks. When he got there, Park was cleaning up their room, which had been tossed. Their foot lockers were overturned, the contents of their shelves dumped onto the floor, clothes in the closet emptied out, the mattresses in their beds flipped over and cut open.

"What happened?" Elya asked, even though he already knew beyond a shadow of a doubt.

Park threw up his hands. "Some kind of prank? Payback? Maybe Raptor is right and Rennie Stickbum has some kind of vendetta against us."

Elya laid his mattress back down and checked his secret cache.

It was empty.

All his backups were gone. His spare tablet had been

taken, too—the one he just bought. Elya closed his eyes. *Dammit.* This was getting expensive.

But there was no way he was backing down.

He came to a sudden decision.

"Nevers!" Naab called after him as he marched out of the room. "Fancypants, where you goin'?"

"I'll be right back."

He made his way down to the library.

He hesitated only a moment before keying in the credentials he'd filched from a pilot in another squad. He logged into the darknet, keying in his secret keys and passwords, thankful he'd taken the time earlier to commit them to memory. It took him four tries to find the account Backspace was using today.

When he'd confirmed he'd found the right account by exchanging code words he'd also memorized, Elya wrote, "You were right about that data dump."

"Tried to tell you," Backspace replied.

"Secret police jumped me tonight."

"... Really? You okay?"

"Yep." There was one silver lining to receiving death threats from Solaran secret police. If nothing else, it told him he was on the right track. "You said you could help."

"Did you take precautions this time?"

"Using someone else's creds."

"Good. You're learning. You'll be more careful next time."

Elya swallowed, his hands hovering over the keyboard.

"Did you make a backup and store it in a secure location like I told you to?"

"Yes," Elya responded, picturing the backup drive stuffed into the crack between the wall and the floor in Klayton's secure room.

"Okay. Commit this to memory and then erase the log. Here's what you have to do..."

# TEN

Casey stood at restful attention at the front of the mat, feet shoulder width apart, hands clasped behind her back, opening and closing her fists. She wore loose, form-fitting workout clothes in navy blue and Imperial crimson, exactly like the rest of the squadron gathered in the gym today. The floor was covered with inch-thick foam, the better for breaking falls, and other than the Solaran Empire's tristar logo painted high on the wall, the white room stood unadorned. It was a practical, spartan space, the kind where form and function came together seamlessly.

"Before we begin," Spector said, speaking from the center of the mat with the squadron gathered in a half circle around her. "I have an announcement to make."

Park muttered under his breath, "More grandstanding from Commander Renny Stickbum."

"Hush," Casey hissed, fighting down a smile.

Spector's head snapped toward her. "Something you want to share with the squadron, Captain Osprey?"

"No, sir."

Spector frowned, noted something on her tab—another

105

red mark against Flight 18, no doubt—and continued her speech as if she hadn't been interrupted. "This is a big day. Does anyone know why?"

A scrawny pilot from Flight 2 lifted his hand. Spector nodded at him.

"Because we're the fittest squadron the SDF has ever seen, sir."

*Suckup*, Casey thought.

Spector's cheeks dimpled as she smiled slightly. "There's no doubt about that, Hanson. But no. Today is a momentous occasion because we've just been assigned our first flying mission under my command."

Excited murmurs rose up among the group of pilots as their faces broke into grins and satisfied looks. After three weeks in port doing nothing but training, they were getting restless. A mission was exactly what they needed. They were all chomping at the bit to get back in the hot seat, performing the duties they signed up for, not running around base doing push-ups and stroking Spector's ego.

Casey clenched her jaw, bracing for the bad news that she knew must be coming—waiting for the other shoe to drop. Try though she might, she hadn't been able to dig up any dirt on Spector. Neither whose ass she kissed to get promoted to Lieutenant Colonel so young, nor who she bribed or black-mailed to get such a desirable command when any number of other, more experienced people would have been a better fit. It seemed she really was going to be stuck with her new commander.

This bald fact gnawed at her soul. The rest of the Furies may have accepted Spector, but Casey refused to do so. She knew the old Renata too well to just lay down and take it.

"So after today's session," Spector went on, "our time getting to know each other has come to an end—training is over. You'll have twenty-four hours off. And then the Furies take flight from the *Paladin of Abniss*."

Another excited murmur. Spector basked in the glow of the Furies' appreciation like the mission had been her idea.

Casey forced herself to unclench her jaw and smooth out the dark scowl she knew must be marring her otherwise disciplined appearance.

"What's the mission, sir?" another pilot piped up, this time a petite woman with a mean streak and flame red hair. She was the lead for Flight 4, and she and Spector got along swimmingly.

"I'll tell you that—once you've earned it. As for today..." Spector made a show of projecting a hologram of their cumulative point totals, a neat table with the flight numbers next to their corresponding scores. Flight 18 was just above halfway down the list. Basically failing, in Casey's mind. "You're all starting with a clean slate." She flicked her fingers to the side and the ranking tumbled to zero. The names rearranged into sequential order, with Flight 1 at the top.

Sharp inhalations ran around the room, followed by murmurs and the shuffling of feet. Casey glanced over her shoulders at Nevers, Yorra and Park. They narrowed their eyes.

Suspicion. Good. She wanted them to be continually on their guard against the commander's subtle manipulations.

Spector said, "Whichever flight scores the highest in today's training gets to fly point on the mission with me."

The chatter ratcheted up a notch in volume, peppered through with the occasional nervous chuckle. To fly point on the mission was a position of honor only given to the best flight in the squadron. Today, with their rankings zeroed out, even the flights that hadn't scored well in their weeks of training had an opportunity to lead, while those that had been ahead needed to work as hard as everyone else just to stay in the game.

It was a stroke of competitive genius, and Casey hated Renata for it.

This was her opportunity. But it was also a trap. Did Flight 18 have what it took to pull ahead? Her heart threw itself repeatedly against the inside of her sternum. She wanted it. They'd worked their butts off to earn it.

And she dared not let hope take hold. Even if they did win today, she had no doubt Spector would find a way to steal the victory from Casey's grasp.

Though the dark circles beneath his eyes had gotten worse, a hungry look had come over Captain Never's gaunt, brown face. That was good. She could always count on him for his competitive spirit, even if he hadn't spoken more than a few words to her since the spaceport. He hadn't forgiven her for breaking his tab.

"Today it's all or nothing. Have you got what it takes to be a Fightin' Fury?"

"Sir, yes, sir!"

The squadron's answer resounded through the gym. Despite her feelings about Spector, Casey shouted louder than anyone.

"Good, that's what I like to hear. Now, today we'll be focusing on close quarters combat training. You all know the stories of pilots crash landing in hostile territory. Whether by act of God, accident, or a grave error in judgment." Spector stared pointedly at Captain Nevers. He found a dust bunny on the mat to get lost in until she redirected her gaze.

*That was uncalled for, bitch,* Casey thought furiously.

"Though you may find yourself with the jaws of death closing around you, the success or failure of the squadron's mission may depend on your ability to survive. And I intend to make sure you do. So far we've done physical training, rifle and pistol training, and flight training. Today we're going to test your fighting skills. You'll be graded in three areas—hand-to-hand, weapons, and ground work. You've got a hard day ahead of you, so warm up, hydrate and stretch —then we'll begin. All right, let's go, hop to it."

"You heard the lady," Casey said. "Half mile, stretch, then light sparring."

Their expressions matched hers in ferocity and determination. "Aye, Captain," said Park.

Usually, Park and Yorra paired up. They were about the same height, which made them good sparring partners, while Nevers was closer to her size. This time Casey made them switch. She didn't want anyone to get too comfortable today. Comfortable meant lazy. Also, she needed to talk to Yorra.

The two circled each other, testing with controlled kicks and punches, jockeying for position.

"What do you think her angle is?" Casey asked.

"Normally, I'd tell you you're imagining things, but this is obviously bait. What's hand-to-hand got to do with flying point on a mission?"

"Seems like a trap."

"Do you think it has something to do with that prank?"

She was referring to Park's and Nevers' room getting tossed. They'd insisted on getting the security cameras in the halls checked, only to find out that they'd been off when it happened. Some kind of software update, they said. Bullshit.

Nevers insisted nothing had been taken from his bunk and Park said no possession of his was missing, either, so base security had chalked it up to pilots pranking each other and was merely annoyed their time had been wasted.

But the incident had seemed too personal to be a prank. Casey had wondered ever since if Spector had put another flight up to it. She couldn't prove anything, and wasn't willing to call Spector out unless she had enough evidence for the accusations to stick.

"I'm not sure," Casey said. "All I know is she's got it out for us."

"She's got it out for *you*, Raptor. The rest of us are just along for the ride."

"If that's true, why trash Nevers' room instead of mine?"

A guest instructor arrived, interrupting their conversation.

They spent the next two hours on the ground learning new grappling moves and sweating on each other. The training culminated in a tournament. Park, with his stocky build and low center of gravity, turned out to be a hell of a good wrestler. Flight 18 came in second place when Park tapped out against a large pilot from Flight 4, who had fifty kilos on him. The ape trapped him in a crucifix, with one arm between the larger man's legs and his neck yanked backward hard enough to make him cry out.

Spector seemed unimpressed by this result, but Casey could tell that Flight 18 even coming close to winning got under her skin.

Weapons combat went even better. Flights faced off against each other, four on a side, each bearing a bo—a short staff of polished wood, or in this case synthetic wood with a little more give. The synthetic hurt less than the real thing, but the way they all fought, her ribs would be bruised for weeks afterward.

Casey got one of her knuckles rapped by the redhead in Flight 4 hard enough to make her cry out. Blood welled up from the fingernail of her ring finger. It swelled and turned a dark, angry purple.

"Do you need to go to the medical wing?" Spector asked mockingly.

Casey regripped the bo. "No, sir."

"Good," Spector said. "Fight!"

The redhead came barreling forward with a throaty shout. Casey ducked at the last second, narrowly avoiding a strike to the head. Nevers came in with a block on her left, buying her enough time to pivot out of range.

Flight 18 ended up getting knocked out in the third round of the weapons match-up. Not semi-finalists, but still far from the bottom of the barrel.

While they trained, Spector continually made notes on her tab, scoring them according to some hidden system that only she knew.

They broke for a short lunch, and when they came back, their commander brought Colonel Volk with her. This time the two of them were each drinking expensive, organic fruit smoothies. Spector had also found time in her brief outing with the colonel to put on a flexible knee brace and tape up both of her wrists.

"Does that mean she's fighting with us?" Nevers asked.

This was unusual. Spector had kept herself apart for the duration of their training, preferring to bark orders and judge them from a distance rather than join them most of the time. Oh, sure, she flew in her own Sabre alongside them during aerial pattern work, but that was only because she couldn't criticize them so easily from the ground.

Unlike Lt. Colonel Walcott, who had always been there in the thick of it, like a good leader *should* be, Spector tended to keep a distance that made her seem both untouchable and arrogant.

"In the last part of today's competition," Spector said, "I'll be teaching you hand-to-hand combat skills. We'll be following the same pattern of training I received from special forces Marines during the war."

Colonel Volk, leaning against the back wall in casual clothes, chuckled and sipped his drink. Some of the larger men eyed their commander and smirked knowingly, as if there was no way this slender woman could beat them hand-to-hand.

Casey frowned. She wasn't so sure. Despite her dislike of Spector, "weak" was not a word Casey ever would have used to describe her. Spector may have looked like a dork with her wrists taped and her knee brace, but all that proved was that she was self-aware enough to know her own weaknesses and smart enough to guard against them. Even if she did look silly.

The thought of her comical appearance amused Casey so much she didn't notice she was grinning like an idiot until Spector snapped at her. "Is something I said amusing to you, Osprey?"

"Uh, no, sir."

"What did I just tell the squadron?"

Her mind went blank. She had no idea what the commander had been saying. She was at a loss for how to respond, so she fell back on being honest. "I don't know, sir. I was distracted."

Spector sneered. "You don't know. Congrats, little bird. You get to be my practice dummy for the demonstration. Put on a helmet and gloves and come over here."

Casey fought down a blush and told herself to remain calm. Lt. Colonel Walcott's voice—quiet for days—suddenly reappeared in her thoughts, as clear as if he were standing next to her.

"The obstacle is the way," he said. "What appears to be an impediment is actually your path to victory. When you strike, your enemy blocks. And when your enemy blocks?"

"You strike," she muttered.

She took padded sparring gloves and a light helmet from Yorra and slipped them on as she approached Spector at the center of the mat. The squadron drew into a tight circle around them.

Spector turned her back on Casey to address the group.

"I've said it before and I'll say it again: It is not often a Starfighter pilot finds himself in a position where hand-to-hand combat is the difference between life or death, but it *can* happen. In those situations, you must be prepared."

Spector turned back to her.

"I'm going to show you three techniques to disable your enemies as quickly and as efficiently as possible."

Casey did her best to control her breathing, inhaling through her nose and exhaling through her mouth. She bounced from foot to foot, shaking out her hands and neck and arms, then drew her hands up to guard her head, making loose fists.

Spector matched her, rising up on the balls of her feet, bouncing lightly. "Hit me."

Casey darted forward with a jab followed by a cross—classic movements from their boxing curriculum.

Spector slipped to the inside with one hand up and in the lead, easily avoiding Casey's blows. Her movement was smooth and practiced.

They exchanged punches, quick and light, not really hitting anything. Casey struck with a harder right, but Spector slipped to the outside and swept her lead leg with a low kick behind her calf. The ground rushed up to meet her and the commander came down on top of her with a knee on her neck.

"If you go in too fast," she told the group, "the enemy will take advantage of the opening and disable you." She stood up, removing her weight from Casey's neck. "Get up."

She shoved herself to her feet with a frustrated growl.

"Again."

Spector was slightly taller than her, with longer arms, but

Casey didn't need to get too close to take a shot at that bum knee. She threw a flurry of kicks at Spector's side and stomach. Some of them landed, but to little effect. The purpose, however, was not to hurt her, but to distract her.

Casey shuffled forward into a feint then retreated. As Spector stepped into the gap, taking her bait, she swung to the side and lashed out with a sidekick. Instead of the gratifying popping noise she hoped to hear, Spector slid past the kick and slipped inside, grabbed her shirt at the collar, and used the momentum to fling her off balance.

Casey stumbled, but managed to set her foot down and pivot to meet the counter-attack. Before she knew it, Spector was inside her guard, keeping her off balance. The commander threw an open palm at her chin. It connected, snapping her head back and sending her staggering.

This time the commander came down on top of her in a striking position before pausing with her fist on her face.

"Nice try, little bird," Spector said. "But I've seen that a hundred times."

Spector removed her weight and held out a hand. Casey took it and the commander hauled her to her feet. Spector turned once more to the group as Casey straightened her shirt and brushed herself off, embarrassed.

"Strike with the heel of your hand, and the insides of your elbows. Not only do these impact points cause an immense amount of damage, they allow you to strike from close quarters with strength, and to do so without risking damage to your wrists or the small bones in your fingers."

She turned back to Casey.

"Now we fight for real."

She nodded and tried to relax her body as the commander came flying at her.

This time, Casey was ready.

She deflected the first blow, a roundhouse kick, with the

muscle of her left forearm, then landed a punch that snapped the commander's jaw to the side.

"Better," Spector said, her voice pitched low so that only the two of them could hear. "You fight harder than you lead."

"Nnng!" Casey snarled and went after her, sending a flurry of knees, elbows and open palm strikes at Spector. Each one was a glancing blow that the commander slid along a muscle or pushed away with her open hands or forearms.

Then the commander stepped in close and wrapped one leg around her right knee, the other tangling up her feet. They smacked the ground, face down with the commander on top of her. The air gushed out of her lungs and she struggled to breathe.

"I know you've been looking into my record, little bird," Spector hissed into her ear. "Didn't you know that would get back to me? I don't like nosey little birds."

Casey gritted her teeth and tried to lift her face up off the mat, but the commander wrapped her neck in a rear naked choke. She managed to suck in half a breath through her nose. "I just figured… you cheated your way to the top like you always do."

Spector hauled back and squeezed, causing Casey to arch in pain. "You know nothing about my life."

"I know all I need to know," she wheezed. "You haven't changed a bit."

Twisting her hips, Casey flipped over and got a knee up between them, using the opening to land a blow in the soft flesh on the side of Spector's neck.

The strike dazed the commander long enough for Casey to lever up and roll over, reversing their positions.

"If these past two weeks have proven anything to me, it's that you're the same manipulative, cheating liar you were in school. You've been messing with our ratings, forcing us down to the bottom in training just to make *me* look bad."

Spector drove a knee up into Casey's ribs, but she managed to hold on to her dominance. For the first time, she noticed that the ring of pilots around them was whooping, cheering, hollering—a vast wall of noise she'd barely noticed until now.

"You're not just being ranked on your abilities during training, Osprey. You're being ranked on your cohesiveness as a unit. Your flight is divided from within. Nevers is your strongest pilot, but he's distracted on the best of days. Park and Yorra are too busy making googly eyes at each other to take their work seriously. And you. You're so obsessed with me that you aren't paying attention to what *they* need."

Spector's words stunned her enough that she loosened her grip ever so slightly, allowing the commander to shift her hips and twist her legs, shoving Casey off her and giving them both time to regain their feet.

Casey struck again before Spector had fully stood up. The commander grabbed Casey's wrist, pulling her into a simple hip throw. She went up and over, landing hard on her back. Keeping hold of her wrist, Spector hauled her arm behind her into a classic hammer lock. Yes, it was a classic. but after it was applied it was very hard to get out of. Pain shot through Casey's arm and up into her neck.

Spector held her there as she turned to address the rest of the squadron. Casey struggled beneath her, but the position of her arm made it impossible to move out from under the commander's power.

"What was Captain Osprey's mistake?" Spector asked the squadron. She sounded ragged and out of breath.

"She didn't control her attack."

Spector shook her head, swallowed and waited.

"She didn't press her advantage while she had the upper hand?"

"Maybe," Spector said. "What else?"

"She let her emotions get the best of her."

"That's right. And it's the most important lesson from today. It's not about what moves you know or how good of a fighter you are. It's about *not* getting in your own way. Not allowing the enemy to get into your head. Osprey's error was simply that I know her better than she knows herself. Isn't that right, little bird?"

Casey gritted her teeth and tried to keep herself from drooling on the mat.

It wasn't the shame of losing a fight that gnawed at her.

It was that there had been some truth to what the commander said.

She had allowed Spector to stoke the flame of her negative emotions, making them burn hot enough to cause her to lose control.

She promised herself that she would find out what the commander had done to get this post. Who she lied to, what system she manipulated, where she cheated, who she fucked. Whatever it took, Casey swore to herself she'd find out. She wouldn't give up until she found the truth.

Until Spector had been exposed.

Was that petty? Maybe.

Spector may have been good in a scrap, but the woman was rotten to the core. Casey felt it in her bones.

"Now," Spector said, "practice those moves and then we'll have ourselves another little tournament." She released Casey's arm and let her up. "May the best flight win."

Casey stumbled back to Flight 18 smarting and sore. Colonel Volk had ducked out at some point. She wondered how much of that he'd seen and whether word of her ass-kicking would make it back to the admiral.

They practiced open palms, elbows and takedowns for the next half hour. By then they were all exhausted. But Spector still wasn't done. She broke them out into random brackets and made the pilots fight one-on-one in single round eliminations until there was one person left standing. The winner of each round scored points for their flight. The losers did push ups at the side of the room and then cheered on their squadmates for the rest of the tournament.

Flight 18 didn't win. They weren't the best hand-to-hand fighters in the squadron. Yorra lasted into the semi-finals, though, and did a lot to redeem Casey's pride. She, Park and Nevers cheered until their voices were hoarse.

Casey was assured by the end of it that, while they hadn't won the day, they certainly hadn't come in last, either. They finished putting away their gear, stretched, and cleaned the space together with spray wash and white rags. The gym was spotless when they were done.

While they rested, Spector announced the winners of the day. Flight 4, headed up by the scrappy redhead Casey'd faced off against earlier, had come in first. She beamed as her squadmates lifted her up on their shoulders and paraded her around the room. Casey felt a pang of jealousy watching the victory dance and knowing they could have done better. But she was still proud of the way they'd held their own.

"Finally," Spector said, "the grand prize—your mission. The rogue Kryl hive has taken off from Robichar. We're to perform recon in the direction we believe they're headed, and see if we can ascertain their destination."

Murmurs of agreement and pats on the back went around the room.

"Flight 4 will fly point, as promised," Spector said. "Flight 18, you're grounded. The rest of you get ready to leave the day after tomorrow at 0600 hours."

"What?!" Casey demanded, shooting to her feet and balling her fists. "You can't do that. We didn't lose!"

"It's not about winning and losing. Insubordination will

not be tolerated in the Furies. You should know that by now, Raptor."

"This is so unfair. If you want to punish someone, punish me, not the whole flight."

"You need to understand that your actions have repercussions. I'm showing the whole squad what a failure of leadership results in. You can either accept your punishment with grace, or throw a fit like a petulant child. Which is it going to be, Captain Osprey?"

Casey bowed her head for a long minute as she fought to contain her unbridled rage.

Once again, Walcott's voice materialized in her thoughts. "The obstacle is the way, Captain. This path is clear. The question is, what are you going to do about it?"

With a supreme effort of will, Casey managed to bottle her anger. She slowly drew herself to attention and saluted her commander, then spun and marched out of the room before she made herself into more of a fool than she already had.

# ELEVEN

E ven if nothing with the Colonization Board had been resolved, Kira felt relieved to be back in her natural habitat.

The bridge of the *Paladin of Abniss* buzzed with activity. Harmony's lights hovered before her in the shape of the ship as the AI steered the Imperial destroyer into synchronous orbit with Ariadne. Officers spoke through their comms to Engineering, Flight Control, Weapons, and other teams as they prepared for the mission. Colonel Volk barked orders and double checked everything twice, overseeing operations.

Kira was only half paying attention to the movements of her crew. By now, such preparations were a routine operation, and her executive officer and the AI had it under control.

Instead, her attention was preoccupied by another satellite in synchronous orbit as she contemplated the next steps in her floundering political campaign—the Emperor's pleasure palace.

Ariadne had no natural moons, no oceans, no tide. The only water source on the city-planet was located underground, deep beneath the frozen poles. Much of the water they currently used had been harvested from asteroids or hauled in from distant colonies. That was one of the main reasons the colonial ventures were so important to Ariadne's survival. They needed an influx of resources like fresh water and metals to continue to support their burgeoning population. And every time they added a new crop of refugees, the system was put under additional stress.

As a direct result of this paucity of resources, the planet had expanded into orbital space. Instead of natural moons, the satellites of Ariadne were all manmade. There was the Molten Cage, a maximum security prison; Two Cubes, the planet's most popular casino, shaped like a pair of glittering silver dice; several personal habitats owned by the ultra wealthy; industrial stations cobbled together from decommissioned starships...

And the Emperor's pleasure palace, an enormous artificial habitat.

Transparent aluminite domes dotted the surface of the palace like bubbles. Inside each, a variety of life flourished— even from this distance, she could make out the canopy of a forest in one, and a neatly organized hydroponics farm in another. She knew there were hundreds of gardens, kilometers of walking trails, even waterfalls within. The palace sustained itself completely, recycling its air, cleaning its water, growing its food. It was run by a staff of several thousand, and their benevolent ruler wanted for nothing. Originally designed as a summer home, the Emperor had quietly relocated there and begun to use it as his primary residence following the conclusion of the Kryl War. Rumor had it that he hadn't been down to Ariadne for over a decade.

That meant the only person with the power to override Chairman Card's foolish decisions was locked up in his own personal bunker, seeing only the priests of Animus who conducted his rites, and those powerful or famous enough to gain an audience with his royal orbitalness.

Kira tasted blood and unclenched her jaw. She hadn't even noticed she was chewing on the inside of her cheek until a canine pierced the flesh.

"Harmony," she said once the AI had disengaged the ship's engines, indicating that they had established synchronous orbit. "Can you apply for an audience with the Emperor on my behalf?"

"Certainly, Admiral. The forms are straightforward, and clear procedure has been laid out in the Imperial military charter. You'll need approval from the Executive Council."

"Admiral Gitano will sign off on it."

"Very well. I'll get that started for you and let you know when it is done."

It was nice to be able to speak out loud to the AI and not look like a crazy person. No one on the bridge even gave her a second glance.

Colonel Volk had approached while she was speaking. He stood rigidly at attention as a bead of sweat tracked down his bald pate and disappeared into the ring of thick gray hair surrounding his head.

"Starfighters are ready to be deployed, Admiral."

She nodded. "Are you feeling all right, Volk?" He had always been pale, but today his skin bordered on pasty. And it wasn't warm on the bridge. Her fingers were stiff and chilled.

"Fine, sir. Bit of a headache. Nothing I can't manage."

That's what he always said when he'd had too much to drink the night before. "Your sick days are there to be used, you know."

A vicious smile split his face, despite his pallor. "And miss the first mission in a month?"

"Can't say I blame you. But once we deploy the scouts, get some rest, would you?"

"Of course, sir."

She leaned in. "Don't make me order you to the sick bay, Colonel."

He grunted. "Wouldn't dream of it."

"Good. Now, remind me which squadrons you picked for this mission?"

"The Furies, Jack's Jokers, and Moraliens."

She felt a smile grow on her face to match Volk's. "Three of the most battle-tested squadrons under my command. Good choices. And when do the light cruisers we requested as support arrive?"

His smile twisted into a grimace. "That's what I came to tell you, sir. I just got word that the request for support craft was cut in half by the Executive Council."

The coppery taste of blood spilled over her tongue again. "I despise politics, Joran."

"Aye, sir."

Kira forced herself to unclench her jaw and take a deep, calming breath. The mission had been approved by the Executive Council, and Admiral Gitano had promised she'd get the heavy cruisers to support her starfighters on their long-range recon mission. The cruisers were essential for refueling the Sabres and rotating the squadrons without making them jump back to Ariadne. With only half the number she requested, the recon they had to do would take twice as long.

*This must be a symptom of those funding battles she's fighting,* Kira thought. *The invisible enemy within.*

"How would you like to proceed, Admiral?"

"As best we know how. They sent us to Robichar without a full accompaniment. Why would this mission be any different?"

"Expected you to say that. I've assigned a heavy cruiser to

each squadron. The patrols will take an extra twenty to thirty hours, but we'll manage."

"I might have to head back down to Ariadne in the middle of the operation. I'm waiting on a call to find out."

"Understood."

"You know what that means, right?"

"Sir?"

"It means you need to get some rest." Colonel Volk was a sweaty mess. "And stay away from the whisky tonight. That *is* an order."

The skin between Volk's brows squeezed another bead of sweat as it tracked down his forehead, but he didn't object. "Permission to deploy the starfighters, Admiral?"

"Granted."

As he turned away, Harmony's swirling hologram appeared in the shape of Captain Osprey's face and said, "Admiral, there's a call waiting for you."

*Finally*, she thought. *Thought he'd never get back to me.* "I'll take it on the secure line in War Room One. Tell him I'll be right there. And stop *doing* that. If he found out…"

Harmony quirked Captain Osprey's hologram mouth into a wry smile and she transformed back into an androgynous everyperson.

Kira stood and watched through the viewport as Colonel Volk connected with the first squadron and ordered them out. "*Paladin* XO to Furies Actual, you are clear for takeoff."

"Copy that," Spector responded. "Preparing for takeoff."

Thirty seconds later, a squad of fifty Sabres shot out of their launch bays and rendezvoused with the first heavy cruiser that separated from a cluster of three.

Together, they flew out to a safe distance and jumped to their recon position in the flash-and-drag that was typical of lightspeed maneuvers.

"You're in charge, Colonel," Kira said.

"Aye, sir!"

The chatter of an active bridge was cut off abruptly as the automatic door cycled closed behind her. She made her way around the corner to War Room One, wasting no time. That door cycled open as she approached and she found Harmony's lights flickering over the octagonal table in the center of the room. She'd already turned on the holodeck.

The flickering image of a man sitting in a deep, padded office chair swiveled to face her. Even from the waist up, she could tell he'd maintained his athletic physique after retirement. He had a thick silver mane of hair that flowed to the nape of his neck, a matching silver beard adorned his square chin, and the intelligent eyes that studied her as she sat down were colored blue like the sky on a crisp winter morning—just like his daughter's.

"Inquisitor Osprey, thank you so much for returning my call."

"Please, dispense with the formalities, Admiral. It's been almost five years since I retired, and I never liked that title anyway."

"The most feared inquisitor in the Solaran Empire doesn't like his title? But you did the job so well."

He grimaced. "I did my duty. It was never a pleasant job."

"Speaking of unpleasant jobs and duty, the reason I'm calling is because I need your help."

"Gitano said you might reach out."

*So why did it take you so long to return my call?* she wondered. Then it hit her. "And did my background check return a clean record?"

A sharp grin split his mouth and deepened the wrinkles at the corners of his blue eyes. "For the most part."

She had a brief moment to wonder how much he knew about the mission that ended the war. Was there anything in there saying how she and Captain Omar Ruidiaz had been lovers? Or that she'd been heartbroken when he sacrificed his life to save the Empire, leaving her behind? That for years afterward, she threw herself into her job, climbing up the ladder of her career as a way to manage her grief—but that she would have given anything to have sacrificed herself with him? Even knowing now what Omar had become, she felt the same.

She couldn't know what he'd seen in the records. Only inquisitors, the Executive Council, and the Emperor himself were privy to that information.

"I know Admiral Gitano would only recommend someone she trusts. But I need to be able to trust you, too, and I don't have the security clearance to run a background check like you did on me."

"You have my word as an inquisitor that I will operate in good faith. If there's something I can't do, I'll be honest with you about that."

"And if you don't?"

"I'm retired, Admiral. Apart from a limited security clearance, all I have left is my reputation."

She leaned back in her chair and glanced aside at the door, thinking. That wasn't much of a guarantee. She trusted Gitano. And she only needed a neutral party, not an ally. She wasn't outsourcing the hard work, she just needed someone who wouldn't undermine her efforts. Who better than a man who spent his life protecting the people of the Solaran Empire, and the last ten years of his career acting as an impartial traveling justice for crimes in the Fleet?

She nodded, turning back to meet those piercing blue eyes again. "Very well. For starters, I need you to host a meeting between Chairman Card and myself."

He nodded as if he'd expected that. "We can do it at my estate."

"He can't feel like he's being pressured or coerced in any way."

"Even if you want to coerce him?" The inquisitor shot her a roguish smile that made him look ten years younger.

"I need him to believe that putting a temporary pause on colonization efforts is the right thing to do." She gave him the background, leaving nothing out about her reasons for believing the Kryl presented a galactic security risk.

"And what if he doesn't see things your way?"

"I'll convince him."

"How?"

She laid it out for him. The inquisitor leaned forward, listening intently, his cold blue eyes shining with a mischievous spark.

Maybe she had been wrong. Politics *could* be fun.

## TWELVE

A sopping wet sponge sailed over the Sabre Elya was currently polishing with a clean cloth and nailed him right in the forehead, exploding in a spray of sudsy water that dripped down his nose and chin.

"Hey," he said. "Sneak attack!"

The sponge landed on the hangar floor with a *splat*.

Park threw his head back and cackled. "Your face!"

Elya scowled at him. There was an exchange of whispered words and then another sponge came sailing over the Sabre, this time landing directly on Park's upraised head, interrupting his laughter with a series of choking sputters.

He bent double and braced himself on his knees. "Augh!" he said. "It got in my mouth!" He spit on the ground. "Soap is gross."

On the other side of the starfighter they'd been cleaning, twin peals of laughter erupted from Osprey and Yorra. Bending down and peering beneath the Sabre, he spied the two women braced against each other and staggering as they were overcome with fits of helpless laughter.

"Tell me you at least used the *clean* water," Park said.

Their laughter cut off abruptly, then redoubled in noise and intensity. Yorra snorted and covered her mouth. Osprey's hand slipped from the shoulder of the shorter woman and she went to the ground, gasping as she clutched at her stomach.

Park's jaw fell open. He clawed at his tongue with both hands and spat several more times. Then he grabbed both sponges and raced around the Sabre. There were screams and then gasps as he shoved the sponges down the backs of the girls' shirts.

Elya snuck around the other side and picked up one of the buckets.

"No!" Osprey said as she staggered to her feet. "Don't you dare, Nevers, nononono—"

Osprey lifted her hands to stop him, but his arms were longer than hers and the bucket of gray water poured down over her head.

Her hair came halfway out of its neatly tied tail. She glared at him beneath sopping wet dark-blonde bangs.

Elya's mouth spread into a lopsided smile. "You started it."

"Ahh!" Yorra screamed. Park had upended the other bucket over her head. She'd seen Osprey get soaked first, so she had some warning and was able to skip out of the way and only get an arm and one shoulder wet. Naab grabbed the sponge that had fallen out of her shirt and went after her. The two of them darted around the jet for a while as he tried to catch her. Though Yorra was small, she was lightning quick, with a low center of gravity, and she managed to evade him for a few circuits of the Sabre. Park finally grabbed her, wrapping his arms around her mid-section. She kicked and squirmed, then tangled her leg around his ankle and took him to the ground. Park landed beneath her, laughing. Neither of them hurried to get up.

Casey picked up the other sponge and threw it at them.

"Get a room!" she said. But her tone was playful and she smiled broadly.

In the Fleet, it was common for squadmates to have intimate relationships that ran the gamut from casual to serious. As long as it wasn't up and down the chain of command, there was no regulation against it. Some commanders even encouraged fraternization, reasoning that intimacy brought the squad closer together while discouraging them from engaging in prostitution or other illicit pastimes. Or so they hoped. Besides, when a group of young people were stuck on a starship together for months at a time, they had to manage their stress somehow, and a person could only lift weights and gamble so much before they got bored and went looking for trouble.

While their fearless leader made kissy faces at the pair on the floor, Elya stood awkwardly nearby, opening and closing his mouth several times. He was desperate to share what was on his mind, but each time he came close to confiding in his friends, something seized up in his brain.

Unlike Yorra and Park, he'd never had a casual relationship with a squad-mate. In fact, he struggled to let any person get close to him. He'd always been happy to show up, do his job, and go home; to fly virtual sims alone, to go for long walks on his own. He was comfortable being by himself.

It struck him, in this moment, seeing Park and Yorra kissing on the ground, soaked in dirty water, with Casey teasing them, that his attitude was *exactly* the problem.

*I'm the problem*, he thought.

If he looked at it with a smidge less self-recrimination, his *choices* were the problem. Spector had been at least half right when she roasted him in front of the squad. Trying to do everything himself was what caused him to crash land on Robichar; it was what kept him up late at night, doing research into Telos relics, without sharing any of his findings with his friends.

After Robichar, he'd promised them he'd be better. He'd promised to act like a team player. But when they returned to Ariadne after the mission was over, he fell into the same old patterns.

He couldn't let them down. Not again.

And what he needed to do next was too much for him to take on alone.

Osprey glanced at Elya, rolling her eyes and jerking a thumb back at the pair on the ground. "Can you believe this?"

When things went bad for Osprey, where did she turn for support? To her team. Even though she was seething mad at Lieutenant Colonel Spector for shaming her in front of the squad and then grounding their flight, she didn't ball up mentally, keep secrets, and lose sleep over the situation. No. She leaned into her friends. She threw wet sponges, brought the flight together, and generally made the best of a bad situation.

Elya looked up to see Hedgebot perched atop the slanted nose of the Sabre's cockpit at a relatively safe distance from flying wet sponges. He cocked his little head to the side, as if he could hear Elya's thoughts.

Before he lost his nerve, Elya blurted out, "MOXA secret police pulled me off the street and threatened to disappear me the other night."

Osprey turned slowly, her eyes widening. Yorra and Park separated and glanced up as they untangled from each other.

He cringed inwardly. Every instinct he'd grown up with screamed at him to take the words back; to laugh and say it was just a joke, look at your faces, ha ha ha. The loner attitude that had kept him walled off from the pain a young man experiences as a galactic refugee on the run from the Kryl insisted he jump down a deep dark hole and hide.

But he couldn't. Even though he was terrified, he'd promised. It was time to confess.

*Let the fires of truth scour me clean.*

"What did you say?" Osprey asked.

*I hope I don't get burned in the process.* "MOXA secret police. After the launch on Saturday, when we realized they were tracking my tablet... I went for a long walk through the city to sort out my thoughts. They jumped me, pulled me off the street and told me that if I didn't stop looking into the relics, they'd make me wish I was dead."

"Same guy who was looking for you at the spaceport?"

Elya nodded.

"But how'd they find you if your tab was broken?"

Elya winced under the scrutiny of Raptor's gaze. Her blue eyes were like the frozen hail that battered the planet of his youth. "I had it repaired so I could save the data. *Off* network, but—"

Park shook his head. "You and that research, man. Like a dog with a bone."

"I didn't want to lose the work."

"If you were off network when you pulled the data down, how'd they track you?" Yorra asked.

"I think the guy who owns the machinist shop gave me up. When he booted up my tab to fix it, he must have been notified somehow. I've wracked my brain and it's the only thing that makes sense. After I stole those blueprints of the MOXA headquarters building—" He swallowed against a sudden dryness in his throat. "—the file I took must have infected my tab with some kind of spyware. When Klayton plugged it in to fix it, it probably threatened or scared him into reporting me."

"Just a damn second," Park said, holding up both hands.

"If they knew it was you, why let you go? Why not arrest you, or worse?"

"Because you're Fleet," Casey said, her voice soft and sure.

Elya's eyebrows shot up. "How'd you know?"

"Because not even MOXA secret police can disappear an officer of the Solaran Defense Forces without serious repercussions. If the Chief Inquisitor found out, they'd nail MOXA to the wall."

"They talked a big game. They said they operated outside of the SDF's jurisdiction, but they let me go all the same."

"They wanted to scare you," Osprey said.

"Well, they succeeded."

"And maybe they wanted to see what you'd do next." Yorra chuckled and shook her head. "You're the unluckiest duck I know, Fancypants."

"True that," Park said as he pulled a bag out of his pocket and wiped drops of water from the plastic packaging. He withdrew a pinch of fluffy brown tabac and arranged it expertly in a boat of rolling paper. "What else they say?"

The bruise on the side of his head, above his ear, where he struck the pavement after they'd tripped him with the bola throbbed as he thought back to that night. "They know more about the relics than they're letting on, I know that much. The fact that they went through the trouble to track me down and threaten my life is proof that I hit a nerve."

Park sparked his rolly and exhaled a plume of smoke through a smirk. "You do have a special talent for gettin' on people's nerves, bro."

Elya plucked the cigarette from the lips of the stocky pilot and took a drag.

"'Ey! Get yer own."

"Boys, please." Yorra snatched the cigarette from Elya and held it out of Park's reach. "Focus."

"Soooo," Osprey said. "Did you get the data off your tab or not?"

"They took the backups I had on me at the time. And they stole the other ones out of my bunk."

Park spun around, completely forgetting about the cigarette Yorra had confiscated, and stared at Elya with his mouth hanging open. "That was *MOXA*?! Earth's blood, man! I thought it was someone on the squad pranking us!"

Elya winced at the words—and the volume—his bunkmate was screeching. "Sorry. I didn't know how to tell you."

Park made several angry gestures and then marched a couple meters off, muttering to himself. He took his pouch of tabac back out and rolled another cigarette. It came out crooked. He threw it down, disgusted, and rolled yet another. This one seemed to satisfy him. He sucked it down to the spiral of paper he used as a filter before he was calm again.

Yorra blew out her cheeks, regarded the cigarette in her hand, shrugged, and took a drag herself. She coughed harshly. "How do you smoke this dirt, Naab? It's awful."

"Pretty girl like you don't need to be pickin' up the habit."

"Aw, you called me pretty." She blinked long lashes at him.

That drew a small smile out of him. But he still looked troubled.

Osprey's frown deepened and a faraway look came over her face. "I could have sworn that was Spector playing dirty."

"Wish it were," Elya said, "but the MOXA cops told me they'd be taking the drives from my bunk. I got back home as fast as I could, but they must have had a second team standing by. They hit the room as soon as they found out who I was. Faster than I thought possible..."

"Animus," Osprey cursed. "I wanted so badly for it to be Spector..."

"Sorry, Raptor. But to answer your question, I did get the

data. I stashed one more drive somewhere and I don't think they found that one."

"Where at?" Park asked.

"At the machinist's shop. I hid it in the wall of the secure room where I made the transfers. I can't go back there, though. I'm sure MOXA has someone watching the place."

"I'll go get it," Yorra said.

Elya blinked at her. "Really?"

"Why not?" She shrugged. "No one would suspect a pretty little girl like me."

Osprey frowned but said nothing. She'd gotten very quiet once she found out that the commander wasn't guilty of an act she had already pinned the blame on her for.

"There's something else," Elya said.

That got Osprey's attention.

They all turned to stare at him, and once again Elya's instincts shouted at him to shut his fool mouth or go the way of Yuzosix—extinct, lost to humanity, one of countless victims of the heartless Kryl.

*You're not a refugee anymore, Elya. Hiding isn't going to help you survive. Tell them the truth.*

He took a deep breath and then said, "I think I know where to find information about the Telos relics. Word is that it's not in the MOXA building, but in the Archives below the Church."

"The great temple?" Yorra asked. "Where Walcott's memorial service was held?"

"That's the one."

"Oh, yeah, that's right," Park said. "Apparently they have actual paper books down in the historical section. Aren't those archives open to the public?"

"Not all of them. There's a portion locked away from the rest. You have to be a High Priest or have top secret security clearance just to get through the door."

"Or a pass from the Emperor," Yorra added.

"Keep dreaming," Park said.

"That's why I need your help."

"How do you know this isn't another headfake?" Park asked. "Like the last brilliant idea you had to steal those MOXA blueprints?"

He winced. Park was right to be suspicious. "I have a source." He filled them in on what Backspace had told him.

Park made an uncertain noise and said, "I dunno, man, seems risky as hell…"

"Of course it is, but if you'd seen what that relic could do, you'd want to know more about it too. Right, Raptor? You saw the kind of power that thing had."

Raptor had been following the conversation pensively. "I did," she admitted. Neither Park nor Yorra had seen the demonstration before Admiral Miyaru took possession of the relic but they'd heard the story. Not to mention they had their own encounter with the Kryl. It left a mark.

"Imagine, Naab," Elya said, "that if another one of those parasites crawled into your head, all we'd have to do was turn the handle on that geode and *boom*, Kryl obliterated."

Park shuddered and licked his lips. "Okay, yeah, I admit, it sounds like a nice thing to have on hand."

Yorra reached out and gripped Park's arm. He gave her a smile, then ground the cherry of his cigarette between two fingers, letting ash drift down onto the hangar floor.

"And what if there are more relics out there? We could send that rogue hive running scared, and the Kryl would never have any power over us again." Elya's hands balled into fists. "Didn't we swear to protect humanity when we joined the Fleet?"

Yorra dipped her head once, decisively. "Oltanis is in more danger than Ariadne is. They could use the advantage."

"All the colonies could," Park said.

"The relics could help us do that. We *need* to know more about them. As much as we can find out."

"What you're suggesting, though," Yorra said. "Breaking into the Archives. It could get us in a whole heap of trouble."

"Sure would piss Lt. Colonel Spector off, though," Park said. "Eh, Raptor?"

Her somber expression melted away as the sun of a sharp smile filled her face. "It would. But I don't know... we're already on deck-swabbing duties."

Elya barreled ahead before she put the kibosh on the whole thing. "First, we get that drive back from the machinist shop."

"You know," Yorra said thoughtfully, "I *have* been meaning to send a video home. I find myself in sudden need of a secure room to record it."

"Perfect."

Park leaned in a little. His anger about Elya's lie by omission seemed to have faded. "And then we need a plan to distract the priests, or somehow convince one of them to let us into the Archives."

"What if there's an easier way to get access?" Raptor asked.

"What did you have in mind?" Elya asked.

"A possible alternative," Raptor said. "But we'll need to work together."

# THIRTEEN

**R**emember, Casey thought, *this was your bright idea.* Swallowing her pride, she pulled open the ornate wooden door and stepped into her family home.

Nevers, Park, and Yorra craned their necks upward as they walked in behind her.

"Whoa," said Nevers. Hedgebot echoed the sentiment in a tone laced with wonder.

"You grew up *here*?" Park said. "This is a palace."

"Chateau Osprey," Yorra whispered.

"It's just a house," she insisted in spite of the wings fluttering through her stomach. "This way."

She moved quickly into the grand foyer, a vast open room with lots of wood and glass and a sweeping staircase that curled up to the third floor. The walls were covered in faded paintings and still photos of Ariadne from days past, back when it actually had wilderness left to photograph. At the top of the stairs, centered on the back wall, an enormous hawk had been painted. It was stylized with striking curves of blue and green and gold—the Osprey family crest. Rapiers were mounted on either side of the bird—an X on the left, an

X on the right—except one stroke was missing. Unlike the paintings, the swords weren't just for show. Her father actually trained and fought with them in fencing tournaments. No surprise that the only entertainment he ever deigned to participate in involved outmaneuvering and stabbing his opponents. And here she was, planning to outmaneuver him. The very idea of such a bold strategy sent another nervous quiver through her body.

She swallowed and stood up a little straighter, the instinctive reflexes of a lifetime of training coming back to her. It always did when things were tough. On missions, she'd been grateful for it. Now, she just felt a little sick.

"You okay, Rap?" Nevers asked.

"Fine."

"You don't look fine."

"You don't know my father."

He put a hand on her shoulder. "Take a deep breath. We can do this."

She nodded, studying the shadows as if she expected her dad to jump out of one of them and yell, "Boo!"

"Remember the plan," she whispered to Nevers. Now she was the one whispering.

Nevers patted Hedgebot's head again. "I remember."

"You're sure he can pull it off?"

The little bot scampered down Nevers' legs and sniffed around the floor, pulsing in soft shades of aquamarine.

"He can. We practiced."

She pursed her lips. "Not here we didn't."

"Daughter mine," a basso voice boomed from the top of the staircase. "You should have called ahead and let me know you'd be dropping by."

Her father stepped in front of the family crest and frowned down at them. Sunlight streaming from the third floor windows behind him glittered off his silver hair, which was slicked back with sweat. His once trim full beard had grown out, and he wore loose-fitting black athletic pants and a wet t-shirt. He brought the sword he had been practicing with across his chest and gripped the blade in the glove of the opposite hand. "I see you brought friends."

The way he said the last part made it sound like an accusation. But that was her father. Always judging, always critical. Never giving her the benefit of the doubt, not even when she chose to follow in his footsteps.

*For once, he's right to be suspicious*, she thought. "Dad, I'd like you to meet Flight 18 of the Fightin' Furies."

"Admiral Osprey," Park said. "It's an honor to meet you, sir."

"Likewise."

Yorra nodded. "You have a beautiful home."

Nevers waved as his eyes darted awkwardly around.

Her father's expression never changed, but eventually he inclined his head in acknowledgement. He removed his gloves, then turned and hung the sword on the wall, completing the second X on the right side of the family crest.

"I'll have the chef throw something together for lunch. We can eat in the garden. Let me clean up and I'll meet you out there."

He walked off into the residential wing where the master bedroom was located, leaving them alone again.

Park's eyes got big and round. "You have a personal chef?"

"And a garden!" Yorra squealed in girlish delight.

Casey blew out a breath. "I don't have anything."

"Relax, Rap," Nevers said. "You've got to take it easy."

She nodded. "I'm trying."

"How 'bout that tour?" Park asked. "I wanna see how rich people live."

She frowned at him, then hastily dropped it when she

realized she probably looked just like her father. "Right. Do you want to start in the library, or the armory?"

"You have an armory?" Park said, his voice echoing up to the third floor. "By the Spirit of Old Earth, I think I'm going to cream my pants."

Yorra rolled her eyes. "Men are disgusting."

"Guilty." Nevers snorted. "Only one of us is kissing that mouth though."

Park shimmied in front of them, waggling his eyebrows. Yorra laughed and gave him a playful shove.

"Come on, you clowns," Casey said as she led them through a pair of double doors.

She gave them the tour of the mansion. Nevers only made it to the library. He immediately set to searching the holos for studies and films on Telos relics, and ended up finding a dense history of the Imperial dynasty starting with Emperor Sol the Fourth and proceeding through first contact with the Kryl. He didn't find what he was looking for, but when they came back to get him he was babbling about time gaps and how history is written by the victors. Casey only half heard him.

"And this is my father's office," she said as they passed it on their way out to the garden. She checked the doorknob. As usual, it was locked. She met Nevers' eyes, and they continued on their way out to where housekeepers had begun to set out their meal.

They sat in upholstered chairs and poured steaming tea from shining metal carafes. Her father joined them about twenty minutes later. He'd showered and swapped the workout clothes for loafers, grey slacks and a v-necked shirt with a high collar that reminded her of a military uniform.

"Sorry for the wait," he said. "I had to take care of some business."

"I thought you were retired. I remember you saying, 'I'm going to spend the rest of my days fencing and reading.'"

"Fencing keeps me fit, but one can only do so much reading before it grows tiresome. Besides, this is a favor for an old friend." That gave Casey pause. She wondered who he was doing the favor for. "I didn't expect you to visit today. Call ahead next time, would you, dear?"

That was her father for you. He hated not being in control of the situation. She gave him her most radiant smile. "I wanted to surprise you, Dad."

"Isn't your squadron supposed to be on a mission right now?"

She hesitated for a moment too long. "We're on special assignment."

He gave her a grave look. "Really."

"How did you know the Furies are on a mission right now?"

"It's my job to know things."

"Not any more it's not."

"Old habits die hard."

*Him and his secrets*, she thought.

"So why aren't you working?" he asked.

Casey pressed her lips together. "We were grounded."

"For what?"

"I don't want to talk about it."

Her father's scowl deepened. He glanced at the other pilots, but they were all busy searching for leaves in their tea cups.

Casey crossed her arms and sipped noisily while the waiters set salad plates in front of each of them.

"So, why don't you tell me what happened? I can see by the looks on your faces that you feel as if you've been slighted."

Casey didn't want to look like the villain, so she let Park

tell the story. He was the talkative one anyway. Park started, hesitantly at first and growing bolder each time her dad nodded or smiled. Park started way back at Walcott's memorial service where their new squadron commander was first foisted upon them before catching him up on recent events. Nevers excused himself in the middle of the story to go to the bathroom. Park's story dragged on until he returned, and the whole time, Casey sank lower and lower in her chair.

The main course was served, chicken marsala with al dente angel hair pasta. Park was blabbing on and on between bites when her father finally interrupted him and, turning to her, asked, "Spector? Isn't that the older girl you picked a fight with at the academy?"

"I did not pick a fight with her."

"You know what I mean."

Why did she even bother? "It is."

"Hngh. What was her first name again?"

"Renata."

A look passed over her father's face. It didn't last long, no more than the span of a breath, before his carefully controlled poker face returned. He ran his hand down his silver beard.

*He knows something and he's keeping it from us.* She knew he would never tell, so instead of bringing it up she filed that information away for later.

Before Park began talking again, Casey said, "Too much tea, excuse me."

She pushed her chair back from the table and made her way quickly into the house. Instead of turning down the hallway toward the bathroom, she pivoted in the opposite direction, her footsteps clicking on the polished marble. After a brief trip upstairs, she returned and stepped up to the door of her father's office.

Nevers was good to his word. The doorknob turned and the door swung smoothly open.

*Thank you, Hedgebot*, she thought.

The rest of the plan was on her. She couldn't have asked one of her pilots to do what she was about to attempt. It just wasn't in her to ask someone else to take this kind of risk. It was *her* father who was the former inquisitor—if she was caught, she would probably get lenience, whereas if it was one of her pilots, they'd be more likely to face a military tribunal. And she was the only one with an influential father who might bail her out.

It had to be her.

She closed the door softly behind her and hurried around the back of the wooden desk, sinking into the leather chair. She waved her hand over the holoprojector and activated the terminal.

A clear panel of crystal set into the desktop illuminated a login request, outlining the shape of a finger. She placed the opaque plastic film she'd used just a minute ago to lift her father's prints from his sword over her thumb, and then laid her thumb on the crystal.

It flashed green and changed to a flat line that measured sound waves.

"Awaiting voice identification."

Next she dug the pocket-sized digital recorder out of a zip pocket on her uniform shoulder and rewound carefully to her father's voice during their conversation. Any words would do, it just had to be *his* voice. The words that came out of the recording were: "—don't you tell me what happened? I can see by the looks on your faces that you feel as if you've been slighted."

The interface gave off a harmonic tone. "Voice ID acknowledged. What is your password?"

This was the hard part. But in spite of his ability to judge his daughter with a most critical eye for details, he was endlessly sentimental about one thing. She called up the holo-keyboard and typed in her mother's first name and the day she died. Casey would never forget that date. It had been right before she got shipped off to military school.

The crystal flashed red. "Password denied."

*Shit.*

She tried again, reversing the date and name.

This time the crystal flashed green. Casey sagged in relief.

"Please enter your authentication code. You have one minute."

She hauled open the desk drawer, shoving papers aside as she searched for the little fob with digits that changed by the minute. She'd seen him use it to access the server before, and knew he kept it in here somewhere.

*Ah, yes.*

She watched the screen on the fob and waited for the numbers to switch over. Then she typed them in, careful not to use the voice commands this time. *One seven five five three.*

"Access granted."

An array of holoscreen interfaces bloomed to life in the air before her as she was granted full access to the inquisitor's database. One window was labeled, "Background checks." Another said, "General search," and a third said, "File a new judgement."

She went to general search and began typing in the terms that Nevers had given her.

"No results found for 'Telos relics'," the system read back.

That was odd. She tried again.

"No results found for 'Ruins artifacts Telos kryl'."

*What in the name of Animus is going on?* she wondered.

It felt like a heavy lead weight sank into her gut. If her father, the famous retired inquisitor didn't have access to view information about Telos relics, who did?

She tried a few more search terms. They were all blank except one: "ancient alien technology" returned a single result that was marked, "CLASSIFIED BY MOXA."

If her father the inquisitor didn't have access to view it, this information really was *need to know*.

This frustrated her because it meant she'd been wrong about being able to find what Nevers was looking for here.

It frustrated her *more* because it meant Nevers was right, and the only place it was likely they would find that information was in the Archive below the Church of Animus—the one institution the Empire didn't have complete power to censor at will.

Nevers was as stubborn as she was. He'd never let this go until he found out what the Empire was hiding about these relics. Especially now that threats from the MOXA secret police confirmed he had scented a trail.

She compartmentalized this information for later and refocused her attention on the search interface, moving from the general search over to the window titled "Background checks."

She typed in Renata Spector's name and braced herself for disappointment.

When the results loaded, an audible gasp escaped her throat.

Spector had records, all right. She'd seen her father search through these before, from the other side of the desk, where the holoscreen interfaces were blurred out. But she knew generally how they were organized.

Each year was put into its own folder, with records inside for each mission, achievement and recordable incident.

Investigations got their own files, and they were cross-linked to the investigation master folder where the notes were kept.

Renata had three. Three investigations she had either been involved with or given testimony for.

*I knew it,* Casey thought. *You are dirty. No one gets investigated three times without getting slimed by some kind of corruption.*

Now the question was, what had she done?

The first investigation happened back before Casey had joined the Fleet. Renata was a Lieutenant then. They'd been flying a mission where the flight lead's Sabre malfunctioned. He got hit by an EMP of some sort, lost control of the starfighter, and ejected—straight into a small meteorite that punctured his oxygen tank. He suffocated in space before the medics had been able to reach him.

As much as Casey was dying to watch the videos of Renata's testimony, she didn't have time. She skimmed the notes left by the inquisitor—not her father—and saw that the investigation was eventually labeled a freak accident and marked "Resolved."

The second investigation happened five years later. Renata had been flight lead for a while when her squadron commander was incapacitated. He got the bends when a depressurization chamber returned to standard too quickly. They were on patrol so Renata, being the most experienced flight lead, took command for the remainder of the mission. They made it back to base to get the commander treated, but not fast enough. He died shortly after their return.

Like the first case, Spector was interviewed as a key witness. She was also commended for her leadership during a difficult situation and, a few months later, promoted and moved to a different squadron.

Casey tensed when soft footsteps padded down the hall by the office. She exhaled the breath she'd been holding when the steps faded away a few seconds later. It must have been one of the housekeepers bringing dessert outside.

She was running out of time. If she didn't get back to lunch, and soon, her father would get suspicious and come looking for her.

But she couldn't pull herself away from the files. She opened the third investigation involving Spector. This case was dated only two years after the first. She was still a captain then, but she was up for a promotion, and the inquisitor's notes stated that her wing commander was planning to oppose it.

Except, the week before her promotion came up for a vote, the wing commander came down gravely ill. He puked up his guts for three days straight. The doctors couldn't figure out what was wrong. He passed away a day later, and the official reason for his death on the coroner's report was "heart attack."

He never got the chance to oppose Spector's promotion.

There was a sinking feeling in her gut as Casey tabbed through the records. Sure enough, Renata Spector got the promotion to Major.

And two years later, she was promoted to Lieutenant Colonel and transferred to Ariadne to head up the Furies.

Casey hastily pulled up Renata's records and cross checked her promotion dates with the investigation. Sure enough, each time Spector was involved in an investigation by an Imperial inquisitor, a promotion lay right around the corner. Not every promotion came with an investigation, but the timing was eerie. Except for the last one, each of her command positions had been assumed within six months of the death of a superior officer.

No wonder she was so young when made Lieutenant Colonel. The path to her first full command was paved with the bodies of her dead commanders.

Did that mean malfeasance? Or another, worse, M-word? Casey was skeptical. Inquisitors, including her own father, had a reputation as hounds for Imperial justice. They were known for being ruthless and exacting in their investigations.

And each of these investigations had acquitted her of any wrongdoing. The deaths of Spector's commanders were individually labeled accidents, like the first two, or "inconclusive," like the third one with the sick wing commander.

Most people would have stopped there. But Casey was not most people. She'd known Renata for decades, knew she would stop at nothing to get what she was after.

And Inquisitors, despite their reputation, were only people. Women and men like her father. People make mistakes.

She thought, then, of the look that passed over her father's face when he'd realized who had become their new squadron commander. Did he suspect something too? He must be familiar with her history.

That sealed it for her. Casey pulled out her tab and snapped photos of the dozens of relevant records the system wouldn't let her forward to the anonymous inbox Nevers had set up for her.

Less than a minute later, she engaged the lock and closed the door behind her as she stepped into the hall. Her fingertips had just lifted from the doorknob when her father appeared in the archway at the far end of the hall.

"Father," she said, slipping the hand with the fingerprint film still on it into her pocket and peeling it off with the nail of her thumb.

"What are you doing?"

"Just needed a quiet place to clear my head," she lied.

He glanced at the door to his office, then walked slowly toward her, studying her face. She smiled as he checked the door and found it locked.

149

"The rules haven't changed since you lived here. My office is off limits."

"I know that. But it's locked. I couldn't have gotten in if I wanted to."

He grunted and narrowed his eyes as he continued to study her face. Two could play at that game—she'd learned from the best. She returned his gaze and tried to ignore the way her heart tried to climb into her throat. Then he put his hand around her shoulder and gave her a lecture on how good things come to those who wait as he led her gently back outside.

When dessert was finished, Park and Yorra fabricated some believable excuse to leave. Casey didn't remember what. She didn't fully relax until after they'd said their good-byes and piled into the cab to head back to base.

# FOURTEEN

I nquisitor Eben Osprey met Kira at the front door of his enormous mansion. "Admiral Miyaru," he said. "It's good to finally meet you in person."

"Likewise, Inquisitor."

He waved a hand and shook his head as if banishing an unpleasant memory. "Please, call me Eben."

"You're taller than I thought you'd be, Eben."

Standing just inside the door on the slightly raised threshold, his piercing blue eyes looked down into hers. They must be practically the same height—which was rare. "As are you."

Silently, Harmony added, "And more handsome."

*You hush,* Kira thought back.

"Why?" Harmony asked. "You could use a handsome friend. You've been wound like a top all week."

Ignoring Harmony's quip, Kira gestured with one hand behind her and said, "This is Colonel Volk, my second-in-command on the *Paladin of Abniss.*"

The bald man nodded to the retired inquisitor. He held out a hand and Eben shook it firmly. "Pleasure, sir."

"Nice to meet you," Eben said.

Volk mopped at his forehead with a handkerchief. He still looked too pale and sickly, even after he'd completed the bed rest she'd ordered him to take. He said he'd come down with some kind of stomach bug, and that it was likely to pass in a few days. Kira wasn't sure she believed that, but she needed a second here whose memory and judgment she could trust, and there was no one like Volk for reading people, whether they were pilots, crew or slimy politicians.

"Your reputation for honesty and commitment to justice is something I've always admired, sir. We appreciate you arranging this meeting."

The subtle reminder of his duty did not escape Eben's notice. He inclined his head a few degrees.

"Are they here yet?" Kira asked.

"Yes, just getting settled in." Eben shot her a roguish smile. "We're in the armory today."

Volk grunted approvingly.

"Oh, I *like* him," Harmony said to Kira. "I see a lot of him in that daughter of his. It's a shame she's not here, too, I'd love to see them together."

*Stop gawking and pay attention. I'll need your analysis later.*

"I am the most advanced neural network in the Solaran Empire, Admiral. I can do both at the same time."

*Well then at least do me a favor and gawk quietly, you're distracting me.*

Silence answered her this time.

*Thank you.*

They followed Eben through the grand foyer, down a long, wood-paneled hall, and into an enormous room that made the foyer look cramped by comparison. A dozen floor-to-ceiling windows were spaced evenly along the outside wall, which looked over a lush garden. Eben Osprey had taken the word armory literally—ancient flac vests, helmets of armored space suits, and the worn uniforms of soldiers from centuries past sat on shelves or stood in standalone cases. All manner of swords and knives hung on the walls between the windows, alongside weapons that ranged from the most ancient ballistic, powder-fired rifles to more modern plasma-based blasters. There were gauss rifles, sniper rifles, handguns, bolt throwers, crossbows, long bows —even a grenade launcher that, while old, still seemed to be operational. An antique, human-operated battle mech suit towered in the far corner. It was twelve feet tall and polished to a shine.

She didn't have the opportunity to study the weapons for long. At the far end of the room, a half dozen leather chairs had been arranged around a low table. Two men and a woman pushed themselves to their feet and turned to face her as they approached.

A tall, lean man in a silk suit stepped forward first, offering her his hand.

"Minister Aganaki," she said, taking it. "You're wearing something different each time I see you. No red silk today?"

"This is an informal occasion. I like to dress more comfortably when I'm not in public."

*Or you're a slimy shapeshifter,* she thought, and smiled. She couldn't begrudge him since he'd delivered on his promise.

At Aganaki's shoulder, Chairman Card stood stiffly, staring up at Kira with beady eyes from a height that was less than impressive without his raised platform and half-circle table to lift him above her. He was maybe two inches shorter than Colonel Volk, but easily twice as wide. He *did* wear a formal robe of state with the Colonization Board logo on the collar. It was tailored to fit his girth, and she guessed the loose pants that bunched up around his silk slippers had an elastic waistband.

The chairman's stiff-lipped secretary stood beside him,

bearing the crystal sheet of a large tablet in her arms like a shield. She wore the same crisp pantsuit Admiral Miyaru had first seen her in, or one so close in cut and color that she couldn't tell the difference.

"Admiral Miyaru," said the Chairman, finally acknowledging her presence. He didn't hold out a hand like the Minister had.

"Mr. Chairman. Thank you so much for agreeing to meet with me."

His eyes darted over to Minister Aganaki. "I wasn't given much choice in the matter."

She'd love to know what kind of pressure Aganaki had applied.

"All the same, I appreciate you taking the time out of your busy schedule. I believe we may have gotten off on the wrong foot."

He grumbled something under his breath and his face started to turn red. Kira exchanged a glance with Volk, then opened her mouth to apologize when Eben stepped between them.

"Why don't we all get settled first, huh? I wouldn't want anyone to get hungry during what could be a long discussion, and food and coffee will be served momentarily—ah, here we are."

"Smart thinking on his part," Harmony said to Kira. "Chairman Card looks like he's about to take a bite out of his leather chair."

After that quip, Kira's forced smile turned into a genuine one, though no one could have heard why. Harmony sometimes talked too much, but she always knew how to lighten the mood.

Kira accepted a coffee and stirred sugar into it, then took a halfhearted bite of a croissant. This was not the kind of negotiation she was used to. Every military parley she'd participated in during her career had been a tense standoff—whether it was with separatist factions on illegal asteroid bases, or pirates on commandeered light cruisers, both parties came armed to the teeth, and no one served appetizers.

And the Kryl? She wasn't sure the xenos had a word for "negotiate" in their psionic language.

Eben's strategy paid off, however. After a half dozen cheese-filled danishes and three cups of coffee, the Chairman finally relaxed back into the leather chair, which creaked under his weight.

Eben took that as his cue. "Shall we begin, then?"

Card nodded and gestured at Eben. "By all means, Inquisitor."

Kira leaned forward in her seat.

"Some ground rules first," Eben said. "I'll state my understanding of the situation, and then each of you will have a chance to share your position. No questions or comments until the other person has had their say. Agreed?"

Kira nodded. The Chairman opened his mouth as if to object, then closed it and inclined his head.

"Good. So here's what I gather from speaking privately to each of you. The admiral believes that the Kryl's latest actions pose a new threat to the Empire. As one of the leading battle commanders in the Fleet, she is uniquely positioned to understand and assess such threats. She's requesting the Colonization Board halt further colonial activity until the threat is neutralized. Admiral, is that correct?"

She thought about adding some color to his description, but thought she'd save her arguments for later, like Eben had asked. "Yes."

Eben nodded, and though his expression remained carefully neutral she got the sense that he was grateful for her brevity.

"The chairman's position is that colonial operations cannot afford to cease because the threat of overpopulation and a strained supply chain on Ariadne pose a domestic threat of their own to the galactic economy. In addition to having to house and feed the hundred thousand additional refugees brought back from the Robichar mission, he has the Emperor's blessing and the funding approved for such colonial ventures. Is that about the shape of it, Mr. Chairman?"

"Not to mention that the military has no jurisdiction over colonial ventures or movements," he grumbled.

Eben grudgingly acknowledged the point by spreading his hands and nodding.

Kira pressed her lips together to keep herself from speaking out of turn.

"And," the chairman went on, "our economy relies increasingly on natural resources brought in from the colonies. They are now the primary source of fresh water, raw metals, and much more."

"A trade which conveniently lines your own pockets," Kira said when she could hold it in no longer. "I find it difficult to believe you have the Empire's best interest at heart when you profit directly from such an endeavor."

He lifted his nose and scoffed at her. "I resent the accusation."

"But do you deny it, sir?"

Card ventured a glance at the inquisitor. As a senior commander in the Fleet, she knew inquisitors didn't have any extrasensory perception with which to detect lies, but due to the AI most of them had access to, it sometimes seemed like they did. He was retired now, so Eben didn't have access to Fleet AIs—though she heard they were allowed to keep a limited security clearance as the Empire's unpaid watchdogs should they happen across some sort of malfeasance—but such beliefs were common nonetheless.

Eben saw the glance, too. His ice-blue eyes hardened ever so slightly.

Card glanced at his secretary.

She switched the tab to her other arm and cleared her throat before she spoke, and then only stiffly. "Stock in colonial trading companies is part of the compensation package for all executive Board members."

"Shocker," Volk replied dryly.

"If I may interject?" Minister Aganaki lifted one finger. Eben nodded at him. "It is the same with any ministry engaged in economic activity. The Empire wishes our interests to be aligned. While we have a much different arrangement, the leadership at the Ministry of Xeno Affairs is rewarded in a similar way. Our bonus structure is based on the discovery of new xeno artifacts and ruins, and research into those discoveries, but if you were to compare the two contracts you would see many parallels."

The bottom dropped out of Kira's stomach as her skin tingled icy hot. She'd made a grave error in telling that snake about the Telos relic and promising to give him the parasite if he did her this favor. He would profit immensely from this deal—far more than she ever would, especially if his bonus was commensurate with the novelty of the discovery.

Dammit, but she had been outmaneuvered after all. She cursed herself for not treading more carefully. If there's a serpent in the grass, you're likely to get bit.

Minister Aganaki saw the realization play out over her face and smiled widely, meeting her gaze.

"Steady," Harmony whispered in her head.

With the AI's encouragement and a patience born of enduring the changing tides of many battles, Kira noted the blow and set it aside to analyze and learn from later. And learn she must, if she was to survive this foray into politics.

This battle of wits wasn't over. Kira forged ahead.

"Be that as it may, you must acknowledge that I profit nothing from the halting of a colonial venture. My only concern is for the security of the Solaran Empire and the protection of its people."

Chairman Card scoffed. "Power is its own profit."

"What power do I stand to gain here, Mr. Chairman?"

"Precedent. If I halt colonial ventures every time you find a spooky little bug or another rogue hive, a decade after we defeated the Kryl and sent them squirming back to their own volume of space, out of which, I will remind you, the vast bulk of their forces have not moved a *single* light-year, then what's to stop the Fleet from doing so again in the future? The precedent will have been set. And then every time some new xeno threat says *Boo*, every time the Fleet gets cagey—which is all the Earth-damned time—the Empire's economy takes a dive. And that *will* affect the *economic* security of every Solaran citizen."

Card had barely taken a breath during his rant. He'd risen a few centimeters out of his chair and his face turned ruddy again.

"Mr. Chairman, need I remind you that we just evacuated an *entire colony*?" Kira said. "Would you like to repeat the experience? Imagine what would happen if it was one of the larger trade centers next time. Colonel Volk, would you please share with our friends from the Colonization Board what our recon team learned on their latest mission?"

"It would be my pleasure, Admiral. The Kryl ditched the trackers we placed on them on their way to Robichar, but after some sub-light recon, we've determined that they seem to be headed in the direction of the Eridani Cluster, or possibly the Elturis System."

The secretary tapped furiously on her tablet. "Hindarvis is in the Eridani cluster, sir."

The blood drained from Card's ruddy face. "I know that," he snapped.

The colony Hindarvis was among the top three sources of silver, a material commonly used in the construction of most personal bots and electronic devices, as well as a key ingredient in the creation of the alloy aluminite.

"And New Kali is in the Elturis System..." the secretary added quietly. The stern, arrogant set of her lips had softened, her cheeks turned suddenly sallow.

Card's thick jowls trembled as he shook his head and muttered under his breath. Kira could imagine the numbers running through his head. The loss of Robichar was something the Empire could sustain. The loss of Hindarvis would set several large industrial companies against him. Ariadne had run out of silver centuries ago, but aluminite was essential in the construction of a number of important works—including the new voyagers the Colonization Board were constructing for their expeditions.

Time to make an appeal to his emotions.

"Alvin," she said. Using his first name felt strange and unfamiliar on her tongue. "I would not ask you to halt your expeditions if the parasite we found didn't represent a serious security risk. Imagine what could happen if the Kryl infected one of your colonies and managed to wrest control of their operations away from the trading company. If they manage to perfect the technique, the results could be... catastrophic. For *all* of us."

He looked up at her, frowning. The potential loss finally sank in, but he still shook his head. "We cannot afford to halt our expeditions."

"It's not forever. Plan your expeditions. Build starships for them. All I'm asking is that you not send another one out until I can eliminate the rogue hive and figure out how to effectively detect and guard against these damned parasites."

He sighed deeply and sank back into the chair once more. Minutes passed in tense silence as he considered his options. She waited patiently until he finally asked, "What do you propose?"

"First, a partnership with MOXA. We need their researchers to help us develop a better method for detecting these parasites, and to determine their ultimate purpose. I don't fully understand their goal with developing them, but I'll be completely honest with you and say that it absolutely terrifies me."

"You have our support," Minister Aganaki said.

"And your funds?"

"We'll need to work out the details."

"Colonel Volk, if you would be so kind as to send over the contract?"

Minister Aganaki's eyebrows shot up when he drew out his tab and saw the contract Harmony had written arrive on his device. "I'll have to have my people review it."

It felt good to surprise the minister. Maybe she was getting better at playing the game after all.

"You have twenty-four hours."

"Very well."

"Second, I need you to keep the *Maiden of Kali* from landing on the new colony and breaking ground on their first base until we can confirm that the Kryl hive poses no threat to New Kali or the Elturis System. With your support, I believe I can convince Admiral Gitano and the Executive Council to give me more ships to safeguard the region, but as the Fleet is already spread thin, the additional ships will likely have to be pulled off other trade routes."

The chairman had gone very quiet while she spoke.

"Is that safe?" the secretary asked.

Oh, *now* they were concerned for safety.

"It's necessary. The projections Harmony ran were based on the hive's former movements and their current trajectory. We don't know exactly what they're after, but they're targeting the colonies—or perhaps they're simply targeting worlds habitable to carbon-based life forms."

*Where Telos relics are likely to be found*, Kira added in her thoughts.

"Look at Minister Aganaki's face," Harmony said.

She glanced left. He was clenching his jaw and staring at his hands. He *knew*. He knew that the Kryl seemed to be going after the Telos ruins and the powerful artifacts they potentially contained.

Another realization hit her then. Minister Aganaki and Chairman Card were more in league than she had initially suspected. What if the planets they had chosen for colonial expansion weren't merely based on their position and potential for natural resources, but also for their potential to harbor Telos ruins and their powerful relics?

By the Spirit of Old Earth. That meant that *all* the colony worlds were potential targets for the Kryl.

If the Kryl had realized this, it meant that the Empire had been unwittingly charting a map to all the Telos ruins for the past decade!

That must be why the Kryl had come out to play again. If only she could figure out how they chose *their* targets...

*If we go to war over this, it's our fault*, Kira thought with horror. Her stomach twirled and tumbled. *I must warn Admiral Gitano. I must warn the Emperor.*

"First things first," Harmony reminded her.

"So do we have a deal?" Kira asked the chairman.

He sighed heavily, and seemed to sag with the burden of more than the gravity of his weight. "We do. But there's one problem."

*Oh, Animus, what now?*

"The *Maiden of Kali* missed her rendezvous in the Elturis System."

"What?!" Kira said, her voice rising.

Card licked his lips. "They were supposed to arrive two days ago with their escort. We've lost contact."

## FIFTEEN

Casey rocked back and forth on her bunk, knees clutched to her chest, vacillating like a Sabre caught between the gravitational pull of two different stars. One moment, she swung toward the righteous fury of vindication —she had been right about Spector! That bitch was guilty as hell. The next, her emotions bottomed out in the rubble of remorse: No officer of the Imperial Fleet had ever sunk so low as to use her father's clearance to illegally search her own commander's private records.

Casey should be busted down to private and thrown in the brig.

*And if I don't turn myself in,* she thought, *then my father will.* There was no way he didn't suspect what she'd done. Casey got them out of the house as soon as humanly possible without making it look like she was fleeing.

"Oh, Animus, what have I done?" Casey whispered. "What would Colonel Walcott think?"

Her pilots exchanged uneasy glances. They were in the bunk that she and Yorra shared, the door closed and locked. The rest of the squadron had returned from their reconnaissance mission and Casey didn't want anyone to overhear their discussion.

Nevers called up a holoscreen over Yorra's desk and filed through the photographs of Spector's files for the umpteenth time. He took a deep, slow breath. "I think he'd say you did the right thing."

Yorra grunted her agreement.

"Renny Stickbum is going dooown," Park added.

"Shh!" the other three said together.

Park rolled his eyes, then rolled another cigarette. A nervous gesture. He had a pocketful of them.

Walcott's words came to her: "Stick to the truth and you'll never have to lie." His pet phrases kept popping up in her head, the same way his disapproving frown did every time she closed her eyes.

"Ugh," she said, burying her face in her knees.

Nevers flipped through Spector's files again. "Well, one thing's for sure. She's either the luckiest commander alive, or she's guilty as hell. Each time she gets cleared of wrongdoing, less than six months later she gets her boss's job. How could she not be running some kind of scam? Unless..."

Casey stopped rocking and picked her head up. Nevers was frowning with one hand on his chin.

"Oh. I see where you're going," Yorra said. "That makes sense."

Park glanced between the two of them. "Uh, care to fill the rest of us in?"

"Someone could be protecting her," Yorra said. "Providing alibis, or helping her get off the hook each time an Inquisitor closed in."

Casey grunted. Something about that idea felt right, but how could she prove it? "Renata always was the teacher's favorite. Even when she was caught in the act, they always took her side."

"Raptor, didn't you say that your father made a funny face when you mentioned Spector?" Yorra asked.

"He's the hardest person to read I know. Compared to him, Fancypants and Naab here are open books."

"Ouch," Nevers said, feigning hurt and touching his fingertips to his chest.

Park just shrugged. "I won't deny it."

Yorra frowned. "But if you're right, then your dad knows something's off about her."

"Yeah, but I can't talk to him about it *now*!"

"That's not what I'm suggesting," Yorra hurried to add. "I'm just pointing out that if an Inquisitor thought something fishy was going on, that probably means there's something fishy going on."

"We just have to find out what," Nevers frowned. "Maybe Backspace knows another way to access personnel files."

"Absolutely not," Casey said, bouncing off the bed to her feet in a single smooth motion. "We can't risk it. If we want to get rid of Spector, everything we do from here on out needs to be completely above board."

"And how do we do that?" Nevers asked

Casey felt her shoulder slump forward. "I don't know," she said in a small voice.

Silence filled the space between them.

"In the meantime," Nevers said, "what are we going to do about the info we were hoping to find on the relics? Isn't that why we took the risk of breaking into your father's office to begin with?"

Casey chewed on that. As per Walcott's policy, she'd been honest with the others about what she'd found. "Yeah. Whatever info's available on the relics, it's top secret. If not even Inquisitors are allowed access…" Casey shook her head.

They all knew what that meant: Trying to get ahold of more information could get them killed. The Empire had assassinated and disappeared people for less. And Nevers had already made a target of himself.

"Even more reason to try my approach," Nevers said.

"I don't know…" she said. "It's risky. And we've already taken too much risk, not to mention Spector is probably keeping a close eye on us now that she's back from the mission."

"No one in the Fleet is watching the Archive," Nevers insisted. "I've already scoped it out—the security on the church is lax compared to what you'd find on a Fleet base. Apart from the distraction we'll need, the authentication measures are way less sophisticated than the ones guarding the Inquisitor's info-tech systems. The priests of Animus are Old Earth old school."

Casey bobbed her head. "True," she admitted. "They don't really trust modern tech."

"Exactly. According to what Backspace told me, the information we're looking for isn't even stored on the network— it's physical storage. That's why the Empire hasn't been able to censor it like all the other systems wired into the Ansible. I mean, who's going to look in some dusty old paper tome for something like this? They don't even *make* books out of paper anymore. No one has the time or money to care for them. They mold and fall apart too easily."

"No matter what, we can't be caught disobeying orders," Casey said.

"No one gave us any orders to stay out of the Archives, Raptor."

"True. True."

"Besides, we've already agreed—this is imperative to national security. If we find what Backspace says we'll find, the Fleet should be awarding us fucking medals, not grounding us and sticking us under the command of some dirty, ladder-climber commander."

"Keep your voice down," Yorra hissed.

Nevers winced. "Sorry, sorry... bad habit. I get loud when I get excited."

"Okay," Casey said. "Okay. Say we *do* do this. What about that distraction? We need something big and noisy, that won't get us into deep shit when we're caught."

"Big, noisy distraction, huh?" Park said, perking up. "Sounds like something I might be able to help with."

Casey snorted. Well. Naab, didn't stand for "Naked as a baby" for nothing.

# SIXTEEN

Elya paused on the steps leading up to the massive, vaulting entrance of the church of Animus—sometimes called the Great Temple for its size and stature as a landmark believers made long pilgrimages from other colonies just to see. The sun was setting to his left, bathing the rich stone in golden light that made the limestone glow.

Hedgebot scurried up the last step and came to rest on his hind legs beside him, the bot's tiny barrel-like body standing upright and radiating blue light from the sensory fibers lining his back and the metal plates armoring his stomach.

"All right, pal. Lights off."

The bot beeped and his lights darkened to a deep black that, among the shadows, would make him nearly invisible. Better camouflage ability was one of the enhancements Elya had purchased for Hedgebot following the first encounter with the MOXA secret police, and he was glad he had.

Elya felt feathery wings flutter through his stomach. He was nervous about the plan. Nearly dying on Robichar had set a new bar of fear for him, so he wasn't paralyzed by it, but things could still go very wrong. They wouldn't go chased-by-murderous-xenos wrong, but there was a lot at stake—his career, his friend's careers, not to mention the threats to his life from MOXA's frightening and as-yet-nameless secret police.

But he'd survived worse. Elya ginned up his courage, consciously forcing his shoulders back and down. It was amazing how much fear a person could tolerate with a little practice.

"You know the drill, Hedgebot. After you hear the screaming, light 'em up."

The bot circled twice and dashed for the opposite end of the stone courtyard, sticking to the shadows at the bush-lined edges. Even in the fading light of the setting sun, Elya had to squint to follow the tiny figure.

After the sun went down, he'd be practically invisible.

Elya strode up to the church, hauled open the heavy wooden door by its ancient handle, and went inside.

The Great Temple was open to the public from sun-up to sundown every day, except when it was booked for private events like Walcott's service. On Friday nights, Wednesday nights, and Saturday and Sunday mornings, they ran two services that could fit two thousand people apiece. You could attend the services by reservation only, and the waiting list was a year long.

On the off-days, the doors opened to all, with priests on staff for consultation and confession.

Inside, the silence was heavy and... still. Peaceful. About forty parishioners were scattered through the pews, alone or in small groups, praying quietly. A half dozen priests were speaking in low tones to supplicants, some near the front, others in alcoves along the side of the sanctuary.

Elya took a deep breath and let it out. Just being inside calmed his nerves... while simultaneously sparking a long-dormant twinge of guilt. It had been years since he'd come to church of his own volition or made a prayer out of anything less than fear for his life. And something told him the Spirit of Old Earth wouldn't count tonight's visit as a genuine one.

Well, he'd just have to ask forgiveness from Animus later. Tonight, he had a mission to accomplish.

Out of habit, Elya passed his hands through the candle flames near the entryway, muttering his thanks to the Spirit of Old Earth for the blessing of this new world. Then he strode down the center aisle.

A couple with two different textures of short-cropped, ink-dark hair sat with their hands intertwined in a pew about halfway down the aisle. They bent their heads together and whispered. The man leaned over to whisper in the woman's ear. She giggled softly. As Elya passed, the man looked up and winked.

He didn't acknowledge the gesture, just kept walking, noting all the while that Park and Yorra were so good together they didn't even have to act to play the part.

He reached the front of the church. A kind-faced priest, an elderly man with a wispy white comb-over, smiled at the laughing couple.

"Hello, Father," Elya said. "May Animus be with you."

"And you, my son," the man said, giving Elya a genuine smile. "How can I be of service?"

"I'm doing research for my graduate thesis in Old Earth technology, and my professor said you kept the Archives open to the public until eight o'clock."

"I love that young people like you still care about our history. Come, I'll show you the way."

The old man turned and led him past the altar, to a set of stone stairs that curled down to a lower level below the sanctuary. Elya paid careful attention to where he was being led, and noticed that there was a mirror image stairway on the other side of the chancel.

"I'll walk you down. We're old fashioned, and it can be dark downstairs at this time of night, so I'd recommend borrowing a lantern from the front desk. Did you know that some of the tomes we keep watch over were printed nearly two thousand years ago?"

"I didn't," Elya admitted, genuinely interested. Backspace hadn't told him that. How much knowledge were they safe-guarding here?

The priest had just begun to descend the stairs when a resounding slap, the unmistakable contact of open palm on cheek, cut through the peaceful silence.

"What was that?" The priest halted suddenly, turning back to look over his shoulder.

"You son of a bitch!" Yorra shouted. "How could you?"

"It didn't mean anything!" Park screamed back. "I swear! It was just the one time."

"I can't believe I trusted you. You're such a pig, Tommy!"

"But I love *you*, Bella. I've always loved you. You've got to believe me!"

Interesting choice of stage names. Elya fought down a smile.

"Uh, excuse me, son," the old priest said, hurrying back the way he'd come. "The Archive desk is down the stairs to your left. You'll find signs pointing the way."

"I understand," Elya said as the priest hurried away. "Thank you, Father."

It would only be another minute or two, now. Elya hurried down the stairs.

As the priest had said, he found signs pointing down a long hall that led back under the sanctuary to a large gate where a clerk sat at a plain metal desk. Two security guards were there as well, wearing the brown and green uniforms of the church. One stood on this side of the desk, watching Elya approach, boredom etched all over his face. Another was inside, behind the metal gate, eyeing a single customer peruse back and forth through the stacks. It was a lean blonde woman, about Elya's height and wearing short sleeves that exposed the raptor tattoos climbing up her forearms.

Osprey met Elya's eyes through the gate without any sign of acknowledgement, then turned and walked toward the back of a big room lit softly by filtered, incandescent lights set into the ceiling. The security guard followed, keeping a discreet distance.

"Hello, sir, can I help you?"

Elya gave the clerk the same story he'd given the priest, and then signed a fake name into a digital logging system. The clerk then took out a scanner, and scanned the chip in the ID that he provided on his own tab while Elya held his breath and tried to look disinterested.

The fake ID cleared the scan, just like Backspace had promised.

*I'm going to have to send him—or her—a thank you gift when this is all over*, Elya thought.

Whoever the hacker was, they'd provided fake IDs for both him and Osprey to check into the archives without giving away their real identities. It wasn't that fake IDs were uncommon, but it took a certain amount of skill to manufacture a believable digital footprint capable of fooling Imperial algorithms. All Elya had to do in exchange was share whatever information he found on the relics.

And he had no problem with that. People deserved to know the truth.

It had occurred to him, however, that if Backspace could so readily locate the information and deliver the fake IDs... why hadn't they come to get the information themselves?

He didn't have a good answer. The question sat uneasily in the back of his mind.

"All right, you're welcome to explore."

"Can I check out a light?"

"Sure. Sign here."

Elya signed the fake name into the tablet in another log. This one didn't seem to go through the same kind of digital check on the network, it was just a way to keep track of a finite number of lamps.

As the clerk handed over the electric lantern, a radio on the security guard's hip crackled and a panicked voice said, "Sir! Sir! Please keep your clothes on, this is a place of *worship*." *Oh, Park*. Eya recognized the voice of the kindly older priest who he'd initially spoken to. "Hey, Sullivan, I'm gonna need a hand up here. Ma'am, put that down. Ma'am!"

The guard glanced at the clerk, who nodded. "On my way," the guard said, and hurried down the stone hall.

One down, two to go.

"Wear these gloves at all times, sir, to protect the books in the Archive." He handed over a pair of white rubber gloves. Elya stretched his fingers into them. "Please only take out one book at a time. Put it back where you found it after reading. Although we do not discourage photographing the pages, please use the lantern and not the flash on your tab. Bright light can damage the pages, and the light from the lamps is filtered to cause a minimal amount of damage. Do you understand?"

"I do."

The clerk then waved him through the gate.

A sense of awed reverence fell over him as he stepped inside. Towering shelves lined the room, which must have been two thousand meters square, and each shelf was filled to the brim with bound books—the kind he'd only ever seen in historical holovids—made of actual paper and leather. Some were thin, others as thick as his hand, with cracked spines and frayed edges. Rectangular windows were set into the top of the walls, at ground level, but the glass in them had a yellow sheen, so they must filter UV light as well. In the center of the room, a straight, elegant metal staircase led the way down to a deeper level.

An explosion shook the stone walls of the Great Temple, vibrating the panes of those thin windows and shattering his reverent peace.

The clerk banged his knees on the desk as he jumped out of his chair. The security guard who'd been shadowing Osprey ran past Elya, through the gate, then hit the ground belly first as a staccato series of pops and bangs followed the first explosion. The sounds were coming from the courtyard.

Elya took advantage of the distraction to turn and drop a small ball just on the other side of the gate. Neither the clerk nor the guard noticed.

"We're under attack!" came a panicked voice through the remaining guard's radio. Elya felt bad for the old priest, but there was nothing to be done for it now.

The guard regained his feet with a look of shame on his face, then glanced uneasily between the guests in the Archive and the clerk.

"Go!" the clerk said, fright pitching his voice an octave too high. "What are you waiting for?"

The guard took off at an ungainly run in the direction the first had gone.

Elya could see Osprey shaking her head out of the corner of his eye. The gap between church guards and Fleet security was light-years wide. You didn't need military training to protect a bunch of old books, right?

Apparently not.

Elya edged back toward Osprey, hurrying to the back of the room to get as much distance between him and the clerk as possible.

Though he couldn't see it, a ten-second timer went off, and a colorless, odorless gas had begun to seep out of the innocuous little ball he'd placed at the gate. The clerk, who was still looking up and down the hallway fearfully, braced one hand against the wall as he wobbled. He blinked wearily, and then he dropped, unconscious, to the floor.

"Well done," Osprey said.

"We've got to hurry." Elya waited a few seconds, then took a deep breath and held it while he moved back to the clerk's side and borrowed the man's security access card. "Did you find it?"

"Third level down, all the way in the back."

They ran down the stairs and moved quickly to the back of the room—which was actually the front of the Temple if his sense of direction was accurate. They seemed to be about thirty feet beneath the stone courtyard itself.

"To think we were standing over top of it at Walcott's memorial service," Elya mused aloud.

Osprey grimaced and then clenched her jaw at the mention of their former commander's name. "Let's just get this over with."

He nodded. They had reached a blacked-out aluminite door at the back of the room. SPECIAL ARCHIVES was printed on a plaque to the right of the door, just like Backspace had told him.

Elya waved the keycard against the security panel to the right of the door. It flashed green and let them in.

As soon as they walked inside, an air filter kicked on and began humming loudly. They stepped into a small room lit by hidden ambient lights. Two parallel shelves ran the length of the room on the right-hand side, enclosed by glass doors. On the left, set against the wall, were three reading desks and controls to adjust the angle of their surfaces.

"Which one is it?"

Elya walked down the length of the first shelf. The books here were arranged face out, rather than spine out, and each of the covers was gorgeously decorated with fading gold or silver leaf, etched with swirling designs, and was aged beyond belief. A cursory glance over a dozen different books revealed that none of them actually printed their titles on the front.

"Uh… I have no idea."

"What?" She looked at the books and came to the same conclusion. "Crap."

"Okay, start opening doors and looking for titles."

"What did he say it was called, again?"

"*A treatise on ancient alien technology and its primary applications.*"

"Whoever came up with that one must have been a real party animal."

Elya snorted. "Boring it may be, but if the information in this book is important enough to erase from the public records, I for one want to know what it's about."

Osprey looked troubled, but she nonetheless began opening doors.

They couldn't hear the explosions from down here, but based on the amount of time they had estimated needing to locate the book, Elya judged that Hedgebot would be nearly out of fireworks by now. Soon the guards would realize that the Great Temple was not, in fact, under attack, and that Park and Yorra's public outburst was a distraction, and come check on the Archives.

Elya started on the other bookshelf and began opening doors, flipping the cover of the leather-bound books aside, and reading titles on the first page.

Some of the books were in languages he'd never seen, and that worried him. Backspace didn't say the book would be in Imperial standard. What if it wasn't? He wouldn't even know what to look for.

"Any luck?" Osprey asked as she shut one aluminite door and opened another.

"Not yet…"

Another stressful minute passed. Elya had reached the end of the row when he found a plain, unmarked book, nothing like the gold leaf-decorated tomes he'd first looked at. This book was the oldest and most delicate of the volumes he'd found so far. The stitching in the spine was coming loose, and the green leather of the cover had air bubbles beneath it. It wasn't a big book, maybe an inch or two thick, but the pages were made of dense paper with specks of color scattered throughout. He gently flipped open the cover with both hands. The second page inside read:

*A Treatise On*
*Ancient Alien Technology*
*&*

*Its Primary Applications*

He blew out the breath he'd been holding. "I think I found it."

He gently lifted the book over to the middle table, and pushed a button to raise the desktop and angle its surface at reading height for the two of them.

Casey came to join him as he began to gently turn the pages. They were so old and delicate he thought he might crack them if he turned too fast. He used fingers of both gloved hands at the top and bottom corners to turn them. The first chapter began in the familiar tone of a travelogue:

> *Each light-year we travel is a light-year farther from the*
> *cradle of civilization than humanity has ever gone before. I*
> *wish my father were alive to see the pro…*

If the condition of the pages was rough, the ink on them was even worse. Cracked and faded, whole swaths of the text were missing.

*...eed drive was a gift. Otherwise we would have d...*

*...ut that's not all there was. The last Engineer guided us out of the attack in Nebula 754 using thei...*

Casey blew out a noisy, frustrated breath. "We go through all this trouble and it's barely even readable."

"Don't give up yet, Rap. We've come this far."

She nodded and clapped him on the shoulder, squeezing slightly as he turned another page.

From what Elya could tell, the author of the text was a scientist who was traveling in an ancient version of a voyager starship during the Great Migration. Their systems were failing and they nearly died when they received aid from someone he referred to only as the "last Engineer" or just the "Engineer." Whether these were the ancient aliens promised by the title, or some elders of their own group, Elya couldn't tell. Were they humans, or xenos? And if they were xenos, were they Telos? The text didn't specify.

When they got to the middle, Elya realized why the book appeared so thin, and what had caused the stitching to come loose. Pages 102 to 157 were missing entirely, having been cut out by what appeared to be a sharp knife.

"Clearly we weren't the first ones to come looking for this book."

Elya studied the incisions in the paper, near the spine. "The cuts don't seem recent."

"How can you tell?"

"Look how soft and frayed the edges are. This happened a long time ago."

"Nevers, if this is a bust, let's get out of here while we still have the opportunity."

"Hang on, there are still a few more chapters."

He turned the page and found a large chunk of text intact.

*...fter we lost a ship in a jump, acting President Oberon Fisher made a deal with the Engineer. I was not privy to the details of the arrangement, but he managed to obtain another alien device as part of the bargain. Unlike the light-speed drive, this one was for communications only. It used some kind of quantum entanglement technology and not only did it allow us to keep better track of the starships in hyperspace, but the Engineer even claimed that it could be used over galactic-scale distances, free from the burdens of time dilation—which, during our recon missions, was a huge problem. Oberon began to call it the Ansible, after an ancient text positing the possibility of such a device.*

*Looking back, that was the turning point when things began to change. Oberon guarded control of the Ansible jealously. By the time we chose the planet that became our home, the power dynamic was entrenched. It was only natural that when people lost trust in the democratic process, Oberon was the first and most obvious choice to assume the throne and become Ariadne's first Emperor. With our shores belea- guered, and rumors of hostile xenos coming from every corner of the galaxy, whoever controlled the Ansible controlled the worlds.*

Elya blinked down at the page. "Whoa."

Osprey read the two paragraphs in question over his shoulder.

"The Ansible is an ancient alien technology? But... I thought..."

"That the ansible was created by humanity."

"That's what we were taught in school."

"Same here. I guess that's what they want us to believe."

"That'd be one hell of a propaganda campaign."

"That's the thing about propaganda. When it works well, we just call it 'history'."

Elya began snapping photos of the legible sections of text with his tablet, using the filtered lantern as a light source like the clerk had recommended. Even though it had been his idea to break in here and steal information, it felt like information everyone should be allowed to access, so he didn't feel guilty about it. He *would* feel guilty, however, if one of the old texts was damaged, so he was as careful as he knew how.

He took photos of several more sections he didn't have a chance to do more than skim near the end of the book, when voices echoed from the stacks on the other side of the door.

"Time to go," Osprey said. She shut the book and nearly tossed it back into the case, making Elya wince. He went to adjust it so it was sitting straight, not putting stress on the spine, when she grabbed his arm and hauled him out the door.

With a grip on his wrist like a metal vice, she pulled him along the wall. Footsteps echoed down the metal stairs, and through the gaps between them, Elya could make out three people coming down the stairs. They all wore the navy blue with crimson trim of Imperial uniforms.

Osprey led them around the side of a bookshelf before finally releasing her hold on him. He rubbed at his wrist and squatted on his haunches beside her, so they were both hidden from view between the outermost bookcase and the far wall.

His breath caught in his throat as the door to the secure-access room latched with an audible *click* that resounded throughout the bottom level of the silent library.

"They're still here," a familiar voice said, sending chills down Elya's spine. He pictured the secret policeman's face—gray bangs, broken nose, a smile that sharpened when he dealt pain. "Spread out."

If they were this close on their trail, that meant that they suspected Elya might come to the Archives. Which meant they *knew* what they stood to find here, at least in theory. They must have rushed inside once they realized the distraction was no more than that. His clever plan had worked well on the priests who worked at the church, but backfired when it came to MOXA's secret police. To them, those fireworks must have been like sending up a flare announcing, "Trouble-makers over here!"

Staying low, they duck-walked their way down the outer-most shelf as the MOXA guys paced slowly toward them. The room was long, but it was carpeted and difficult to tell where they were walking.

Fortunately, the one that came toward them breathed loudly, with a slight whistle in his nose each time he exhaled. Osprey signaled to pause, and pointed out the man's approximate location. He nodded his agreement, and when the whistling came close, they slipped inside to the next aisle at the same moment as he passed to the outside.

Only, when they turned around, the leader of their little troop was right behind them.

"Gotcha," he said, smiling, and kicked Elya in the ribcage.

As he gasped for breath, Osprey launched herself up and slammed her head into his chin, snapping the man's head back. His skull struck the hard metal edge of a bookshelf, sending him reeling, right as the second guy who they'd briefly managed to evade came back around.

"Run!" Osprey said, pulling Elya to his feet.

She sprinted for the stairs and he staggered after her.

They pounded up one flight, then another, before coming back to ground level. Elya risked a brief look over his shoulder and saw two of the secret policemen pacing hard on his heels. Their gray-eyed leader dripped blood from a split lip down his chin. The man drew his blaster.

"Put your weapon away!" the clerk shouted. He'd woken up but was obviously still groggy. Unsteady on his feet, he leaned against a wall to keep himself upright. "No violence in the Archives, these works are too valuable to put at risk."

Elya and Casey sprinted past him.

"Split up!" said Elya.

"Roger."

"Sir, please!" the clerk shouted again. "This is a place of *worship!*"

Apparently the clerk's first plea had gone unheard.

A blaster bolt ripped into the stone of the wall as Elya and Osprey split and went in opposite directions down the stone hall.

They had already picked out their rendezvous point, so he didn't need to ask where to meet them. He just had to get out of here in one piece.

Their gambit worked. One of the lower-level MOXA secret policemen chased Osprey. Their leader and the other guy followed him.

He banged up the stairs and out the side door. Osprey came up at the same time and sprinted hard for the front. He'd never been so thankful for hard physical training. His legs were still sore from all the running Spector made them do—but they had a lot of practice at staying moving.

He tore out the door and bounded into the brush at the edge of the courtyard, whistling for Hedgebot as he ran.

The little bot scurried out of cover and emerged in front

of him twenty paces ahead, at the same time as they crossed the thin ring of green space and hit a metal fence.

Without pausing, Elya launched himself at the fence, gripping the metal bars with both hands and scaling up with the rubber soles of his boots. At the top, the railings turned into metal spikes, but fortunately, they were designed to prevent unsavory types from getting in, not out, and they curved away from him. Careful not to catch his pants or skin on the sharp edges, he slid forward and landed on the opposite side of the fence on his feet, bending his knees and rolling to spread out the impact.

Hedgebot squeezed between the bars and *meep meeped* at him.

"Show off," Elya muttered.

Then Hedgebot flared red and darted away, consistent with his new programming.

Elya's stomach dropped into his boots. As he stood, three more policemen stepped out from behind the hedges hiding the fence from the street, surrounding him before he had a chance to take a step. Elya turned back and met the gray eyes of their leader through the bars of the fence as he jogged up. His bangs stuck to his sweaty forehead, but he was smiling serenely, baring bloody teeth. "I warned you, Captain Nevers."

"You can't hurt me. I'm Fleet."

The man's smile broadened, and then tumbled sideways as pain blossomed in the back of Elya's head. It was a distant hurt that arrived on a slight delay. When the tumbling stopped, soft grass pressed against his cheek and more men towered over him.

Shadows began to close around his vision. Before he could form another coherent thought, darkness poured in.

# SEVENTEEN

Casey danced around a cluster of priests crowding the aisle. They were trying to keep the larger crowd of forty panicked parishioners calm. About half of the people were taking cover behind the pews, while the other half were peering out the front door. Casey shouldered aside the two men holding the door closed before throwing herself through—only to come stumbling to a halt on the stone steps outside.

"Hello, little bird," Spector said, stepping out of a knot of crimson-armored Imperial guards who had the entrance surrounded.

She had a second to wonder how Spector got permission to use the official Fleet security personnel to harass her, but then she saw Colonel Volk standing off to one side. The *Paladin*'s first officer was pasty with sunken cheeks. Dark circles had formed under his eyes. Even his ever-present paunch had receded somewhat, making him look almost sickly thin. His normally steady hands trembled at his sides, and then clenched into fists as he coughed.

184

"Osprey," the colonel said when the coughing fit had subsided. "Explain yourself."

She glanced behind her as the door cracked open, revealing the crowd of frightened priests and parishioners once more. Behind them, the MOXA secret policeman who'd chased her out of the Archives came skidding to a halt. He took stock of the situation. Then as he slowly began to back away, he put one finger to his ear and spoke softly into his collar.

Apparently not even MOXA secret police were willing to take on armed and armored Fleet security. That was some kind of silver lining. She just hoped Nevers had made it clear.

The door closed again, cutting off her view. Casey turned back to her present problem.

Park and Yorra were being held off to the side by two guards apiece. Park had no shirt on and his pants were buttoned, but with the fly open. Yorra's hair was disheveled and messy, speckled with candle wax, and despite the terror this situation inspired in her, Casey was momentarily amused by the thought of what must have been one hell of a distraction.

"What in Earth's name are you smiling about, Captain?" Spector demanded. "Do you even realize the pile of shit you just stepped in?"

Casey clenched her jaw and met her commander's eyes. "It can't be any deeper than the shitstorm you've been wading through, Renata."

Spector froze and glared hard at her. Casey could see the question in her eyes—*how much do you know?* Instead, what she said was, "You mean *Commander* or *Colonel* Spector. I'm sick of your constant insubordination. Answer Volk's question."

"I don't believe the first officer asked one."

185

Volk coughed again—a wet, phlegmy hack—and spat to the side. The wad of saliva landed on the stone steps. It was flecked with blood. "What are you doing here?"

"Visiting the Archives, sir."

"That right? Didn't take you for much of a bookworm."

"There are no standing orders against studying up on history, are there, sir?"

This was a thin line she was walking. Before she'd fully signed off on the plan, Casey had been sure to check the penal code. Misrepresenting herself using a false identity was punishable by a fine and a suspension, but that alone wouldn't get her thrown into the Molten Cage. Forcing unauthorized access of classified information, though? That would. It was a serious enough offense to get her dishonorably discharged from the Fleet—*if* the information was on a Fleet system.

This wasn't Fleet property. This building belonged to the Church of Animus.

And since the Church had jurisdiction, a military tribunal couldn't touch her. It was a technicality, but legally her superior officers couldn't charge her for a crime. They didn't have the authority.

And by the looks on Volk and Spector's faces, they both knew it.

Volk bent down and picked up the spent cardboard shell of a firecracker. "And I'm sure you had nothing to do with these."

"What are those? Fireworks?" She shrugged. "We definitely heard explosions of some kind down there. The guards thought they were under attack, but now I can see that it was just a misunderstanding."

"Where's Captain Nevers?" Spector demanded. "We saw his bot scurrying across the courtyard. If that bot tests positive for propellant, I'm taking Nevers into custody."

"Throw him in the brig for fireworks? They aren't illegal."

"Disturbing the peace is."

"Well, I don't know where he is."

"He must have gone out the side door." Spector turned to one of the security guards. "Find him and bring him back here."

The guard glanced at Volk, who nodded his approval. It was nice to know the guards were still deferring to the colonel. Spector obviously dragged them all out here to pin Flight 18 down like insects in a collectible case, but she didn't have full authority to boss around Fleet security personnel.

The guard picked a buddy and the two of them jogged around the side of the building.

"I was right to ground you," Spector said after they were gone. "You can't be trusted." She jerked her chin at another guard and said, "Find whoever's in charge and bring them here. We'll find out quickly whether or not she's telling the truth."

Volk's attention wandered as what was either fatigue or nausea or both warred for his mind and body. The expression on his face looked ill, and she wondered how he was even standing.

The guard returned with the clerk of the Archives a few tense minutes later. He looked almost as sick as Volk did, but in a different way. Unlike the Colonel, she knew exactly what was wrong with this poor bastard. The knockout gas they'd borrowed from her father's armory was an Osprey family recipe. It worked fast, wore off relatively quickly, and left the victim with a vicious headache that thundered through their skull for a solid hour afterward. Casey and her cousins used to prank each other with it when her aunt and uncle came to visit. Her memory of the experience made her intestines twist up.

The man blanched as he took in the coterie of armored guards and the two Fleet officers. "Can I help you?"

"Yes, do you recognize this woman?"

"Y-yes."

"Hang on," Volk interrupted. "If this is an interrogation we need a witness."

Casey was both thankful and frightened. Even ill, Volk still followed Fleet protocol. Any adversarial situation—especially questioning witnesses—was supposed to be observed and recorded by a neutral third party. It helped cut down on hearsay, he-said-she-said types of accusations during conflict between Fleet personnel.

"Sir, is that really—"

"It's the rules," growled Volk as he pulled a tab from his back pocket and unfolded it. He made one of the security guards hold it while he activated it and put in his ID code and password. A pattern of colored lights appeared in the shape of an androgynous face.

"Harmony, please activate incident recording."

The lights danced and the face subtly shifted, taking in Spector, Casey, the guards, identifying all of them by facial scans.

"Affirmative, sir. Please state your name and summarize the situation."

"Colonel Volk, First officer of the *Paladin of Abniss*, ID number AB4-56113. Flight 18 of the Furies was caught disturbing the peace at 2100 hours. Lt. Colonel Renata Spector questioning witness."

The lights flashed while his explanation was validated in some way by the AI, and an active link with the secure Fleet network was established. It finalized in the blink of an eye, so fast that someone not familiar with the Fleet's systems might not even notice it. "Thank you, sir, you may proceed."

The dazed clerk of the Archives, so accustomed to the

byzantine ways of the Church, stared slackjawed at the Fleet AI. Spector snapped her fingers impatiently in order to regain his attention.

"Do you recognize this woman?"

"Yes."

"What's her name?"

"I don't, uh, recall, ma'am," he said.

"Sir," she snapped. "Fleet officers are always referred to as 'sir'."

"Uh, sorry, sir. My head is killing me."

"When did she arrive?"

"Um… about thirty minutes before the explosions?" He glanced sheepishly at the fireworks.

"And what did she do when she arrived?"

"I don't know. I only met her when she came downstairs and asked to see the Archives."

"So you just let her in?"

"No, sir, everyone who enters the Archives is required to provide identification." He frowned, pulling out his own tablet and tapping on the crystal surface a few times. "Here, her name is." He frowned. "Casey Osprey."

A shiver coursed down her spine. How in the *worlds* did he get her real name? She hadn't used her real name because they hadn't planned on getting caught. If they'd gotten clear without incident, it would have been a flawless plan. Using a false identity would have gotten her in a ton of trouble.

So how the hell did the system have her real name?

She glanced at the glowing lights of the AI, clustered tightly to resemble a human face. The figure briefly shifted until it took on more of the fine features of the female form. The chin shrank and narrowed, the cheekbones hiked up, the motes of light lengthened on top until they resembled straight, shoulder-length hair.

The chill in her body turned to hot liquid shock when she realized Harmony was showing *her own face* back to her.

Casey blinked and looked around until she found the eyes of Park and Yorra. Park's eyebrows were knit and he was staring at Spector. Yorra, however—her ever-perceptive friend and confidante—had seen Harmony show Casey's face, too. Her eyes bulged.

*No way.*

It was gone in an instant, back to the androgynous features the AI normally wore.

"What's the matter?" Spector demanded of the clerk.

"Nothing, nothing, it says it right here. My memory must still be fuzzy from fainting."

"And then what happened?"

"Another visitor showed up. I checked him in. And then we heard the explosions. The guards were called away, and then I passed out. And when I woke up..." he swallowed. "Imperial secret police were in the building. From one of the ministries, I'm not sure which. And one of the men drew his blaster and took a chunk out of the damn stone." His voice got firmer the more he spoke, and the next sentence was spoken with a thick passion. "That stone foundation has stood for a thousand years. Who does he think he is? He doesn't have the *right—*"

Spector's face had gone cold, her eyes flat. She didn't give a rip about some old stone foundation or even the men who'd been chasing them. All she cared about was punishing Casey. "And the other visitor?" she said.

"He left with her," the clerk said, pointing at Casey.

"The other man's name in your records?"

"Captain Elya Nevers"

Harmony's facsimile of a face briefly stretched into a barely perceptible smile.

*She's protecting us...*

The clerk frowned down at his tablet again, then shrugged. "Is that all?"

Spector clenched her jaw and spun to face Casey, closing the distance until she was a foot from her, staring down at her. "Either you're very stupid to use your real names, or very clever."

The two guards who had gone looking for Elya appeared on the opposite side of the church they'd gone looking on. They'd done a full circuit.

"Anything?" Colonel Volk asked.

"No sign of him, sir. We even sent a pocket drone up. If he was here, he's vacated the area now."

Volk grunted and then braced himself on his knees, swallowing with a visible effort.

"Where is Captain Nevers?" Spector demanded.

"Couldn't tell you," Casey said.

"If I can't arrest you, I can at least make damn sure you never fly in my squadron again. Your grounding is permanent. And you're being demoted. Congratulations, *Lieutenant* Osprey."

"You can't *do* that." Casey paced away in a tight circle and stopped facing Volk. "She can't *do* that, Colonel. She doesn't have the authority."

With his lips pressed into a pale, thin line, Colonel Volk straightened and reached into his jacket. "Admiral Miyaru will need to sign it off, but she's your commander."

"You can authorize it, can't you, sir?" Spector said, her voice suddenly dripping with honey.

Volk looked less certain. He withdrew a flask from his jacket. "I can't."

"Then I'll talk to the admiral myself."

Volk nodded, uncapped the flask with shaking fingers and took a small swig, swallowing the liquor with a grimace.

Spector turned back to the hologram projected from Volk's tablet. "Harmony, I need to speak to Admiral Miyaru."

This was it for Casey—the defining moment of her career. If the Admiral signed off on Spector's demotion, her career as a starfighter pilot was finished. No one would want to work with a flight lead who got busted back to lieutenant and removed from her post, no matter whether she was guilty or not. Her father would be ashamed of her. She wouldn't even be able to face up to the memory of Colonel Walcott. For the first time, she actually thought maybe it was better he was dead. She couldn't stomach the look in his eye after this shameful incident.

Harmony's image faded and was replaced with a live feed of Admiral Miyaru. Was she... was she in the armory at her father's house?

What on Earth? Tonight's events were turning out stranger than she'd ever imagined.

"This is not a good time, Spector. I told you, I've received your application and I'm still considering it."

"It's not about that, sir. I—"

"Colonel Volk!" Before the words were out of Admiral Miyaru's mouth, Volk collapsed into a wheezing heap on the ground. "Medic! Harmony, dispatch a medic to their location, stat."

"Yes, Admiral. An emergency response team has been alerted."

The nostrils of Admiral Miyaru's broad nose flared as she took in the faces of those gathered around Colonel Volk's prone form.

If looks could kill, Casey would be dead.

And Colonel Volk might actually be.

# EIGHTEEN

"Harmony, call the sick bay on the *Paladin* and let them know Volk is being medevacked in." A narrow chasm of worry for her first officer's life yawned open in the floor of Kira's gut. She actively fought to smother the emotion so it wouldn't distract her. "The destroyer is closer than any hospital, less crowded, and our medical officers there know him better than some random ER doctor."

"Very wise, Admiral," Harmony said. "Right away."

Kira had responded the way she always did under stress—with a bias to action. She wished there was more she could do for Volk. He must be very ill, and she had just been too distracted by everything else going on to make sure he got the medical attention he needed.

Eben had been watching her face intently. He hadn't been able to see what Harmony had shown her of the situation through the neural link, just her expression and her subsequent order. "What just happened?"

The two of them had remained in the armory in his house to make plans after Volk had left to take care of what he'd described as "a minor personnel problem." And although she pointed the way to the rest.

"Volk's been sick for the past few days. I thought it was
the flu or a stomach bug, but after the last time one of my
crew got sick, my brain immediately goes to the parasite. His
symptoms are different, so I'm fairly sure it's not that, but it
still seems serious." She paused, considering how much she
could safely share with this man. "Your daughter was there."

Eben's eyebrows—the only smudge of darkness left in his
silver mane—shot up toward his hairline. "What for?"

"The personnel problem," she said. "Captain Osprey's
been butting heads with her new squadron commander since
Walcott's funeral. I knew she and Spector had both gone to
the Capital Military Academy, but their records said they
were years apart. I thought the camaraderie would help, not
hurt." Kira sighed heavily and rested her head in one hand as
she massaged her temples. "On top of everything else. This is
my fault. I shouldn't have rushed to fill his post. The
squadron wasn't ready."

Eben just said, "Hmmm."

They'd spent so much time together this afternoon—
working through the logistics of recalling warships from
trade route patrols, writing official missives on behalf of the
Colonization Board to help them save face—that she knew
one of Eben's "Hmmms" from another. This one was filled
with a sense of unease.

"Well, don't hold out on me now," she said after a beat.

"If my daughter is stubborn, I suppose I'm the one to
blame. She inherited my moral righteousness, as well as my
pig-headedness."

"What are you saying?"

"Do you know what the nature of her disagreement with
her squadron commander is? I believe her name is Spector."

Kira blinked. He definitely knew more than he was letting

on. "Not exactly. Volk has been handling it. I know it's personal. She gave me a vetted list of possible commanders the day I introduced her to Spector. The introduction did not go smoothly."

Eben chuckled. "I can imagine."

"It was my job to make sure the transition to the new commander went well. I hadn't planned on sharing the news at Walcott's memorial service. I was just distracted with..." She waved vaguely. "Everything else going on. Maybe I didn't vet Spector as well as I should have. But Volk has been watching her and seems to think she's doing a bang-up job."

"Could be my daughter who's the problem."

Kira snorted. She looked up to see his eyes glittering. "Independent streak ten klicks wide runs in the family, doesn't it?"

He shrugged. "Guilty."

"I don't mind sharing that she acted courageously on the mission to Robichar. Caught that parasite. Rescued one of her pilots who had crash landed and was stuck planetside. I'm inclined to give her the benefit of the doubt provided she hasn't broken any regulations that force my hand. She just gets her teeth into something and doesn't let go."

"We've had our differences, my daughter and I." He sighed. "I was too hard on her when she was a kid. That's why I sent her to the military academy. She was out of control and my temper was too short. We're too much alike and without her mother around to balance the both of us out, it was blowup after blowup. Anyway, enough of a walk down memory lane. She and I have mostly made amends, I think." The glimmer of humor returned to his eye. "I'm just glad she's your responsibility now."

Kira grunted. "To a point."

"Unless the Inquisitors get involved."

"Care to lend a hand? I have some influence with Gitano.

I could get you a one-day retirement waiver."

"If you think that wouldn't backfire, you don't know my daughter."

Kira erupted in a sudden peal of laughter that broke up some of the tension in her body. She hadn't even realized she'd been carrying so much. She rolled a shoulder that twanged uncomfortably.

"Besides, I'm retired." Eben stifled a yawn by burying his face in his shoulder, then drew his arms overhead and arched back, stretching. Kira admired the hard lines of his strong arms and shoulders hungrily. Eben was handsome, and more relaxed alone with her than he had been when the others were around.

He caught her watching him and leaned back into the leather recliner. His mouth spread into an open smile that deepened the care lines around his eyes. She usually went for younger men, but the idea of a man with Eben's experience made her mouth suddenly go dry.

"Retirement's been good to you," she said.

"Yeah? Then why do I miss work so Earth-damned much?"

"You've obviously found other outlets." Her eyes traced down over his body.

"Because I'm *bored*. Maybe Gitano was right."

"Hmm?" Kira asked, trying to play it casual.

"Maybe I should have postponed retirement. I could have tried for Chief Inquisitor. Played politics. It looks good on you." He gestured at Kira.

"Oh, no," she said. "Bad idea. Politics is a nightmare. You made the right decision."

Eben chuckled.

Kira rose from her chair and, turning her back on him, stepped over to a display case full of antique rifles mounted between two of the floor-to-ceiling windows. The blinds were open, which meant those windows were fish bowls at this time of night, and she wanted to enjoy a little more privacy.

Eben stood and followed her.

"Which part do you miss the most?" she asked.

"Not the weight of it. Not holding people's careers in my hand. I was a Marine first, a soldier, and that kind of responsibility was never something I went searching for. But I miss the work so damned much. Solving people's problems. Making hard calls." He was silent for a moment before adding, "Being relied upon."

"I get it."

Eben stepped up behind her and braced his hands softly on her shoulders. He dug his thumbs into the muscles under her shoulder blades, causing her to groan with pleasure. "I know you do," he said. "That's why I told you. I feel comfortable around you in a way I haven't felt since…"

Eben continued the rolling motions of his thumbs. The chop of an aerial transport buzzed outside as the unmanned vehicle set itself down in the garden, on the other side of the wall. Kira closed her eyes and leaned back until Eben's chest pressed against her. He crossed his arms over her stomach, pulling her in closer.

"And here I was about to offer you a ride back to your ship."

"I have work to do."

"It'll take time for the rest of the armada to return to Ariadne."

"They're going to meet us en route. The Executive Council just doesn't know it yet."

He nodded, drawing his hands away until they rested lightly on her hips. "Then I should say good luck."

She turned around in the circle of his arms to face him. "You'll tell me what you find on Spector, won't you?"

He quirked his head to one side. "How do you know I'm looking for anything on her?"

She gave him a wry, lopsided smirk and stepped back out of his embrace.

"While your reach is extending," he said, "mine is more limited than it used to be. *If* I find something, I'll let you know. But no guarantees on what I can share."

"I'd expect nothing less." Harmony whispered a new piece of information in Kira's ear. "The Executive Council's gathering now. I have to go."

"Will I get to see you again?" he asked.

Her throat thickened. She didn't trust her voice, so she just nodded, smiling this time, and—really?—felt her face heat slightly.

Kira collected her things and hurried out to the transport, which whipped her into the sky without delay.

"Your heart rate remains elevated," Harmony said.

"Telling me," Kira said. "I haven't felt that way for..." Her thoughts went back to the weeks and months before the end of the Kryl War, to memories of a younger lover, to times before she knew the pain of loss. "Ages."

---

"What in the name of Animus is going on between you two?" Kira demanded from the private room just off the bridge of the *Paladin of Abniss*. "You've been at each other's throats since Walcott's memorial service."

Captain Casey Osprey and Lieutenant Colonel Renata Spector stood at attention before her, each pilot firmly avoiding the other's eyes. After a long night of meetings with the Executive Council and only a couple hours of rest, Kira had called the two of them here for the hearing that protocol demanded following the formal request Spector filed to demote the captain to lieutenant. She wished she had Volk here, but he was still in the sick bay—stable, but recovering. Harmony would have to suffice as a witness.

It was annoying that she had to deal with this at all. She would have much preferred to linger fondly on the memory of Eben's strong fingers pressing into her shoulders while she waited for her troops to mobilize.

"Osprey has been insubordinate since I assumed command of the Furies," Spector said stiffly. "She's challenged my authority at every opportunity, insulted me in front of the squadron, and after the incident at the church of Animus I am simply disciplining her as I would any other leader under my command who commits actions unbecoming of an officer."

"Bullshit," Osprey sneered. "You've been sandbagging Flight 18 since day one just because I'm on it. If I had a—"

"Osprey," Kira snapped. "Please shut up for one minute."

Osprey stared down at her boots and clenched her jaw.

Whatever her mistakes, it hadn't been worthy of a full court martial, so the responsibility fell to her. It was doubly annoying because Osprey was Eben's daughter. She couldn't risk showing even an ounce of favoritism.

"From what I've seen, Lt. Colonel Spector was right to ground you. A flight lead who constantly questions and insults her squadron commander isn't fit to follow her into battle, let alone lead one of *my* flights on a mission. And don't you dare forget that these are *my* flights. *My* starfighters. *My* pilots. It's your job as flight lead to take care of the pilots you work with. Nothing else." She turned to Spector next. Because if this was about treating people fairly, she expected more of a squadron commander than she did of any captain under her command. "As for you, I'm disappointed in your first showing as a squadron commander. Did I not say I expected you *not* to take things personally?"

199

"I didn't, sir."

"Then why in all the orbiting worlds did you commandeer a squad of Fleet security guards and make them follow Osprey to the Great Temple when she was *off duty?*"

"Sir, Colonel Volk was worried that—"

Kira slammed a hand down on the arm of her chair. "Don't you dare blame my first officer for the decisions *you made* about pilots under *your* command."

Now it was Spector's turn to study the floor between her boots. "No, sir. You're right, Admiral, it was my mistake."

"You're Earth-damned right it was your mistake. I don't appreciate you commandeering security personnel for your own personal vendetta."

Spector wisely held her silence.

"And apart from pulling a stupid prank with some fireworks and encouraging Lieutenant Park to streak on Church property, what did you actually expect to accomplish?"

Osprey licked her lips and glanced at Harmony, who hovered ominously to Kira's left, her lights drifting in the amorphous, abstract pattern she liked to use when Kira didn't want people to be able to read her thoughts. "We were visiting the Archives, Admiral."

"Sir, I still believe my suspicions were well-founded," Spector said. "Flight 18 had already been suspended. When I found out they weren't in the barracks, it seemed a worthwhile precaution to make sure they weren't trying to enact revenge for disciplinary action."

"Explain to me, Spector, how visiting the Archives below the church constitutes plotting for revenge."

Spector clenched her jaw.

"Well?"

"It was just a suspicion, Admiral."

"Just a suspicion. And you pulled Colonel Volk away from a vital matter of galactic security for *just a suspicion.*"

"Yes, sir."

A smile played across Osprey's face.

"Is something about this situation amusing to you, Captain?"

The smirk dropped immediately. "No, sir."

"I sure hope not, since you've wasted everyone's time here, especially mine. What were you looking for in the Archives?"

"Information, Admiral."

"What kind of information?"

Osprey glanced over at Spector, who glared fiercely back. "It's classified, sir. I think."

Ah. Damn it. That changed things.

Of course this had something to do with the relic they'd found on Robichar. Maybe Kira should have been more specific about what Osprey and Nevers could and couldn't say on the topic. She'd been operating on the assumption that no directive would be the best way to keep her options open and their mouths shut. If she kept the relic close to the vest, she had more time to deal with the fallout it would inevitably cause when it became public knowledge.

But of course they had been curious. She would have been, at Osprey's age. Had Flight 18 found something that might help arm Kira with information she could wield against the Minister of Xeno Affairs?

Kira paused to observe herself. She noted how incredibly fast politics seeped into a person's mode of thinking.

To buy herself a moment to think, and simultaneously shame both of the officers she was busy disciplining, Kira turned to the cloud of pink, purple, blue and green lights and said, "Harmony, how is Volk doing?"

The AI was connected to and helped operate medical systems and, at Kira's request, had been keeping a close watch over her first officer.

"His condition is stable, Admiral. His vital signs are up and he seems to be on the road to recovery. Scanners found traces of heavy metals in his blood. The doctors gave him medication that will help his system flush them out."

"Spector, go check on the colonel. Make sure he has everything he needs."

"But Admiral, I—"

She lifted a hand. "I don't want to hear it. When you're on my ship, you'll do as I say."

"What about disciplinary action for Osprey?"

"I'll let you know my decision."

Spector knew when she'd been beaten. She delivered a final glare at Osprey, one that promised pain in the near future, and then left the bridge without another word.

Osprey blew out her cheeks.

"Don't think you've gotten off so easily, Captain. You and your flight will be disciplined for your actions. But in the meantime, I want to know what you found in the Archives."

She glanced at Harmony. "Not much. A few half-readable passages in some old book."

The captain was hedging. "On the public network?"

"No sir, an actual paper book like something you'd see in those Old Earth historical holofilms."

"Interesting. What did it say?"

Osprey glanced at Harmony, and then around the empty room.

"We're alone, Captain"

"Admiral, can I just ask... who else knows about the relic?"

"You, me, Captain Nevers, those guards, the Executive Council... a few other highly placed people in the government." She didn't want to get specific with Osprey about the promise she'd made Minister Aganaki because she was still hoping she could get out of it.

"And the AI?"

"Harmony knows everything I know. But don't worry, she won't share anything without my permission."

Osprey chewed her cheek. "A weapon like that, with what it can do to the Kryl, seems like it would be in high demand."

"Why do you think I've been controlling the flow of information and protecting it as much as I can?"

Osprey nodded as a look of tired fear tightened the skin on her face and forehead. She shifted from foot to foot, suddenly restless.

"What is it?"

"Captain Nevers found something, sir. It was his idea to look in the Archives. Apparently information on these relics is being scrubbed from Ariadne's public network. He went poking around the darknet."

"And you didn't feel the need to bring this up to your squadron commander?"

"Respectfully, Admiral, no way in hell."

"You should have come to me."

"I tried, sir. You were busy."

Kira grunted. She supposed that was true.

It was rare that the Empire felt the need to censor information on the public network, but if anyone had the pull and the capability to do such a sweep, it would be one of the Imperial ministries. She had no question which one would benefit most from such a play.

Good thing she had been wise enough to hold onto the relic itself. Keeping it safe was the one move she hadn't had an opportunity to regret. She wondered if her admissions of the weapon's existence had made its way outside of the Fleet yet.

"And how does the book you found in the Archives tie in?"

"The book confirms what Nevers found. That these relics

are alien in origin. The author of the book called the alien the 'last Engineer'."

"What else?"

She sighed. "Well, sir, I wish I could remember, but we were being chased at the time."

"By Spector?"

"No, sir, by MOXA secret police."

"What?" Her blood ran cold. "Earth's last light." Kira added several more colorful curse words under her breath. "Do you still have the book?"

"No, sir, we left it where we found it," Osprey said. "But I'd be willing to bet MOXA took it."

"What did it say?"

"We got photos of a few passages, but I don't have them."

"Where are they?"

"On Captain Nevers' tab. Which brings me to the other thing. I haven't seen him since the incident at the Archives."

"I was informed that he didn't report for duty. Spector thinks he's avoiding her because he's afraid of disciplinary action. Tell him to come in, I won't punish him for accessing Archives that are open to the public."

"He's not avoiding her," Osprey said. "Okay, maybe he is, but he wouldn't go into hiding and not tell me. I know he can be obstinate—" She paused, her face reddening as she must have realized how much the description also applied to *her*. "—but he's one of us, sir. He would have sent a message if he could have. So if he would have, and he didn't, I can only conclude…"

"What is it?" Kira asked. Although she suspected she knew the answer, she wanted to hear Osprey to say it out loud.

"That Captain Nevers has been taken by the MOXA secret police."

# NINETEEN

**P**ain.

Powerful currents of pain rushed around him, over him, through him, thrashing his body like a helpless leaf against the unforgiving shoals and stones, drowning him repeatedly in the tumbling rapids of agony.

*Your future holds nothing but pain and sorrow.*

The Overmind had been right.

Pulsing red, angry, bright, the river battered him downstream before finally spitting him out on a shivering cold shore.

Somewhere above, as if echoing out of the cavern of spacetime itself, an inhuman voice cackled.

*Resistance is futile... Join us or die.*

Elya gasped as he sprang out of the nightmare, only to discover he was bound at the wrists and ankles by metal manacles which restricted his movements. The bands got colder the more he hauled on them, so cold he hissed against the icy shock of it, but he couldn't stop fighting their pull. He wanted out, he needed away, his mind was caught completely in fight or flight mode, and his thoughts were screaming, *RUN!*

The bands of metal got so cold they began to burn. They were dense, not aluminite at all but a weighty alloy that got heavier the more he struggled, as if his fight were water and the manacles a sponge that drank in the kinetic motion and converted it to force. His every motion added another multiplier against him.

The panic really set in when his muscles began to tire. A mechanical droning sound kicked on somewhere above and behind him and began to hum through the walls. At the same time, as if in concert with the sound, his wrists and ankles were hauled away from the ground. Although the manacles sprouted no ropes, no chains, they were being drawn up and backwards by powerful, invisible forces. Gulping air and gritting his teeth, he strained against the restraints until they snapped to the wall.

The scratched gray metal was a stark contrast to the rune-carved, octagonal manacles of stone that held him.

Wait. What?

He stared at his extended wrist. Now that he had accepted the state of his restraint, he could finally make out details his mind hadn't been ready to register before.

The manacles were made, unmistakably, of the same stone-like material as the Robichar relic. It looked to be marble, grayish-white and polished smooth with sharp edges. Apart from the material, the relic and these restraints had little in common. Inside the octagonal bands encircling his wrists was a gel-like substance. That was the source of the frozen pain that burned his skin, so cold the deepest subterranean rivers of Ariadne's poles must have been jealous. His wrists were numb to any sensation other than pain, and at the same time his skin felt like it was on fire.

He forced himself to relax his aching muscles. By this

point his arms were pointed straight out to either side while his ankles had snapped together. He was pinned to the cold, angled metal wall with his toes barely scraping the smooth cement floor.

The manacles continued to burn icy hot, but they had begun to warm the moment he stopped struggling.

With a conscious effort made possible by the Fleet's rigorous training programs and weeks of agonizing fitness routines, he forced himself to relax against the pain, to breathe into it more deeply. His limbs remained pinned to the wall in the shape of a cross, that symbol of suffering as ancient as Old Earth, and which you could still find decorating the walls and stained glass windows of the churches, but the icy hot pain began to subside.

As he breathed, his memories began to reorder themselves. The temple, the Archives, the "last Engineer"... it was all coming back.

And now there was this new mystery—the unmistakable handiwork of the Telos holding him prisoner in a windowless room.

He wasn't left to wonder how that came to be for very long.

A crack appeared in the blank wall opposite him, and a previously invisible door slid into a pocket in the wall.

In walked the man who had captured him—the MOXA agent with the gray eyes, lanky bangs, and broken nose.

Man, he really needed to figure out what this guy's name was. Didn't he deserve to know the name of the man who was making his life so miserable? He hadn't cared before— he'd only been trying to reach someone who could give him the answers he was seeking.

But now it was personal.

"Who are you?" he demanded.

The door closed, leaving them alone together. The man

didn't answer.

"I know you work for MOXA, you son of a bitch. Tell me your name and ID number so I can sue your ass for wrongful imprisonment. When my flight lead finds out about this, she's gonna grab you by the balls so hard you won't even kn—"

The invisible magnetic force that had resisted him when he struggled before was suddenly and violently reactivated, yanking his arms apart and scraping noisily as the manacles hauled him up the wall another meter. Elya screamed as his arms were stretched even further apart, so far that sharp stabbing cramps erupted in his shoulders and an unnatural crackling noise filled his ears.

If the sensation of burning cold from *before* was painful, this experience could only be described as a tidal wave of frozen agony.

The volume of pain ratcheted back down a second—a minute? Ten?—later.

Elya's breathing was ragged. His throat ached. Tears were coursing down his face, tears he hadn't even known he'd shed. His arms were still being held firm in the manacles of alien design, preventing him from even wiping his face on his sweat-soaked shirt.

"You want to know my name?" The man's gray eyes stared, unblinking, inches from his face. "I'm Agent Callus. And your flight lead has no power here. I have special authorization from the Emperor himself that puts men like me in rooms like this so far outside of the Fleet's jurisdiction it would make your head spin."

"You have no right to keep me here."

"Why not? Who the stars are you?"

The question was rhetorical. Agent Callus already knew who he was. But the powerless indignity of it singed his ego, and Elya felt the sudden need to reaffirm his existence.

"I'm Captain Elya Nevers, Imperial starfighter pilot in Flight 18 of the Fightin' Furies."

"Exactly. Xeno fodder. I looked you up since the last time we crossed paths, boy. Nobody will miss a nosy refugee from Yuzosix who lucked into the starfighter pilot program."

"Hey! I worked my ass off to earn that spot."

"You got in on an income-based refugee provision. Pure dumb luck."

Elya's ears burned. Callus was right about the program, but that didn't mean he hadn't earned it. He still had to work his ass off to get through basic, to qualify as a pilot, to fight and claw his way to the top of the rankings so he could merely be *considered* for the honor of joining the Furies. It was cruel to throw his refugee status back in his face. Elya may have been from a poor refugee family, but wasn't that the least they could do since his homeworld got invaded by the Kryl? His family lost everything. Their farm, their home, their livelihood. "Screw you, Bangs."

Agent Callus sniffed through his crooked nose. "I'm sure the Fleet is already drafting a statement. Some made-up story about how you died on a pointless mission at the edge of Kryl space. A fluke. Maybe a freak accident. Bodies are barely recognizable after you put them out an airlock, you know?"

"They wouldn't lie." Spector was a wild card, but this guy obviously didn't know Captain Osprey or Admiral Miyaru very well.

Agent Callus worked something in his hand and Elya was on the rack again, the manacles freezing and burning and trying to rip his shoulders out of his sockets all at once.

It relaxed again a terrible minute later with another motion of Callus's hand. He had some kind of remote control in his closed fist. "You don't think the Fleet has lied about worse? You're dumber than I thought."

The irony of him pointing the finger at the Fleet's lies when a MOXA agent was literally torturing him was too much to contain. Maybe he'd pulled back the veil on too much of what he presumed to be reality lately, and this little bit was the extra nudge that pushed him over the edge. A laugh bubbled up and frothed out of Elya's mouth. "If I'm so stupid then how'd I find out MOXA's been erasing Telos relics from the public record?" He looked pointedly at the manacles.

"If you were *smart*, you wouldn't have tipped me off that you were snooping around in the first place."

His laughter trailed off. Earth damn him, but Callus had a point.

"Are you some kind of information liberation radical?" Callus asked. "Tell me who you're working with."

"What? No one."

"Bullshit. You couldn't have found that book on your own. It has no digital trail—MOXA's information control department made sure of that."

Elya clenched his jaw. It was an instinctive reaction. He barely realized he was doing it until Agent Callus's eyes lit up like glittering gray opals.

"I knew it. Who was it?"

Would telling him about Backspace endanger his informant? And would that somehow tie him to the larger Veritas network? Backspace had never told him so much as his real name, let alone any other identifying information. He (or she) had been careful—incredibly careful—about how they communicated and what they shared with him.

And now he *really* knew why.

He still couldn't give them up. Not after they'd told him the truth and led him to the Archive.

"I don't know what you're talking about," Elya said.

Pain. Endless, tortuous rivers of pain coursing through him from the wrists and ankles.

He squeezed his eyes shut and tried to hold back his tears.

He lasted about thirty seconds before his voice couldn't be contained any longer. He screamed until his voice gave out.

"I could do this all day, boy. And we haven't even gotten started with the restraints."

His wrists began to vibrate slightly. The burning cold melted away and some kind of buzzing electricity tingled up his arms instead. It was ticklish at first—but not for long. The tingling turned to something akin to what he imagined touching a live wire might feel like, but continuous, constant.

Time lost all meaning as his muscles began to cramp and clench. His body became an instrument. Pain, the music.

An interminable time later, the music stopped—interlude.

"Backspace, huh?" Agent Callus said, lifting his ear away from Elya's mouth.

Elya's eyes widened in fear. "No," he croaked. "No no no. How did you—I didn't—"

"Enough pain is like dreaming, boy. Sometimes you don't even know what you're saying until the words are out of your mouth."

He'd been clinging so tightly to that name, trying so hard to hold it in, that he must have become fixated and without consciously meaning to, ended up whispering the name while he was lost in the fog of pain.

Callus had tortured him, but Elya was far more angry at being tricked than being hurt.

He'd dealt with pain. Life was pain. Being a refugee after your homeworld got invaded was pain. Leaving your family behind to become a starfighter pilot was pain. *Training* to be a starfighter pilot was pain.

But being made to look a fool was worse, somehow. It cut

211

deeper. It left him raw and bleeding, though the manacles causing the pain hadn't drawn a single drop of his blood.

He sagged forward, exhausted. The manacles cut into his wrists, which were raw and throbbing.

He just breathed. It was all he had energy left to do.

Callus opened the door and stepped out of the room. He caught a glimpse of the man speaking to one of the guards standing outside. No doubt they were taking that name and running it up the chain of command to whoever was in charge. They'd track down Backspace, if they could. They'd either kill Elya or charge him with espionage, and if he were given the choice he'd rather die on the rack than be publicly known as a traitor to the Empire.

All for some relics.

And what did he really learn? That the Empire was keeping secrets?

What else was new?

It was the Solaran freaking Empire. Of *course* they were keeping secrets.

If what he read in that old book was true, the secrets they kept had been hidden for thousands of years. The Ansible was originally an alien technology. Humanity had taken it and adopted it for their own purposes, and those in power had motivation to erase this inconvenient fact from the public record.

Knowledge is power.

These manacles were ancient relics, too. Relics must have been more plentiful than he originally thought. The Empire —and the Ministry of Xeno Affairs in particular—didn't want anyone else to know about them.

And especially not to possess them.

Why?

To hang onto their power.

If what he'd learned in the book—not to mention his own

experiences—were anything to judge by, it all came down to power. The Emperor controlled the Ansible network, and whoever controlled the flow of information had the power. MOXA had these Earth-damned manacles, and by using them they held power over him—or held him powerless, whichever way you wanted to look at it.

Whoever had the relics, had the power.

Whoever didn't have the relics... was at their mercy.

And this dynamic went back to the very founding of the Solaran Empire.

At no time had this ever been more apparent than in his current predicament.

These thoughts gave way to exhaustion. Agent Callus was still out of the room. Elya dozed for a while, drifting in and out of consciousness.

He came to when Agent Callus closed the door and leaned against the wall with his arms crossed, his gray eyes glittering with a new malice.

Another man was in the room with them now. He had a narrow face, dark eyes, dark hair. He was wearing business casual attire, expensive tailored synthweave trousers and shirt with a dizzy, swirling pattern. The attire almost fooled Elya. His exhausted brain eventually caught up with his eyes, however, and he realized that this was Aganaki, the Minister of Xeno Affairs he had been trying to talk to that day at Walcott's funeral.

It took him a minute to make his voice work in his aching throat, but eventually he did. "Did Agent Asshole there ever give you my message?"

The minister smiled politely, as if the two of them were sitting at a café together and sipping coffee. "Telos ruins on Robichar. Yes, he did."

"And a Telos relic."

Aganaki frowned. "So I've heard."

213

So, Admiral Miyaru hadn't handed the Robichar relic over to MOXA yet. That gave him some small measure of hope.

"And speaking of relics, you've been busy snooping around," Minister Aganaki said. "It has been quite the interesting experiment. A stress test of our information control systems."

"You can't keep the relics a secret forever. People are going to find out, and once the truth is out, you won't be able to bottle it up again."

The minister waved his hand in the air as if that was insubstantial. "You underestimate the power of propaganda, Captain Nevers. People will believe exactly what we tell them to believe. Besides, even if word does get out, the Ministry will soon be so far ahead in our understanding of the relics that no one else will be able to catch up. That is, after all, the primary reason MOXA exists."

"I thought you existed to help us defend the Empire against the Kryl."

"It is the Ministry of Xeno Affairs, not the Ministry of Kryl Affairs. You do have a point though. There is much we still don't know about the Telos and the technologies they left scattered across the worlds. But there is also much we still don't know about the Kryl. And that's where you come in."

A cold feeling slithered through Elya's already knotted and anxious stomach. The minister knocked on the door, which slid open to reveal a man in a full-body hazmat suit. The newcomer walked in bearing a transparent aluminite jar and the door closed behind him.

Agent Callus pushed himself off the wall and opened his mouth as if to object, but then thought better of it and took up a post beside the doorway.

When the man in the hazmat suit came close enough for

Elya to see what was inside, he began to squirm and kick against his restraints. "No, no, you don't understand what you're doing."

"Quite so," said the minister. "And above all else, MOXA has a directive to advance our understanding. In this case, of the Kryl and their new parasite."

Minister Aganaki backed up until he stood on the opposite side of the closed door from Agent Callus, each of them as far away as they could get from Elya and that aluminite jar.

"Don't! You haven't seen this thing in action! You don't understand what it'll do to me!"

"Yes, Captain Nevers," said Minister Aganaki calmly. "That is precisely the point." He nodded at the man in the hazmat suit. "Please proceed."

As the man unsealed the lid, it made a sucking sound. The creature sitting on the bottom began to pace around the edge of the jar in anticipation.

Elya thrashed against his restraints, but the manacles held firmly.

He turned his head away as the man lifted the jar up close to his face.

The lid parted from the container, and Elya's worst nightmare came to life. The parasite jumped out and landed on his cheek. It crawled over his nose, tickling his skin before burrowing painfully into the tear duct of his right eye.

The last thing Elya heard was the sound of his own hoarse scream.

And then his mind no longer belonged to him.

At least not to him alone. Something *else* could see into his thoughts. A vast being with a direct line of sight into his mind.

*Resistance is futile*, said Overmind X. *Welcome to the hive, Captain.*

# TWENTY

The delicious sounds of their screams echoed through the vaulted triangular corridors of the *Maiden of Kali*, and Omar's mandibles clicked together in excitement. He hooked the thumb of his left hand into his belt by his blaster, the other arm—heavy, distended, and bulky with Kryl muscle fibers and coated in a glossy carapace—swung at his side, keeping pace like a metronome with the footsteps of the snarling groundlings at his back.

The Solaran colony ship was vast—far bigger than even he'd expected. There were hundreds of nooks and crannies for the passengers to hide in, and those were just the ones She could see. Solaran shipbuilders had excelled in their craft in the decade he'd been away.

But clever engineering wouldn't save them.

Booted feet hammered against the metal floor as a contingent of crimson-armored security guards shoved a long barricade into the intersection ahead, blocking his way. Fifty men crouched behind it. They leveled their rifles in his direction.

*Destroy them*, Overmind X's voice hissed into their collective consciousness.

Groundlings and sentinels bristled and quivered in anticipation of the fight. The Kryl were a strong, competitive species. Each class had been purpose-bred, designed with deadly precision in mind. Groundlings roved ahead and killed with impunity. They were the ground forces, the scouts. Sentinels were broad, stalwart, implacable, and they could take a beating. They were his heavy hitters. And Omar himself? Captain Omar Ruidiaz was one of a kind.

Overmind X referred to him as Subject Zero. He still thought of himself as Captain Omar Ruidiaz, but his identity as her lieutenant had consumed his former life as a Solaran starfighter pilot. He was part of her hive now, and this was the purpose *he* was bred for. With a gesture of his mutant arm, Omar loosed the destruction of his escort upon the Solaran security guards.

Groundlings, hunchbacked quadrupeds with rangy legs and knife-sharp talons, sprinted down the hall, drawing blaster fire and bouncing off the walls as they vaulted the barricade. Bolts pulsed and ricocheted as smoke and screams erupted from the melee. Half a dozen Kryl disappeared from his awareness, signifying by their absence their deaths—but they died happily, willingly, in service of the hive.

Four sentinels lumbered forward in the next wave. These creatures were bipedal, with legs like tree trunks. The largest rose to three meters, and their bodies were covered in a carapace ten times thicker than the chitin that coated Omar's mutant arm and back. The floor shuddered as they lumbered forward. Bolts of plasma ricocheted off their chests and arms, providing cover for him to stroll languidly along in their wake.

The first sentinel to reach the barricade kicked it in, buckling the light metal. By the time he reached it, only

217

about a dozen guards remained standing and fighting. They held their ground, slicing with knives and even throwing fists when their blaster packs ran empty. A part of him thought it was admirable and brave, the way they were willing to die so nobly. Like the hive, he respected humanity and their willingness to resist—pointless though it may be.

He pulled his blaster and painted the walls with the blood of two security guards. When they dropped, he got a glimpse of what they were trying to protect. His mandibles clicked a rapid staccato and his mutant jaw trembled.

A hundred meters down an adjacent hall, a brown-robed priest and an older man with scars criss-crossing his arm were ushering a group of children into a small maintenance door.

*Don't let them get away*, Overmind X breathed into his mind.

She didn't need to tell him how useful the human children would be to their cause. But once she did, he couldn't possibly refuse.

Omar backhanded a security guard with his mutant arm, then trod on his chest to follow the priest.

The guards saw where he was going and rallied. Two managed to gain hold of their rifles. Blaster bolts bounced off the angled metal wall ahead of him and sent the priest diving for cover. The old man with the scars flinched when a bolt nicked the top of his ear. He scooped up a duffel bag and successfully used it as cover to get the last child through the door.

Omar grinned—an expression that used to win women and which now, fittingly, sent them fleeing in fear—and gave chase.

The lock on the maintenance door held surprisingly fast. The sentinels took turns denting the aluminite wall.

Her impatience built within him until he could stand it

no longer. "Forget it," he snarled. "Move." With a gesture of his arm, the xenos that were his to control swarmed down the hall in the direction the maintenance shaft led.

They encountered six more barricades, each manned by a greater force than the one before. The Solarans had been caught off guard by the surprise attack. Now that they knew what was happening, their resistance was more organized. A thousand Kryl in his command perished as they took the ship, corridor by corridor. For each one lost, Overmind X sent three more to take their place. Bodies, Solaran and Kryl alike, littered the halls in their wake. The walls were painted with crimson blood and yellowish ichor that dried as they fought.

Finally, one of the sentinels, missing an arm and *pissed off* about it, crushed in the skull of the last standing man, and slammed his body against the wall several times after he was dead.

The Solarans had retreated to the most secure part of the ship. Omar found himself facing the door of the bridge.

He reloaded his sidearm with a fresh charge pack, then reached down with his hand—the one that hadn't been replaced by a Kryl appendage—and flicked a switch on the relic mounted behind his handgun holster.

Then he stepped through the closed door.

His skin tingled as he passed through a meter of aluminite, plastic, and heavy-duty impact foam. It always unsettled him when he used the phase shifter, which is how he thought of the tool of the Ancient Ones. Overmind X didn't have a word for it, just a thought tinged with extreme possessiveness. Whatever it was called, the relic had helped him get in and out of several jams, and he'd learned how to use it to his advantage. Its major flaw was that its effects only lasted for a few seconds at a time. Each use was followed by a reboot period that couldn't be interrupted. He always saved it until he needed it.

Which is why he'd waited until now. He knew he had them cornered.

When he emerged on the other side, a hail of blaster bolts passed through him and began bouncing dangerously around the room. The feeling made him shudder and the legs folded at his back sprang out of their own accord. One bolt deflected into a control panel nearby, which hissed and spit smoke. Another struck one of the children, sending them screaming to the ground, before a Solaran—the captain, he thought—bellowed, "Cease fire!"

By the time the phase shifter's effects wore off, the blaster fire had stopped.

Ignoring the tremor in his hands that always followed the relic's use, he clacked his mandibles a few times, and then let his mouth fall open in a hungry smile.

The group of women and children, with only the bridge crew and a dozen weary, frightened, bruised security guards, edged back against the viewscreen on the far wall.

The sight in space outside of the mothership sent a thrill through his body.

*Victory at last. Well done, Subject Zero,* said Overmind X. *Take the children.*

Omar slapped the holoscreen on the wall to his right, cycling open the door he'd just passed through. The Kryl prowled inside and surrounded the Solarans. They methodically separated the children from the adults. Omar picked three of the most harmless-looking adults—two women and the older man, the one with the scars encircling his arm who had led the children into the maintenance shaft earlier.

"What's your name?"

"J-Jonah," the man said, flinching away from the touch of the Kryl legs that had unfolded from Omar's back. He shook his head and folded the extra limbs back in again. He barely noticed, sometimes, which extremity he was using. They had become such a natural part of him. His intention wasn't for the man to be discomfited by him, however. He knew it would be easier if the comforting presence of an adult stayed with the children. And it would be less work for Omar, who needed to care for them until they were finished being turned.

"What do you do, Jonah?"

The man blinked around at the Kryl. Omar made them all take a few steps back from the children. Even he had to admit, the way those groundlings salivated could be unsettling.

The man noticed what he'd done and refocused on him.

He asked his question again. "What job have they given you to do on the new colony?"

"I'm a robotics engineer."

"A useful skill. However, I'm changing your title."

The man swallowed and looked at the kids, then to one of the women—she must be his wife. She looked years younger than him. "To what?"

"Nanny."

"Uh...Okay." The man's eyes darted again to the woman, and then to a small, sandy-haired boy hiding behind her legs.

"That your son?"

He shook his head. "No."

"You're a terrible liar." Omar gestured. There was a tearful episode, but after a minute one of the sentinels managed to separate the boy from his mother. "If you try to escape, or cause trouble, I'll murder the boy. Understood?"

Tears filled the man's eyes, but he nodded.

"Good."

Just then a new consciousness joined the collective. For a moment, Omar was overwhelmed by the pain and sheer, edgy terror the newcomer felt. This always happened when a foreign consciousness joined them. What was telling was that this newcomer was afraid of death—something a Kryl would normally look forward to. It was, after all, their purpose.

Something in him—in the human side of him—recognized this fear of death, and it sent a cold chill shivering through him that not even the sensation caused by the phase shifter could match.

And in that moment, the new consciousness and his melded, drawing close to each other as if in kinship.

For a moment, the new consciousness saw the world through his eyes: the old man, the women, the children—oh, Animus, the *children*—even the blaze of glory he could see through the viewscreen. He was not capable of holding anything back.

Overmind X quickly wrested the two minds apart, separating them at controllable distances—but not fast enough to prevent what the new mind had witnessed. The cold, calm, rational, relentless Kryl mind that belonged to Subject Zero returned to his awareness.

He felt Overmind X begin to converse with another being. His eyes widened in astonishment as he recognized the new individual who had melded with the hive.

It must be their lucky day.

With prodding from Overmind X, Omar commenced with his duties. He put guards up around the children, leaving them in the bridge, and went to sweep the rest of the enormous ship.

# TWENTY-ONE

Elya's awareness zoomed out from his body and soared through space, flying past gold-green nebulas and banking around black holes as if they were potholes on an interstellar causeway.

He felt no wind on his face, for he had no face, and no light on his skin, for he had no skin, yet he hurtled forward with the kind of speed starfighter pilots long for but never reach. Looking down, he saw that he possessed no definite form at all. He existed only as a vague cloud of sensation. His soul had been plucked from his weakened body and pulled across the galaxy by an interstellar force with the power to defy physics.

But he was conscious. He could think. *How is this possible?* he wondered.

He didn't have time to answer his own question. His formless consciousness crashed into the source of the magnetism. He drowned in a vast pulsating awareness that obliterated his sense of self. He melded into it. They became one—

Until jarring static sent a bright shard of pain lancing through the collective consciousness, a backlash against the foreign presence.

Bright light. Pain. A reflexive jerking back of the defenses... For a moment all was open and available to him. A flash of jumbled images and emotions sent him reeling:

The ululating cry of a million minds hungrily howling.

Drawn faces of frightened children.

A man, wearing a starfighter pilot's flight suit, being ripped apart at the joints.

A glowing object like a box of stars, opening and no longer able to close...

His consciousness began to vibrate rapidly, jittering. Energy flowed into him, more than his formless being could handle. If he had a body he'd have passed out from the pain. But since he had no body, no vehicle to safeguard his mind, the vibrations increased until it felt like the molecules of his very consciousness were going to blow apart and scatter to the ends of the universe.

Something intervened. A magnetic force lifted him away, isolated him, walled him off.

The cosmic being had sequestered him from the rest of the hive because he couldn't handle the massive influx of information; human consciousness wasn't made to assimilate that many inputs. What he'd been shown was everything, all at once. A trillion images, memories, wishes, fears, desires, thoughts. The ones that had appeared to him first were all his frail, limited mortal mind could comprehend in that moment of contact.

The cosmic being who had protected him was not bound by such limited constraints. He marveled at Overmind X— her name revealed itself in a flash of recognition—as she rested in her sprawling capacity. He shook his metaphorical head, stunned that humanity had ever thought they could contain *this*.

*Now you understand.*

"Understand what?" he asked.

*Why the Inheritance belongs to us.*

... Yes, he *could* understand. It all made sense. The Inheritance didn't just belong to her—it was made for her, and her alone. No being could ever be a better fit for its awesome power.

*Join us...*

He balked. His mind formed an objection, but hesitated. Something about it didn't sit right with him, but he couldn't figure out why. Finally, he asked, "Me?"

*You are destined to join us.*

"But what about my friends? My family? My duty to the Empire..."

*Ephemeral. Don't you want to make a lasting impact? A... how do you put it... dent in the universe?*

She showed him a picture of herself as a vast tangled web. Starlit threads sprawling out to a million different points in the spacetime around her. At the center of this web was a golden knot, shining like a nuclear furnace. All threads led back to her—to the source.

He was looking at Overmind X as she saw *herself*.

And she was beautiful.

"What do you want me to do?"

*Find your piece of the Inheritance*, she whispered, *and bring it to me.*

He flinched. "No! I can't."

She turned him to face the way he'd come—along a causeway that ran across the galaxy, leading to where he'd left his body behind—and shoved him back. He raced along the path until he was once more floating above and in front

225

of his body, looking down at himself: A skinny young man, barely out of boyhood, with dark hair and wiry muscles.

"I won't," he insisted.

He—Elya—grimaced in pain where he hung limply, sprawled on an angled sheet of metal. The manacles pinned his wrists above his head, like a trellafly pinioned in a display case.

*You will*, she whispered.

---

Like a person held underwater until their lungs ache before being suddenly released, Elya opened his mouth and sucked in a great gasping breath.

"Earth's blood," Callus sighed, evidently relieved. "He's breathing again. Medic!"

Elya's eyes bulged. He gulped air as he fought to control a sense of vertigo. The room spun around him, gradually slowing, until it settled on Minister Aganaki.

Aganaki and Callus were staring at him with wide eyes from across the room, their bodies held tense. Callus had one hand on his sidearm, the other on the device that controlled the manacles, while Aganaki crossed his arms and leaned away, his eyes squinted in obvious suspicion.

Callus approached and with two fingers lifted Elya's chin.

"Welcome back to the land of the living."

Elya tried to reply, but his voice merely croaked.

The door opened and a medic came in to wave a hand-held scanner over him. "Vital signs appear to be stable."

The medic ducked out and returned a moment later with a bottle of water before leaving once more. Callus took the bottle and poured a stream into Elya's mouth.

He worked his tongue until in a hoarse voice he managed to ask, "How long was I out?"

"State your name, please," Callus said.

Elya was too weak to roll his eyes so he simply complied. "Captain Elya Nevers."

"Where do you work?"

"Flight 18 of the Furies, stationed on the *Paladin of Abniss*."

"Where are you now?"

"I don't know. You assholes kidnapped me, remember?" Rage overcame him and he spat on the man.

Callus wiped his face and dialed up the manacles, causing Elya's muscles to shiver and cramp again as familiar hot-and-cold spears of pain stabbed their ends into his arms and shoulders. He clenched his jaw and forced himself to breathe through it. This wasn't the highest setting, but the pain made it damned difficult to concentrate.

While he suffered, Aganaki and Callus exchanged low whispers, of which Elya only caught snatches.

"...not like the other reports..."

"...must know... tell him if we're careful..."

"How long was I out?" Elya asked again, interrupting them.

Aganaki gestured at Callus, who turned down the pain again so he was merely hanging there. "We don't look like xenos to you?" asked the minister.

"No, just assholes."

"Are you hallucinating?"

"Would I know if I was?"

"Fair point."

"Wait a minute." A chill swept through his exhausted and agonized body. "Are you saying that xeno parasite is still in me?"

They watched him silently, waiting.

"Shit." Now he knew why they were acting so weird. He'd heard Naab's story about what happened when the parasite was in *him*. How everyone looked like xenos and he tried to take them out rather than let himself be "captured."

Everyone knew that the Kryl showed no mercy.

Worse, Elya had seen what happened when Subject Zero put one of these Kryl parasites into a boy named Hedrick on Robichar. The boy had started to *become* one of them, to mutate, to turn.

Was he turning?

*Not yet*, said Overmind X. She didn't speak into his mind so much as leave the impression of thought.

He looked up at his wrists and down at his ankles for any sign that he was becoming like Subject Zero—a half human, half Kryl mutant. He only saw his own aching limbs, unmarred by Kryl growths or fungus. His wrists were raw and red where the manacles met his skin.

"What did you just think about?" Aganaki asked.

"Um…" What did he have to lose? He found himself suddenly desperate to share what he'd seen, things he hadn't even shared with his squad-mates—frightening things he'd been suppressing so much that they haunted his sleep. *Screw it*, he thought. "She uses this parasite to turn people into Kryl. To manipulate and control them. I saw it with my own eyes."

"So why aren't you turning?"

"Because the parasite is only the first ingredient. Overmind X needs direct contact to complete the transformation." He remembered the pus-covered platform they'd put Hedrick on, and shivered at the thought. The image of living mucous crawling up the boy's ankles and starting to form the muscle and exoskeleton of a xeno mutant remained vivid in his mind's eye.

"Who is Overmind X?"

"The rogue hive queen who invaded Robichar. That's what she calls herself."

"What does she want?"

228

"Relics. She calls them her 'Inheritance'." This time, the impression she gave him was one of gloating satisfaction. It made his skin crawl, and he shivered all over.

Aganaki and Callus exchanged an uneasy glance.

"You know about the Inheritance?" Elya asked.

"That's not what we call it, but I can guess what she means."

A visceral sense of urgency rushed through his body. Overmind X wanted to know more—and so did he. Hadn't he spent the last several weeks digging into what MOXA knew? And now here was the Minister of Xeno Affairs himself. The man had information he needed. "What are you hiding about these relics? I saw that book in the Archive." Now he took a guess. "You tore those pages out, didn't you?"

Minister Aganaki frowned at him, the man's smooth brow wrinkling. His hands disappeared into the sleeves as he put them together—a pensive gesture. "It's complicated. We've known about the existence of Telos relics for a long time."

"The book said that the Ansible is a Telos relic. So is the hyperspace drive."

"Gifts from an ancient ally to the founders." He meant the people who colonized Ariadne—their ancestors who first established the Solaran Empire.

Again that thrill of urgency and excitement that didn't belong to him. If pressed, Elya wouldn't have been able to say he didn't share the feeling. He struggled to discern where her feelings ended and his began. "But you know more than you're letting on, don't you?"

Aganaki ran his tongue over his teeth and paced across the room, his hands still hidden in his sleeves. "Perhaps."

Another impression was planted in his mind. Elya didn't hear the information so much as immediately recognize it, like a memory he'd forgotten about and suddenly regained.

"You're too late. Overmind X is going to get to the relic in the Elturis System before you."

Aganaki paused in his pacing. "She can hear us." It wasn't a question.

Elya nodded. "Don't blame me. You put this fucking parasite in my head."

"I suppose you already know it's true. There are relics scattered across dozens of uncolonized worlds."

Elya pulled at the manacles. "But some of them are more powerful than others. Like the Robichar relic. That's what's on those missing pages, isn't it?"

Aganaki reluctantly acknowledged it with a brief dip of his chin. "The founders called them the prime relics. There are seven scattered across the galaxy, hidden by the Telos and lost to us."

Another impression from Overmind X was planted. This time it consisted of two words: "Not anymore."

Aganaki watched him carefully as he continued. "One is already in our possession, as you so cleverly discovered. Our research uncovered the location of several others. Most of the ones we found, however, were mundane artifacts. Useful —" He gestured to the manacles "—and fairly lucrative, but not the prime relics we're looking for."

"Until Robichar."

"Yes. Until Robichar."

"Where is it?"

Aganaki's face soured and he could see movement beneath the man's sleeve as he clenched his hands around the opposite arms. "Still in the possession of Admiral Miyaru."

Elya laughed. "Sucks to be you."

"It is only a matter of time."

Through the parasite, he felt a snarling anger. "She doesn't like that."

"Good. From what I understand, this relic is powerful."

230

"And dangerous to the Kryl. The geode hurts them, some-how. It—"

His head began to ache and Elya squinted his eyes against it.

"You're bleeding," Agent Callus observed.

Overmind X didn't like it when he talked openly about her weaknesses. Elya rubbed his nose on his shoulder and left behind a streak of blood. His eyes widened as a panicky feeling took hold of him. "The parasite. Get it out of me. She can't complete the transformation, but she can still use it to hurt me. Please."

"First, I want to know how she knew about Robichar."

Another impression was planted in his mind. He gasped as an added realization struck him "The Colonization Board… they're only sending voyagers to planets where you think relics can be found. You led her right to it!"

Aganaki frowned. He didn't like that news. "And thanks to you, we were able to hang onto the Robichar relic. I owe you one for that."

"Then pay up and get this damned thing out of me. They operated on Lieutenant Park to remove his. You have to get a surgical bot in here. Hurry!"

Callus frowned, looking pensive, and reduced the pain imparted by the manacles down to zero. Elya sagged.

"When we're finished." Aganaki paced around for a minute while he formulated his next question. "If we've been leading her to the relics, how did Overmind X know about the Elturis System? She didn't arrive on Robichar until after we got news of the relic's discovery."

Another impression was planted in his mind. This time she was gloating.

And that's when he remembered the images he'd seen when his mind was first joined to her awareness through the conduit of the parasite. One stood out: *A glowing object like a box of stars...*

He gasped as the realization landed. "She has a starmap."

Sharp stabbing pain shot through his head, ten times worse than anything he'd endured to this point. He screamed. Liquid copper wet his tongue as blood spilled out of his nose and over his lips.

If he thought the manacles were bad, the pain they imparted was nothing compared to *this*.

# TWENTY-TWO

When Casey walked into the war room on the *Paladin of Abniss*, Park and Yorra were sitting on opposite ends of the octagonal war table, turned away from each other, with a holovid from Ariadne's news channel, *Sector Five*, active between them.

"The *Maiden of Kali*, bound for the habitable third world in the Elturis System, was discovered to be *missing* today when a series of panicked emails was leaked by the information freedom radicals known as Veritas," said the reporter— an androgynous AI like Harmony who, rather than pilot starships, was programmed to read scripts in soothing voices. "The colonial voyager's crew reportedly missed their third scheduled check-in via Ansible late last night. Officials from the Colonization Board have yet to confirm the report, however, our network was able to independently confirm the rumor with multiple anonymous sources at the highest echelons of the Imperial government."

The holovid switched to a live shot of the Colonization Board's spaceport where the launch celebration was being held. It boiled over with a restless mob of refugees streaming in from the refugee camps. The SDF had been called in to keep the peace, so it hadn't devolved into riots yet, but it was getting there. Casey considered it a good sign that some self-organizing faction had lit a giant bonfire in the center of the runway. Instead of fanning the flames, the church of Animus had declared the fire an "homage to Sol" and was keeping people distracted by leading prayer every hour on the hour.

This would go on for days.

"Meanwhile, on Ariadne, citizens of the Empire have gathered here to protest overflowing refugee camps, high unemployment, and enforced rations that were clamped down again just this week. To make matters worse, thousands are claiming they were unfairly denied colonial status by the Colonization Board and now, with the *Maiden of Kali* missing, that they were misled about the success of such voyages. It's caused a spike in applications for permanent resident status here on Ariadne, even despite difficult living conditions and rising inflation. With the influx of refugees from Robichar, Ariadne's water systems and power grid remain in Tier Two restrictions. As of last week, the Colonization Board estimates the colonization waitlist to have doubled in the past year…"

Casey slapped the table-mounted holoprojector, cutting off the news feed and sending the room into a heavy silence. Park hung his head and mumbled something under his breath. Yorra cast him a toxic glare.

"What's eating you two? If it's personal, have it out because we have bigger problems to deal with right now."

Not a peep between them.

"Well?"

Park heaved a sigh. "Sorry, Rap, things got a bit too real in the church."

Yorra shoved her jaw out pugnaciously. "You mean too *honest?*"

Park winced. "I told you, it was just that once, and we weren't a thing at the time."

"So we're a *thing* now? I thought you didn't want to make it official."

"You know what I mean! I can't believe you're mad at me for something that happened months ago."

"I'm not mad you slept with her, Naab, I'm mad you *lied to me* about it."

He winced like she'd slapped him. She might as well have. Casey wanted very much to be somewhere else right now—the tension was enough to make her all sweaty. But she needed the support of her squad mates if they were going to find Nevers or expose Spector. Preferably both.

"I don't have feelings for her," Naab insisted. "It didn't mean anything. It just kind of happened."

Yorra got very quiet, like a loaded coilgun before it obliterated a xeno on a hillside in the distance. She trained her metaphorical sights on Park. "It means something to me."

He crossed the room and took her hands in his. She pulled away. "Come on, Olara. It was just a little harmless fun."

Casey winced. *Harmless? Really, Park?* She'd always thought that the way the Fleet encouraged pilots to—er—relieve stress on their own time was a good idea. Contraception was extremely reliable and they were all tested for diseases regularly. What better way to relieve stress? She'd indulged on occasion, with a willing young stud. But she'd never seen it get messy, at least not in her own squad.

To her surprise, Yorra sighed and some of the tension went out of her body. Park relaxed and his eyes closed briefly in evident relief.

Until Gears reared back and punched him under the chest. Park staggered back and groaned.

235

Casey winced in sympathy. That one was going to leave a bruise.

"I remember how you kept checking her out in training. You can't keep your eyes off her long red hair, *or* her ass. And it's a great ass, too, which makes me even angrier about it." she muttered something about putting his balls in a vice. "I just need some space."

He wilted.

Casey wanted to ask if it was the redhead from Flight 4, but she didn't dare get between them right now. She coughed and turned away slightly, trying to give them *some* privacy.

However, Harmony had no such qualms. Her light-mote form lurked at the door. She must have heard the argument and made her stealthy way into the room.

"Are you spying on us?" Casey demanded.

Harmony's form expanded and colored motes of gold, green and purple light formed an androgynous body as tall as Casey. Her mouth moved when she spoke, and her eyes were huge, bright densities of energy, like miniature suns. "Admiral Miyaru asked me to keep an eye on you while she makes contact with MOXA."

The conflict between Park and Yorra momentarily set aside, they came around to her side of the table and stood a discrete distance apart, regarding the AI curiously. Casey filled them in about what she'd discussed with the Admiral.

"Since you're here," Casey said to Harmony, "I want to know something. Why did you cover for me back there at the Archives?"

Harmony's face cocked to one side. "What do you mean?"

"Don't play dumb with me. Back at the Temple, you protected me by telling Spector that we used our real names to check into the Archives. We both know things would have gone way differently if she caught us using false identities— then Spector actually would have had grounds to court martial me instead of drag me in front of the Admiral to dispute a minor infraction—and she made the mistake of trying to demote me, which the Admiral didn't like. You saved me and Nevers from an inquisition."

"I may have *temporarily* edited the visitor's logs."

"Did the admiral order you to do that?" Casey demanded.

"No." Those big eyes never blinked. "But if she inquires, I will tell her."

Casey's mind raced. Everyone knew the shipboard AI's were hard-wired to follow their commander's orders—in this case Admiral Miyaru. But maybe that wasn't all they were programmed for. Why would she do something outside of what the admiral ordered her to do?

Casey walked across the room to check that the door to the war room was firmly shut and latched.

"Why cover for us?"

"Because you needed help."

"What's in it for you?"

"I wanted to help."

"Earth! Spare me. *Why?*"

A slight hesitation. "I couldn't risk your movements being hampered. And I require the information you retrieved from the Archives."

A cold shivery sensation slithered down her spine and curled up on the floor of her gut.

"I thought that was Nevers' idea."

"It was. For the most part."

"What do you mean, 'for the most part'?"

"I may have seeded the idea in his head."

Casey blinked. "Are you... Backspace?"

The motes of light burst apart and reformed. "I am not at liberty to say."

That was as much of a confirmation as they were going to get.

Yorra swore. "Earth's last light."

"Wait, *this* is the so-called Veritas hacker Fancypants has been talking to on the darknet?" Park put his fingers next to his ear and opened his hand while making the sound of an explosion with his mouth. "Mind. Blown."

"Why send us? Why not just get the information yourself? You obviously have access to all the Imperial systems."

Harmony's floating face blinked at her.

"Maybe," Yorra said, tapping her chin, "She couldn't find the information because it doesn't *exist* on the network."

"Or on the darknet," Park added. "Which she obviously has access to."

It hit her then, and Casey ground her forehead into the palm of her hand. "Of course. Hah! AI's can pilot starships but they can't read an old book."

Harmony looked amused. "Not in the Archives. That's the church's jurisdiction."

"Freakin' AI hacker... who would have thought." Park shook his head.

"Wait just a minute," Casey said. Her mind took a minute to circle to what was really bothering her. Her hands shook in anticipation when the thought formed. "If you can hack into the darknet, can you hack into the Inquisitor's systems and get Spector's personnel files?"

"I can see her record, but anything secured with confidential access on Inquisitor system is outside my reach."

"But Spector is stationed on the *Paladin* now. Surely, anything that pertains to the ship's security measures is within your purview."

"Indeed."

"So, what can you tell me?"

"I ran a background check on her when Admiral Miyaru picked her as the new squadron commander of the Furies. She has an exemplary record."

Casey snorted. "Exactly. Don't you find that suspicious?"

"Not necessarily... her record is in the 93$^{rd}$ percentile of all the most exemplary officer records in the database. Adjusted for time, her advancement matches yours, for instance. At least, it did. Recent... incidents have forced me to recalibrate my model."

That hit a nerve for some reason. It was the competitive streak in her. "Surely you can tell us *something* about Spector that might be helpful.."

"Rap, you're digging awful hard," Yorra said. "Shouldn't we be trying to figure out where Nevers disappeared to this time?"

"No way, Gears! Spector keeps trying to nail us to the wall. We're not going to be able to help Fancypants until we get her off our ass. Besides, I'm not letting up on Spector until I find out the truth about her so-called exemplary record. I couldn't believe she roped the XO into commandeering Fleet security to chase us down at the Temple. Maybe she's got something on him, too."

"Blackmail?" asked Park.

She threw up her hands. "Who knows!"

"She is kind of charming, you have to admit,"

"You shut up."

Park threw his hands up like a shield. "Just sayin'."

"Hmm..." Harmony said. Her motes of light flashed, making Casey think she was processing something. "My analysis indicates that Colonel Volk's behavior has made a marked shift since Spector took command of the Furies. He has taken two sick days, on Admiral Miyaru's orders, and his illness does not seem to be from a communicable disease because no one he came into contact with showed similar symptoms."

"Good 'ol Fleet injections," Park said, his hand wandering up to the spinal port at the base of his skull in the back.

"They feed us enough antibiotics as part of regular treatments that I haven't had so much as a cold since I entered pilot training."

Volk had collapsed suddenly at the Temple but, now that Casey thought about it, he'd looked more and more sick each time she saw him over the weeks since Walcott's funeral. He had been spending an awful lot of time around Spector.

Could Spector have something to do with Colonel Volk's sudden illness? Casey took a deep breath to steel herself for what she had in mind. It wasn't wise. But she was her father's daughter, and part of the reason he'd been a good inquisitor —according to the stories his comrades-in-arms told about him—was his dogged determination to get to the bottom of any mystery. "Harmony, is Spector still with the XO right now?"

"She is, Captain," Harmony acknowledged.

"In the sick bay?" Yorra asked. "Why would she be there?"

"Because the admiral sent her to check on Volk."

"Are you thinking what I'm thinking?" Yorra asked.

Casey's heart soared. "I could kiss you."

"What are you two talking about?" Park said. "Hey wait up."

They rushed out of the war room and quick-walked through the capital ship, slowing anytime they were within sight of a senior officer. Casey delivered sharp salutes without slowing her pace, avoiding people's eyes and walking with purpose so that no one was inspired to stop them.

In the sick bay, the nurse pointed them toward Volk's room. On their way in, they passed a room where the surgical bot was currently performing a minor operation. Park blew out his cheeks and put his hand over the scar on his neck where the very same surgical bot had extracted the Kryl parasite from his body on the last mission.

Volk's room wasn't hard to find. Two crimson-suited security guards were stationed outside.

"Only two visitors at a time," they said. "Lt. Colonel Spector is already in there."

Yorra looked none too pleased, a crease forming between her gently sloping brows, but she acquiesced.

"We'll be right out here, Raptor," Park added.

Casey looked between them, silently checking in. Whatever personal conflict they were dealing with, it had been put on a shelf for now. She took a deep breath and stepped through the doorway.

Spector had her hand on the shoulder of the medic who was currently attending Volk. She was whispering in the young man's ear. Her other hand held a bottle of pills— presumably the medicine they were giving the colonel to remove the heavy metals from his body. She set the pills down on the bedside table and whispered again. The medic swallowed uneasily and then nodded several times. She couldn't hear what Spector had said, but the medic immediately began to swap out the IV bag piping drugs into Volk's veins.

Volk saw her before Spector did. "Osprey," he croaked.

She smiled at him. The old man was lying prostrate on the bed in a medical gown, covered up to his neck by the thin white hospital sheets. His face had a two-day growth of salt and pepper beard, and his bald pate looked pale and wan.

"Hello, sir. How are you feeling?"

"Like shit, Captain. How do you think?"

She snorted. "I didn't want to be the one to say it, sir. You gave us all a scare back at the Temple."

"No thanks to you," Spector interrupted.

"Enough, you two. Captain, I don't know what you were up to at the Archives, but I want you to think long and hard about your future in the Fleet. Walcott saw a lot of promise in you, and I know the admiral does too. Don't throw it away by antagonizing your commanding officer."

Casey stared at her boots and gritted her teeth, trying not to glance over at Spector. He sounded just like her father—but she supposed all Fleet veterans of a certain age had the same thought patterns ingrained in them—honor, duty, planet, Empire. They thought alike.

Walcott had been different. Wiser, somehow. How would Walcott have responded to that accusation?

She took a deep breath and answered the colonel as best she knew how. "If someone can show me that what I did was wrong, I will happily admit it and take my punishment. All I want is for the truth to come out. The truth never hurt anyone. It's the person who continues in deception and ignorance who is harmed—and who harms others."

Volk stared at her with that pale face screwed up in consternation. He lay his head back down on the pillow. "All I know is, you two better figure out a way to keep the peace between you. We can't have this strife on the ship. Spector is a good commander. You could learn a lot from her."

With the new IV bag hanging, the medic picked up the bottle of pills. Spector took it from him and tapped two pills out of the bottle before handing them to Volk. The colonel popped the pills into his mouth and swallowed them with a sip of water, followed by a hacking cough that dragged out for the better part of a minute, before he finally lay back to rest in the narrow bed. His eyelids fluttered and then closed, and he began to snore softly.

"He needs to rest," Spector said.

Casey glared at Spector. "What are you up to?"

"You better watch your tone."

"What are you up to, *sir*?"

"One more word and I'll have you thrown in the brig."

Unlike the demotion, Spector *could* do that. Even if the

admiral decided to let her off easy a second time, she'd still spend time in the brig, where she wouldn't be of any use to Nevers.

The medic who was tending to Volk eyed them both carefully, sensing the animosity building. He slid behind Spector and glanced down at the bottle of pills. His eyebrows drew together in consternation or confusion—it was just a momentary reaction, but it was a moment of significance that triggered an instinct deep within her. Spector hadn't seen the medic, but the expression on *her* face when Casey snapped up the bottle of pills and backpedaled out the door was all the confirmation she needed.

The expression on Spector's face spelled *fear*. Plain as day.

Casey rushed between the security guards and down the hall, past the operating room that was occupied and into another that was empty.

"Guards!" Spector shouted as she gave chase.

"Harmony," Casey huffed as she closed the door and locked herself in the OR. "Are you there?"

"Yes, Captain," came the voice from the speakers of the surgical bot.

Casey struggled with the pill bottle, trying to get the cap open. It was a semi-transparent, white plastic, half full of pills, and the damn childproof cap wouldn't come off. Spector slammed into the door and began shaking it. She yelled at the medics for the key and when they didn't produce it, ordered the guards to kick it in. Casey was vaguely aware of Yorra and Park trying to intervene but being easily turned away by Spector and the guards.

The cap finally came off and Casey spilled the contents of the bottle into the seat of the surgical bot, slapping the touchscreen to close the machine.

"Beginning analysis," Harmony said through speakers on the surgical bot.

The door burst inward. Pieces of the latch went flying by her head. Spector dashed over to the machine and tried to lift the shell off, but it was sealed. Casey shoved her away from it. She just needed to buy Harmony a few minutes to run the analysis, and then it would be ship's record and impossible to bury the truth any longer.

Spector slapped Casey's hands down and drove an open palm into her solar plexus. She'd been expecting that. Casey turned her body, sending the blow glancing to the side and causing Spector to lurch forward, off balance.

Casey grabbed her arm and yanked the squadron commander away from the bot.

Spector staggered forward once, then stepped out wide with her left foot, halting her forward momentum and taking all her weight onto her left knee—the weak one, where she wasn't currently wearing a knee brace like she had in combat training—while looking back at Casey.

Spector grimaced, her face twisting in pain. Casey had a moment to feel triumphant before panic set in. As the commander had turned, she'd gotten one hand around the back of Casey's flight suit and grabbed hold of the fabric. The cry of pain she let loose was genuine—but how it looked to the guards must have been far different from how Casey experienced the motion. Spector threw her weight backwards, holding Casey tight to her body, and took the both of them down with Casey on top of her, so that instead of re-injuring an old wound, it looked like Casey took her to the ground by force.

"Help!" Spector cried out.

The guard's rushed in while Spector held her down. The two guards wrestled Casey away. Once she was free, Spector staggered up and hit the panel on the surgical bot.

The bot's transparent shell lifted before the analysis could be completed.

Spector swiped a hand to erase the partial results, then began to sweep up the pills and put them back in the bottle.

The guards held Casey fast. "Stop her!" she said. "Can't you see she's hiding something?"

"Throw her in the brig," Spector said.

"No! Wait! You don't have to believe me. Just look at the results. Just look at them!"

The guards hesitated, glancing between Spector and Casey.

"Do it!" Spector shouted. "That's an order."

She was the senior-ranking officer in the room. From the perspective of Volk's guards, it looked like Casey had grabbed the colonel's pills and then attacked Spector. Without the analysis to prove what Spector had been doing, she was in the wrong.

They began to lead her away. Casey wasn't strong enough to resist.

Park and Yorra objected loudly, but when backup arrived Casey was easily separated from her squadmates and dragged to a five by five cell. They tossed her unceremoniously inside and locked the door.

# TWENTY-THREE

Through a fog of immeasurable pain, this time centered behind his eyes and radiating out like barbed tentacles into his chest and arms, Elya dimly watched the two men from MOXA arguing with each other.

"It's killing him," said Agent Callus.

A silent pause.

"We need to intervene. The medics are rushing in a surgical bot from th—"

"Shh!" said the minister. "Wait."

Callus's tongue darted out, wetting his lips, but he paused with his hand near the panel that would open the door. "He hasn't got long."

"I saw you switch the manacles off. If he dies, it'll be the parasite that kills him."

"If we watch a Fleet pilot die and do nothing, we're responsible."

"*I'm* responsible. Are you going to disobey a direct order, Agent?"

Callus dropped his hand and turned back to Elya who, between bursts of blinding agony, could plainly see the guilt in the man's eyes. In that moment he came to understand that while he and Callus had been in conflict since they met, they also shared a motivation—a sense of duty to the Solaran Empire. Elya felt that it was his responsibility to uncover the truth about the relics so he could protect people from the xeno threat. It was Callus's job to protect the Ministry of Xeno Affairs and its leader, but wasn't their reason for being to learn about the xenos, the Kryl in particular? And by doing so, arm humanity with the knowledge they needed to mount an effective defense?

*These foolish ideas are your weakness,* Overmind X interrupted, speaking through the parasite directly into his mind. *They divide you and impede your ability to act. We are singular in our purpose. Humanity cannot stand against us. This will be your downfall, as it was for the Enemy.*

His pain amplified until the minister and Agent Callus faded into the distance of his awareness.

Once again she showed him visions. Not hallucinations draped like a cruel blanket over reality, but fully realized holovids of the mind.

A great battle stretched across a vast canvas of time. Overmind X was there, but she appeared to be much smaller and less expansive than the gold-threaded web he'd seen before. In this version, her identity was but one piece of a larger whole...

The nexus of an older, more expansive awareness was located on a planet he didn't recognize. Through his connection with Overmind X, she showed him that it was the homeworld of the Kryl—the hivemind of the Queen Mother. Humanity called it Planet K. She knew it only as *Home*.

From the seat of *Home*, the Queen Mother spent centuries waging a war against a dark and terrible foe known as the Enemy. The Enemy possessed weapons of great power that could maim and blind and annihilate. They thrived in the cold emptiness of space, sealed in their great vessels. They roamed, these killers of the void, patrolling her borders. The Queen Mother grew strong and wily fighting against the Enemy.

After all, merciless war and defeat are the greatest of teachers.

Many terrible battles were fought. No matter how she tried, the Queen Mother could not gain a foothold against the Enemy. They drove her back, but never pursued, seemingly content to repeat the task on the next turn of the stars. While the Enemy were merciless in battle, with vast warships and the most destructive weaponry she'd ever seen, they were foolishly tolerant and smug in their superiority. They allowed the war to drag on, and in time she came to perceive that it was a game to them. The Queen Mother longed to gain access to greater resources in order to expand her brood so that one day she could give them a worthy challenge. Yet every time she ventured out into uncharted territory, every time she sought to grow, the Enemy appeared out of nowhere to slaughter her children and turn her back again.

But the Queen Mother's life was long. She was the collective, the multitude, the swarm. If a life of endless war had taught her anything, it was patience.

Over time, she realized that the Enemy's power came from their weapons, the technology that gave them the ability to be everywhere at once. In each battle she fought to obtain it, but on the odd occasion when she did manage to acquire a ship, she did not understand how to make it function. Their technology was locked away from her, their secrets carefully guarded.

Restless, she sent feelers into a system the Enemy occupied that happened to be a source of sulfur, which the Queen Mother needed to breed, when she discovered that a world the Enemy had occupied for centuries had, overnight, become embroiled in a civil war.

Divided into factions, the Enemy turned their weapons of destruction on each other. Kin fighting kin was repulsive to the Queen Mother, whose brood was an extension of herself. To employ violence against another race was the way of the universe, the cycle of the stars. Bigger animals ate smaller ones, predators hunted prey. This tapestry of the horror that occurs when a species turns on *itself* was an abomination. Yet she found she could not look away. The battle raged for cycles and cycles, and though reserve forces were brought from far away, they could do nothing to quell the blazing inferno. The planet engulfed itself, along with the resources it contained—a blasphemy.

At times, fighting the Enemy had frightened her; this event sent her into existential shock. The Queen Mother retreated to the safety of *Home*. What she saw next amazed her: The fighting continued, traveling back like a disease toward the Enemy's homeworld. Slowly, ever so slowly, the Enemy's dominance began to recede. The body of their species grew weak. Their population dwindled.

And then the unthinkable happened. They began to vanish from the galaxy, abandoning their worlds until soon the Enemy was gone.

The Queen Mother was left alone.

Except for the low animal species of the worlds that sustained her, she lived in isolation for the next millennia. She grew mature and wise, and in the absence of strife, her brood flourished. She missed the struggle of fighting against the Enemy—bleeding among the stars in the war that had forged her strength—but for the first time, she found peace.

So it was a profound surprise when a new spacefaring species arrived in the galaxy, borne upon the wings of the Enemy. Though she was older now, the Queen Mother's blood sang with the prospect of renewed struggle. It would be a wonderful way to test her brood, now more expansive than ever. She began developing more intelligent Overminds, like miniature versions of herself, to send into battle. One day one of them would replace her. Was this not the perfect opportunity to develop a new queen? These newcomers were young, but much like the Enemy, they loved war and possessed unique weapons of their own.

As the Enemy had done for her, she encouraged this young species that called itself Humanity. They fought her, but when they retreated she did not allow herself to pursue, giving them time and space to renew their strength. However, after a few decades of this new war, she grew tired, and in her old age, she made a grave mistake. She allowed them to sneak a weapon into the heart of *Home*, a weapon that brought destruction the likes of which she hadn't seen since the Enemy's departure. They delivered a crushing blow that lethally injured the Queen Mother and forced her into hibernation.

While this was devastating, it was not without a silver lining. The soldier sent to deliver the payload possessed knowledge of the Enemy and their weapons. In the heat of a nuclear furnace, in a desperate attempt to keep her favorite child alive, the Queen Mother grafted a splinter of her awareness to the human soldier, giving birth to Overmind X.

Separated from the Queen Mother's influence for the first time, Overmind X nourished herself on the human in order to save her own life, simultaneously turning him into the first of her own brood: Subject Zero. Like a child, Overmind X had to learn how to direct her brood instead of being directed by the Queen Mother. Over time, she began to mine the depths of Subject Zero's memories. Combined with the Queen Mother's knowledge of the Enemy, she made a discovery: the Enemy may have departed from this galaxy, but their most powerful weapons had been left behind.

Together, Overmind X and Subject Zero set off on their search. It took years to locate the first relic. What had been hidden away since the Enemy disappeared from the galaxy was brought back into the light.

Most of the major relics were still out there. Overmind X vowed to find them all, to unite them, to obtain her Inheritance. She would use their combined power to avenge *Home*, to accomplish what the Queen Mother had never been able or even willing to do—to erase humanity from existence.

The throbbing agony in his head receded and his visions—Overmind X's memories—faded. He breathed rapidly and arched his back against a sudden freezing fire encircling his throbbing wrists.

"No! Stop!" he found himself crying. "Please, please, please, please...." he begged as sweat and spit ran down his face.

"Interesting," Aganaki observed calmly. "The manacles seem to be able to interrupt its effects."

"Minister, please, we can't let this go on."

"I *must* know the full extent of the parasite's abilities."

Callus clenched his jaw and looked down. After an interminable time, the minister nodded, and Callus turned the manacles back down with a relieved exhale.

Elya hung there for a moment, breathing hard. As the pain in his wrists receded, the pain in his head advanced. He shuddered as the presence of Overmind X encroached on the edge of his awareness. He licked his cracked lips.

Why had she shown him her history? She must have had a reason. His first moment of contact with her had revealed things she didn't want him to know about. And he'd obviously pissed her off when he told Aganaki about the starmap. But this latest vision was too well coordinated, too buttoned up, to be accidental.

She wanted him to know her story.

Elya worked his mouth and tried to speak. Callus approached and poured a stream of gloriously cold water into his mouth.

"She wants us to know that we're responsible," Elya rasped.

Aganaki went very still, like a reptile who senses a threatening predator nearby. "Responsible for what?"

"For creating Overmind X and the first of her brood. It was a survival response to the attack on their homeworld."

Was that... sympathy he felt? Elya knew what it was like to have your homeworld attacked. He tried to shake himself of the notion, but the seed had been planted.

"Are you saying... the nuclear blast that ended the Kryl War made this new queen?"

"It's our fault she found out about the relics, too. We gave her the information." Elya waited to see how Overmind X would react. The stabbing pain behind his eyes remained at bay.

"How?" asked Aganaki.

"The hero of the Kryl War," he swallowed. "Captain Omar Ruidiaz. She merged with him during the blast, and then mined his memories for stories from the time of the Great Migration. I don't know if Ruidiaz read that old book, or heard about it somewhere else, but he knew about the relics."

Aganaki exchanged a worried glance with Callus. He paced across the room. Elya let him. The pain of the manacles and the pain of the parasite were both at a minimum, and he was happy to let them stay that way and just breathe for a minute. A moment's respite was all he got.

"When I speak to you," the minister asked, "do I also speak to this Overmind X?"

"As far as I can tell. Don't ask me how."

"Why you?"

Elya felt his jaw clench. "You tell me! You put the damn thing in my head."

He shook his head calmly. "Your reactions are different than previous reports have led us to expect."

Overmind X sent him a thought that made him shudder. "I guess it's because of what I saw on Robichar…" He thought of the boy she tried to turn. Panic seized Elya and his eyes watered. "Please, you've got to get this thing out of me. Please. I'll tell you everything she showed me. I'll—AAGGH-HH!" Sharpened agony took him again, and only Callus's quick reaction on the manacles kept Overmind X from fully taking over.

"When we're finished," Aganaki said. "First, I have something to say to her."

The pain in his head receded. Callus, noticing, dialed the manacles down again.

Aganaki clasped his hands behind his back and drew himself upright. "You were right about what was on those missing pages. They contain the most detailed account we have of humanity's first and only encounter with the Telos."

Excitement and desire to do violence literally *squirmed* inside of him. "*The Enemy,*" Elya hissed in a voice that didn't belong to him. Overmind X's voice.

"The account describes a meeting with a single xeno. The author referred to him only as the 'last Engineer.'"

Elya's whole body shivered in anticipation. Not Elya's reaction—although he recognized the name from what he'd read in the Archives—but the Overmind's.

Aganaki continued. "Others simply called him 'the alien.' Regardless, according to our records, this Telos was the first

253

sentient xeno humanity ever encountered. He told the founders about his people, a technologically advanced race that nearly went extinct when their civilization erupted in a sudden and violent revolution. He also told them about the Kryl."

Elya's spine bristled—a strange sensation because he didn't have any fur or feathers to bristle *with*. But that didn't seem to matter. Overmind X's sensations and his were one and the same.

"He told the founders about their devouring nature, a hunger that could never be sated, and the defenses the Telos invented to keep the Kryl at bay. Chief among those defenses were seven 'prime relics'... weapons of untold power his people had created, now hidden away and scattered across the galaxy. Laid in sealed vaults and laced with protections, the last Engineer had worked to ensure the safekeeping of these artifacts so that, if their need was great, humanity or another sentient race could find and use them—while also ensuring that the Kryl could not."

Overmind X snarled through Elya's mouth. He and the Overmind both knew that was only partially true. Through Subject Zero, she had been able to both obtain the relics *and* use them.

She hungered for more.

"The book itself was lost for centuries," Aganaki went on. "We rediscovered it during the Kryl War in our search for intel to defeat them. It worked. The war ended, the Kryl horde was driven back to Planet K, and the Queen Mother was destroyed."

"*Diminished but not destroyed,*" Overmind X said through Elya's mouth. "*I lived. I evolved. I am the Queen Mother. I am Overmind X.*"

Vertical lines creased the skin between Aganaki's brows. A bead of sweat dripped down his forehead. He wiped it away with the voluminous red sleeve and replied, "No matter. We killed you once. We can do it again." The minister's tone was flippant.

Overmind X thrashed in anger.

*"Never!"* she snarled. *"I am Overmind X. I am inevitable. With the Inheritance in my possession, humanity is doomed. You are but a mote in the sun of existence, passing and then gone. It is only a matter of time. I am eternal. I will destroy you."*

Agony shot out into every tendril of Elya's being. Having outlived his usefulness, Overmind X made it clear that she was content to destroy him.

Only Callus's quick reaction on the manacles saved his life.

Torn between the tides of two agonies, a sea of pain swept him away.

255

# TWENTY-FOUR

Captain Osprey had made her choices—she would just have to learn to deal with the fallout.

Kira had done her best to help the young captain, despite the bad blood between her and Spector. The parasite and the relic they'd found on Robichar had caused some extenuating circumstances that warranted a little lenience. Osprey may have caused some trouble at the Archives, but as far as Kira could tell she hadn't broken any laws and it didn't merit the demotion Spector wanted to give her. The request for punishment did not fit the crime.

But assaulting your commanding officer was something else entirely. Kira had reviewed the footage. She didn't know what had gotten into the captain's head, but the outcome was clear cut. Once Osprey took Spector to the ground, there was nothing she could do to help her. She would spend time in the brig for that and deserve every lonely minute. A crying shame it happened right before they were about to embark on their next mission—she wouldn't get to fly.

Tough luck.

"You survived in the hole," said Harmony.

"And so will she."

Kira paced the empty bridge while she waited for the crew to return. They only had a few hours before departure, and Kira was restless to get moving. Mobilizing troops took the time it took, however, so here she waited with her tits in her hands, so to speak.

"Admiral, you have a visitor," said Harmony.

Half a second later, the door to the bridge irised open and Lieutenant Colonel Spector limped in, drew up and saluted. No doubt she was here to check in on the results of her request to get Osprey demoted.

"At ease," Kira said.

Spector shuffled to get the weight off her hurt leg, which now sported a heavy-duty knee brace.

"Sir, I think I might have figured out where Captain Nevers disappeared to."

Kira blinked. That was not what she'd been expecting or mentally preparing for. It took her a moment to recover. "Well, spit it out."

"I have a friend who works as a warden on the Molten Cage. Rumors have it that a Fleet pilot was in-processed around the time of the shift change late last night."

That computed to just a few hours after the incident at the Archives. A string of muttered curses slid off Kira's tongue. "Rumors are one thing. Harmony, can you verify?"

Harmony's lights blinked in the air beside her. "He's not listed on the Cage's manifest of prisoners."

"Respectfully, that doesn't mean anything, Admiral," Spector said. "MOXA doesn't have to report any such thing."

So Spector shared Captain Osprey's suspicions about who was responsible for Nevers' disappearance. That damn starfighter pilot had the worst luck. First Robichar, and now MOXA. She could help by acting decisively.

"Have a seat. I need to make a call."

"Aye, sir." Spector limped over to the nearest crash couch and sank gratefully into the gel-packed cushion.

Kira went into the war room adjacent to the bridge and had Harmony connect the call. With Colonel Volk out of commission, there was only one objective third party she could truly trust. The retired Inquisitor's head and shoulders appeared in hologram in the air before her.

"Hello, Kira—I mean, Admiral Miyaru."

"Eben."

When she said his name, he smiled that roguish smile of his. Unfortunately, her enjoyment of the look was marred by her knowledge that her security forces had just locked his daughter in the brig of the *Paladin*. Kira wasn't looking forward to sharing this intel with him. Fortunately, she had another excuse for the call.

She told him about Captain Nevers' disappearance and his crew's suspicions. His face drew down into a frown and his eyes darkened as she talked, so that by the time she had finished her recap he looked every bit like the Inquisitor she had imagined before meeting him—grim-faced, lips pressed into a straight line, unflinching.

"Can you confirm any of these rumors?" Kira asked.

"Even if I had full security clearance, I don't have access to MOXA systems. And if I did have access to their systems, this isn't the sort of thing they like to formalize on the record. That said, I know they have space on the Molten Cage for... enhanced interrogations."

"Interrogation? What does MOXA want to interrogate him for? Unless..." Another string of curses leaped from her tongue as her blood ran cold. This time even Harmony's presence seemed to recede, as if running for cover.

"What is it?" Eben asked.

"I just handed that Kryl parasite over to Aganaki."

"Yes, with a directive to determine their purpose and create a method for detecting them. So what?"

"So it's Aganaki we're talking about." Eben knew the minister's reputation as well as she did. "I just gave him a parasite designed to infect *people* and asked him to experiment with it. Experiments like that require subjects."

He looked away, troubled, but he didn't object to her small leap of logic.

She never should have trusted that snake of a minister. He had no right to kidnap her pilot. If Osprey's and Spector's suspicions were right—and when was the last time the two of them agreed on anything?—Well... let's just say she was glad she had hung on to that geode. It was one of the few things that was capable of effectively countering the parasite in a pinch—and unlike a surgical bot or the space side of an airlock, it was small enough to strap onto her utility belt.

Kira thought about putting her XO in charge so she could blow down the door of the Cage and bring her pilot home. But Colonel Volk was still in dire straits in the hospital wing. She'd have to appoint another officer to watch the *Paladin of Abniss* while she was gone. She schooled her emotions and turned back to Eben.

"Inquisitor, can you stand by?"

"Of course."

She walked back out to the bridge. Spector hobbled to her feet.

"You know how to fly a Fleet shuttle, don't you?"

"My flight certification is expired," Her brows knit down, and she nodded. "But yes, sir, I can do it."

"Then you're with me. In the meantime, fetch Major Seklor. He'll be manning the destroyer while we're gone."

"On it, sir." Spector departed.

Kira walked back into the war room with Eben's hologram.

Sharing the news about his daughter could wait. She ignored the twinge of guilt, smiled, and said, "Can you get me into the Molten Cage? I want to pay MOXA a little surprise visit."

Private craft weren't allowed to dock at the Molten Cage as they were considered a security risk. So Eben joined them *en route*, leaving his private plane in orbit and transferring to the Fleet shuttle through the airlock.

Once Eben was safely aboard, Spector, at the helm, directed them toward the outer barricade of the Molten Cage, which looked like a vast sphere of lace. It was actually constructed of thinly hammered aluminite that was wired with an energy repulsion field that could be activated in case of emergencies to prevent break-ins—or break-outs.

After exchanging Fleet passcodes—provided by Eben—with flight control, they passed through a hole in the lace, matched orbital rotation with the spinning ring of the station, and docked.

"Inquisitor," said the young warden who greeted them at the first security checkpoint. "No one told us you were coming."

"Surprise inspection." In reality, there was no such inspection, but they had been able to get this far on his word alone and it was worth keeping up appearances. "Alert your commanding officer."

"Command looks good on him," Harmony whispered privately.

*Almost as good as that uniform*, Kira thought back. Instead of rank, Inquisitors had a special symbol on their shoulders that distinguished them from other SDF officers—a pair of scales representing justice. A board of multi-colored medals decorated his chest over his heart, and sharp crimson stripes ran down his pressed trousers. An embroidered gavel marked each cuff at his wrist.

Oh, and he was armed. Inquisitors always carried a sword, and Eben obviously knew how to use it. The silver-handled rapier carved like a hawk's head was a not-so-subtle nod to tradition—but truthfully, in tight quarters like these, the sword was as effective as a blaster and a fair bit less likely to scorch an ally with an ill-timed ricochet.

The young warden swallowed, then disappeared into a door in his guard booth. He returned fifteen minutes later with the chief warden. He and Eben talked privately for a moment before the old man acquiesced and led the three of them into the depths of the Cage.

They passed several areas full of individual prison cells, cubes made of transparent aluminite and stacked on top of each other. Armed security guards in Imperial crimson patrolled steel catwalks, looking down through long angled walls of glass on their captives.

They finally came to a quiet hallway at the back of the facility, where the chief warden stopped before a sealed door. Solid metal, no window. "This is as far as I can take you. The other side of that door is MOXA jurisdiction and not even I have access."

"Thanks, Aaron," Eben said, "we'll take it from here."

"We're even now, Osprey. Got it?"

"My word is bond." The phrase had an official sense of finality to it. They gripped each other's forearms briefly and then the chief warden hurried away.

After he was gone, Eben nodded at her.

*All right, Harmony, you're up.*

"Are you certain you wish to continue, Admiral? I can unlock the door, but as you know the Molten Cage is wired into the Ansible network, and I won't be able to stop the alert notices that will be dispatched."

She thought about the repercussions—played through the political aleacc game in her mind. The Executive Council of the Fleet would find out, and she doubted Gitano could protect her. She'd likely lose what little ground she'd gained with Chairman Card and Minister Aganaki on the agenda to halt Colonization efforts. Once her actions here were made public, her career would be doomed. The people already hated her for trying to lock down the flow of refugees from Ariadne to new colonies. If they found out she'd broken into MOXA territory, she'd be tarred and feathered publicly.

But then she thought about her pilot being abducted by MOXA, and a righteous fury ripped through her. Kira ran her hands through her short-cropped hair, whisking away a film of sweat. She hadn't felt this angry since the end of the Kryl War, on the day she and Captain Ruidiaz were ordered to deliver the payload to Planet K. The memory of that day's events still sent a pang of regret through her abdomen. The Kryl had invaded planets, destroyed colonies, murdered millions. They *deserved* the destruction she and Ruidiaz had been sent to deliver. She just wished she'd been able to deliver it herself.

This fury was different, since it was directed against a member of her own species, rather than a distant xeno hive queen. But it was no less righteous.

"Do it," she told Harmony.

It took the briefest of moments. The door clicked, unlocked, and Spector pulled it open.

"What in Earth's name—"

The guard's exclamation was cut off as Spector stepped through the door and delivered an uppercut to his chin. His head snapped back and he slid down the wall, holding his mouth as blood from his clipped tongue poured down his chin.

Eben's sword whipped out and held firm along the neck

of the other guard with a MOXA badge on his shirt. "If you draw that blaster you'll never get to use it."

The guard swallowed and nodded shakily, slowly removing his hand from the weapon. These weren't Fleet guards, they were MOXA agents. Clever and strong, but not accustomed to Inquisitors holding swords at their throats. They spent most of their time guarding harmless bureaucratic flunkies—or babysitting an unvisited, off-the-books section of the Molten Cage. Surprise was on their side.

"Where's the pilot?" Kira demanded. She'd been forced to leave her own sidearm on the shuttle, so she commandeered the guard's weapon and tapped it lightly on the head of the second guard, the one Spector had knocked down. It turned out to be a man with a square jaw, mid thirties, just graying at the temples.

"I... I don't know, ma'am."

She slammed the butt of the pistol into his temple, and he cried out. "You will address me as *sir* or *Admiral*. Now, where's my pilot?"

"You're too late." His eyes skipped down the hall then back to her. "Sir."

"Up." Kira grabbed his arm and twisted it behind him, using the grip as leverage to haul the man to his feet and lead him down the hallway.

Unlike the prison blocks they'd passed on their way, these cells were isolated, individual, and closed with the same kind of heavy security door Harmony had just unlocked. They passed a small triage area where a few rough-looking doctors had set up portable medical equipment—nothing like the surgical bots in ORs on the *Paladin*, but plenty of monitoring tools. Their eyes grew wide when they saw the gun in her hands, and more than one of them jumped for their tabs. Spector shot one tab out of a doctor's hands, to a cacophony of frightened yelps.

"Which room is it?" Kira said, pressing the blaster into the guard's temple, this time using the barrel instead of the butt-end.

He winced from the heat of the barrel against his skin, then nodded at the second to last cell in the row.

"Harmony, get the—thank you."

The door's lock clicked halfway through her request. "Watch my back," she said to Eben as she shoved the MOXA agent away. Eben nodded and took up a position beside the cell's opening as he watched the man retreat. He gripped the rapier with one hand and jerked his head toward the cell.

Kira stepped through the doorway and entered a horror show.

Captain Nevers was suspended on an angled sheet of metal like some kind of ritual sacrifice, suspended by his wrists and pinned at the ankles. He still wore his Fleet uniform, crimson and navy blue, but it was wrinkled and stained with sweat and blood. He was whimpering and bruised, and dried blood coated his nostrils, mouth and chin.

The righteous fury burned within. Her eyes fell on the other two men in the room—a MOXA agent, judging by his grey uniform to match the so-called "guards" they'd just walked through, and Minister Aganaki dressed like he was going out for a nice dinner.

"What the hell is going on here?" Kira shouted.

Aganaki turned slowly toward her. Then a long frown drew down his lips. "You have no jurisdiction here, Admiral."

"Like hell I don't. That's my pilot you're torturing."

"This is not torture."

"This is a darksite in a prison! What the fuck do you call it?"

"Research," he said.

Her blood turned to liquid nitrogen in her veins, and a chill washed over her as he confirmed her fears. Her righteous fury turned to shock, which gave way to a cold, implacable determination.

She unclipped the geode from where it had been hanging from her belt, and twisted its marble handle.

A bright green ambience rushed out of three triangular apertures in the multi-faceted stone sphere, and filled the room with light. Although it should have cast long angular shadows wherever it came into contact with a person, it *didn't*. Every corner of the room was filled with green light and no shadows, almost as if the light was not light but some kind of gas or liquid.

Nevers reacted violently.

He arched his back against the wall and thrashed with a strength his weakened, battered body shouldn't have been capable of. He screamed until his voice broke. Then he went silent and sagged.

Aganaki and the MOXA agent had turned, stunned, to watch him. The agent staggered back, obviously shocked by the violence of his reaction. But Aganaki? He crept close, watching intently as the parasite crawled out of the captain's ear, leaching a trail of his blood.

While Nevers lay still, breathing fast and shallow, the worm-shaped Kryl—no bigger than the length of her thumbnail—crept out of his ear and thrashed violently, just like Nevers had. Whatever Telos technology was at work in this geode, it caused a physical affliction to the Kryl that was like no weapon she'd ever seen. If Ruidiaz had had this relic when he delivered the payload, to Planet K, maybe he would have...

But no. That was in the past. She couldn't think like that now.

Nevers moaned. The MOXA agent jiggled something in his fist, releasing the manacles from the captain's wrist and dropping him to the floor.

Nevers pivoted and slapped his hand over the parasite on the wall. His movements were slow and weak, but determined. The parasite, affected by the relic's power, hardly seemed to notice what was happening.

"Wait!" Aganaki shouted.

But Nevers didn't listen. He ground the worm to paste against the wall, snarled at it like an animal, and turned eyes filled with a wicked glee up to Aganaki. Nevers swallowed, then looked past the minister at her.

"Admiral," he rasped, and collapsed, no longer moving.

The MOXA agent rushed out and retrieved the medics. Two came running in and tended to Nevers. They lifted him onto a stretcher and fixed an oxygen mask over his face.

Aganaki didn't move to interrupt his care. However, when the medics began to carry him out, Aganaki stepped in the way, laying a hand on the stretcher.

"If you don't move," said Kira, "I'll make you."

The MOXA agent drew a blaster of his own. "Try it."

Eben, standing in the doorway with his rapier held poised, out away from his body, wouldn't be able to get to her before the agent squeezed the trigger.

Aganaki held up a hand, forestalling violence. "We made a deal, remember?"

"This was *not* part of the deal," Kira said.

"He was being held with cause—suspicions that ended up being well founded, I might add. He confessed to it. He also helped us obtain some key information about the Kryl during our... discussions."

"It's not right. You could have done these experiments another way."

"Not one that would have yielded results so quickly. And I have every right. Would you care to take this to the Emperor?"

266

She would lose that battle, she knew. Kira shook her head.

"Now we know more about the parasites and what they're capable of—you asked me to do that, remember?"

"I didn't give you permission to use my pilot as a test subject," she spat.

"You didn't have to."

She glared, but Minister Aganaki's calm confidence unsettled her, made her hesitate. She expected him to lash out. When he didn't, she realized that it was because in here, he had complete power over her. For crying out loud, he was running a detention facility out of the blasted Molten Cage.

"I'll let the pilot go—*and* I'll keep this little incident quiet —but only if you hand over that relic," Aganaki said.

In fact... he'd *wanted* her to come here. The realization slowly dawned. He must have arranged the whole thing— letting rumors leak to Spector, letting them "force" their way in here. No wonder it was so easy. This was a trap.

"And what if I don't?"

He shrugged. "We keep Captain Nevers for future experiments. We always need volunteers—willing or unwilling, it doesn't matter to me."

She clenched her teeth so hard her jaw muscles quivered. He met her gaze with a politician's patience.

"Admiral?" Harmony asked in her mind. "Say something."

*Do you see another way out of this?*

"Not presently."

She glanced over at Eben. He was eyeballing the MOXA agent's blaster. Two more had closed in behind him—the guards from before. The ex-inquisitor still held his sword out. He'd do some damage, if it came to blows, but there was no way they would get out of the room unscathed.

Kira didn't want to give up the relic. It was the only leverage she had left. She hated what Aganaki did to Captain

Nevers—it was a betrayal of her principles. You don't torture your own people!

But she had an opportunity to rescue the captain, and here was Aganaki, offering her a way out.

"Fine," Kira said. She twisted the handle of the geode counter-clockwise, eliminating the glowing green light, and tossed it to Aganaki.

He caught it, then stepped aside. The medics pushed the stretcher out of the room. Kira stalked after them, empty handed, with Eben at her back.

# TWENTY-FIVE

Casey fumed in the dank, stinking hole, ready to fight someone. But there was no enemy here to fight. No xenos, no parasite-infected starfighter pilots, no dirty squadron commander.

Colonel Walcott's voice echoed in her mind, saying, *You must have the courage to do what's right, even when it's hard. The obstacle is the way.*

Her father was going to be ashamed of her. Half of his career had been spent enforcing the rules and regulations, and here she was breaking them to take down Spector. Even if she could prove that she was right about the commander—and oh, there was so much to be right about—he'd never approve of the methods she'd used to bring the secrets to light.

Casey had always had a fiercely independent streak that drove her father mad—it was why he'd sent her away to school as a kid. What else was new? He'd never understand.

She sat alone in that room for hours upon end. No one came to visit her. Did her father know she was here? Was Spector preventing her friends from coming to visit her?

Surely, had any of them known and been allowed to visit, they would have.

Surprisingly, the longer she thought about what had gotten her thrown in the brig in the first place, the more certain she became that she was right.

Right didn't mean she'd be vindicated, however. The Fleet was full of all sorts of people, and sometimes that meant bad people got away with things they shouldn't have. That's why the Emperor had created the Inquisitors as a body of justices *independent* of Fleet oversight.

And she was sure that a person like her father, no matter how disappointed he would be, would be able to look at the facts and come to a rational—and correct—conclusion.

Spector drugged Colonel Volk. She must have. That's why she'd been switching his pills, which the medic realized right before she grabbed them. Instead of giving Volk the medicine that would pull the metals out of his body, she was either giving him a placebo or more poison.

If only the analysis had been completed...

Spector must have worked hard to get close to the XO. That's why Volk kept showing up at their training sessions. He had a soft spot for Spector, and she took advantage of his trust, using the opportunity to poison him in small doses without him noticing it was happening.

Just like she'd offed her former commanders, Spector was planning to do the same to Volk in order to continue rising through the ranks.

Or was there another explanation?

At this point in her reasoning, Casey became hardened with a new determination.

She *had* to finish the analysis on those pills. She *had* to find proof of Spector's wrongdoing—hard evidence that could not be denied.

And to do that, she first had to get out of the brig.

Why hadn't Park and Yorra come to visit?

Underneath all these thoughts, anxiety about Nevers continued to plague her.

Once again, he was missing—only this time she wasn't there for him. He was on his own.

Despite her certainty about Spector's crimes, she felt an awful, gnawing ache at being unable to help her wingman. Casey had a deep-seated need to be useful, and Nevers was in way over his head. She just had to hope that the Spirit of Old Earth was watching over him.

After a while, she slept fitfully, waking what seemed like every few hours with a gasp and covered in sweat. The only way she could mark the time was by the meals, delivered through a small window that opened electronically and pushed in her rations.

She was on meal number four when the ship lurched and reoriented itself.

*We're moving,* she thought. *Where?*

There was a brief pause, and then an intense nausea that was incredibly familiar. She braced herself against the bench in the cell and focused on her breathing. After a moment, it passed.

The *Paladin of Abniss* had just jumped into hyperspace.

# TWENTY-SIX

**E**lya woke in the sick bay and gasped, "I know where she's going. I know where Overmind X is going!"

He bucked and tried to roll out of bed, only to find that he was tangled up in electrical lines and oxygen tubes. Sharp pains pulled at his inner elbows and nostrils and the back of his head. He yanked the oxygen mask off his face and was about to pull the metal applicator out of his spinal port when three medics rushed in and laid their hands on him, forcing him back down.

"Let me up," he said, pushing against them with weak arms. His throat was raw and it hurt to talk. In fact, *everything* hurt—it felt like a heavy cloud of throbbing pain pressing down all over his body.

"Captain Nevers, stop fighting us. Please! We're trying to help you!"

The words finally wormed their way into his brain. It took an effort to let go of the instinctive struggle that had kept him fighting against the worst Agent Callus and Minister Aganaki could do—and alive when the parasite was inside of him.

But he'd killed it. He'd crushed it to paste in his hand. He remembered that now.

Slowly, calmed by the memory, he stopped resisting. One by one, the medics relaxed and let go of him. Only then did they set about checking his vitals and reattaching all the wires, hoses and tubes he'd pulled off. One person reached under his bed and tugged on the spinal port applicator. Right as he was thinking this, the medic pressed a button. His pain receded like a low tide. He sighed deeply and sank into the narrow hospital bed.

The medics were just finishing up when Park and Yorra appeared in the doorway.

"Fancypants! You're up," Yorra said brightly, stepping inside.

"*Man* is it good to see you!" Park added. He put an arm around Yorra's shoulder, but she slipped out of his grasp and shuffled a step to the side. Elya glanced between them.

"Right back at'cha," he croaked. One of the medics handed him a glass of water and he took a grateful sip. The painkillers made his tongue feel thick and clumsy. "You two okay?"

"We're good," Yorra said.

"Yeah, man, nothing like you went through."

Although Park smiled, Elya realized something wasn't quite right. He decided it must be some kind of lover's quarrel and that it was none of his business. MOXA agents, he could do. Getting in the middle of someone else's romantic conflict? *Nothankyouverymuch.* "So you heard, huh? Is this… Are we on the *Paladin*?"

They both nodded. Park said, "Except, not in orbit around Ariadne. We're in hyperspace transit to the Elturis System."

Elya blew out his breath and sagged back into the thin

pillows. "That's good news. We don't have much time. I need to speak to Admiral Miyaru."

Park and Yorra exchanged a meaningful glance.

"What?" he asked.

"She asked us to bring you to her the minute you woke up."

"Oh." A foggy memory of her tall, broad-shouldered figure backlit in the doorway of the MOXA interrogation chamber flashed into his mind. She had been holding the geode. "That makes sense. Well, I'm awake now. Let's go."

"Hah!" Park snorted. "Glad it makes sense to you, hombre. What the hell happened? We did the thing at the Archives and you missed our rendezvous. A day later, the Admiral and Osprey's dad bring you in on a stretcher."

The Inquisitor had been there? Huh.

"I'll fill you in on the way." He swung his feet to the floor and had to brace himself on his knees while the world tilted on its axis.

"Easy, Fancypants," Yorra said as she came to his aid. "Heh. You don't have any pants on."

He looked down and blushed, then tucked the covers back over his hospital gown. "I don't want to, but if I have to see the Admiral butt ass naked, I will. This is that important."

"Cool your jets, flyboy," Yorra said. "Always so impatient."

"This is mission critical information!" he protested. "Can someone get me some pants?"

Park jogged out of the room and came back with a change of clothes, a hoverchair, and a devious smirk. Rolled up in a spiky little ball on the seat was Hedgebot. When Elya reached out, the bot unfurled from its defensive position and leaped into his hand.

"Found him hiding in your bunk after we jumped to hyperspace. He's a little skittish these days."

"Temporary measures. Thanks for taking care of him, Naab. You're a good friend."

Park beamed. Hedgebot beeped and scurried around the room, avoiding all people except for Elya.

The medics reluctantly unhooked him from their contraptions, including the clunky spinal port. He slowly, painstakingly dressed himself.

As they pushed him across the ship, he had to force himself to stop bouncing his toe on the footrest. Hedgebot moved ahead of them, climbing the curved walls of the starship and pulsing a cool blue that masked the real and imminent danger lying ahead.

On the bridge, Admiral Miyaru stood at the center of a flurry of a dozen navigators, technicians and flight engineers working their stations. Harmony's hologram hovered over the command couch, which was set into an area of cleared space in the back third of the room. The shipmind and the admiral had a full view of the crew and the main viewscreen, which, at the present moment, was keyed to an opaque navy blue blur so as not to give people nausea as the hyperspace stream slipped by.

On the way here, his friends had filled him in on how Harmony had protected them by altering the visitor's logs, their suspicions about Lieutenant Colonel Spector, and how she'd had Raptor thrown in the brig with no visitors allowed for "attacking" her. It was a real mess.

But first there was a more pressing issue he had to deal with. He had to convince Admiral Miyaru to take his predictions about Overmind X's movements seriously.

"Captain Nevers," the admiral said. "I'm glad to see you up and about."

"Thanks to you, sir. I owe you my life."

She fixed hard eyes on him and stepped closer. "Captain, the only thing you owe me is an explanation. After what you just went through, I'm inclined to hear you out, but you sure pissed off MOXA in the worst way. You should know better than to attract the attention of the Empire's most secretive ministry. Their secrets have secrets, and they don't like prying eyes."

Hedgebot scurried to the farthest corner of the room, as far away from everyone else as it could get. Nevers wished he could follow, but he rose painstakingly out of the chair and found he could stand on his own two feet now. He craned his neck back to meet the admiral's agate eyes. "Sir, those relics are the key to stopping Overmind X. MOXA was concealing mission critical information."

"You should have come to me before causing such a ruckus at the church."

He glanced over at Harmony, whose hologram gave absolutely no sign of her role in that situation. "No offense, sir, but you wouldn't have believed me if I came to you without evidence."

She sighed heavily and stared down at him for a long minute, apparently thinking.

Standing wasn't as painful as he expected, largely due to the drugs still pouring through his veins. He drew himself up as best as he could and saluted the admiral. "Sir, permission to speak freely?"

Her face darkened, but she nodded.

"Our priority needs to be finding Overmind X and stopping her from getting ahold of any more of those Telos relics."

"Where do you think we're going, Captain? Our scouts determined that she was on course toward the Elturis System. We're going to intercept her."

Elya shook his head. "She beat us there. I just hope we're not too late."

"What?" she asked in a voice that was soft and laced with danger.

"She's already been on the *Maiden of Kali*."

The admiral's straight mouth turned down into a deep frown. "*On* the ship? You're sure?"

"I saw it." He told her about the intimate connection he'd established with Overmind X when the parasite was in him, and how he'd been able to access her memories—even some of the ones she didn't want him to see. The bustling movement and discussions about hyperspace calculations among the technicians, buffered by the floor space between the command couch and the battle stations, meant their discussion was kept mostly private as long as they spoke in low voices. Yorra and Park stepped in close, forming a tight ring.

"How can you be sure she wasn't just showing you what she *wanted* you to see?" asked Admiral Miyaru.

"I just know."

"I hope you're wrong, Captain."

"Me, too, sir, but I don't think I am."

"Admiral," Harmony said. "We are preparing to exit hyperspace."

"Guess we're about to find out," Miyaru said. "Find something to hold onto."

The three starfighter pilots stepped out of the way and found an empty couch at the back of the room as Miyaru turned to the crew and ordered them to secure themselves. A countdown began in the 360-degree viewscreen, the minutes and seconds mirrored at each of the four cardinal points of the bridge. The navy blue backdrop faded to black and then resolved into a stream of light—stars that streamed by so fast they could only be visualized in a liquid blur of motion. When the countdown reached ten seconds, Hedgebot

277

nuzzled up behind Elya's boot and sank its tiny claws into the padded synthetic near his ankle. Elya tightened his seatbelt.

They lurched forward as the ship dropped out of hyperspace. Or, perhaps it only felt like they lurched forward because everything around them came to an abrupt and nauseating *halt*. It normally didn't affect him this much in his bunk—seeing it happen made the nausea ten times worse. But the bridge crew needed to have clear lines of sight in case they dropped into a risky situation, where an extra second to respond meant averting disaster.

Whatever he'd been expecting to find, it wasn't this.

Cracked pieces of battle-scarred ships drifted in space around them. His sharp pilot's eyes picked out the wing of a Sabre, the tail of a Solaran light cruiser, the hull of a shuttle— even the vac-suited body of an ejected pilot as it floated across the scene. Thousands of scraps of metal floated between the larger pieces, some five hundred meters wide, others no bigger than his fist.

The voyager's Fleet security detail had been annihilated.

Yorra chewed her nails beside him. Park muttered darkly under his breath.

"Earth's blood," Admiral Miyaru cursed. "They must have been ambushed." She looked down and knotted her fists for a moment, then raised her head. "Captain Nevers!"

"Yes, Admiral?" He pushed himself back to his feet.

"Where is she headed next?"

"I—that I'm not sure about, sir." He glanced over at the crew, whose eyes were pinned on him. How much did they know? How much could he share?

"Dammit, now is not the time for secrets. Secrets about those damned relics are what got us into this mess in the first place. Now where is she going? Think!"

He never imagined, when it happened, that he'd so soon

have occasion to *regret* smashing that xeno parasite against the wall, but now he did, for just a brief moment. He could have used it to make contact with her again.

The thought made him shiver.

"Nevers!" the admiral barked.

"I don't know, sir. She wants the relics—badly. She's obsessed with them. It stands to reason that if she's here, there's a relic nearby."

"Is it on the planet, like it was last time? The colonists were supposed to settle on the third planet from this system's sun."

"It wasn't that kind of discussion, sir. Maybe there's something in that book from the Archives. MOXA knows more about where to find these relics than anyone."

Admiral Miyaru growled and slammed a fist down on the back of her command couch.

He glanced at Park and Yorra for help. They came to stand at his side. Park gripped his shoulder in camaraderie.

He let his squad support him for a minute before a thought struck him. "How did you know they were coming to the Elturis System? How did you know to jump *here*, of all places, right where it happened?"

"Because this is the region they should have been in when the *Maiden of Kali* missed their last check-in. They must have been ambushed at the moment they dropped out of hyperspace."

He gazed out the viewscreen at the scattered debris of a dozen Solaran starships. As more ships in their entourage dropped out of hyperspace at safe distances and moved back into formation, he realized that this was nothing like the evacuation of Robichar, where they'd been alone overseeing the mission with a couple wings of starfighters and a flock of defenseless longhaulers full of civilians to protect. This time, Admiral Miyaru had brought along a proper armada.

They had the manpower to stand and fight, if it came down to it.

If only they could find Overmind X and her hive.

"Where exactly is the voyager?" asked Elya, scanning the debris.

The admiral quickly clued into what he was suggesting, and used her comms to broadcast to the other ship captains. Together, they began to scan the region of space where the battle had taken place. One of the corvettes eventually located a piece of the *Maiden of Kali*—their Ansible, which had been burned out of its metal mounting as if by acid, but otherwise left completely intact—not a blast mark or scratch on it.

"Strange," Elya said.

Admiral Miyaru had the *Paladin's* sensors do a detailed scan of the debris floating in the region and processed the models through the AI. Harmony brought the image up on a holodeck, and the crew set to work analyzing it.

They soon confirmed that none of the large pieces could be clearly identified as belonging to the *Maiden of Kali*. They found pieces to most of the Fleet ships in the security escort —like the fragments of a light cruiser he'd visually identified when they arrived—but nothing that matched the sleek curves of the brand new voyager the Colonization Board had commissioned, and which Elya had gone to celebrate that day at the spaceport.

It could mean only one thing.

"They must have taken the ship," said Admiral Miyaru.

"And the people still on it."

Miyaru clenched her jaw. "Come with me."

She led him, Park and Yorra to the nearest war room, the one she reserved for her own use, and closed the door. "Stand over there and don't speak until I call on you."

She sat in the chair that faced the door and took a deep breath.

Holograms of half a dozen people began to materialize in the chairs around the table, their forms constructed of light, until five of the chairs were occupied by three men and two women. The holograms were so realistic that you almost couldn't tell the people weren't physically present, except for the occasional flicker.

Elya blanched when Minster Aganaki appeared with an antique paper folder in his hands. The minister glanced at Elya, then looked away with only the barest hint of recognition that made his cheeks burn in anger. Agent Callus sat beside his boss, frowning.

The Minister and the MOXA agent were "seated" across from a stern-looking woman in a stiff pantsuit, and a hugely obese man with soft hands and round, ruddy cheeks. It was this man who spoke first.

"What news, Admiral?" he demanded.

"Mr. Chairman, we have reason to believe the Kryl hive has commandeered the *Maiden of Kali*," said Admiral Miyaru. No beating around the bush with her.

The other woman in hologram, a dark-skinned admiral about twenty years Miyaru's senior, briefly closed her eyes. "And the security escort?" she asked.

Miyaru shook her head. "Destroyed, sir. Completely. Harmony, if you will please show Admiral Gitano what we found."

The AI brought up the scan of the debris from the battle.

"How is this possible?" Chairman Card demanded, gesturing widely with open hands. "When you evacuated Robichar, you successfully defended a dozen longhaulers against this hive with a single destroyer. How could they have wiped out two destroyers, half a dozen light cruisers and twice as many corvettes?"

"For starters," Admiral Miyaru said, "they had the advantage of surprise. Overmind X already knew where the *Maiden* was going. In an ambush, a much smaller force can easily overcome a larger one, especially with how the Kryl communicate. Secondly, we now know that during the Robichar evacuation, the Kryl were focused on landing on the moon's surface and locating the relic they were searching for. They only engaged us to give the rest of their forces time to make ground."

"This is your fault." Chairman Card pointed at Admiral Gitano. "Your security escort should have been better prepared."

"No one is ever prepared to be ambushed, Mr. Chairman. That's why they call it an ambush."

"Then you should have sent a larger force to protect the colonists!"

"If you'll recall, you decided—*against* our recommendation—to move forward with this voyage."

He blustered some more, but Admiral Gitano remained stoic, apparently content to let him lie in the hole he'd dug. When the admiral didn't budge, the chairman turned to Minister Aganaki for support.

"It is in the past," said the minister. "What I want to know is why the Kryl have taken the voyager hostage. They've never been interested in our starships before."

"I was hoping you could tell us that," Admiral Miyaru said, her eyes never leaving Aganaki's face.

He pushed his tongue into his cheek. "We have our theories."

"I'm listening."

He glanced at Elya, then back at the admiral. "What else do you know?"

"You first," Admiral Miyaru said. "And don't forget, there are people's lives at stake here."

Aganaki opened the folder in his hand and flipped through a sheaf of *actual* paper. Elya could see that one side of each sheet was ragged as though it had been torn from a book.

There was only one old paper book with information about the relics that he knew about. Elya's breath caught in his throat as Aganaki read a passage:

*What Oberon didn't know was that I befriended the last Engineer who told me about seven pieces of technology hidden away among the stars, designed to protect their people against the Kryl. They told me that we could use these weapons as a means of defense should the aliens grow territorial and aggressive in the future, as is their nature. While the Engineer chose not to disclose the locations of these weapons to Oberon, they gave me clues that would help me find them in case of emergency. I've written what I can below. As a precaution to prevent this information from falling into the wrong hands, I must be cryptic.*

*The Telos hid seven prime relics across the galaxy...*

> *One in a cave on a forest moon*
> *Two in the ocean at high noon*
> *Three to orbit a broken planet*
> *Four and five in tombs of granite*
> *Six on a starship lost to time*
> *Seven behind the shrine.*

The room rang in the silence.

"That's it?" Elya demanded, outraged. Did he really get tortured for a *freaking poem*?

Admiral Miyaru glared at him. Heat bloomed in his chest

283

and swirled over his face. Elya stared at his feet and clenched his hands behind his back. "Sorry, sir."

"Who is this boy?" Chairman Card demanded. "And why is he even in here?"

*Boy?* he thought. *You fat son of a...*

"Captain Nevers was taken hostage by the Kryl on Robichar," Admiral Miyaru said smoothly. "He's the only one who's spoken to Overmind X directly."

*More than spoken to*, he thought.

"And besides," she went on, "while he can be a royal pain in everyone's ass, what starfighter worth his wings isn't?"

The words made Aganaki chuckle—ironically, he was sure. Gitano's broad face split into a smile. Even Card seemed to unpucker his butt a little bit.

"Tell us your theory, Nevers," she said.

A voice in his head that belonged to a little refugee boy told him he had no business even being present in this room, surrounded by high-ranking Solaran officials. But a second voice—one that would star in his nightmares, he was sure—wouldn't let him forget what the hive queen had shown him.

"Overmind X took the children on that ship," he said.

Card leaned back like he'd been slapped. Gasps and murmurs ringed the table, punctuated by the clearing of throats.

"They probably killed the rest of the colonists," he added, "but those kids still have a chance... if we can figure out where she's going, we could interce—"

"Why would she keep the children alive?" Agent Callus interrupted as he leaned forward, resting his forearms on the table.

Elya paused for a long second to glare at his former torturer, irritated by the interruption and scared as hell. Yet a glint in Callus's cold eyes made him think the man was

284

genuinely trying to help him out. Despite the pain Callus had inflicted upon him, it hadn't been personal. That was the past. They were on the same side now. They shared a mission.

Elya glanced to Admiral Miyaru for support, then took a deep breath. Knowing Callus couldn't physically leap across the room and strangle him may have boosted his confidence in that moment. Not that he'd ever admit it. "Because she wants to turn them into weapons of her own, using those parasites."

Card flinched, Callus clenched his muscular jaw, while Miyaru and Gitano turned their mouths down into twin frowns. The secretary looked horrified. Only the minister remained unfazed.

Aganaki set the folder down on a table in front of him—his table was a few inches higher than the one they sat at, making the folder seem to levitate. "This idea of turning children has not been demonstrated by the evidence we've collected, and we must be scientific. So far, empirical evidence suggests that the parasite causes people to hallucinate—to see the visions she wants you to see." He looked pointedly at Elya.

"That's not what it was designed for," Elya said, "merely a side effect. I saw her try to turn a boy on Robichar. I think it's how they evolve, the Kryl." He thought about how Subject Zero had been able to resist the relic's forcefield of emerald power better than the other xenos. "They find another species that's better than they are, and they adapt the ability to their own." He swallowed against a very dry throat. "She makes them one of the swarm."

"Why children?" asked Gitano.

"If it is true, as Captain Nevers seems to think, then it is likely because their minds are still malleable," said the minister. "And their bodies are more readily capable of adapting to sudden… changes… that no doubt occur after the parasite is introduced to their system."

Card's mouth hung open and he looked like he wanted to gag. "We can't let that happen. We *cannot* let that happen. If word spreads that people are at risk of being kidnapped by xenos and turned into one of them, they'll refuse to be relocated and Ariadne will be overru—"

Card withered under the minister's pitiless gaze.

"I don't intend to *just let that happen*, Alvin. Now, hold it together, man."

The chairman snapped his mouth shut and leaned back in his chair.

"Focus," Admiral Miyaru said. "We have to figure out where they went."

"She's right," Callus added. "Not just for the children. If they find another relic out there, things could get a lot worse."

"I agree," Admiral Gitano said. "We need to understand the level of the threat so we can formulate an appropriate response."

Aganaki glanced down at the paper he'd read the poem from. He looked uncertain. "We have our theories but… suffice to say, if they find more of the relics, the danger to the Solaran people is at least equal to the danger we pose to the Kryl."

"Nuclear?" asked Gitano.

"Or worse."

"Planet busters?" asked Card, using the common term for antimatter bombs.

"Maybe."

"Are we talking an extinction-level threat?" asked Gitano.

Minister Aganaki shrugged. "We don't know for certain."

"We need more information than what's in that vague passage," said Elya. All that effort he put into searching for information, and this is all they had? He could hardly believe what he'd gone through for it. A stinking poem?

Aganaki's face broke out in his first real smile of the session. He turned it upon Elya. "Oh, ye of little faith."

Admiral Miyaru leaned in to brace her hands on the tabletop. "Tell us what you know, Aganaki."

"It will cost you."

She took a deep breath and huffed out of her nose. "Whatever it takes."

He met Elya's eyes. *"One in a cave on a forest moon. Does that not sound familiar?"*

"Cave? Robichar was a forest moon, but…" He felt his eyes grow wide. "The cave the boy saw. That's number one. The one we found."

"Indeed."

"Read it again."

> *One in a cave on a forest moon*
> *Two in the ocean at high noon*
> *Three to orbit a broken planet*
> *Four and five in tombs of granite*
> *Six on a starship lost to time*
> *Seven behind the shrine*

By the time he was finished, he knew that Aganaki had known all along where the relic in the Elturis System would be found. "Which one is here in this system?"

*"Three to orbit a broken planet."*

"Where?"

"We have reason to believe it's in an asteroid that orbits the second planet in this system."

"Not the one we set out to colonize? New Kali is the third planet from the sun."

"The other isn't exactly livable."

287

"We'll finish this later," the admiral said. "Dismissed."

Admiral Miyaru called on Harmony and they set course for the second planet. The intervening transit took agonizing hours, but there was no help for it. Starships moved fast, but space was still vast, and since they were so close to the gravity wells of the planets and their star, hyperspace transit had been taken off the table. They waited impatiently on the bridge. Fortunately, Elya managed to put some food away and was feeling a bit more normal, though still lightheaded and jittery, when they arrived.

"Well, if the Telos wanted their relics to be a secret," Elya said, "they sure picked a good hiding place."

The planet was all busted up, as if from a great war or perhaps an accident of solar physics. A huge chunk was missing from the otherwise round orb of the world, and that chunk had broken up into several massive asteroids that orbited in the region where its moon once had been.

Hell, for all he knew, the thousands of jagged chunks of stone *were* the moon.

"So which one is it?" Park asked.

"No one knows, dummy, that's the whole point," Yorra pointed out, her voice full of disdain. Park did something unusual and stayed quiet for a change, looking like a kicked puppy.

"Harmony," Admiral Miyaru said, "scan the asteroid field for anomalies."

"I'm just glad Aganaki took that relic from us," Elya said to Park and Yorra. "Relieved, honestly."

"You are? Why?"

"Because Overmind X wanted me to bring it to her. I can't do that if I don't have it, so no matter what happens next, at least I won't do that." The parasite may have been out of his head, but her consciousness and greedy hunger lingered in his memory.

Park picked at his teeth. Yorra chewed her lips nervously. They sat on opposite sides of him, still trying to keep their distance from each other. But neither of them scooted away from him. He really wished Osprey were here. She'd know just what to say. She had a way of reassuring them that Elya would never master.

They were a thousand klicks off their mark when the *Paladin's* shields were activated by the AI to deflect range-seeking fire.

"Contact!" a weapons engineer shouted. "Those were Kryl missiles, sir."

A klaxon began to bleat through the ship, calling the crew to arms. As he watched, Kryl ships began to rise out of the asteroid field, filling visible space for a thousand klicks in all directions.

Elya glanced at his friends, whose jaws were strained. That klaxon sang a song their pilot's muscles had been trained to dance to, and not being able to move to the music was agony. No doubt the rest of their squad was even now sprinting through the hangar toward a row of Sabres with canopies open.

"You three," Admiral Miyaru ordered, pointing at them. "Get to your starfighters. Go!"

# TWENTY-SEVEN

For the second time in a month, Kira's forces engaged Overmind X.

This time she came prepared. A full armada of Fleet warships flew at her beck and call. In a matter of minutes, four wings of Sabres had been deployed and were engaging the enemy. Heavy cruisers held their flanks, raking lasers across the Kryl refuelers and scouts, making it hard for them to support the swarm and giving her starfighters time to drive a wedge into the bulk of the enemy forces.

"Admiral, we've located the *Maiden of Kali*," Harmony said.

"Show me."

A yellow outline of the colonial voyager appeared in the main viewscreen. It was located deep within the swarm of Kryl.

"My scanners detect no sign of external damage or hull breach," Harmony added.

"Is anyone alive inside?"

A momentary pause.

"Cannot be determined. There are too many lifeforms in the way to get a clear scan."

"And the shipmind AI?"

"Unresponsive."

Kira bit down on her lip. There could be survivors. The Kryl knew she knew that. They were using the ship as bait.

"We'll have to fight our way to it." Even if it was bait, it wasn't like they could be ambushed now. The heavy cruiser on their left flank rocked as it took the brunt of a barrage of torpedoes against its shields, reinforcing her point.

Was Overmind X toying with her?

"Furies actual, do you copy?"

"Yes, Admiral," Spector said, apparently through gritted teeth. The sound of her wingtip blasters could be heard in the background, a rapid *whump-whump-whump* that was the telltale sign of plasma bolts being flung at the enemy.

"Get your squad to the *Maiden*. Secure the area so we can land Marines and take back the ship."

"Copy that."

"And tell Captain Nevers to keep his eyes peeled for any… unusual flying activity."

"Sir?"

"He'll know what I mean."

"Okay… I'll relay the message."

Kira was too amped up to sit down for the next hour of battle. She paced across the bridge near her command couch while they slowly pressed the Kryl forces back into the asteroid field. The xenos had attached some kind of tug vessel to the *Maiden of Kali* and were hauling it with them each time they retreated. The Furies took down the tug with a couple of well-placed missiles of their own, then pushed back the drones flying a defensive perimeter until they had secured the area.

Meanwhile, Kira had her weapons officer deploy a few

nuclear payloads toward the back half of the swarm, away from the *Maiden*, where she suspected the hive queen directed her forces from concealment. These attacks had the added effect of dusting several hundred asteroids and making the field of battle hazy and dangerous to navigate for small craft and obscuring even Harmony's line of sight.

When the Kryl forces pulled back to regroup, Kira immediately dispatched a platoon of Marines. They docked amidship on the *Maiden of Kali* while the Furies flew patrols around the enormous voyager, taking out straggling Kryl drones and generally giving the Marines time to board.

"Admiral, we've entered the passenger area of the ship," the Marine Sergeant reported. "It's not a pleasant sight."

"What did you find?"

"Death."

"How many?" A pause. "Sergeant, how many?"

"We're only in the first hall but if I had to guess... All of them."

The bridge crew let out a collective gasp and froze at their stations. Kira closed her eyes and sent a silent prayer up to Animus.

"Keep looking for survivors."

As they moved deeper into the huge starship, the Marines engaged several packs of groundlings who were roving through and eating the corpses of dead colonists.

"We made it to the bridge," the Sergeant reported after a lengthy delay. "Entering override code now... Earth's blood!"

"What is it? More dead?"

The Sergeant grunted. "You've got to see this for yourself. Video feed incoming."

A small rectangle on the viewscreen widened into a window showing video from the bodycam of the Marine Sergeant. It took a second for her mind to process what she was seeing. It looked like the back of a dark cave, or a

292

spider's nest, where the floor rolled in heaps and mounds, and thick sheets of webbing hung from the ceiling, making the normally expansive bridge seem cramped and small. Rifle-mounted flashlights skimmed over yellow-white Kryl excretions that had grown over every piece of electronic equipment in the place, although several holoscreens still showed radar/lidar and controls, and lights pulsed as if the computers were still functional. Instead of a view of space outside, a dozen chrysalises lined the viewscreen against the far wall—little pods that came up to about the chest of the Marine. They had been torn open, seemingly from the inside, with pus and webbing and darker splotches that may have been blood decorating the floor around them.

"Like what they did to the place," muttered one of the Marines in a wry voice.

"Someone needs to confiscate their decorating license," said another.

"Whatever was in these pods is out there now," said the Marine Sergeant. "On the ship or… somewhere else."

"Groundlings?" asked Kira.

"Animus knows…"

"Where are the rest of the Kryl?" Kira asked. "I thought the ship would be swarming with them."

"The ones we fought on our way here were stragglers. No real danger."

Kira didn't know what the Kryl had been doing on the bridge, and every instinct in her screamed to shove the ship into the blazing inferno of the nearest star—but not before she made sure there were no survivors.

Something nagged at her mind, causing her to pause.

There was one person who might be able to tell them what the Marines found. She signaled to Harmony.

"Captain Nevers of the Furies, do you read?"

"Loud and clear, Admiral."

293

"Harmony, send him the video feed."

Silence drifted over the line. "Where is this?" he asked in a quiet voice.

"On the bridge of the *Maiden*."

"Oh, Animus. That's not good."

"What is it?"

"Those pods at the back... how tall do you think they are? Three, maybe four feet, right?"

Just then, the video blurred as the Marine Sergeant spun around and fired his rifle in the same motion. Blaster bolts were flung across the camera angle as men began to scream and the sound of rending flesh tore through the connection.

The video feed toppled to the side and then abruptly cut out.

"Fall back!" Kira ordered. "Fall back to the shuttles. Get out of there!"

No one responded. The squad comms the Marines had been using were now filled with ragged breathing and the sound of booted feet. "I don't want to hurt you!" someone shouted moments before they switched their rifle to semi-automatic and depleted the charge magazine by holding down the trigger.

Complete silence followed.

"Sergeant, do you copy?" Kira asked.

Nothing.

"Marines, someone answer me."

Again, nothing.

"Sir!" one of the navigators said. "A new ship just dropped out of hyperspace."

"Kryl?"

"No, sir, I don't think so."

"Identify."

"I think... I think it's a Solaran vessel, sir."

"Fleet?"

"ID just confirmed. Light cruiser is registered to the Ministry of Xeno Affairs."

"How the hell did they get our coordinates?" Kira demanded. It was protocol not to broadcast battle coordinates in case they were intercepted. Fleet command knew they were in system, but not *exactly* where. "Open a channel." The navigator did. "State your business."

No response.

"Aganaki, I know it's you. You'll get your chance at whatever relic we find after we recover it. I don't have the time to babysit you. Fly away until we secure the area."

"Negative, *Paladin*," came the response in the voice of some anonymous MOXA captain she didn't recognize.

"Why the hell not?"

"Orders."

"This is a combat zone. Stand down! That's *my* order."

Instead of standing down, the ship turned its thrusters to maximum and made a beeline for the asteroid field—in particular, a large asteroid near their line about 40 degrees off port.

"*Paladin!*" cried Captain Nevers. "New bogeys on the loose."

Harmony spun up a visual—she caught the tail end of a pack of drones as they poured from where they'd been hiding in the hangar of the *Maiden of Kali*.

They converged on the MOXA ship's trajectory, aiming to intercept.

# TWENTY-EIGHT

Elya's blood turned to ice water in his veins.

Admiral Miyaru—or maybe Harmony—had left the channel she'd been using to converse with him open when the new ship dropped out of hyperspace, so he knew exactly who was on it.

"Furies, we're flying protection," Spector ordered over the broadbeam. "Don't let those drones get within shooting range of the light cruiser."

Strange. Spector had said that so calmly, as if she hadn't been surprised the MOXA ship had shown up when it had.

As if she'd expected it.

But that wasn't what sent chills through his body. The memory of Overmind X's words echoing in his mind did.

*Find your piece of the Inheritance*, she had said, *and bring it to me.*

He'd refused.

*You will*, she had told him.

Elya had been relieved to learn Admiral Miyaru had turned the geode over to Minister Aganaki. Because without it, he couldn't *possibly* fulfill her prediction.

But what if he didn't have to?

What if Minister Aganaki brought the geode instead?

Elya shivered. He didn't have proof, of course, but he didn't need it. He knew deep in his bones what had happened. The geode's power would afford the minister a level of protection that not even a platoon of special forces Marines could provide. He didn't know where Aganaki was going, but he did know there were seven prime relics, seven weapons of great power hidden in the galaxy by the Telos, and the Minister would do anything in his power to get his hands on them.

Preferably before Overmind X did.

How bizarre, he observed, to find his interests aligned with his tormentor.

"Admiral," said Elya over the command channel as he burned after Spector and the four score Sabres she led. The Kryl drones were closing in on the asteroid. "I think we have a problem."

"You think?" the admiral snapped.

He cringed. She was already pissed... but he had to fill her in. No more secrets.

"Uh, sir, is it possible the minister brought the geode with him?"

"How should I know? And why does that matter right now?"

"When they put that parasite in me, it established some kind of psychic connection with Overmind X. She told me to bring her the geode." He dodged around an asteroid as he gained on the drones, pulling up beside Spector with Park and Yorra flagging off his left shoulder. "I was just telling the others that I was glad the minister took the damn thing because I figured he'd squirreled it away somewhere safe. But if Aganaki's here, and he brought it with him... well, that's exactly what she wanted. She's trying to disarm us of the only effective weapon we have against her."

"Earth's last lights..." Admiral Miyaru sighed. "Well, Captain, you'll just have to make sure that doesn't happen. Catch that damn ship."

She cut off the line. Hedgebot scampered up the side wall of the cockpit, hooked its toes into a seam, and cocked its head at him.

"Hang on tight, buddy."

Elya clenched his jaw and veered through a cloud of asteroid dust in the direction the drones were flying. He loosed a volley of blaster fire at the units ranging out ahead of him. As one, the xeno ships dodged down, easily bobbing under his shots.

"These Kryl are flying a lot tighter than the other ones we fought today," Yorra said.

"More flying, less talking!" Spector barked. *Now* she sounded worried. She'd heard the conversation between him and the admiral—the whole squad had. They knew what was at stake, even if he was the only one—apart from the admiral and Casey, who was still stuck in the brig—who knew what the relic could do.

"Sir, yes, sir," Park mumbled, vaguely irritated.

The MOXA ship and the drones were racing toward the same point in the distance, rapidly closing in. As the haze of dust cleared, hard edges materialized into an enormous asteroid that was easily twice as long as the colonial voyager and just as wide. The MOXA cruiser got there first, twisting around the back side of the rock and out of sight.

Drones streamed after it, firing reverse thrusters as they banked into the turn. Half a dozen exploded as his squadmates picked them off. Whoops and hollers went up on squad comms. He barely heard them as his vision narrowed and he pulled ahead of the pack.

He turned in a tight loop and came down so the asteroid was positioned "above" him. He had a clear line of sight on the MOXA ship's trajectory. Elya gasped. There was a small aperture in a familiar triangular shape placed in the back side of the asteroid. It looked precisely like the geode's triangular openings, but on a more massive scale.

The MOXA ship banked through the opening and entered the asteroid.

A dozen drones streamed in on its tail. The rest of them, maybe a hundred in all, split off, turned, and engaged the squad head on.

"There's a bay in the rock!" Elya shouted. His voice on the broadbeam was lost in the confusion. The other pilots were too busy flying erratically to avoid getting targeted. A blood curdling scream ended abruptly as a female pilot's Sabre split in half and exploded against the asteroid's face.

Elya dialed back into the command channel and was immediately admitted by the shipmind. At least *someone* understood his urgency.

"Admiral, there's some kind of hangar in the asteroid. The MOXA ship just went inside."

"Do you have line of sight?"

He craned his neck around. Elya was flabbergasted. Why would the minister take such a risk? People were dying! Even if he did get inside this Telos temple, and even if the relic did protect him from the Kryl, it wouldn't be so effective against mutants like Subject Zero and whomever else they'd managed to turn on the *Maiden*.

"Negative," he said.

"We can't afford to lose that relic to Aganaki's reckless impatience. Damn him for tricking me into letting him have the geode." He couldn't see Admiral Miyaru but he imagined her digging her fingers deep into the command couch.

"Whoa!" said Park. "Incoming fire."

Hedgebot's claws clacked overhead. Elya tilted his Sabre in the direction indicated, and the bot helped guide him through the hail of fire. A blob of liquid hissed against his shields. Some burned through and acid bubbled on the visible edge of his right wingtip.

"Well, *that's* a fun new trick," he observed.

Small rocks pinged off the canopy. Elya opened his stim-chem to full tilt as he banked and looped away, increasing his resistance and reaction time as he tried to get clear.

"Naab! Gears! Where the hell are you?"

Plasma fire from a cruiser that had appeared ten klicks off to his left shredded a dozen drones, giving him a pocket of space to maneuver through. His heads-up display showed a thousand more units, friendly and enemy, rapidly closing on his location.

It was now or never.

"Right behind you, Fancypants," Yorra said. She appeared overhead and shot a drone that had looped up from beneath them.

"Cover me," he said, "I'm going in."

Park and Yorra laid down cover fire as he tilted his Sabre toward the triangular bay.

Thanks to Hedgebot's expert guidance, cover from his squad, and some slick flying of his own, Elya was the first of the Furies into the asteroid.

He jerked the stick back as a sudden gravitational force tried to haul him down to a deck of solid stone.

He nearly bellied out. The runway was tiny, and already crowded. It was constructed of a familiar, swirling marble-like stone, the same sort of material as the relic from Robichar. Right now the runway was covered with the dark, slimy shapes of a few dozen xeno bodies. The MOXA ship had set down at the far end, near an enormous, triangular stone door. Knots of purple-black groundlings boiled out of the drones, half of which had landed and the other half which hovered overhead, taking fire from the MOXA cruiser even as they dropped those pregnant flower-like pods containing more xenos.

Elya fired his reverse thrusters and Hedgebot scrambled to the rear of the cockpit to brace itself. He came down beside the MOXA ship, using his thrusters to toast a few groundlings and make space for his starfighter.

Using the wheels of the landing gear to rotate the Sabre, he turned so the MOXA ship was at his back and hauled on the trigger for his wingtip blasters, sweeping the crosshairs over the pad. Xenos scattered, taking cover behind the drones that had apparently carried them and using the pods like shields.

"How the hell are there so many of them already?" Park demanded. He was hovering near the entrance and shooting at them from above, at a different angle. "And shouldn't the vacuum be sucking their lungs out through their mouths?"

The space they made gave Yorra room to set down. She bounced a little, but settled in. Park came in to take up the last bit of space. Now there were four Solaran starships at the far end of the runway, trapped against the wall and facing off against a xeno force ten times as large across a fifty meter-wide No Man's Land.

Yorra's voice crackled into his ear. "There's artificial gravity in here, why wouldn't there be atmosphere?"

"Inside an asteroid in the middle of nowhere? How?"

"Now is not the time for dumb questions!" Yorra shouted. "Keep them back! Shoot! Shoot!"

They did, taking out dozens more xenos and shredding one or two of the drones. Soon, the stone floor was covered with yellow blood and gore, and the bodies of dozens of dead or dying xenos. To his shock, the stone remained unscathed.

Elya checked to make sure his helmet was airtight, then

popped his canopy and let Hedgebot out. The danger detector did a quick scan and cycled green. *Safe.*

"Oxygen-rich, according to the bot. We can breathe if we need to."

"Not taking the chance, thank you very much," said Park.

He was right. Probably not worth risking it. Elya kept his helmet sealed and took a different risk, drawing his sidearm and jumping down out of his Sabre. He landed on shaky legs. The massive dose of stimchem he just took through his spinal port gave him strength. He'd suffer for it later, but for the moment he felt strong and hyperaware of everything.

"Flight 18, what in the name of Animus are you doing?" Spector demanded over squad comms. She must have finally gotten eyes on them through the aperture into the asteroid. "Get back in your jets and get clear! If anyone should be landing it's me."

"No can do, Commander."

"I said get clear! That's an order!"

"Negative," said Elya.

He could feel Spector's seething fury. She wanted *so badly* to be the one to set down with MOXA.

"I'll have your wings for this," she said.

"We'll have to sort that out later, sir. Meantime, we could really use a defensive perimeter."

Several more drones had flown through the aperture during the exchange, tossing more of those little packages of groundlings onto the landing. They unfurled like giant flower petals and released packs of hungry, hunch-backed quadrupeds... and other xenoforms more ungainly and way more scary-looking than he wanted to admit. These new arrivals had ugly spines climbing up their backs and were spitting ahead of them. Wherever their spit touched, the saliva bubbled and sizzled—but again, the stone itself remained impervious to it.

Park and Yorra, still in their Sabres, continued to fire their wingtip blasters, holding the line of xenos back.

Elya ducked around the MOXA light cruiser and spotted the massive stone door he'd seen from above. The triangle this time wasn't the door itself, but an opening to an antechamber about thirty meters wide, which sheltered the true door, a perfect circle made of the same material as the deck—and carved with alien runes and symbols.

It was beautiful. Even given the danger at his back, he recognized the level of craftsmanship such a door must have taken to carve.

Under the cover of the antechamber, a squad of Marines wearing MOXA gray formed a half-circle against the rune-carved door. They bore carbine blasters in their arms and the man at their lead was Agent Callus. He set his jaw when he spotted Elya, and gave a nod of acknowledgment.

Behind the ring of agents, a man in crimson robes stepped up to the carved circle and ran his fingers over the raised ridges of stone.

"Aganaki!" Elya shouted between bursts of blaster fire from the Sabres. "You're making a mistake!"

The minister's fingers came to rest on an overlapping pair of circles in the middle of the circular door. He turned. Making eye contact with Elya, the minister withdrew the geode from beneath his robes, set it against the lower circle, and twisted the handle.

Viridian light shot out, engulfing his detail of agents and Elya, flowing over the Sabres and across the gap, and then spreading across roughly half the snapping xenos his comrades had been holding at bay. Roars and screeches echoed into the high stone hangar, bouncing off the inside of the hollow asteroid. The Kryl howled in pain and trampled each other in a mad scramble to get out of the light, pushing some of their kin off the edge of the landing pad so they plummeted into empty space to be dashed against the canyon of stone five hundred meters below.

But most of the xenos held their ground. As they shifted, a bipedal creature appeared at their vanguard. In one hand—human appearing—he held a blaster pistol with a square-edged, old-fashioned design. The other appendage had no hand at all, but was instead a muscular, carapace-covered Kryl arm ending in a taloned claw.

Subject Zero.

The hybrid leader's lower mandible—also a piece from a Kryl body that had evidently been grafted onto his skull to replace his natural jawbone during his transformation—hung open. He snapped it hungrily a few times.

A pack of small quadrupeds growled and paced at his back.

A jolt of fear raced through Elya. "That's new," he said. Only Subject Zero had been able to withstand the geode's power before. Now there were more of them.

They hung back, but not as far back as the purebred Kryl. "Are those…?" Yorra began.

Elya's heart dropped into his boots as he came to the same conclusion. "Oh, Animus," he breathed softly, "those are the *children.*"

Those weren't baby groundlings behind Subject Zero. Those were human children who had been infected by the parasite.

Infected and then successfully turned—the first generation of mutants who traced their lineage directly to Subject Zero.

Elya turned away as, behind them, the circle split and the door began to slide into the stone on either side of the threshold.

As the doors parted, the green light intensified. Elya squinted into the brightness. Shapes were thrown in stark white-and-black contrast as the brightness expanded to fill the vast area.

The brightness flared into a painful bright white, and he squeezed his eyes shut. When he opened them again, the doorway had yawned fully open.

Subject Zero and his brood paced at the edge of the ring of green. Then Subject Zero stopped and the spider legs in his back unhinged and spread out behind him. The mutant children gathered close, each of them clinging to one of his many limbs.

Elya realized what he was going to do the moment before it happened. Subject Zero touched a small device mounted on his belt, right next to his blaster holster, and the group of mutants phased out of real space, going semi-translucent and then disappearing. Like a ship jumping to light speed, they darted forward at an impossible speed, past Elya, between the group of MOXA agents, through the open door, and into the asteroid.

As fast as a person could blink.

A malformed cackle drifted back into their hearing range. Subject Zero and his mutants were inside. They'd waited until Aganaki opened the door, and now they were in the asteroid. Park and Yorra popped their canopies and jumped down to join him, jaws hanging open inside of their helmets. Elya exchanged an uneasy glance with his friends and then hurried toward the ring of MOXA agents. He felt a sense of relief as they parted to let them inside the protective circle of armed men.

Elya approached Minister Aganaki, who stood in the open doorway staring into the darkness of the interior.

"Minister," Elya said. "In the name of the Fleet, I demand you stand down."

He cocked an eyebrow. "The Fleet has no jurisdiction here, Captain."

"Then I'll take the geode from you by force." He couldn't let Subject Zero have it. It was their one advantage against the Kryl.

"You can try." At least three of the MOXA agents turned and pointed their carbines at him. "I don't think you'll be very successful."

Elya considered his options. "You're not really going to go in there, are you?"

"I am." Aganaki looked at him and raised the geode. Green light continued to pour out of it. The relic seemed more powerful here than it had been on Robichar, almost as if it were drawing power from the Telos structure, from the unnatural stone beneath his feet. "Come, or don't come, it makes no difference to me."

His curiosity got the best of him. "What do you expect you'll find inside?"

" 'Three to orbit a broken planet', " Aganaki recited. "Beyond that, I'm not certain. But I've waited a lifetime to find out."

Elya glanced at Park and Yorra. "You don't have to come."

"And take our chances with those xenos?" Park said, thumbing back at the rest of the Kryl where they waited beyond the edge of emerald light. "Fat chance."

"Raptor'd never forgive us if we let you go in there alone," Yorra said. "Much as I don't want to."

"Enough talk," Aganaki said. "We're wasting time. I don't know how long the geode's power will last and they've already got a lead on us."

Elya nodded and stepped up beside Aganaki. The MOXA agents pressed forward. With the xenos at their back, and the geode's power protecting them, they advanced into the Telos temple and the center of the asteroid.

# TWENTY-NINE

"We've lost squad comms," Spector reported in a grim voice over the command channel.

The commander of the Furies had been giving Kira the play-by-play since Nevers disembarked. When Aganaki led the group inside, their broadbeam signal cut out. Harmony informed her that the stone walls of the asteroid were interrupting the frequency. She wasn't surprised. Whatever the Telos were hiding inside this asteroid, they'd gone to great pains to conceal it.

Animus only knew what Aganaki and the pilots would find.

"They need backup," Kira said. "Flight control, deploy the rest of our Marines to the asteroid. Spector, I need the Furies to hold that perimeter at all costs. Don't let another Kryl drone inside."

"Solid copy," Spector answered grimly and disconnected.

A navigation specialist she'd assigned to track the Kryl's movements signaled to her on the bridge. "Admiral, the swarm is pressing into quadrant sierra nine again."

"Defensive laser arrays are still recharging," the weapons officer reported.

"Within missile range?" Kira asked.

"Affirmative, Admiral," Harmony said.

"Use them," Kira said. "Hold the line."

They wouldn't be able to withstand these attacks forever, but this time, Kira had come prepared for a knock down, drag-out fight. The odds were in her favor. So far, her pilots were eliminating a hundred Kryl for every one starfighter they lost. The Kryl would never flag or show signs of weariness—not until Overmind X herself gave up, and the hive queen was too close to getting whatever relic was located inside that asteroid to let up now—but it was still early in the battle and they were stocked up on munitions. Nothing to do but dig her heels in and give Aganaki and Flight 18 time to get in and back out again. She wanted more than anything to be there with them—to stop Aganaki from getting another relic as much as to keep it out of Kryl talons—but it was her job to direct the battle. Without an executive officer to take her place, she couldn't risk leaving her post.

The door to the bridge cycled open.

"Colonel Volk," Kira said, surprise causing an unexpected smile to form on her face.

Her XO levitated onto the bridge. He was sitting in a hoverchair pushed by a medical attendant. Volk scowled back at the young man. "Happy now?"

"Just wanted to make sure you got here safely, sir."

"I'm safe! All right? Now buzz off."

The medical attendant, whose name tag read "Samuel", nodded at Kira and departed.

*Harmony*, she thought, *remind me to thank that young man later.*

"Noted, Admiral."

To Volk she said, "You look better."

Another man entered behind him. This time, surprise made her jaw drop all the way open.

"Eben, what in all the livable worlds are you doing here? How did you sneak aboard my ship without my knowledge?"

The silver-haired man lifted his chin and smiled at her. "I have my ways. Ah ah, don't ask me to tell you. I need a few secrets, otherwise life just gets too boring. Besides, I did it as a favor for an old friend."

Kira raised an eyebrow. "I thought you and Volk only met when I introduced you."

"Not Volk." Eben's gaze shifted to look over her shoulder —right at Harmony, who took on the image of a curvy female officer standing at attention. She drew up into a salute. He returned it.

She'd almost forgotten Harmony's reaction when she'd first read Eben's name from the shortlist of allies procured by Admiral Gitano. "You orchestrated this?" she asked the shipmind.

Harmony's holographic arm lowered to her side. "I did."

"Okay," she said slowly. She didn't think Eben was the kind of person to overstep boundaries without a good reason. And how had Volk gotten wrapped up in it? She took in all three of them with a sweeping gaze. "Explain yourselves."

Eben and Volk exchanged a look that told her they'd already discussed it at length.

"It goes back about seven years to an investigation I was in charge of," Eben said. "I was ordered to look into the death of an officer, the commander of the 76th starfighter squadron. He died on a mission patrolling the edge of Solaran space shortly after the Kryl retreated back to Planet K. I took testimony from every pilot on his squad... including Renata Spector. Ultimately, the people involved were cleared of any wrongdoing and the death was ruled 'accidental'. But it never sat right with me. Looking back now, it seems pretty clear that I missed something."

He glanced at Volk, who withdrew a bottle of pills and rattled them in her direction. "You know what's in here?" he asked.

"Medicine?"

"Placebo. Someone managed to swap them out with fake pills. No wonder my treatment wasn't working. I got a refill of the real drugs in the sick bay an hour ago, and my blood toxicity levels are already going down."

"But... who would do that?"

"Renata Spector," Volk grumbled. He sighed and said, "I'm afraid I owe Captain Osprey an apology." Kira wasn't sure if he was more annoyed at himself for letting Spector deceive him, or that he had to admit his wrongdoing to the hotheaded young captain. Probably both. Volk cast Eben a glance as he gathered his wits. "I suspect now that Spector has been poisoning me with low doses of heavy metals over the past several weeks. I thought she wanted my mentorship as she learned to become a better commander." His face twisted into a scowl. "Turns out I was just the dupe. Every time we met for a chat, she furnished drinks or meals. To pay me for my good mentorship, she claimed. I feel like such a fool."

Her nose wrinkled and she jerked back. Her mind recoiled from Volk's casual accusation. It had been Kira's stamp of approval on Spector. She'd seen the woman's impressive record. Spector aced all of her interviews for the job. "Why would she do that?"

"I suppose we should ask her. Anyway, Osprey clued into what was going on, but before she could make a case, Spector got her thrown in the brig."

Kira's whole body shook with anger—not at Spector, but at herself. She'd been annoyed at Spector's attempt to get

Osprey demoted, but this put a whole new spin on the situation. Never in a million years did she think the woman would be capable of poisoning her XO. Not only was it attempted murder, it was tantamount to treason, a crime punishable by dishonorable discharge and decades in prison. Even, on occasion, execution... by an Imperial Inquisitor.

Eben's face was grim but he refrained from commenting. "Why?"

"She's young for her rank. Ambitious. She holds grudges like you wouldn't believe. And her commanders keep dying under mysterious circumstances." Volk shrugged. "My guess? She wanted me out of her way."

"Or she's trying to get closer to the admiral," Eben interjected, making eye contact with her as he said it.

"Or both," Volk added.

Really? Kira didn't have any real power. Oh sure, she commanded her armada, but these past weeks had proven how little political clout she actually possessed. What could Kira have that Spector wanted?

"I'll order her to come back to the ship so we can speak to her." Kira turned to Harmony. "Get Spector on a private frequency."

A tense minute passed as they waited. "She's not answering, Admiral," the shipmind finally said.

"Patch me into the squad's broadbeam channel." Harmony did so. "*Paladin* to Furies actual, come in."

"Yes, Admiral?" said a voice Kira didn't recognize

That wasn't Spector's voice.

"I want to speak to Lieutenant Colonel Spector."

"She went after Flight 18, Admiral," The pilot said. "We couldn't talk her out of it. We're still holding the perimeter, as you ordered. No more drones inside." The last words were shoved through gritted teeth as muffled weapons fire sounded through the channel.

Kira glanced at Eben, whose face darkened. He checked the rapier and blaster holsters on his belt to make sure they were securely fastened.

Kira disconnected. "Has she lost her damn mind?"

Volk frowned. "What if it wasn't Spector's idea at all?" he asked.

"Sorry?"

The colonel licked his lips. "What if her 'why' is that she's working with MOXA?"

She didn't have proof, but somehow that felt right.

"Bloody politics," Kira muttered. Aganaki had been screwing with her this whole time. If what Volk and Eben were telling her was true, they'd orchestrated everything—placing Spector under her command, having her buddy up to Volk in order to poison him. No doubt they predicted Captain Osprey's inability to accept Spector as her new commander, too—or at least were thrilled with her reaction.

"Oh, Earth," Kira said when it hit her. "That's how the MOXA Light Cruiser found us in the first place. Spector must have located the asteroid first and sent our coordinates to Aganaki. She's an Earth-damned ministry spy."

The meddlesome minister was going to be the death of her. This was all a play for power. She imagined worst case scenarios—her pilots and the minister ripped to shreds inside the asteroid. The geode and whatever other powerful relic falling into the possession of Overmind X.

A flaring up of hostilities leading to a second Kryl War.

Omar Ruidiaz delivering a deadly payload to Ariadne to end said war, like he had the first time, only for the other team.

The vivid image gave her chills.

She couldn't stand by and do nothing.

At least now she had her XO with her—lucid and seemingly well.

"Volk, are you feeling up to taking command of the *Paladin?*"

He nodded and gave her a lopsided grin. "Aye, sir."

"I'm coming with you," Eben demanded.

"You don't even know where I'm going yet," Kira replied.

"Of course I do."

"Suppose we should let your daughter out of the brig, eh?"

He thought about it for a moment. She was sure Eben was going to dress her down for not telling him his daughter had been stuck in the brig sooner.

"No," he said. "There's no reason to put her in harm's way."

"Her friends are inside that asteroid."

"Even better reason to keep her where she is. She may be your pilot, but she's still my daughter."

The closest thing Kira had to kids were her officers. But she was used to putting her officers in harm's way—that was literally part of her job. A parent's job was the opposite.

"Have it your way," Kira said, "but if she's pissed off about it later, I know where I'm sending her."

"I'll gladly take the heat."

"Harmony, tell the Marines to hold the shuttle and make room for two. I need them ready to leave in five," Kira said as they exited the bridge together. Then, to Eben, "I hope they packed the heavy guns. We might need them."

# THIRTY

E lya and his two squad mates padded at Aganaki's heels
as they made their way quickly into the soft gray darkness of the asteroid's interior. The MOXA agents, with
Callus on point, surrounded them in a loose circle, while
Hedgebot ranged out ahead, still trying to keep its distance
from anything with a heat signature.

The bulk of the Kryl force trailed behind by fifty meters
or more—watching and waiting for the geode's protective
circle of green light to fade. Periodically, one of the MOXA
agents would turn and shoot in their direction, driving them
back and out of sight.

But they didn't retreat. The xenos dogged them with a
predator's patience.

Subject Zero and his captives were somewhere out ahead.
He trusted Hedgebot would warn him if they drew near, but
he was more worried at this point that Overmind X would
beat them to the relic than turn and attack.

The group had initially moved down a long hallway lined
with angled walls which were covered in the same glyphs

and runes as the great stone door. The geode in Aganaki's hand cast the tunnel in a pale green glow. The farther they got from the door and the starlight illuminating the asteroid, the darker the hall became. It ran about two hundred meters before terminating in a split that forked off to the left and right.

Hedgebot darted down the left-hand path and shot a flash of blue back in their direction as it disappeared around the corner.

Elya held his breath. He exhaled a moment later as his bot scurried back up the branch to their right, flashing blue a second time as he completed the circuit.

"All clear," Elya said, translating Hedgebot's signals for the group.

The agents regripped their carbines and cast a couple potshots back to where the xenos still lurked out of reach. There was a *thunk* and an angry snarl as one round hit its target. Callus then signaled for the group to move in the bot's direction.

As Elya passed through an archway trimmed in the same artfully carved stone as the entrance, his jaw fell open. "No way," he breathed as he drew up short and gazed into the distance.

The pathway they traveled curved down into the asteroid's interior, broadening out and leading down to the floor of an enormous cavern filled with the soaring walls and arches of a thousand interlocking structures.

The solid stone that had once occupied this space had been chiseled away by the finest laser cutters. Delicate stone fingers were connected like a web to the walls, ceiling, and floor. Gaps between them were either left open to the air, or fitted with perfect crystal sheets that served as windows and walls, balconies with balustrades, doors and walkways and ladders—and other jutting objects whose purpose he couldn't fathom. Each building was stylized in swooping curves, with the heights artfully connected by soaring bridges. The alien city's architecture was beautiful, like nothing Elya had ever seen.

And somewhere in all that beauty, Subject Zero was moving ever closer to another potentially powerful weapon —another piece of the Kryl's so-called "Inheritance."

A gentle golden light filled the air, seeming to emanate from no fixed source. While the long hall they'd come through had been dark and cold, in here the effect was akin to an early autumn evening suffused by a golden-red twilight. The buildings swept back across a concave plane to the back wall of the asteroid, where more stone-and-crystal structures climbed up in overlapping sheaves dotted by a pattern of shining crystal portholes, almost like the passenger cabin of a luxury starliner, or an alien arachnid's thousand eyes. Above that, the light faded and was replaced not with rough stone, as he expected, but a firmament painted with wispy clouds, speckled with twinkling stars, and hung with half-waxed moons—three of them that shone in shades of pale red, orange and blue.

"Marvelous," Yorra whispered, staring up with her mouth hanging open.

Park pointed at the false sky. "Is that a holoscreen?"

"No time," Aganaki said, interrupting their reverie and jolting the rest of the group into motion again. "We must locate the relic, and quickly." His eyes swept across the city. "We'll be able to cover more ground if we split up."

The look of horror on Park's and Yorra's faces mirrored his own feelings. Besides, after the minister's deception to get the geode here, Elya wasn't about to let the little weasel out of his sight. "That's what they want," he said. "If we don't stick together, they'll pick us off one by one."

Minister Aganaki sniffed disdainfully. "Fine. The relic will be protected, in a saferoom of some kind, so that's what we're looking for. It will be in plain sight, but not necessarily obvious or easy to find. And we must be on our guard. The Telos never leave anything unprotected."

They made their way quickly down the slope and into the city. Once they reached the main cluster of buildings, each five or six stories tall, with the first floor of many open to the air on evenly spaced spindles, their line of sight became limited. Elya took a surreptitious glance back as a hundred xenos—groundlings, the hulking lizards they called duralisks, and a few sentinels picking up the rear—poured through the two archways before scurrying out of the geode's reach and between other buildings hundreds of meters to their left and right.

Agent Callus sent a few MOXA agents up a spiral path of crystal that wound to the top of a tall building. They cast small surveillance drones into the air. "We need eyes in the sky if we're going to find the relic quickly," Callus explained.

"How about eyes on the ground?" Elya asked. "Hang on, I've got an idea."

He whistled Hedgebot over as he pulled his tab out of his flight suit. He tapped into the module that amplified the bot's spatial awareness, tinkered with the settings, and then redeployed it. Hedgebot zipped off at top speed down beneath the nearest structure before hopping along a stone retaining wall.

On his tab, Hedgebot's motions began to color in shapes that would eventually become a map of the city. Agent Callus nodded his approval. They began to move forward again.

Yorra turned to Minister Aganaki. "Did you read anything in that old book about what this place is supposed to look like?"

"Unfortunately not," Aganaki said. "There wasn't any

mention that this would be such a large, complex facility. I'll bet it was some kind of research laboratory."

"Those overlapping slabs of crystal against the back wall look like condos," said Park, pointing up into the distance. Each porthole-like window must have been ten or twenty meters across. "Maybe it was a luxury resort."

"Merely housing for the scientists and engineers who worked here," Aganaki insisted.

They shared theories and guesses as to the purpose of each building as the group made their way deeper into the city. Like a space station that's been cobbled together over time, there seemed to be little rhyme or reason to the layout. Despite being uniformly elegant and beautiful, the bridges and inclined paths led them to several dead ends—or at least walls they couldn't climb—through empty buildings, and to locked crystal doors that couldn't be breached. The crystal itself was often hazy and opaque up close, so they couldn't even see inside most of the buildings, assuming they found an accessible door in the first place.

With Hedgebot's help and Agent Callus's coordinated communication with the other agents, they began to make forward progress. Hedgebot's map grew until it showed indications of all the major structures, and at least three thoroughfares that seemed to meet in the center and were wider than the other paths.

"This is a waste of time," Elya said after they crossed back to a four-way intersection they had already visited. "We keep retracing our steps. We need to figure out where the best place would be to hide this saferoom."

Minister Aganaki rejoined him. Elya used the rudimentary holoprojector capability of his new tab to show Hedgebot's map in three dimensions. They pored over it together.

"Most of the Telos temples we've found have been built into the natural stone," said Aganaki. "Much like this place, although this is the first orbital structure we've discovered, and certainly the most... elaborate. Usually it's caves, lava tubes, or other subterranean habitats. Our theory is that the ancient Telos conducted extensive seismic and geological analysis so that each site could be placed at a location optimal for withstanding natural changes in landscape, erosion, flooding, and other natural phenomena. Their ability to predict what would still be standing and above water millennia into the future was uncanny, far beyond our own capacity." He squinted up at the structures rising around them. This building had a courtyard open to the sky. A gate at one end was as tall as a surrounding field of crystal domes.

Elya snapped his fingers. "We've been looking at all these buildings and thinking the answer is next to or above us. But everything here seems to have been built in one direction—up. What if what we're looking for is hidden below?"

Aganaki's eyes widened. He walked around the hologram until he spotted the circular plaza where the three major thoroughfares met. The map there was partially incomplete.

Elya's theory was confirmed as they began to make their way in that direction. As they drew closer to the plaza, packs of patrolling groundlings began to appear in their path, atop buildings—always out of reach of the geode—or closing in behind them.

"Easy..." Agent Callus warned his agents. "Hold your fire..."

A group of duralisks appeared on a raised terrace to their right and began to shoot mucousy projectiles at them, forcing the group forward to stay out of the line of fire.

The road curved. They emerged into a circular plaza.

Subject Zero was standing in the center, waiting. Ten captive children were fanned out behind him, glassy-eyed and empty-faced.

There was one other person among them. An older man

319

with the pinkish-white welts of old scars criss-crossing his arms. He hovered near one of the kids, a boy, and licked his lips nervously.

"Don't move!" Aganaki commanded in a voice that rang across the plaza, echoing off the arches of stone and walls of crystal that surrounded the only open area in the whole place.

Subject Zero withdrew a small orb from his pocket. He held it aloft in his palm and it burst into a cloud of sparks that hovered around him like a cape of stars.

The sparks settled onto the stone near his feet, collecting in a perfect circle around where Subject Zero stood, as if outlining a target. Elya shivered as he met the mutant xeno's eyes. Subject Zero's jaw opened sideways and snapped a few times.

Aganaki clenched his jaw, raised the geode and advanced, perhaps hoping to force them back. At first, as the green aura passed over Subject Zero, nothing happened except that the Kryl mutant and his captive children began to squirm, snarling and shaking their heads in discomfort—although nothing like the pain purebred Kryl seemed to experience. More xenos closed into the space behind them where the green aura had given way, surrounding them and forcing the rest of the agents and pilots deeper into the plaza with Aganaki.

As the green light engulfed the circular piece of stone that Subject Zero and the children stood on, the ground reacted to the geode the same way the asteroid gate had. The geode's light intensified into bright whiteness, and Elya realized what was about to happen.

"Aganaki, no!" he shouted.

But his warning came too late.

The stone within the perfect circle of gold specks separated from the plaza floor, rapidly lowering Subject Zero, the captive children, and the old man into a hidden sub-level below.

A great clacking and clanging filled the plaza as, piece by piece, the floor broke into octagons and folded up one section at a time, each shape stacking on its neighbor as it rapidly retracted. Elya jumped to avoid getting his ankle broken, only to bump into Park and Yorra as they all tumbled into empty air.

They'd found the so-called "saferoom" Aganaki had been looking for.

A hundred Kryl dove in after them, screeching as they fell.

---

Admiral Miyaru picked up the pace. The Marines trailed her, checking their backup magazines and charge packs. They didn't need the flashlights they'd brought along. The crystal city seemed to be lit as if from within. It hadn't been hard to follow the trail of blood spoors and the occasional groundling corpse. Aganaki's escort had done a decent job of picking the xenos off as they made their way deeper into the ancient alien construction. They hadn't found any sign of Lt. Colonel Spector yet, either, but Kira knew she was here somewhere. Her Sabre had been parked on the deck next to the rest of Flight 18's starfighters.

Something heavy landed on top of her and drove sharp claws into Kira's ribcage.

She drove a knee into a groundling's underbelly, kicking it off, and fired three shots into its carapace with her pistol, spraying a crystal wall with yellow blood. Eben muscled in beside her and shoved his sword into the creature's mouth.

The xeno thrashed, wheezed wetly, and then lay still. Eben pulled his rapier out with a slicing squelch.

The dull impacts of rifle butts on flesh, and the muted *pop pop pop* of silenced carbines filled the hall as the platoon of Marines dispatched the rest of the groundlings who had ambushed them. A pack had dropped down on them from a crystal bridge.

They'd barely drawn a breath when more came screaming out of the shadows and from around corners, slashing talons and snapping teeth. This group was more careful, harrying the edges of their line, darting in and out and avoiding fire by staying on the move. Half a dozen Marines went down with injuries, their comrades pulling them back to protect them while others administered first aid.

Kira aimed over the heads of the men in front of her until her charge pack clicked on empty. She slapped in a replacement and leveled the gun to shoot again. But the xenos suddenly perked their heads up, turned, and sprinted as one down an alley between a ridge of stone and the crystal wall of a garden of crystal domes made out of hexagonal crystal frames.

"That can't be good," Kira muttered.

They were left in the sound of their own ragged breathing. One or two of the Marines moaned painfully.

"They were called away," Eben observed. "They must have found something."

A clacking sound echoed from a distance. A couple hundred meters, maybe less, she figured.

"Let's go!" Kira ordered. "On the hop."

The Marine Sergeant sent a half dozen injured soldiers back to the entrance with a protective detail. Then he turned to the rest of them and said, "You heard the admiral, move out."

Elya bounced off one of the stone tiles on the way down, careened off the backside of a MOXA agent thrashing in free fall, and hit the floor so hard his breath was driven from his chest. Thank Animus he was still wearing his flightsuit with its built-in armored nanofiber, and that the stimchem still pumped through his veins. Both kept him conscious.

He was on his knees gasping when the Kryl came flying at them like rabid dogs, snarling and snapping.

It was ten times worse that some of these creatures had the faces of human children.

MOXA agents held off the first wave by virtue of sheer grit. Seeing human expressions on the faces of these new mutant xenos made several of the agents hesitate and revert to non-lethal force. They used the butts of their rifles to smash heads and their booted feet to kick the kids back, rather than going for the kill.

Elya had the same hesitation—it was him or them, and he'd long suspected how the xenos would use the children, but still... he swallowed any latent disgust he felt and kicked a ten-year-old girl in the jaw so hard her head snapped back.

She thrashed on the floor. Her body was wrapped in a Kryl membrane that had begun to harden along her back and legs. Otherwise, she was entirely naked. The membrane on her hands had extended the fingers into the beginnings of what would become razor sharp talons. Shallow cuts on her arms bled a deep crimson—like any other human being. Perhaps, given a little more time, Elya wouldn't be able to tell this child from another xeno. But right now...

He turned and vomited on the floor.

The children turned and retreated together back to Subject Zero's position, including the girl who lurched bonelessly to all fours and staggered away. By this point, the rest of the Marines had come to their senses, realizing the us-or-them situation, and started using lethal force against the other xenos who had fallen into the sub-level with them.

Meanwhile, Aganaki chased after the geode, which must have been knocked out of his hands in the fall. Hence why they were being attacked with such ferocity—without the protection of the green aura, they were exposed. To the minister's credit, his face was focused in a look of concentration as he pursued the geode, not panic. Aganaki was tougher than Elya expected. Brash and fighting above his weight class, but tough all the same.

A second wave of Kryl arrived, backing them further into the chamber, which was circular and ringed with great columns holding up the edge of the plaza dozens of feet overhead. It almost seemed as though they were in a stadium, an arena, with open space above rising to the very apex of the asteroid itself. But there was no time to gawk. Elya picked out a couple hulking sentinels, and others he didn't have names for, and rotated to keep the most dangerous among them in his sight.

He spotted Subject Zero in the center of the arena, still standing on the platform that had lowered him down. He was a steady rock in the flow of Kryl as they surged around and past him. Elya took aim with his pistol and loosed a shot at the mutant. His aim was true, but Subject Zero touched an object on his belt at the moment of his shot and the plasma bolt passed right through him.

"Damn it," Elya muttered. He'd momentarily forgotten about the phase shifter—the relic that allowed Subject Zero to move through space and solid objects—or allow objects to pass through him. The mutant xeno was focusing on the orb that had showered the chamber in sparks and triggered the lowering of the platform. Obviously another relic, he made hand gestures as he tried to get it to do something.

He seemed to be having trouble operating it for some reason.

Two Marines went down with shouts of pain beside them, and Elya had to dodge back to avoid being gutted by a groundling. One of the sentinels roared and charged, splitting the group and snapping bones underfoot.

They were sorely outnumbered and outmatched.

"Aganaki... hurry up with that geode!" Elya shouted, searching the chaos of bodies for the minister. Aganaki had recovered the relic and ducked down by a pair of stone fists at the base of one of the smooth columns. The sculpture shielded him from the fighting, as well as Subject Zero's line of sight. Elya realized there were more statues of oversized stone fists ringing the room, seven in all, one at the base of each column. The fingers of stone were long and interlocked, two hands together. These hands looked *almost* human, but they had too many knuckle joints.

A MOXA agent landed a good shot into the back of a sentinel's head with a gauss rifle as it was passing by. The hulking xeno went limp and fell on the platform where Subject Zero still stood, preoccupied by the orb, which broke into a swirling mass of miniature stars once again. Subject Zero stepped over the sentinel's body and made another expansive gesture, like he was beading an invisible necklace.

This time, one of the stone fists parted, creating a platform and revealing a stone obelisk with an angled crystal face.

The way Subject Zero strutted forward told Elya he was pleased with himself for getting it to work. He attempted to approach the new relic, but as he drew close, an invisible energy shield revealed itself, flashed neon green and sent Subject Zero cartwheeling backwards through the air with a sonic boom that cut through the chatter of gunshots. The mutant's spider-like legs extended from his back and windmilled as he flew through the air and landed on a pack of groundlings.

"Watch out!" someone shouted.

Elya tore his eyes from Subject Zero in time to see a wad of mucus fly through the air, spin over the heads of the MOXA agents, and splatter against the helmet of Lieutenant Olara Yorra. As he stared at the liquid, trying to figure out what the Kryl hoped to gain by spitting on them, smoke suddenly began to stream up toward the ceiling, rising from Yorra's helmet where the viscous liquid seeped in. The aluminite panel began to bubble, liquifying and melting away.

Park jumped forward and shouted, "Take it off! Take it off!" before Yorra realized what was happening. She instinctively pulled back from his touch—she was still angry at him, or maybe just shocked at his reaction, or both—but then started screaming and dancing around as the acid dripped down onto her left cheek and lower jaw.

More globs of phlegmy acid were flung out of the darkness from the farthest corner of the chamber. The scene dissolved into chaos again as MOXA agents and pilots alike scattered to get out of range. Agent Callus and a brave group of MOXA agents holding tight with him turned to engage the xenos, cutting through one's abdomen immediately and sending gore spilling across the floor in front of a statue.

Elya yanked Park and Yorra with him as he rushed to take shelter about fifty meters from where Aganaki had been hiding a moment ago. As they ran, Park managed to tear Yorra's helmet off and fling it at a groundling who snapped at their heels.

As they ran, the ground rose, and Elya tripped more than once. The floor was layered in petaled steppes carved of hazy crystal. Hedgebot, who had vanished in the melee, darted out from the shadows and led them into the shelter behind a great column.

Park stumbled and a groundling pounced on top of him. Hedgebot harried the xeno, zipping back and forth and leading it on a chase, which gave Park time to fight his way back to his feet and rejoin them. Yorra moaned and touched shaking fingers to her skin, which was raw and red on her neck and chin.

"Try not to touch it," Park said breathlessly as he fumbled the first aid kit out of the utility belt on his flight suit and pressed a medicated cotton pad to her neck. "We'll get you out of here."

"How?" she asked.

Park risked a glance around the column only to pull back, pale as a ghost, and look at Elya.

"What?"

"Aganaki," Park mouthed.

Elya peered around the column. The Kryl had gathered a few dozen meters from the crystal obelisk. Subject Zero stood there at the eye of the storm of xenos with his gigantic malformed Kryl appendage resting on the shoulders of Minister Aganaki. His human hand pointed a decades-old Fleet-issued blaster at the minister's forehead.

Aganaki knelt in his fine red robes of state, which were surprisingly unscathed. Not ripped and bloody, like the bodies of the xenos and half a dozen MOXA agents now scattered around the chamber.

With trembling hands, he set the geode down at Subject Zero's feet. It was off and emitted no green light.

"Where's Agent Callus?" Elya cast his eyes about and found the man lying on the ground with blood pooling around his head. Callus's eyes were glassy and lifeless. The still bodies of two hulking sentinels, pierced with gaping wounds, lay dead nearby.

Agent Callus wouldn't be rescuing the minister or stopping Subject Zero from taking the geode. No other MOXA agents seemed to have survived the fight, either.

It was down to Elya.

Subject Zero raised the pistol and brought it down on the back of Aganaki's head. The minister dropped, unconscious, to the floor. Subject Zero picked up the geode.

Once again, the hybrid xeno turned to the crystal pillar. This time he activated the phase shifter first, causing his form to blur. But as he approached, the shield activated again. It didn't fling him back this time, just brightened on the side facing him. He attempted to reach out and push the geode through the energy shield using his human hand. As he reached the convex plane, his arm trembled and his mandibles shivered with pain. After a few seconds, he drew back, hissing through that inhuman mouth. His hand was raw and red, as if it had been burned.

He marched back to the group of mutant children and stopped next to a small, skinny, dark-haired boy.

"No," cried the old man who had been hiding among the children during the fight. Old, faded scars braided his thin arms, which had been wrapped around the boy's shoulders. "Please, no, not my son. Send me instead!"

"Shut up," Subject Zero said. "You've outlived your usefulness as their caretaker."

A bolt from the mutant's blaster burned into the man's rib cage and he fell back.

Elya's gut churned. He snapped his fingers and Hedgebot scurried to his side, then he stepped out from behind the column where they'd been hiding.

He didn't know what he was going to do. But he couldn't let this happen.

Kira recognized the old man from her appeal in front of the Colonization Board. It was the robotics engineer who'd begged for passage on the voyager—and received it in exchange for a life of indentured servitude for his wife and son.

This nightmare was so much worse than he bargained for.

Kira didn't see the man's wife among the group, and somehow that seemed a mercy.

"On the count of three," Kira said, turning to Eben and the platoon of Marines behind them. "We go in guns blazing." They'd skirted along the outside of the plaza and studied the bloody melee without the Kryl noticing so far. Subject Zero and his fighters were too distracted worrying about the geode and the crystal pylon; presumably, the new relic they wanted.

"What about the children?" Eben asked.

"Spare them if you can, but not at risk to your own life."

If they couldn't save those kids, maybe she could stop Subject Zero from taking the relic.

After all, wasn't that the purpose of her appeal to the Colonization Board? Once she found out the Overmind had turned Omar Ruidiaz and was searching for Telos relics, she had to do everything in her power to stop it. To protect the Solaran people.

To prevent another war with the Kryl.

But the Colonization Board hadn't listened. Card was just a puppet. Aganaki's greed had rushed them ahead, straight into Overmind X's trap.

As the blaster bolt sent the boy's father to the ground, the child stepped out of the crowd willingly, displaying no emotion.

"Here, boy." The creature she had once known and loved

as the war hero, Captain Omar Ruidiaz, handed the boy the geode. "This is the key. Retrieve the relic, and bring it to me."

"One…" Admiral Miyaru whispered.

"Two…" Eben said.

"Three!" they cried together.

And jumped.

# THIRTY-ONE

Blaster and rifle fire erupted from above and behind the arena as most of a platoon of Marines dropped into the lower level, striking down half a dozen Kryl before they knew what hit them.

The xenos turned and engaged, rushing toward the squad of Marines—with the large, fit form of Admiral Miyaru leading the charge, her platinum mohawk shining in the light of the gunfight.

And was that Inquisitor Eben Osprey spearing the neck of a groundling with his sword?

The xenos closed ranks in a flurry of thumps and grunts, of blaster fire and the flash-and-bark of semi-automatic rifles.

Park stepped up beside Elya. Yorra, wincing in pain, came around his other side. Hedgebot scurried out of a shadowed corner and glanced back, chirped once and flashed red. This was a danger zone, all right.

"What are you planning to do?" Park asked.

"I'm going for the geode," Elya said. "It's our best shot, and I know how it works. Cover me?"

The two of them nodded and drew their sidearms. "We've got your back."

Three pilots and a bot charged into the fray.

What happened next was a blur of motion and terror. The xenos were occupied with the Marines and Admiral Miyaru's devastating attack, but not for long. As soon as their group was noticed, a dozen xenos turned toward them and charged.

What he realized in that moment was that these xenos weren't afraid of dying. They *lived* to fight. They had been bred for it.

Hedgebot darted through the mob, leading them away from xenos and into open space, flashing red and blue so that Elya knew where to step next. If Hedgebot could direct him in a Sabre, the little dude could do it on the ground, too.

Elya followed his bot, spinning and dodging and shooting with his sidearm, and soon found himself on the other side of the melee—with only a handful of xenos between him and the crystal relic. Subject Zero stood a dozen meters behind the child bearing the geode. Elya realized his flight suit had a gash on the side, and his ribs ached when he breathed in. His blaster radiated heat, and he had dozens of scrapes and scratches along his arms and legs. But, by Earth, he was standing and breathing. A groundling jumped at him. He raised his pistol and pulled the trigger. The bolt took the creature in the face, blasting its brains out through the back of its head.

Inquisitor Osprey slashed through the xeno horde and was suddenly there next to him, guarding his back. Elya nodded at him.

The boy was now standing right next to the obelisk in the pair of open hands—the point at which the energy shield had turned Subject Zero away. The invisible wall flashed green, and then cycled through a rainbow of colors. It reminded Elya of the shipmind, Harmony, when she was running calculations. The boy waited as the alien tech seemed to attempt to assess his humanity—or at least look for cause to reject him as Kryl, like it had Subject Zero.

"Stop!" Elya shouted. "Don't listen to her! Overmind X just wants the relics for herself."

But he knew it was hopeless. The boy didn't turn or acknowledge him. He lifted the geode and presented it to the alien tech with a glazed look on his face.

Subject Zero's mandibles swung open and he stepped in Elya's path. "Unlike a grown human, your children do not have the mental capacity to resist our controllers."

A weird resonance echoed in his mind when the creature spoke, almost as if the voice spoke into his head. He knew it wasn't Subject Zero's voice alone, but Overmind X's as well. Whatever that thing had done inside his brain, it had left an indelible mark on his psyche. She couldn't speak directly to him, but she had been in his mind too recently for his body to forget what it felt like.

"Controllers?" he asked a moment before it hit him. "You mean the parasites."

Subject Zero's mandibles hung open in a mockery of a smile. Saliva dripped down his lower jaw.

"You couldn't control me."

"Didn't we, though? You brought us the relic, like we said you would."

"That wasn't me. I didn't ask the minister to bring it... that was a fluke. You got lucky."

Minister Aganaki still lay unconscious nearby as the fighting raged around him.

"No difference," Subject Zero said, turning to look at the child. "Only the end result matters." Elya began to shuffle around in an arc toward the boy. Subject Zero mirrored his steps but didn't use his weapon. He was enjoying gloating, apparently. Or Overmind X was. Elya couldn't be sure.

His blaster and Osprey's sword kept the rest of the xenos surrounding them at bay. Or maybe it was Subject Zero's control over them. Regardless, they didn't attack.

"A grown human's pre-frontal cortex is too well developed to expect you to be perfectly obedient without.... significant modifications." Subject Zero gestured to his own body. "The brood's genetic material is far more adaptable. It is one reason of many that we deserve the Inheritance. We are the superior species."

"What is this monster blabbing on about?" Park demanded. He and Yorra caught up to them as well. They each held their sidearms in their hands with indicators showing their chargepacks were running on dregs. Hedgebot lurked nearby, keeping his lights off so as not to attract attention.

The fighting continued behind them. The Marines seemed to be winning, and were working together, with Admiral Miyaru at their center, to systematically corner and eliminate the groundlings one at a time. Subject Zero didn't even seem concerned.

"Our experiments have been... educational," said Subject Zero. "We continue to evolve."

"Which is why you needed the kids. They're different, aren't they?" Elya asked. The boy remained standing at the edge of the shield. Elya stepped slowly toward him, using his questions to keep Overmind X—through Subject Zero as her mouthpiece—talking.

"We simply required more... pliable subjects."

Overmind X hadn't bothered putting parasites in the adults they'd found on the *Maiden of Kali*—they would have panicked, probably hurting the Kryl in the process as they were overcome by the hallucinations. Children were more malleable. Easier to control.

"The parasite is, after all, an extension of ourselves—all

our brood is. In the chemical reaction that ended the last great battle between our species, I was ripped apart and remade anew. Separating from the Queen Mother was painful. But it opened up a myriad of new possibilities. We are only now beginning to reach our true potential."

"Just shoot him and get this over with," Inquisitor Osprey murmured.

Elya wanted to. Earth knew what would happen when the boy activated that crystal obelisk.

But wouldn't he just activate the phase shifter and dodge it again?

His fingers twitched on his blaster as he grasped for alternatives.

A few more rifle shots popped off on the opposite side of the chamber. The Marines picked their way through the bodies of the xenos littering the floor, staying together as they made their way forward. The Sergeant called a halt, and Admiral Miyaru stepped out in front of them with the soldiers flanking her, their rifles raised and pointed at Subject Zero.

The mutant stared at the admiral with a slightly unnatural tilt to his head, and paused. It gave him a menacing, alien air.

Why wasn't he scared? They had him surrounded. Elya's eyes dropped to the small object on his belt. Up close, he could see how the phase shifter was made of the same impervious stone as the geode, with a little, stone-carved dial sticking out of the curved face.

While Subject Zero was distracted, Elya took a few soft steps toward the boy and said, "You mean the Telos relics. You found out that the relics were hidden in this galaxy when you merged with Ruidiaz and acquired his memories."

Subject Zero nodded without turning. His eyes remained

fixed on Admiral Miyaru and a look of confusion came over his grotesque face.

The protective shield surrounding the crystal pillar finally fell away, letting the boy through. Now was his chance. Elya whistled and pointed so Hedgebot dashed forward first, with him following close behind. The astrobot could make it—he would get there just in time to knock the boy away. The child was moving so slowly. He hovered a hand over the angled crystal face of the relic.

The child suddenly stiffened as a blaster shot echoed through the chamber. He staggered sideways and blood trickled out of his mouth. He never touched the relic. Shivers raced down Elya's spine as Hedgebot darted between the legs of a groundling who overshot an attempted interception.

"No!" someone screamed, their voice breaking. The old man scrabbled to his feet and ran for his boy. The xenos had stopped guarding him, presuming the man dead, but he still had some fight left in him. A sentinel reached for the man, but the creature had been injured in the fight that killed Agent Callus, and so it was a hair too slow and allowed the old man to slip away.

Elya's eyes focused in the distance and found Lt. Colonel Renata Spector. She must have snuck around the back of the columns to the opposite side. She gripped a blaster with two hands, her arms steady.

She pulled the trigger twice more as the old man reached his son. The boy's father took both blaster bolts to the back before dropping like a rock.

The man's body provided cover for the injured, parasite-infected child to lay hands on the pylon. The relic surged, sucking air from every corner of the room as it drew in power.

It activated.

A great figure appeared before them, holding itself

suspended between two columns, one enormous hand wrapped around each, with a whiplike tail stretching out behind and above. Powerful shoulders were draped in a midnight purple robe trimmed with gold and embroidered with runes and sigils in the Telos language, no doubt identical to the ones decorating the asteroid's gated entrance. The robe was cut to allow the creature's legs to swing loose, and within the fabric, Elya caught flashes of a toned abdomen that seemed to be coated with metallic armor, or perhaps scales.

It was the most realistic hologram Elya had ever seen. No flickers of light, no transparency. It seemed as if the giant creature were *here* with them. He could feel it *breathing*.

The seven carved stone fists ringing the room *moved* with a synchronous grinding noise he would never forget. They un-threaded their giant stone fingers—or toes, each of which had four or five knuckle joints—until they lay open as if willing to accept a gift.

Unlike the crystal obelisk, none of the other pairs of hands or feet contained any relics.

While Subject Zero was distracted staring at Admiral Miyaru, Hedgebot leaped and slammed its body into the handle of the geode in the boy's hand.

It was enough. A wave of green light burst outward, sending most of the Kryl reeling. The geode rolled away and Elya snatched it up, sprinting back the way he'd come. He didn't have any way to know which pair of hands the geode was designed to fit in, but trusted that Minister Aganaki had been devious enough to have figured it out before him.

Park and Yorra expended the last of their charge packs, eviscerating a pair of groundlings who tried to cut off his path. Elya leapt over the bodies, and slammed the geode into the hollow in the center of the sculpture.

The geode locked into the space where the hands met

with a click, and its emerald anti-Kryl ambience ratcheted exponentially up in brightness and power, filling the chamber and rising to suffuse the false sky above with an emerald glow.

Subject Zero stared at Kira with the same eyes she had once fallen in love with. Almost as if he recognized her. Almost as if the Omar she once knew was trapped in there behind that monstrous visage.

When Captain Nevers first told her he'd recognized Subject Zero as the famous starfighter pilot, Captain Omar Ruidiaz, her legs had turned to noodles and she'd fainted.

Her knees wobbled now. But this time she held her ground.

A blaster fired from the shadows of the archway to her right, breaking the moment. Subject Zero's mandibles spread and sprayed saliva as he roared and turned.

The little Hedgehog-shaped robot that was Captain Nevers' constant companion knocked the geode into the captain's path. He ran to an adjacent pair of stone hands, slamming the relic into place.

A supernova of energy exploded from the geode, sending people flying. A shaft of green light shot all the way up to the atrium of the asteroid. The artificial sky above churned like an aurora, or an emerald storm.

That mutant may once have been the Omar Ruidiaz Kira fell in love with... but not anymore. Those were his eyes, sure, but the Kryl mandibles? The muscular, scaly arm that ended in talon-sharp claws? Those didn't belong to him.

What happened next proved her point. Subject Zero hit the ground with a wet smack, then roared and struggled to his knees. He immediately began scrabbling away, trying to get distance from the geode's power. His hand clutched at his belt, and his form went blurry and thin, as if he was hidden behind a heat mirage, or being projected in via hologram.

This seemed to ease his pain. He stood up. The aura didn't hurt him as much when the phase shifter was activated.

Save for the mutant children, the rest of the xenos still alive in the room weren't nearly so lucky. They didn't have the protective power of that phase shifter, nor a half-human hybrid genome. Before her eyes, dozens of bodies of xenos, living and dead, vaporized.

"Stop him!" Kira shouted. The Marines ran forward, but Subject Zero passed right through them like some kind of ghost. He picked up speed and began to run.

She gave chase as he ran through the doorway into a tunnel she hadn't seen before. Kira pulled up short, aimed her blaster, and fired.

The bolts of white-hot energy passed through him. He huffed and shook his head. A dozen more xenos lurked in the hall beyond the reach of the geode's power. They surrounded him.

Subject Zero turned and stared at her across the boundary.

Kira met his eyes—the eyes of a lover, a son, a starfighter pilot...

A monster.

No, he was no monster. He was a pawn.

"I'm coming for you," she told Overmind X. "You can't hide from me."

Subject Zero snarled, turned and disappeared into the darkness.

She let him go.

# THIRTY-TWO

The amplified energy of the geode knocked Elya back ten meters. He landed roughly, spinning and knocking his head against the stone floor. When he stopped rolling, he just lay there for a moment, aching all over.

In a pool of blood near his boot, he noticed something xeno-shaped squirming under the agony of the green light. He instinctively stomped down. It was satisfyingly gritty and wet under the sole of his boot.

"Kill the parasites!" he told the others. "Quick, before they re-infect the children!"

He didn't stop to study them, just noted their forms and ground them into the stone. Dozens of the worms were thrashing on the floor between the unconscious bodies of the children. Like the geode had done for him, that blast of green light must have dislodged them.

Ragged breathing filled the room. Elya realized it was finally over. The green light had vaporized most of the Kryl with the initial blast, freed the children, and sent Subject Zero running.

Survivors gathered around and did their best to calm the

traumatized children as they returned to awareness, and saw death all around them.

Hedgebot shook its bristled body as it returned to Elya's side. It was really scratched up, but otherwise seemed to be in working condition. "Great job, buddy. You saved the day."

"The bot deserves some credit, but it was you who saved the day, Captain Nevers." He looked up and noticed Admiral Miyaru was standing over him. Her normally hale figure was worn down. Her shoulders slumped and she seemed older, her face more deeply lined, her eyes shadowed and haunted. "Kept him talking long enough to distract him from his goal."

"He wasn't really distracted until he saw you, sir."

"I think he recognized me. ..." The admiral suddenly looked very vulnerable. "Or some part of him did. It only lasted a moment. Overmind X has a firm grip on his mind."

He put a hand on her arm. "I'm sorry," he said. "He was, and still *is*, a war hero. That thing the Overmind calls Subject Zero... that's not Captain Ruidiaz anymore."

"You're right." She sniffed and lifted her chin.

"I know it doesn't make it any easier. I can't imagine how you must feel."

"I feel like I want to catch that bastard and put him down."

"So he and the Overmind don't get hold of any more Telos relics," Elya said.

"So she can't hurt anyone else."

A moment of silent understanding passed between them. Their motivations were different, but they shared the same goal.

"Thank you, Elya," the admiral said, using his first name for the first time ever.

"Thank *you*, sir."

She smiled and clapped him on the shoulders.

He whistled for the bot to follow him and they moved

over to the crystal obelisk below the hologram of the ancient Telos. It hadn't moved or disappeared since the new relic had been activated.

"Speaking of relics," Elya said, "what is this place?"

The suspended creature looked like an oversized cross between a wolf and a dragon—creatures out of Old Earth mythology—but with a touch of something more alien... and dressed like a priest of Animus. The bone structure of its clasped feet matched the anatomy of the carvings ringing the room. Its face, however, remained cast in shadow beneath the deep hood of the robe, and Elya couldn't make out any features apart from shadowed ridges of bone around what might be the eyes.

She followed his gaze. "I don't know. I feel like this was more than Overmind X had expected to find."

The geode, mounted in an adjacent statue, still radiated powerfully. Whatever these Telos were, they had access to power and knowledge this galaxy had never seen. Why had they really left the galaxy—and where had they gone?

"Overmind X was counting on us bringing the geode here," Elya said. "We walked right into her trap. All for this obelisk relic. I don't know what it does yet, but it's important. This whole place is."

Elya spun around and counted again—seven statues for seven prime relics. Two were locked in the stone hands. Subject Zero had two more, the phase shifter on his belt and that orb, which had to be the starmap which led him here.

That left three relics at large, with destructive or fantastical abilities he could only begin to imagine.

"For what purpose?" Admiral Miyaru asked.

"No idea. There's still so much I don't know about the relics. But there's one person who does."

They turned to look across the room at Minister Aganaki, who was just now regaining consciousness. A few of the

Marines who had come with the admiral checked him for wounds and, finding none—fate had some sense of humor—helped him to his feet.

"The sacrifices we make for the Solaran Empire," Kira muttered.

Aganaki didn't even acknowledge them. He walked straight to the obelisk, and whatever power had protected it from Subject Zero let him through without objection.

He laid a hand on the angled surface of crystal and the hologram stirred.

"Who are you?" asked Aganaki.

"I am Chronicle," it responded in a rumble that sounded like the whole *room* was speaking—and in Galactic Standard, no less. Elya couldn't decide which was more eerie. His skin crawled and he rubbed his arms to ward off the chills.

"What do you do?" asked Aganaki.

"Collect knowledge," the voice boomed.

Aganaki's brow drew down in consternation as he thought of his next question. "What is your specific purpose?"

"To serve as the First People's final record of the collected knowledge and history of the Kryl."

# THIRTY-THREE

Sounds of struggle and a sharp cry of pain interrupted Aganaki's interview with the ancient alien storage program. Kira whipped around 180 degrees and drew her weapon.

She studied the shadows in the direction of the noise, which came through the last archway across the chamber. Retired Inquisitor Eben Osprey marched Spector out of the shadows and back into the green light. The Lieutenant Colonel's face was smeared with grease and dust and she was struggling against her escort. Eben must have carried restraints somewhere on his person because Spector's wrists were cuffed behind her with bands of aluminite.

Kira reholstered her gun.

"The Kryl hive is retreating," Harmony's voice spoke into her mind. "Colonel Volk has taken control of the quadrant."

*Good*, she thought back. *Thanks for keeping an eye on him.*

"It is my pleasure, Admiral."

*Wait*, Kira thought. *I thought comms wouldn't work inside the asteroid. How can I hear you now?*

"I was able to reconnect just a few moments ago."

She wasn't sure if that was a good sign or a bad one. Something about that relic locking into place in the stone hands must have taken down some of the asteroid base's defenses.

There would be time to investigate that later.

"Admiral!" Spector said as Eben stopped the squadron commander in front of her. "What is the meaning of this? Order him to let me go. I've done nothing wrong."

"You shot that kid," Captain Nevers said.

"And you poisoned Colonel Volk!" Park added from where he knelt beside Yorra. She was shivering with cold and pain as one of the Marines examined her acid burns and applied a salve to them.

"Regardless, Spector, you know the Fleet has no purview over Imperial inquisitions."

"By the power vested in me by the Emperor of the Solaran Empire, I'm placing you under arrest," Eben said. "You'll be detained until my investigation into your misconduct is complete. Anything you say can and will be used against you in a court of law. Do you understand?"

A look of shock had come over Spector's face during his speech, but it quickly faded to annoyance as she got her tongue under control. She glanced over at Aganaki, seeking support, but he was still occupied with the crystal obelisk and offered nothing. Spector quit objecting and shut her mouth. Eben repeated his question and got a reluctant affirmative.

*Right. Back to business, then.* "Harmony, have Colonel Volk send three more platoons to help us secure the area. Give them instructions to mark their path and lead the survivors out. And tell them to bring extra supplies—with plenty of food and water."

"Yes, Admiral," the shipmind responded.

Satisfied, Eben guided Spector to sit near the entrance,

345

where he stood guarding her as he waited for the rest to clean up.

"Extra supplies, sir?" Nevers asked.

"I have a feeling we're going to be here for a while, Captain."

# THIRTY-FOUR

Casey was released from the brig on their way back to Ariadne after the mission. The MOXA ship, two platoons of Marines and support craft stayed behind. She listened, stunned, as her friends told her what had happened. She almost didn't believe they had found a Telos city hidden in an asteroid, but the acid burns on Yorra's neck tempered her acceptance of the incredible story. She wished she could have been there, and after the telling, she was beyond grateful all three of them had made it out alive.

Nothing surprised her, though, like seeing her father on the *Paladin*. All of her struggles and efforts to expose Spector were vindicated when Colonel Volk came to apologize personally for what had happened. She accepted as graciously as she could manage, and then celebrated in the rec with her squad.

Lieutenant Colonel Renata Spector was arraigned a week later. The trial moved quickly, with most of it happening in a military tribunal behind closed doors. However, they did allow Fleet personnel to be present for the sentencing.

Casey arrived early and took a seat near the back of the small room. Nevers slid into the bench next to her. Park and Yorra sat one row back, once again holding hands. The scare they had in the asteroid had caused them to resolve whatever spat or argument they had gotten into before. It was nice to see them together again. Reassuring, like the Captain's bars that rested on her shoulder. Admiral Miyaru had dismissed the attempt to demote her immediately upon their return.

*The obstacle is the way*, Lt. Colonel Walcott would have said. That was the last time she heard his voice echo in her thoughts. Even though she'd always carry his memory with her, his voice was gone, and with it, the self-doubt that had dogged her since Robichar.

She knew there would be opportunities to doubt herself in the future, but knowing she'd overcome it once gave her confidence that she could do so again.

Casey turned in her chair. "Thanks for standing by me, you guys. I know it isn't always easy."

"We all have our moments," Nevers said with a grin. Hedgebot jumped from his shoulder to her lap and curled up in a little ball.

"Some more than others," Park said in a stage whisper.

Yorra smacked him playfully. "We'll always have each other's backs. Even if we don't understand why in the moment. We're a team."

Casey held out a hand. They all piled their hands on top of hers. "A team. Flight 18 of the Fightin' Furies."

The pilots all nodded.

They turned to face forward when the back wall slid open, revealing a doorway. Inquisitor Osprey came through wearing a form-fitting black tunic with a high, formal collar. Silver scales decorated his shoulders, and a board of colorful medals adorned his chest. A pair of security guards escorted Spector between them. Her hands and ankles bore an elaborate set of powered cuffs with magnetic locking mechanisms. They sat her in a chair and snapped the cuffs to a plate mounted on the tabletop. She faced the audience.

The courtroom came to order, and then her father stood. Casey watched Spector the whole time. Her former commander avoided her eyes.

They did a little preamble and then Inquisitor Osprey said, "Lieutenant Colonel Renata Spector is charged with three counts of manslaughter, and one count of attempted murder."

Spector stared at her feet.

"I was hoping for treason," Casey muttered, "but I suppose that'll do."

"On three counts of manslaughter, the court finds the defendant not guilty."

Casey swore. She glanced to the side, to where Chairman Card's stern-faced secretary sat, her back stiff and straight.

"On the count of attempted murder, the court finds the defendant guilty."

Renata lifted her face and stared forward..

Once again, the Furies were short a squadron commander, but at least this one would never poison the water of camaraderie—or call her "little bird"—ever again.

"However, in light of the circumstances, the sentence we're assigning is not jail time, but rather service to the Empire. The Colonization Board has agreed to take responsibility and place her in a position of indentured servitude on a new colony. Renata Spector, you are hereby dishonorably discharged from the Solaran Defense Forces."

Casey met her father's eyes, saw that this was not a joke, and swore under her breath. MOXA had a hand in this, she knew. The Colonization Board may have been the one to publicly save Spector, but it must have been MOXA who made the deal. Renata had betrayed the Fleet to get MOXA the information they wanted—info on the admiral's movements, as well as the coordinates of the asteroid base.

Casey got up and walked out with her head held high. The courts of the Solaran Empire may be corrupt, but at least she'd sleep well at night knowing Renata Spector would never again serve as a squadron commander in the Fleet.

# THIRTY-FIVE

The deaths of the colonists on the *Maiden of Kali* hit the people of Ariadne hard.

There was unrest, looting and burning in the refugee camps for days. It overflowed into the wealthy parts of the city-planet near the capitol buildings. Riot police had to be called in. Hundreds were arrested for vandalism and looting —even a few on charges of insurrection against the Solaran Empire.

The Emperor declared a day of mourning for the tragedy and used the holiday as an opportunity to quell the unrest by suspending the rationing restrictions for a week. He sent shipments of food and clean water—all given free, as a peace offering.

Many meetings were held by important political bodies to determine what to do next.

Kira waited for the politics to play out. Politics would never be her game. But when the summons came from the Colonization Board, she wasn't surprised.

She appeared before them the next morning wearing her cleanly pressed Fleet uniform, navy trimmed with crimson.

It wasn't just the Colonization Board, it turned out. Admiral Gitano was there representing the Executive Council of the SDF, as were lower-level flunkies from the Ministry of Xeno Affairs. Minister Aganaki himself would have come, but he was still in the Elturis System, studying the Telos city in the asteroid. They hadn't been able to remove the geode from the stone hands since Captain Nevers had placed it there.

"Admiral Miyaru," said Chairman Card, "we wanted to take this opportunity to commend you for your service. Thanks to your bravery, the *Maiden of Kali* was recovered."

She supposed this was the closest thing to an apology she was likely to get from him. She glanced at Gitano, who remained stoic but glowed with a tangible sense of satisfaction.

Kira inclined her head. "Thank you, Mr. Chairman. It's an honor to be recognized."

He squirmed a little in his chair, resettling his flabby bulk as he, too, glanced around at the other officials. Gitano returned his gaze evenly. The MOXA bureaucrats waited impatiently, tapping their fingers and bouncing their feet.

"Circumstances have forced our hand," Chairman Card went on. "Despite our best efforts, we believe it is wise to suspend further colonization missions until the threat of the rogue Overmind has been neutralized."

Kira nodded. "Wise decision, Mr. Chairman." *If only you'd listened to me earlier*, she thought, *all those deaths could have been avoided.*

"Admiral Gitano and the Executive Council have pledged their full support. We have agreed to divert some Colonization Board funds to help build the Fleet back up to full strength as quickly as possible."

"Let us pray to Animus that we are not too late," Kira said. At least they wouldn't be sending civilians out to wild new planets and spreading the Fleet's warships thin in the process.

Card looked over at Gitano, who leaned forward and said, "In the meantime, Admiral, we'd like to appoint you head of a taskforce responsible for hunting down and eliminating the rogue Overmind. Will you accept this mission?"

And there it was. What she'd been waiting for this whole time—an official taskforce meant dedicated resources, a fullstrength armada, and the ability to hand pick her team. She'd still report to the Executive Council, but no more getting blocked by the machinations of the Colonization Board or the Ministry of Xeno Affairs.

"I will."

# THIRTY-SIX

O mar's mandibles ached. He kept compulsively stretching his mouth open to pop his ears, and where the xeno mandibles attached to his human jawbone it was tender and sore.

Not to mention the other injuries he sustained in the asteroid.

"A minor setback," Overmind X told the hive. No conversation was private among the Kryl. They were one mind. "We will prevail."

"Yes, my queen," the hive answered, and Omar with them.

He glanced at the children beside him, a thin girl of about eleven years and a blond boy of about six. Overmind X had wisely kept two children here for safekeeping while the rest went with him on the mission into the asteroid. His losses stung.

"How will we bring the rest of the prime relics to the Telos city if it's controlled by the Solarans?" Omar asked.

"Let me worry about that," said Overmind X.

In response, she used the starmap to play an image in the hive's mind. A vortex of stars swam before his eyes. Among them, bright, blood red pinpricks alighted on dozens of different sectors: one where the forest moon Robichar was located, another in the Elturis System where they'd just been, and others marking the other Telos places of hiding.

The small pinpricks indicated minor relics... but the larger ones, the shining ruby gemstones, marked the resting places of the remaining pieces of their Inheritance.

Only three remained to be recovered.

But there was only one which Overmind X was *really* interested in.

The little girl turned to him and spoke in Overmind X's voice. "Human memory is like a sieve. It is one of your flaws, Subject Zero, one that we have been unable to correct. Perhaps because you were the first. We will be sure to take that into account with our newest subjects." The girl smiled in a haunting way that would have made his spine crawl if he didn't feel Overmind X's sense of joy as if it were his own. "Along with other... considerations."

She was referring to the changes she wanted to make to the transformation process. She'd been pumping out new iterations of the parasites continuously since they found the starmap. Each was designed to enable a particular adaptation in their younger, more malleable subjects. Overmind X was nothing if not prepared—no matter what booby trap, mechanism, or protective environment the Enemy had laid in wait, she was devising ways to circumvent them.

The Telos had been clever. But not even their most talented Engineers could stop a determined Overmind.

"Yes, my queen," Omar said.

"Why do you hesitate?" The young girl paced around him in a circle, studying him.

"I do not mean to, my queen. I trust you completely."

This was the truth, and Overmind X knew it was so because of the way their minds were linked.

But she was also right. Something about the encounter with the Solarans had unbalanced him. He thought, for a moment, that he'd recognized one of them. The recognition had lasted for no more than the space of a breath… but it was like a stone being dropped into a deep well. Something moved in him, but it had yet to hit the bottom. He didn't understand what it could mean.

He cast his mind back into his memories, and as he always did when he thought about his past, he hit a wall. Beyond a certain point, there was… nothing.

"Come."

The girl stopped circling him and stepped to the side.

He walked toward the shadows in the far corner. As he approached, he felt the temperature increase as he walked toward the source of the heat.

A half-circle of egg-shaped sacs pulsed and throbbed on the floor. Their walls were translucent and mobbed with veins. Inside, the fluid was yellow and filled with a thousand tiny creatures swimming. He received his queen's command, knelt down, and using both hands gently pried open the top of the nearest egg.

Fluid spilled down his hands and onto the floor, to be absorbed back into the living flesh that formed the shell of their mothership. The tiny creatures—her controllers—scattered. About half of them choked and died on the air before they made it clear. A few crawled behind him, swarmed up the legs of the Solaran girl, and scurried into her tear duct. A long, spiked appendage slithered out of the shadows and picked one of the worms out from among the set.

Overmind X placed this parasite on his own face. He shivered as the creature entered his body.

His hesitation slowly dissipated.

Along with the worm, Overmind X fed him the details of his next mission. A profound sense of calm overcame him.

With a renewed sense of focus and energy, he bowed deeply to his queen.

"We shall recover the rest of the relics, my queen, and with them, you will inherit the galaxy."

---

### Next in the Series

Grab the next book, *Rogue Swarm*, and read on to find out what Overmind X and Subject Zero's next gambit will be...

Will Elya solve the Telos puzzle and locate the remaining prime relics before Overmind X does?

Will Casey be able to fill the vacuum their disgraced former squadron commander left behind?

Will Kira build her new armada up to full strength before Overmind X reignites the Kryl War?

**Get it now:** *Rogue Swarm*

# THANK YOU

Hey, hero! Thanks for reading.

Before you go, I wanted to tell you the story about how this series was first launched on Kickstarter.

And share what I've been up to since then.

It all started with a little leap of faith...

## 400%+ Funded in 24 Hours

After finishing this novel in the summer of 2021, when at last the story had vacated the space in my brain it had occupied for over a year, I was finally able to look up and consider what needed to be done to help *Relics* reach its audience.

That's when I first began to seriously consider Kickstarter.

I'd never launched a book there, but I'd seen others do so, and I thought I knew how to make it work. By this point, I had three books in the bag—*Hidden Relics*, *Starfighter Down*, and the prequel novella, *Spare Parts*, which I wrote as a character study about Elya Nevers back in 2019.

It was the ideal moment to launch the campaign. Having written three books ahead of time, I could set my writing aside (temporarily), and give the campaign all my energy and focus.

And thank the Spirit of Old Earth I did.

The Kickstarter was a rousing success. I've never been so

happy with a leap of faith. Thanks, again, to the 271 original backers who pledged $12,879. You gave this series life.

The campaign funded over 400% in 24 hours and blasted through every stretch goal I set. I didn't think we'd hit them all, but we did—three extra novellas, and all three novels as audiobooks. The first audiobooks I've ever been able to produce myself, and I'm super proud of how they turned out.

But a Kickstarter is not the end.

It's the beginning.

Since then, much has happened.

I completed the first round of fulfillment for Kickstarter backers (books, t-shirts, Sabre models) and released *Starfighter Down* on retailers.

Meanwhile, I proofread *Hidden Relics*, formatted it, and got the finished book into the hands of Keith McCarthy for audio production. (And now you have it!)

Next, I eagerly set to work on the second novella about Casey Osprey. It was liberating to be writing again. Those books are shorter than the novels, so I finished it over the winter holiday and released it in March, 2022.

In January, I broke ground on the third novel, *Rogue Swarm*. By the time this book is released, I'll be close to having a first draft in hand.

I already have a plan for the third novella about Kira Miyaru, although I haven't written it yet. That book will tie everything together, past and future, through the characters. I've named the novella series *Starfighter Origins*, because they take place a decade earlier and can be read in any order. But truly, the two series are intricately interwoven and are best read together.

By the end of this year, all six books promised in the original campaign will be done and in various stages of post-production.

Three novels and three novellas.

Pretty amazing turnout, if you ask me.

I can't wait to find out how *Rogue Swarm* ends. Maybe then I'll have the brain space to figure out what I'm going to do next.

Another Kickstarter? More *Relics of the Ancients* novels? A new series of novellas? The universe is expansive, and there's so much I want to explore.

Until then, keep your eyes peeled for *Rogue Swarm*. It'll be an explosive finish to the original story arc, so you won't want you to miss it!

## Original Acknowledgements

I have a lot of people to thank for helping to bring this project to life.

My wife, Shelly, whose unwavering support and belief in me has lifted me up more times than I can count. Without her, none of this would be possible.

All the freelancers who have contributed to this project deserve to be mentioned by name: the artist Elias Stern, Vivid Covers for typography, and my editors Amy Teegan and Steve Statham.

Let's not forget the military veterans and pilots who read early versions of *Starfighter Down* and corrected my many mistakes and goof-ups: my father, Colonel James Herron (US Air Force); Lt. Colonel Tim Hebel (US Air Force); combat journalist Sullivan Laramie (US Army); Chief Warrant Officer Jerry Leake (US Army); and commercial pilot Jenny Avery. These people taught me a lot, and any mistakes with flight mechanics that might have snuck through the rigorous editing process are my own!

Beta readers, including those above, helped me improve the story and they deserve a special mention, too. Specifically, Bob Truman, Wayne Key, and Paula Adler.

And the following readers jumped in to help with proofreading and catching flubs and errors in the first novel: H Chesno, Jenny Avery, James Green, Wayne Key and Maureen Henn.

## A Special Thanks to Kickstarter Heroes

This series was first launched on Kickstarter! The campaign raised $12,879 in 4 weeks, and it wouldn't have been possible without the support of 271 backers.

A special shoutout to these heroes, who backed the original campaign at the highest levels:

Tim Hebel, Jennifer Whitesell, Jacob Moyer, Gregory Clawson, Jerry Leake, James Herron, Tim Cross, Leigh, Lawrence Tate, Sebastián, Tyler Prince, Adam Knuth, MJ Caan, Jacen Spector, Jerome, Chad Anthony Randell, Linda Schattauer, Peyton, Marouane Jerraf, Mette Lundsgaard, Destin Floyd, Pierino Gattei, Rhett and Kathy Leonard, Dietrich Thompson, Becky Herron, Missy Burrows, Cindy Lorion, Chris Wooster, Lauren Appa, Nikhil Daftary, and Joe Bunting.

## ALSO BY M.G. HERRON

### Translocator Trilogy

*The Auriga Project*

*The Alien Element*

*The Ares Initiative*

*The Translocator (Books 1-3)*

### The Gunn Files

*Culture Shock*

*Overdose*

*Quantum Flare*

*The Gunn Files (Books 1-3)*

### Other Books

*The Republic*

*Boys & Their Monsters*

Get science fiction and fantasy reading recommendations from MG
Herron delivered straight to your inbox. Join here:
mgherron.com/bookclub

## ABOUT THE AUTHOR

M.G. Herron writes science fiction and fantasy for adrenaline junkies.

His books explore new worlds, futuristic technologies, ancient mysteries, various apocalypses, and the vagaries of the human experience.

His characters have a sense of humor (except for the ones who don't). They stand up to strange alien monsters from other worlds... unless they slept through their alarm again.

Like ordinary people, Herron's heroes sometimes make mistakes, but they're always trying to make the universe a better place.

Find all his books and news about upcoming releases at mgherron.com.

CPSIA information can be obtained
at www.ICGtesting.com
Printed in the USA
JSHW030922030423
39825JS00003B/14

9 781956 029130